The King's
Achievement

right, beside which the lamp extinguisher hung, grimy with smoke and grease. The yard dog came out at the sound of the hoofs, dragging his chain after him, from his kennel beneath the little cloister outside the chapel, barked solemnly once or twice, and having done his duty lay down on the cool stones, head on paws, watching with bright eyes the door that led from the hall into the Court. A moment later the little door from the masters chamber opened; and Sir James Torridon came out and, giving a glance at the disappearing servants, said a word or two to the others, and turned again through the hall to meet his sons.

The coach was coming up the drive round toward the gatehouse, as he came out on the wide paved terrace; and he stood watching the glitter of brasswork through the dust, the four plumed cantering horses in front, and the bobbing heads of the men that rode behind; and there was a grave pleased expectancy on his bearded face and in his bright grey eyes as he looked. His two sons had met at Begham, and were coming home, Ralph from town sites a six months' absence, and Christopher from Canterbury, where he had been spending a week or two in company with Mr. Carleton, the chaplain of the Court. He was the more pleased as the house had been rather lonely in their absence, since the two daughters were both from home, Mary with her husband, Sir Nicholas Maxwell, over at Great Keynes, and Margaret at her convent education at Rusper: and he himself had had for company his wife alone.

She came out presently as the carriage rolled through the archway, a tall dignified figure of a woman, finely dressed in purple and black, and stood by him, silently, a yard or two away, watching the carriage out of steady black eyes. A moment later the carriage drew up at the steps, and a couple of servants ran down to open the door.

Ralph stepped out first, a tall man like both his parents, with a face and slow gait extraordinarily like his mother's, and dressed in the same kind of rich splendor, with a short silver-clasped traveling cloak, crimson hose, and plumed felt cap; and his face with its pointed black beard had something of the same steady impassivity in it; he was flicking the dust from his shoulder as he came up the steps on to the terrace.

Christopher followed him, not quite so tall as the other, and a good ten years younger, with the grey eyes of his father, and a little brown beard beginning to sprout on his cheeks and chin.

Ralph turned at the top of the steps

"The bag," he said shortly; and then turned again to kiss his parents' hands; as Christopher went back to the carriage, from which the priest was just stepping out. Sir James asked his son about the journey.

"Oh, yes," he said; and then added, "Christopher was late at Begham."

"And you are well, my son?" asked his mother, as they turned to walk up to the house.

"Oh, yes!" he said again.

Sir James waited for Christopher and Mr. Carleton, and the three followed the others a few yards behind.

"You saw her?" said his father.

Christopher nodded.

"Yes," he said, "I must speak to you, sir, before I tell the others."

"Come to me when you are dressed, then. Supper will be in an hour from now;" and he looked at his son with a kind of sharp expectancy.

The courtyard was empty as they passed through, but half a dozen servants stood crowded in the little flagged passage that led from it into the kitchen, and watched Ralph and his mother with an awed interest as they came out from the hall. Mr. Ralph had come down from the heart of life, as they knew; had been present at the crowning of Anne Boleyn a week before, had mixed with great folks; and what secrets of State might there not be in that little strapped bag that his brother carried behind him?

When the two first had disappeared, the servants broke into talk, and went back to the kitchen.

*L*ady Torridon, with her elder son and the chaplain, had to wait a few minutes on the dais in the hall an hour later, before the door under the musicians' gallery opened, and the other two came in from the master's chamber. Sir James looked a little anxious as he came across the clean strewed rushes, past the table at the lower end where the household sat, but Christopher's face was bright with excitement. After a word or two of apology they moved to their places. Mr. Carleton said grace, and as they sat down the door behind from the kitchen opened, and the servants came through with the pewter dishes.

Ralph was very silent at first; his mother sat by him almost as silent as himself; the servants sprang about noiseless and eager to wait on him; and Sir James and the chaplain did most of the conversation, pleasant harmless talk about the estate and the tenants; but as supper went on, and the weariness of the hot journey faded, and the talk from the lower tables grew louder, Ralph began to talk a little more freely.

"Yes," he said, "the crowning went well enough. The people were quiet enough. She looked very pretty in her robes; she was in purple velvet, and her gentlemen in scarlet. We shall have news of her soon."

Sir James looked up sharply at his son. They were all listening intently; and even a servant behind Ralph's chair paused with a silver jug.

"Yes," said Ralph again with a tranquil air, setting down his Venetian glass; "God has blessed the union already."

"And the King?" asked his father, from his black velvet chair in the center.

There fell a deeper silence yet as that name was mentioned. Henry dominated the imagination of his subjects to an extraordinary degree, no less in his heavy middle-age than in the magnificent strength and capacity of his youth.

But Ralph answered carelessly enough. He had seen the King too often.

"The King looked pleased enough; he was in his throne. He is stouter than when I saw him last. My Lord of Canterbury did the crowning; Te Deum was sung after, and then solemn mass. There was a dozen abbots, I should think, and my Lords of York and London and Winchester with two or three more. My Lord of Suffolk bore the crown."

"And the procession?" asked his father again.

"That, too, was well enough. There came four chariots after the Queen, full of ancient old ladies, at which some of the folks laughed. And then the rest of them."

They talked a few minutes about the coronation, Sir James asking most of the questions and Ralph answering shortly; and presently Christopher broke in —

"And the Lady Katharine —" he began.

"Hush, my son," said his father, glancing at Ralph, who sat perfectly still a moment before answering.

"Chris is always eager about the wrong thing," he said evenly; "he is late at Begham, and then asks me about the Princess Dowager. She is still alive, if you mean that."

Lady Torridon looked from one to the other.

"And Master Cromwell?" she asked.

"Master Cromwell is well enough. He asked me to give you both his respects. I left him at Hackney."

*T*he tall southern windows of the hall, above the pargetted plaster, had faded through glowing ruby and blue to dusk before they rose from the table and went down and through the passage into the little parlor next the master's chamber, where they usually took their dessert. This part of the house had been lately re-built, but the old woodwork had been re-used, and the pale oak panels, each crowned by an elaborate foliated head, gave back the pleasant flicker of the fire that burned between the polished sheets of Flemish tiles on either side of the hearth. A great globe stood in the corner furthest from the door, with a map of England hanging above it. A piece of tapestry hung over the mantel-piece, representing Diana bending over Endymion, and two tall candles in brass stands burned beneath. The floor was covered with rushes.

Mr. Carleton, who had come with them as far as the door, according to custom, was on the point of saying-good-night, when Sir James called him back.

"Come in, father," he said, "we want you tonight. Chris has something to tell us."

The priest came in and sat down with the others, his face in shadow, at the corner of the hearth.

Sir James looked across at his younger son and nodded; and Chris, his chin on his hand, and sitting very upright on the long-backed settle beside the chaplain, began rather nervously and abruptly.

"I — I have told Ralph," he said, "on the way here and you, sir; but I will tell you again. You know I was questioning whether I had a vocation to the religious life; and I went, with that in my mind, to see the Holy Maid. We saw her, Mr. Carleton and I; and — and I have made up my mind I must go."

He stopped, hesitating a little, Ralph and his mother sat perfectly still, without a word or sign of either sympathy or disapproval. His father leaned forward a little, and smiled encouragingly.

"Go on, my son."

Chris drew a breath and leaned back more easily.

"Well, we went to St. Sepulcher's; and she could not see us for a day or two. There were several others staying with us at the monastery; there was a Carthusian from Sheen — I forget his name."

"Henry Man," put in the chaplain.

"— And some others," went on Chris, "all waiting to see her. Dr. Bocking promised to tell us when we could see her; and he came to us one morning after mass, and told us that she was in ecstasy, and that we were to come at once. So we all went to the nuns' chapel, and there she was on her knees, with her arms across her breast."

He stopped again. Ralph cleared his throat, crossed his legs, and drank a little wine.

"Yes?" said the knight questioningly.

"Well — she said a great deal," went on Chris hurriedly.

"About the King?" put in his mother who was looking at the fire.

"A little about the King," said Chris, "and about holy things as well. She spoke about heaven; it was wonderful to hear her; with her eyes burning, and such a voice; and then she spoke low and deep and told us about hell, and the devil and his torments; and I could hardly bear to listen; and she told us about shrift, and what it did for the soul; and the blessed sacrament. The Carthusian put a question or two to her, and she answered them: and all the while she was speaking her voice seemed to come from her body, and not from her mouth; and it was terrible to see her when she spoke of hell; her tongue lay out on her cheek, and her eyes grew little and afraid."

"Her tongue in her cheek, did you say?" asked Ralph politely, without moving.

Chris flushed, and sat back silent. His father glanced quickly from one to the other.

"Tell us more, Chris," he said. "What did she say to you?"

The young man leaned forward again.

"I wish, Ralph —" he began.

"I was asking —" began the other.

"There, there," said Sir James. "Go on, Chris."

"Well, after a while Dr. Bocking brought me forward; and told her to look at me; and her eyes seemed to see something beyond me; and I was afraid. But he told me to ask her, and I did. She said nothing for a while; and then she began to speak of a great church, as if she saw it; and she saw there was a tower in the middle, and chapels on either side, and tombs beside the high altar; and an image, and then she stopped, and cried out aloud 'Saint Pancras pray for us' — and then I knew."

Chris was trembling violently with excitement as he turned to the priest for corroboration. Mr. Carleton nodded once or twice without speaking.

"Then I knew," went on Chris. "You know it was what I had in my mind; and I had not spoken a word of Lewes, or of my thought of going there."

"Had you told any?" asked his father.

"Only Dr. Bocking. Then I asked her, was I to go there; but she said nothing for a while; and her eyes wandered about; and she began to speak of black monks going this way and that; and she spoke of a prior, and of his ring; it was of gold, she said, with figures engraved on it. You know the ring the Prior wears?" he added, looking eagerly at his father.

Sir James nodded.

"I know it," he said. "Well?"

"Well, I asked her again, was I to go there; and then she looked at me up and down; I was in my traveling suit; but she said she saw my cowl and its hanging sleeves, and an antiphoner in my hands; and then her face grew dreadful and afraid again, and she cried out and fell forward; and Dr. Bocking led us out from the chapel."

There was a long silence as Chris ended and leaned back again, taking up a bunch of raisins. Ralph sighed once as if wearied out, and his mother put her hand on his sleeve. Then at last Sir James spoke.

"You have heard the story," he said, and then paused; but there was no answer. At last the chaplain spoke from his place.

"It is all as Chris said," he began, "I was there and heard it. If the woman is not from God, she is one of Satan's own; and it is hard to think that Satan would tell us of the sacraments and bid us use them greedily, and if she is from God —" he stopped again.

The knight nodded at him.

"And you, sweetheart?" he said to his wife.

She turned to him slowly.

"You know what I think," she said. "If Chris believes it, he must go, I suppose."

"And you, Ralph?"

Ralph raised himself in his chair.

"Do you wish me to say what I think?" he asked deliberately, "or what Chris wishes me to say? I will do either."

Chris made a quick movement of his head; but his father answered for him.

"We wish you to say what you think," he said quietly.

"Well, then," said Ralph, "it is this. I cannot agree with the father. I think the woman is neither of God nor Satan; but that she speaks of her own heart, and of Dr. Bocking's. I believe they are a couple of knaves — clever knaves, I will grant, though perhaps the woman is something of a fool too; for she deceives persons as wise even as Mr. Carleton here by speaking of shrift and the like; and so she does the priests' will, and hopes to get gain for them and herself. I am not alone in thinking this — there are many in town who think with me, and holy persons too."

"Is Master Cromwell one of them?" put in Chris bitterly.

Ralph raised his eyebrows a little.

"There is no use in sneering," he said, "but Master Cromwell is one of them. I suppose I ought not to speak of this; but I know you will not speak of it again; and I can tell you of my own knowledge that the Holy Maid will not be at St. Sepulcher's much longer."

His father leaned forward.

"Do you mean —" he began.

"I mean that His Grace is weary of her prophesyings. It was all very well till she began to meddle with matters of State; but His Grace will have none of that. I can tell you no more. On the other hand if Chris thinks he must be a monk, well and good; I do not think so myself; but that is not my affair; but I hope he will not be a monk only because a knavish woman has put out her tongue at him, and repeated what a knavish priest has put into her mouth. But I suppose he had made up his mind before he asked me."

"He has made up his mind," said his father, "and will hold to it unless reason is shown to the contrary; and for myself I think he is right."

"Very well, then," said Ralph; and leaned back once more.

The minutes passed away in silence for a while; and then Ralph asked a question or two about his sisters.

"Mary is coming over to hunt tomorrow with her husband," said Sir James. "I have told Forrest to be here by nine o'clock. Shall you come with us?"

Ralph yawned, and sipped his Bordeaux.

"I do not know," he said, "I suppose so."

"And Margaret is at Rusper still," went on the other. "She will not be here until August."

"She, too, is thinking of Religion," put in Lady Torridon impassively.

Ralph looked up lazily.

"Indeed," he said, "then Mary and I will be the only worldlings."

"She is very happy with the nuns," said his father, smiling, "and a worldling can be no more than that; and perhaps not always as much."

Ralph smiled with one corner of his mouth.

"You are quite right, sir," he said.

The bell for evening prayers sounded out presently from the turret in the chapel-corner, and the chaplain rose and went out.

"Will you forgive me, sir," said Ralph, "if I do not come this evening? I am worn out with traveling. The stay at Begham was very troublesome."

"Good-night, then, my son. I will send Morris to you immediately."

"Oh, after prayers," said Ralph. "I need not deprive God of his prayers too."

*L*ady Torridon had gone out silently after the chaplain, and Sir James and Chris walked across the Court together. Overhead the summer night sky was clear and luminous with stars, and the air still and fragrant. There were a few lights here and there round the Court, and the tall chapel windows shone dimly above the little cloister. A link flared steadily on its iron bracket by the door into the hall, and threw waves of flickering ruddy light across the cobble-stones, and the shadow of the tall pump wavered on the further side.

Sir James put his hand tenderly on Chris' shoulder.

"You must not be angry at Ralph, my son," he said. "Remember he does not understand."

"He should not speak like that," said Chris fiercely. "How dare he do so?"

"Of course he should not; but he does not know that. He thinks he is advising you well. You must let him alone, Chris. You must remember he is almost mad with business. Master Cromwell works him hard."

*T*he chapel was but dimly lighted as Chris made his way up to the high gallery at the west where he usually knelt. The altar glimmered in the dusk at the further end, and only a couple of candles burned on the priest's kneeling stool on the south side. The rest was dark, for the house hold knew compline by heart; and even before Chris reached his seat he heard the blessing asked for a quiet night and a perfect end. It was very soothing to him as he leaned over the oak rail and looked down on the dim figures of his parents in their seat at the front, and the heads of the servants below, and listened to the quiet pulsation of those waves of prayer going to and fro in the dusk, beating, as a summer tide at the foot of a cliff against those white steps that rose up to the altar where a single spark winked against the leaded window beneath the silk-shrouded pyx. He had come home full of excitement and joy at his first sight of an ecstatic, and at the message that she had seemed to have for him, and across these heightened perceptions had jarred the impatience of his brother in the inn at Begham and in the carriage on their way home, and above all his sharp criticism and aloofness in the parlor just now. But he became quieter as he knelt now; the bitterness seamed to sink beneath him and to leave him alone in a world of peaceful glory — the world of mystic life to which his face was now set, illuminated by the words of the nun. He had seen one who could see further than he himself; he had looked upon eyes that were fixed on mysteries and realms in which he indeed passionately believed, but which were apt to be faint and formless sometimes to the weary eyes of faith alone; and as a proof that these were more than fancies she had told him too of what he could verify — of the priory at Lewes which she had never visited, and even the details of the ring on the Prior's finger which he alone of the two had seen. And then lastly she had encouraged him in his desires, had seen him with those same wide eyes in the habit that he longed to wear, going about the psalmody — the great *Opus Dei* — to which he longed to consecrate his life. If such were not a message from God to him for what further revelation could he hope?

And as for Ralph's news and interests, of what value were they? Of what importance was it to ask who sat on the Consort's throne, or whether she wore purple velvet or red? These were little matters compared with those high affairs of the soul and the Eternal God, of which he was already beginning to catch glimpses, and even the whispers that ran about the country places and of which Ralph no doubt could tell him much if he chose, of the danger that threatened the religious houses, and of Henry's intentions towards them — even these were but impotent cries of the people raging round the throne of the Anointed.

So he knelt here now, pacified and content again, and thought with something of pity of his brother dozing now no doubt before the parlor fire, cramped by his poor ideals and dismally happy in his limitations.

His father, too, was content down below in the chapel. He himself had at one time before his marriage looked towards the religious life; and now that it had turned out otherwise had desired nothing more than that he should be represented in that inner world of God's favorites by at least one of his children. His daughter Margaret had written a week earlier to say that her mind was turning that way, and now Christopher's decision had filled up the cup of his desires. To have a priest for a son, and above all one who was a monk as well was more than he had dared to hope, though not to pray for; if he could not be one himself, at least he had begotten one — one who would represent him before God, bring a blessing on the house, and pray and offer sacrifice for his soul until his time should be run out and he see God face to face. And Ralph would represent him before men and carry on the line, and hand on the house to a third generation — Ralph, at whom he had felt so sorely puzzled of late, for he seemed full of objects and ambitions for which the father had very little sympathy, and to have lost almost entirely that delicate relation with home that was at once so indefinable and so real. But he comforted himself by the thought that his elder son was not wholly wasting time as so many of the country squires were doing round about, absorbed in work that a brainless yeoman could do with better success. Ralph at least was occupied with grave matters, in Cromwell's service and the King's, and entrusted with high secrets the issue of which both temporal and eternal it was hard to predict. And, no doubt, the knight thought, in time he would come back and pick up the strands he had dropped; for when a man had wife and children of his own to care for, other businesses must seem secondary; and questions that could be ignored before must be faced then.

But he thought with a little anxiety of his wife, and wondered whether his elder son had not after all inherited that kind of dry rot of the soul, in which the sap and vigor disappear little by little, leaving the shape indeed intact but not the powers. When he had married her, thirty-five years before, she had seemed to him an incarnate mystery of whose key he was taking possession — her silence had seemed pregnant with knowledge, and her words precious pieces from an immeasurable treasury; and then little by little he had found that the wide treasury was empty, clean indeed and capacious, but no more, and above all with no promise of any riches as yet unperceived. Those great black eyes, that high forehead, those stately movements, meant nothing; it was a splendid figure with no soul within. She did her duty admirably, she said her prayers, she entertained her guests with the proper conversation, she could be trusted to behave well in any circumstances that called for tact or strength; and that was all. But Ralph would not be like that; he was intensely devoted to his work, and from all accounts able in its performance; and more than that, with all his impassivity he was capable of passion; for his employer Sir Thomas Cromwell was to Ralph's eyes, his father had begun to see, something almost more than human. A word against that master of his would set his eyes blazing and his voice trembling; and this showed that at least the soul was not more than sleeping, or its powers more than misdirected.

And meanwhile there was Chris; and at the thought the father lifted his eyes to the gallery, and saw the faint outline of his son's brown head against the whitewash.

Chapter II
A FORETASTE OF PEACE

It was not until the party was riding home the next day that Sir Nicholas Maxwell and his wife were informed of Chris' decision.

*T*hey had had a fair day's sport in the two estates that marched with one another between Overfield and Great Keynes, and about fifteen stags had been killed as well as a quantity of smaller game.

Ralph had ridden out after the party had left, and had found Sir Nicholas at the close of the afternoon just as the last drive was about to take place; and had stepped into his shelter to watch the finish. It was a still, hot afternoon, and the air over the open space between the copse in which they stood and the dense forest eighty yards away danced in the heat.

Ralph nodded to his brother-in-law, who was flushed and sunburned, and then stood behind, running his eyes up and down that sturdy figure with the tightly-gaitered legs set well apart and the little feathered cap that moved this way and that as the sportsman peered through the branches before him. Once he turned fierce eyes backwards at the whine of one of the hounds, and then again thrust his hot dripping face into the greenery.

Then very far away came a shout, and a chorus of taps and cries followed it, sounding from a couple of miles away as the beaters after sweeping a wide circle entered the thick undergrowth on the opposite side of the wood. Sir Nicholas' legs trembled, and he shifted his position a little, half lifting his strong spliced hunting bow as he did so.

For a few minutes there was silence about them except for the distant cries, and once for the stamp of a horse behind them. Then Sir Nicholas made a quick movement, and dropped his hands again; a single rabbit had cantered out from the growth opposite, and sat up with cocked ears staring straight at the deadly shelter. Then another followed; and again in a sudden panic the two little furry bodies whisked back into cover.

Ralph marveled at this strange passion that could set a reasonable man twitching and panting like the figure in front of him. He himself was a good rider, and a sufficiently keen hunter when his blood was up; but this brother-in-law of his seemed to live for little else. Day after day, as Ralph knew, from the beginning of the season to the end he was out with his men and hounds, and the rest of the year he seemed to spend in talking about the sport, fingering and oiling his weapons through long mornings, and elaborating future campaigns, in which the quarries' chances should be reduced to a minimum.

*O*n a sudden Sir Nicholas's figure stiffened and then relaxed. A doe had stepped out noiselessly from the cover, head up and feet close together, sniffing up wind — and they were shooting no does this month. Then again she moved along against the thick undergrowth, stepping delicately and silently, and vanished without a sound a hundred yards along to the left.

The cries and taps were sounding nearer now, and at any moment the game might appear. Sir Nicholas shifted his position again a little, and simultaneously the scolding voice of a blackbird rang out in front, and he stopped again. At the same moment a hare, mad with fright, burst out of the cover, making straight for the shelter. Sir Nicholas' hands rose, steady now the crisis had come; and Ralph leaning forward touched him on the shoulder and pointed.

A great stag was standing in the green gloom within the wood eighty yards away, with a couple of does at his flank. Then as a shout sounded out near at hand, he bolted towards the shelter in a line that would bring him close to it. Ralph crouched down, for he had left his bow with his man an hour earlier, and one of the hounds gave a stifled yelp as Nicholas straightened himself and threw out his left foot. Either the sound or the movement startled the great brown beast in front, and as the arrow twanged from the string he checked and wheeled round, and went off like the wind, untouched. A furious hiss of the breath broke from Nicholas, and he made a swift sign as he turned to his horse; and in a moment the two lithe hounds had leapt from the shelter and were flying in long noiseless leaps after the disappearing quarry; the does, confused by the change of direction, had whisked back into cover. A moment later Nicholas too was after the hounds, his shoulders working and his head thrust forward, and a stirrup clashed and jingled against the saddle.

Ralph sat down on the ground smiling. It gave him a certain pleasure to see such a complete discomfiture; Nicholas was always so amusingly angry when he failed, and so full of reasons.

The forest was full of noises now; a crowd of starlings were protesting wildly overhead, there were shouts far away and the throb of hoofs, and the ground game was pouring out of the undergrowth and dispersing in all directions. Once a boar ran past, grumbling as he went, turning a wicked and resentful eye on the placid gentleman in green who sat on the ground, but who felt for his long dirk as he saw the fury on the brute's face and the foam on the tusks. But the pig thought discretion was best, and hurried on complaining. More than one troop of deer flew past, the does gathered round their lord to protect him, all swerving together like a string of geese as they turned the corner of the shelter and caught sight of Ralph; but the beaters were coming out now, whistling and talking as they came, and gathering into groups of two or three on the ground, for the work was done, and it had been hot going.

Mary Maxwell appeared presently on her grey horse, looking slender and dignified in her green riding-suit with the great plume shading her face, and rode up to Ralph whom she had seen earlier in the afternoon.

"My husband?" she enquired looking down at Ralph who was lying with his hat over his eyes.

"He left me just now," said her brother, "very hot and red, after a stag which he missed. That will mean some conversation tonight, Minnie."

She smiled down at him.

"I shall agree with him, you know," she said.

"Of course you will; it is but right. And I suppose I shall too."

"Will you wait for him? Tell him we are going home by the mill. It is all over now."

Ralph nodded, and Mary moved off down the glade to join the others.

Ralph began to wonder how Nicholas would take the news of Chris' decision. Mary, he knew very well, would assent to it quietly as she did to all normal events, even though they were not what she would have wished; and probably her husband would assent too, for he had a great respect for a churchman. For himself his opinions were divided and he scarcely knew what he thought. From the temporal point of view Chris' step would be an advantage to him, for the vow of poverty would put an end to any claims upon the estate on the part of the younger son; but Ralph was sufficiently generous not to pay much attention to this. From the social point of view, no great difference would be made; it was as respectable to have a monk for a brother as a small squire, and Chris could never be more than this unless he made a good marriage. From the spiritual point of view — and here Ralph stopped and wondered whether it was very seriously worth considering. It was the normal thing of course to believe in the sublimity of the religious life and its peculiar dignity; but the new learning was beginning to put questions on the subject that had very considerably affected the normal view in Ralph's eyes. In that section of society where new ideas are generated and to which Ralph himself belonged, there were very odd tales being told; and it was beginning to be thought possible that monasticism had over-reached itself, and that in trying to convert the world it had itself been converted by the world. Ralph was proud enough of the honor of his family to wonder whether it was an unmixed gain that his own brother should join such ranks as these. And lastly there were the facts that he had learnt from his association with Cromwell that made him hesitate more than ever in giving Chris his sympathy. He had been thinking these points over in the parlor the night before when the others had left him, and during the day in the intervals of the sport; and he was beginning to come to the conclusion that all things considered he had better just acquiesce in the situation, and neither praise nor blame overmuch.

It was a sleepy afternoon. The servants had all gone by now, and the horn-blowings and noises had died away in the direction of the mill; there was no leisure for stags to bray, as they crouched now far away in the bracken, listening large-eyed and trumpet-eared for the sounds of pursuit; only the hum of insect life in the hot evening sunshine filled the air; and Ralph began to fall asleep, his back against a fallen trunk.

Then he suddenly awakened and saw his brother-in-law, black against the sky, looking down at him, from the saddle.

"Well?" said Ralph, not moving.

Nicholas began to explain. There were a hundred reasons, it seemed, for his coming home empty-handed; and where were his men?

"They are all gone home," said Ralph, getting up and stretching himself. "I waited for you It is all over."

"You understand," said Nicholas, putting his horse into motion, and beginning to explain all over again, "you understand that it had not been for that foul hound yelping, I should have had him here. I never miss such a shot; and then when we went after him —"

"I understand perfectly, Nick," said Ralph. "You missed him because you did not shoot straight, and you did not catch him because you did not go fast enough. A lawyer could say no more."

Nicholas threw back his head and laughed loudly, for the two were good friends.

"Well, if you will have it," he said, "I was a damned fool. There! A lawyer dare not say as much — not to me, at any rate."

Ralph found his man half a mile further on coming to meet him with his horse, and he mounted and rode on with Nicholas towards the mill.

"I have something to tell you," he said presently. "Chris is to be a monk."

"Mother of God!" cried Nicholas, half checking his horse, "and when was that arranged?"

"Last night," went on Ralph. "He went to see the Holy Maid at St. Sepulcher's, and it seems that she told him he had a vocation; so there is an end of it."

"And what do you all think of it?" asked the other.

"Oh! I suppose he knows his business."

Nicholas asked a number of questions, and was informed that Chris proposed to go to Lewes in a month's time. He was already twenty-three, the Prior had given his conditional consent before, and there was no need for waiting. Yes, they were Cluniacs; but Ralph believed that they were far from strict just at present. It need not be the end of Chris so far as this world was concerned.

"But you must not say that to him," he went on, "he thinks it is heaven itself between four walls, and we shall have a great scene of farewell. I think I must go back to town before it takes place: I cannot do that kind of thing."

Nicholas was not attending, and rode on in silence for a few yards, sucking in his lower lip.

"We are lucky fellows, you and I," he said at last, "to have a monk to pray for us."

Ralph glanced at him, for he was perfectly grave, and a rather intent and awed look was in his eyes.

"I think a deal of that," he went on, "though I cannot talk to a churchman as I should. I had a terrible time with my Lord of Canterbury last year, at Otford. He was not a hunter like this one, and I knew not what else to speak of."

Ralph's eyes narrowed with amusement.

"What did you say to him?" he asked.

"I forget," said Nicholas, "and I hope my lord did. Mary told me I behaved like a fool. But this one is better. I hear. He is at Ashford now with his hounds."

They talked a little more about Chris, and Ralph soon saw on which side Nicholas ranged himself. It was an unfeigned pleasure to this hunting squire to have a monk for a brother-in-law; there was no knowing how short purgatory might not be for them all under the circumstances.

It was evident, too, when they came up with the others a couple of miles further on, that Nicholas's attitude towards the young man had undergone a change. He looked at him with a deep respect, refrained from criticizing his bloodless hands, and was soon riding on in front beside him, talking eagerly and deferentially, while Ralph followed with Mary and his father.

"You have heard?" he said to her presently.

"Father has just told me," she said. "We are very much pleased — dear Chris!"

"And then there is Meg," put in her father.

"Oh! Meg; yes, I knew she would. She is made for a nun."

Sir James edged his horse in presently close to Ralph, as Mary went in front through a narrow opening in the wood.

"Be good to him," he said. "He thinks so much of you."

Ralph glanced up and smiled into the tender keen eyes that were looking into his own.

"Why, of course, sir," he said.

*I*t was an immense pleasure to Chris to notice the difference in Nicholas's behavior towards him. There was none of that loud and cheerful rallying that stood for humor, no criticisms of his riding or his costume. The squire asked him a hundred questions, almost nervously, about the Holy Maid and himself, and what had passed between them.

"They say the Host was carried to her through the air from Calais, Chris, when the King was there. Did you hear her speak of that?"

Chris shook his head.

"There was not time," he said.

"And then there was the matter of the divorce —" Nicholas turned his head slightly; "Ralph cannot hear us, can he? Well — the matter of the divorce — I hear she denounced that, and would have none of it, and has written to the Pope, too."

"They were saying something of the kind," said Chris, "but I thought it best not to meddle."

"And what did she say to you?"

Chris told him the story, and Nicholas's eyes grew round and fixed as he listened; his mouth was a little open, and he murmured inarticulate comments as they rode together up from the mill.

"Lord!" he said at last, "and she said all that about hell. God save us! And her tongue out of her mouth all the while! And did you see anything yourself? No devils or angels?"

"I saw nothing," said Chris. "I just listened, but she saw them."

"Lord!" said Nicholas again, and rode on in profound silence.

The Maxwells were to stay to supper at the Court; and drive home afterwards; so there was no opportunity for Chris to go down and bathe in the lake as he usually did in summer after a day's hunting, for supper was at seven o'clock, and he had scarcely more than time to dress.

Nicholas was very talkative at supper, and poured out all that Chris had told him, with his usual lack of discretion; for the other had already told the others once all the details that he thought would interest them.

"They were talking about the divorce," he broke out, and then stopped and eyed Ralph craftily; "but I had better not speak of that here — eh, Chris?"

Ralph looked blandly at his plate.

"Chris did not mention that," he said. "Tell us, Nick."

"No, no," cried Nicholas. "I do not want you to go with tales to town. Your ears are too quick, my friend. Then there was that about the Host flying from Calais, eh, Chris? No, no; you said you had heard nothing of that."

Chris looked up and his face was a little flushed.

"No, Nick," he said.

"There seems to have been a great deal that Chris did not tell us —" began Ralph.

Sir James glanced swiftly from his seat under the canopy.

"He told us all that was needed," he said.

"Aha!" broke out Nicholas again, "but the Holy Maid said that the King would not live six months if he —"

Chris's face was full of despair and misery, and his father interrupted once more.

"We had better not speak of that, my son," he said to Nicholas. "It is best to leave such things alone."

Ralph was smiling broadly with tight lips by now.

"By my soul, Nick, you are the maddest wind-bag I have ever heard. All our heads might go for what you have said tonight. Thank God the servants are gone."

"Nick," cried Mary imploringly, "do hold your tongue."

Lady Torridon looked from one to the other with serene amusement, and there was an odd pause such as generally fell when she showed signs of speaking. Her lips moved but she said nothing, and ran her eyes over the silver flagons before her.

When the Maxwells had gone at last, and prayers were over, Chris slipped across the Court with a towel, and went up to the priest's room over the sacristy. Mr. Carleton looked up from his lamp and rose.

"Yes, Chris," he said, "I will come. The moon will be up soon."

They went down together through the sacristy door on to the level plateaux of lawns that stretched step after step down to the dark lake. The sky was ablaze with stars, and in the East there was a growing light in the quarter where the moon was at its rising. The woods beyond the water were blotted masses against the sky; and the air was full of the rich fragrance of the summer night. The two said very little, and the priest stopped on the bank as Chris stepped out along the little boarded pier that ran out among the rushes into deep water. There was a scurry and a cry, and a moor-hen dashed out from under cover, and sped across the pond, scattering the silver points that hung there motionless, reflected from the heaven overhead.

Chris was soon ready, and stood there a moment, a pale figure in the gloom, watching the shining dots rock back again in the ripples to motionlessness. Then he lifted his hands and plunged.

It seemed to him, as he rose to the surface again, as if he were swimming between two sides. As he moved softly out across the middle, and a little ripple moved before him, the water was invisible. There was only a fathomless gulf, as deep below as the sky was high above, pricked with stars. As he turned his head this way and that the great trees, high overhead, seemed less real than those two immeasurable spaces above and beneath. There was a dead silence everywhere, only broken by the faint suck of the water over his shoulder, and an indescribably sweet coolness that thrilled him like a strain of music. Under its influence, again, as last night, the tangible, irritating world seemed to sink out of his soul; here he was, a living creature alone in a great silence with God, and nothing else was of any importance.

He turned on his back, and there was the dark figure on the bank watching him, and above it the great towered house, with its half-dozen lighted windows along its eastern side, telling him of the world of men and passion.

"Look," came the priest's voice, and he turned again, and over the further bank, between two tall trees, shone a great silver rim of the rising moon. A path of glory was struck now across the black water, and he pleased himself by traveling up it towards the remote splendor, noticing as he went how shadows had sprung into being in that moment, and how the same light that made the glory made the dark as well. His soul seemed to emerge a stage higher yet from the limits in which the hot day and the shouting and the horns and the crowded woods had fettered it. How remote and little seemed Ralph's sneers and Nicholas's indiscretions and Mary's pity! Here he moved round in a cooler and serener mood. That keen mood, whether physical or spiritual he did not care to ask, made him inarticulate as he walked up with the priest ten minutes later. But Mr. Carleton seemed to understand.

"There are some things besides the divorce best not talked about," he said, "and I think bathing by starlight is one of them."

They passed under the chapel window presently, and Chris noticed with an odd sensation of pleasure the little translucent patch of color between the slender mullions thrown by the lamp within — a kind of reflex or anti-type of the broad light shining over the water.

"Come up for a while," went on the priest, as they reached the side-entrance, "if you are not too tired."

The two went through the sacristy-door, locking it behind them, and up the winding stairs in the turret at the corner to the priest's chamber. Chris threw himself down, relaxed and happy, in the tall chair by the window, where he could look out and see the moon, clear of the trees now, riding high in heaven.

"That was a pity at supper," said the priest presently, as he sat at the table. "I love Sir Nicholas and think him a good Christian, but he is scarcely a discreet one."

"Tell me, father," broke out Chris, "what is going to happen?"

Mr. Carleton looked at him smiling. He had a pleasant ugly face, with little kind eyes and sensitive mouth.

"You must ask Mr. Ralph," he said, "or rather you must not. But he knows more than any of us."

"I wish he would not speak like that."

"Dear lad," said the priest, "you must not feel it like that. Remember our Lord bore contempt as well as pain."

There was silence a moment, and then Chris began again. "Tell me about Lewes, father. What will it be like?"

"It will be bitterly hard," said the priest deliberately. "Christ Church was too bitter for me, as you know. I came out after six months, and the Cluniacs are harder. I do not know if I lost my vocation or found it; but I am not the man to advise you in either case."

"Ralph thinks it is easy enough. He told me last night in the carriage that I need not trouble myself, and that monks had a very pleasant time. He began to tell me some tale about Glastonbury, but I would not hear it."

"Ah," said the chaplain regretfully, "the world's standard for monks is always high. But you will find it hard enough, especially in the first year. But, as I said, I am not the man to advise you — I failed."

Chris looked at him with something of pity in his heart, as the priest fingered the iron pen on the table, and stared with pursed lips and frowning forehead. The chaplain was extraordinarily silent in public, just carrying on sufficient conversation not to be peculiar or to seem morose, but he spoke more freely to Chris, and would often spend an hour or two in mysterious talk with Sir James. Chris's father had a very marked respect for the priest, and had had more than one sharp word with his wife, ten years before when he had first come to the house, and had found Lady Torridon prepared to treat her chaplain with the kind of respect that she gave to her butler. But the chaplain's position was secured by now, owing in a large measure to his own tact and unobtrusiveness, and he went about the house a quiet, sedate figure of considerable dignity and impressiveness, performing his duties punctually and keeping his counsel. He had been tutor to both the sons for a while, to Ralph only for a few months, but to Chris since his twelfth birthday, and the latter had formed with him a kind of peaceful confederacy, often looking in on him at unusual hours, always finding him genial, although very rarely confidential. It was to Mr. Carleton, too, that Chris owed his first drawings to the mystical life of prayer; there was a shelf of little books in the corner by the window of the priest's room, from which he would read to the boy aloud, first translating them into English as he went, and then, as studies progressed, reading the Latin as it stood; and that mysteriously fascinating world in which great souls saw and heard eternal things and talked familiarly with the Savior and His Blessed Mother had first dawned on the boy there. New little books, too, appeared from time to time, and the volumes had overflowed their original home; and from that fact Christopher gathered that the priest, though he had left the external life of Religion, still followed after the elusive spirit that was its soul.

"But tell me," he said again, as the priest laid the pen down and sat back in his chair, crossing his buckled feet beneath the cassock; "tell me, why is it so hard? I am not afraid of the discipline or the food."

"It is the silence," said the priest, looking at him.

"I love silence," said Chris eagerly.

"Yes, you love an hour or two, or there would be no hope of a vocation for you. But I do not think you will love a year. However, I may be wrong. But it is the day after day that is difficult. And there is no relaxation; not even in the infirmary. You will have to learn signs in your novitiate; that is almost the first exercise."

The priest got up and fetched a little book from the corner cupboard.

"Listen," he said, and then began to read aloud the instructions laid down for the sign-language of novices; how they were to make a circle in the air for bread since it was round, a motion of drinking for water, and so forth.

"You see," he said, "you are not even allowed to speak when you ask for necessaries. And, you know, silence has its peculiar temptations as well as its joys. There is accidie and scrupulousness and contempt of others, and a host of snares that you know little of now."

"But —" began Chris.

"Oh, yes; it has its joys, and gives a peculiar strength."

Chris knew, of course, well enough by now in an abstract way what the Religious discipline would mean, but he wished to have it made more concrete by examples, and he sat long with the chaplain asking him questions. Mr. Carleton had been, as he said, in the novitiate at Canterbury for a few months, and was able to tell him a good deal about the life there; but the differences between the Augustinians and the Cluniacs made it impossible for him to go with any minuteness into the life of the Priory at Lewes. He warned him, however, of the tendency that every soul found in silence to think itself different from others, and of so peculiar a constitution that ordinary rules did not apply to it. He laid so much stress on this that the other was astonished.

"But it is true," said Chris, "no two souls are the same."

The priest smiled.

"Yes, that is true, too; no two sheep are the same, but the sheep nature is one, and you will have to learn that for yourself. A Religious rule is drawn up for many, not for one; and each must learn to conform himself. It was through that I failed myself; I remembered that I was different from others, and forgot that I was the same."

Mr. Carleton seemed to take a kind of melancholy pleasure in returning to what he considered his own failure, and Chris began to wonder whether the thought of it was not the secret of that slight indication to moroseness that he had noticed in him.

The moon was high and clear by now, and Chris often leaned his cheek on the sash as the priest talked, and watched that steady shining shield go up the sky, and the familiar view of lawns and water and trees, ghostly and mystical now in the pale light.

The Court was silent as he passed through it near midnight, as the household had been long in bed; the flaring link had been extinguished two hours before, and the shadows of the tall chimneys lay black and precise at his feet across the great whiteness on the western side of the yard. Again the sense of the smallness of himself and his surroundings, of the vastness of all else, poured over his soul; these little piled bricks and stones, the lawns and woods round about, even England and the world itself, he thought, as his mind shot out towards the stars and the unfathomable spaces — all these were but very tiny things, negligible quantities, when he looked at them in the eternal light. It was this thought, after all, that was calling him out of the world, and had been calling him fitfully ever since his soul awoke eight years ago, and knew herself and her God: and his heart expanded and grew tremulous as he remembered once more that his vocation had been sealed by a divine messenger, and that he would soon be gone out of this little cell into the wide silent liberty of the most dear children of God.

Chapter III

THE ARRIVAL AT LEWES

Ralph relented as the month drew on, and was among those who wished Chris good-bye on the afternoon of the July day on which he was to present himself at Lewes. The servants were all drawn up at the back of the terrace against the hall, watching Ralph, even more than his departing brother, with the fascinated interest that the discreet and dignified friend of Cromwell always commanded. Ralph was at his best on such occasions, genial and natural, and showed a pleasing interest in the girths of the two horses, and the exact strapping of the couple of bags that Chris was to take with him. His own man, too, Mr. Morris, who had been with him ever since he had come to London, was to ride with Chris, at his master's express wish; stay with him in the guest-house that night, and return with the two horses and a precise report the next morning.

"You have the hares for my Lord Prior," he said impressively, looking at the game that was hanging head downwards from the servant's saddle. "Tell him that they were killed on Tuesday."

Sir James and his younger son were walking together a few yards away in deep talk; and Lady Torridon had caused a chair to be set for her at the top of the terrace steps where she could at once do her duty as a mother, and be moderately comfortable at the same time. She hardly spoke at all, but looked gravely with her enigmatic black eyes at the horses' legs and the luggage, and once held up her hand to silence a small dog that had begun to yelp with excitement.

"They must be going," said Ralph, when all was ready; and at the same moment Chris and his father came up, Sir James's arm thrown over his son's shoulders.

The farewells were very short; it was impossible to indulge in sentiment in the genial business-atmosphere generated by Ralph, and a minute later Chris was mounted. Sir James said no more, but stood a little apart looking at his son. Lady Torridon smiled rather pleasantly and nodded her head two or three times, and Ralph, with Mr. Carleton, stood on the gravel below, his hand on Chris's crupper, smiling up at him.

"Good-bye, Chris," he said, and added with an unusual piety, "God keep you!"

As the two horses passed through the gatehouse, Chris turned once again with swimming eyes, and saw the group a little re-arranged. Sir James and Ralph were standing together, Ralph's arm thrust through his father's; Mr. Carleton was still on the gravel, and Lady Torridon was walking very deliberately back to the house.

*T*he distance to Lewes was about fourteen miles, and it was not until they had traveled some two of them, and had struck off towards Burgess Hill that Chris turned his head for Mr. Morris to come up.

It was very strange to him to ride through that familiar country, where he had ridden hundreds of times before, and to know that this was probably the last time that he would pass along those lanes, at least under the same circumstances. It had the same effect on him, as a death in the house would have; the familiar things were the same, but they wore a new and strange significance. The few men and children he passed saluted him deferentially as usual, and then turned fifty yards further on and stared at the young gentleman who, as they knew, was riding off on such an errand, and with such grave looks.

Mr. Morris came up with an eager respectfulness at Chris's sign, keeping a yard or two away lest the swinging luggage on his own horse should discompose the master, and answered a formal question or two about the roads and the bags, which Chris put to him as a gambit of conversation. The servant was clever and well trained, and knew how to modulate his attitude to the precise degree of deference due to his master and his master's relations; he had entered Ralph's service from Cromwell's own eight years before. He liked nothing better than to talk of London and his experiences there, and selected with considerable skill the topics that he knew would please in each case. Now he was soon deep on the subject of Wolsey, pausing respectfully now and again for corroboration, or to ask a question the answer to which he knew a good deal better than Chris himself.

"I understand, sir, that the Lord Cardinal had a wonderful deal of furniture at York House: I saw some of it at Master Cromwell's; his grace sent it to him, at least, so I heard. Is that so, sir?"

Chris said he did not know.

"Well, I believe it was so, sir; there was a chair there, set with agates and pearl, that I think I heard Mr. Ralph say had come from there. Did you ever see my lord, sir?"

Chris said he had seen him once in a narrow street at Westminster, but the crowd was so great he could not get near.

"Ah! sir; then you never saw him go in state. I remember once seeing him, sir, going down to Hampton Court, with his gentlemen bearing the silver pillars before him, and the two priests with crosses. What might the pillars mean, sir?"

Again Chris confessed he did not know.

"Ah, sir!" said Morris reflectively, as if he had received a satisfactory answer. "And there was his saddle, Mr. Christopher, with silver-gilt stirrups, and red velvet, set on my lord's mule. And there was the Red Hat borne in front by another gentleman. At mass, too, he would be served by none under the rank of an earl; and I heard that he would have a duke sometimes for his lavabo. I heard Mr. Ralph say that there was more than a hundred and fifty carts that went with the Lord Cardinal up to Cawood, and that was after the King's grace had broken with him, sir; and he was counted a poor man."

Chris asked what was in the carts.

"Just his stuff, sir," said Mr. Morris reverentially.

The servant seemed to take a melancholy pleasure in recounting these glories, but was most discreet about the political aspects of Wolsey, although Chris tried hard to get him to speak, and he would neither praise nor blame the fallen prelate; he was more frank, however, about Campeggio, who as an Italian, was a less dangerous target.

"He was not a good man, I fear, Mr. Christopher. They told some very queer tales of him when he was over here. But he could ride, sir, Master Maxwell's man told me, near as well as my Lord of Canterbury himself. You know they say, sir, that the Archbishop can ride horses that none of his grooms can manage. But I never liked to think that a foreigner was to be sent over to do our business for us, and more than ever not such an one as that."

He proceeded to talk a good deal about Campeggio; his red silk and his lace, his gout, his servants, his un-English ways; but it began to get a little tiresome to Chris, and soon after passing through Ditchling, Mr. Morris, having pointed across the country towards Fatton Hovel, and having spoken of the ghost of a cow that was seen there with two heads, one black and one white, fell gradually behind again, and Chris rode alone.

They were coming up now towards the downs, and the great rounded green shoulders heaved high against the sky, gashed here and there by white strips and patches where the chalk glared in the bright afternoon sun. Ditchling beacon rose to their right, a hundred feet higher than the surrounding hills, and the high country sloped away from it parallel with their road, down to Lewes. The shadows were beginning to lie eastwards and to lengthen in long blue hollows and streaks against the clear green turf.

Chris wondered when he would see that side of the downs again; his ride was like a kind of farewell progress, and all that he looked on was dearer than it had ever been before, but he comforted himself by the thought of that larger world, so bright with revelation and so enchanting in its mystery that lay before him. He pleased himself by picturing this last journey as a ride through an overhung lane, beautiful indeed, but dusky, towards shining gates beyond which lay great tracts of country set with palaces alive with wonderful presences, and watered by the very river of life.

He did not catch sight of Lewes until he was close upon it, and it suddenly opened out beneath him, with its crowded roofs pricked by a dozen spires, the Norman castle on its twin mounds towering to his left, a silver gleam of the Ouse here and there between the plaster and timber houses as the river wound beneath its bridges, and beyond all the vast masses of the Priory straight in front of him to the South of the town, the church in front with its tall central tower, a huddle of convent roofs behind, all white against the rich meadows that lay beyond the stream.

Mr. Morris came up as Chris checked his horse here.

"See, Mr. Christopher," he said, and the other turned to see the town gallows on the right of the road, not fifty yards away, with a ragged shape or two hanging there, and a great bird rising heavily and winging its way into the west. Mr. Morris's face bore a look of judicial satisfaction.

"We are making a sweep of them," he said, and as a terrible figure, all rags and sores, with blind red eyes and toothless mouth rose croaking and entreating from the ditch by the road, the servant pointed with tight lips and solemn eyes to Hangman's Acre. Chris fumbled in his purse, threw a couple of groats on to the ground, and rode on down the hill.

His heart was beating fast as he went down Westgate Lane into the High Street, and it quickened yet further as the great bells in the Priory church began to jangle; for it was close on vesper time, and instinctively he shook his reins to hasten his beast, who was picking his way delicately through the filth and tumbled stones that lay everywhere, for the melodious roar seemed to be bidding him haste and be welcome. Mr. Morris was close beside him, and remarked on this and that as they went, the spire of St. Ann's away to the right, with St. Pancras's Bridge, a swinging sign over an inn with Queen Katharine's face erased, but plainly visible under Ann Boleyn's, the tall mound beyond the Priory crowned by a Calvary, and the roof of the famous dove-cote of the Priory, a great cruciform structure with over two thousand cells. But Christopher knew it all better than the servant, and paid little attention, and besides, his excitement was running too high. They came down at last through Antioch Street, Puddingbag Lane, and across the dry bed of the Winterbourne, and the gateway was before them.

The bells had ceased by now, after a final stroke. Mr. Morris sprang off his horse, and drew on the chain that hung by the smaller of the two doors. There was a sound of footsteps and a face looked out from the grating. The servant said a word or two; the face disappeared, and a moment later there was the turning of a key, and one leaf of the horse-entrance rolled back. Chris touched his beast with his heel, passed through on to the paved floor, and sat smiling and flushed, looking down at the old lay-brother, who beamed up at him pleasantly and told him he was expected.

Chris dismounted at once, telling the servant to take the horses round to the stables on the right, and himself went across the open court towards the west end of the church, that rose above him fifty feet into the clear evening air, faced with marble about the two doors, and crowned by the western tower and the high central spire beyond where the bells hung. On the right lay the long low wall of the Cellarer's offices, with the kitchen jutting out at the lower end, and the high-pitched refectory roof above and beyond it. The church was full of golden light as he entered, darkening to dusk in the chapels on either side, pricked with lights here and there that burned before the images, and giving an impression of immense height owing to its narrowness and its length. The air was full of rolling sound, sonorous and full, that echoed in the two high vaults on this side and that of the high altar, was caught in the double transepts, and lost in the chapels that opened in a corona of carved work at the further end, for the monks were busy at the *Opus Dei*, and the psalms rocked from side to side, as if the nave were indeed a great ship plowing its way to the kingdom of heaven.

There were a few seats at the western end, and into one of these Christopher found his way, signing himself first from the stoup at the door, and inclining before he went in. Then he leaned his chin on his hands and looked eagerly.

It was difficult to make out details clearly at the further end, for the church was poorly lighted, and there was no western window; the glare from the white roads, too, along which he had come still dazzled him, but little by little, helped by his own knowledge of the place, he began to see more clearly.

*H*igh above him ran the lines of the clerestory, resting on the rounded Norman arches, broken by the beam that held the mighty rood, with the figures of St. Mary and St. John on either side; and beyond, yet higher, on this side of the high altar, rose the lofty air of the vault ninety feet above the pavement. To left and right opened the two western transepts, and from where he knelt he could make out the altar of St. Martin in the further one, with its apse behind. The image of St. Pancras himself stood against a pillar with the light from the lamp beneath flickering against his feet. But Christopher's eyes soon came back to the center, beyond the screen, where a row of blackness on either side in the stalls, marked where the monks rested back, and where he would soon be resting with them. There were candles lighted at sparse intervals along the book-rests, that shone up into the faces bent down over the wide pages beneath; and beyond all rose the altar with two steady flames crowning it against the shining halpas behind that cut it off from the four groups of slender carved columns that divided the five chapels at the extreme east. Half-a-dozen figures sat about the nave, and Christopher noticed an old man, his white hair falling to his shoulders, two seats in front, beginning to nod gently with sleep as the soft heavy waves of melody poured down, lulling him.

He began now to catch the words, as his ears grew accustomed to the sound, and he, too, sat back to listen.

"Fiat pax in virtute tua: et abundantia in turribus tuis;" *"Propter fratres meos et proximos meos:"* came back the answer, *"loquebar pacem de te."* And once more: *"Propter domum Domini Dei nostri: quaesivi bona tibi."*

Then there was a soft clattering roar as the monks rose to their feet, and in double volume from the bent heads sounded out the *Gloria Patri.*

It was overwhelming to the young man to hear the melodious tumult of praise, and to remember that in less than a week he would be standing there among the novices and adding his voice. It seemed to him as if he had already come into the heart of life that he had felt pulsating round him as he swam in the starlight a month before. It was this that was reality, and the rest illusion. Here was the end for which man was made, the direct praise of God; here were living souls eager and alert on the business of their existence, building up with vibration after vibration the eternal temple of glory in which God dwelt. Once he began to sing, and then stopped. He would be silent here until his voice had been authorized to join in that consecrated offering.

He waited until all was over, and the two lines of black figures had passed out southwards, and the sacristan was going round putting out the lights; and then he too rose and went out, thrilled and excited, into the gathering twilight, as the bell for supper began to sound out from the refectory tower.

He found Mr. Morris waiting for him at the entrance to the guesthouse, and the two went up the stairs at the porter's directions into the parlor that looked out over the irregular court towards the church and convent.

Christopher sat down in the window seat.

Over the roofs opposite the sky was still tender and luminous, with rosy light from the west, and a little troop of pigeons were wheeling over the church in their last flight before returning home to their huge dwelling down by the stream. The porter had gone a few minutes before, and Christopher presently saw him returning with Dom Anthony Marks, the guest-master, whom he had got to know very well on former visits. In a fit of shyness he drew back from the window, and stood up, nervous and trembling, and a moment later heard steps on the stairs. Mr. Morris had slipped out, and now stood in the passage, and Chris saw him bowing with a nicely calculated mixture of humility and independence. Then a black figure appeared in the doorway, and came briskly through.

"My dear Chris," he said warmly, holding out his hands, and Chris took them, still trembling and excited.

They sat down together in the window-seat, and the monk opened the casement and threw it open, for the atmosphere was a little heavy, and then flung his arm out over the sill and crossed his feet, as if he had an hour at his disposal. Chris had noticed before that extraordinary appearance of ease and leisure in such monks, and it imperceptibly soothed him. Neither would Dom Anthony speak on technical matters, but discoursed pleasantly about the party at Overfield Court and the beauty of the roads between there and Lewes, as if Chris were only come to pay a passing visit.

"Your horses are happy enough," he said. "We had a load of fresh beans sent in today. And you, Chris, are you hungry? Supper will be here immediately. Brother James told the guest-cook as soon as you came."

He seemed to want no answer, but talked on genially and restfully about the commissioners who had come from Cluny to see after their possessions in England, and their queer French ways.

"Dom Philippe would not touch the muscadel at first, and now he cannot have too much. He clamored for claret at first, and we had to give him some. But he knows better now. But he says mass like a holy angel of God, and is a very devout man in all ways. But they are going soon."

Dom Anthony fulfilled to perfection the ideal laid down for a guest-master in the Custumal. He showed, indeed, the "cheerful hospitality to guests" by which "the good name of the monastery was enhanced, friendships multiplied, enmities lessened, God honored, and charity increased." He recognized perfectly well the confused terror in Christopher's mind and his anxiety to make a good beginning, and smoothed down the tendency to awkwardness that would otherwise have shown itself. He had a happy tranquil face, with wide friendly eyes that almost disappeared when he laughed, and a row of even white teeth.

As he talked on, Christopher furtively examined his habit, though he knew every detail of it well enough already. He had, of course, left his cowl, or ample-sleeved singing gown, in the sacristy on leaving the church, and was in his black frock girded with the leather belt, and the scapular over it, hanging to the ground before and behind. His hood, Christopher noticed, was creased and flat as if he were accustomed to sit back at his ease. He wore strong black leather boots that just showed beneath his habit, and a bunch of keys, duplicates of those of the camerarius and cook, hung on his right side. He was tonsured according to the Benedictine pattern, and his lips and cheeks were clean-shaven.

He noticed presently that Christopher was eyeing hum, and put his hand in friendly fashion on the young man's knee.

"Yes," he said, smiling, "yours is ready too. Dom Franklin looked it out today, and asked me whether it would be the right size. But of the boots I am not so sure."

There was a clink and a footstep outside, and the monk glanced out.

"Supper is here," he said, and stood up to look at the table — the polished clothless top laid ready with a couple of wooden plates and knives, a pewter tankard, salt-cellar and bread. There was a plain chair with arms drawn up to it. The rest of the room, which Christopher had scarcely noticed before, was furnished plainly and efficiently, and had just that touch of ornament that was intended to distinguish it from a cell. The floor was strewn with clean rushes; a couple of iron candlesticks stood on the mantelpiece, and the white walls had one or two religious objects hanging on them — a wooden crucifix opposite the table, a framed card bearing an "Image of Pity" with an indulgenced prayer illuminated beneath, a little statue of St. Pancras on a bracket over the fire, and a clear-written copy of rules for guests hung by the low oak door.

Dom Anthony nodded approvingly at the table, took up a knife and rubbed it delicately on the napkin, and turned round.

"We will look here," he said, and went towards the second door by the fire. Christopher followed him, and found himself in the bedroom, furnished with the same simplicity as the other; but with an iron bedstead in the corner, a kneeling stool beside it, with a little French silver image of St. Mary over it, and a sprig of dried yew tucked in behind. A thin leather-bound copy of the Little Office of Our Lady lay on the sloping desk, with another book or two on the upper slab. Dom Anthony went to the window and threw that open too.

"Your luggage is unpacked, I see," he said, nodding to the press beside which lay the two trunks, emptied now by Mr. Morris's careful hands.

"There are some hares, too," said Christopher. "Ralph has sent them to my Lord Prior."

"The porter has them," said the monk, "they look strangely like a bribe." And he nodded again with a beaming face, and his eyes grew little and bright at his own humor.

He examined the bed before he left the room again, turned back the sheets and pressed them down, and the straw rustled dryly beneath; glanced into the sweating earthenware jug, refolded the coarse towel on its wooden peg, and then smiled again at the young man.

"Supper," he said briefly.

Christopher stayed a moment with a word of excuse to wash off the dust of his ride from his hands and face, and when he came back into the sitting room found the candles lighted, the wooden shutters folded over the windows, and a basin of soup with a roast pigeon steaming on the table. The monk was standing, waiting for him by the door.

"I must be gone, Chris," he said, "but I shall be back before compline. My Lord Prior will see you tomorrow. There is nothing more? Remember you are at home now."

And on Christopher's assurances that he had all he could need, he was gone, leisurely and cheerfully, and his footsteps sounded on the stairs.

Mr. Morris came up before Chris had finished supper, and as he silently slipped away his plate and set another for the cheese, Chris remembered with a nervous exultation that this would be probably the last time that he would have a servant to wait on him. He was beginning to feel strangely at home already; the bean soup was strong and savory, the beer cool; and he was pleasantly exercised by his ride. Mr. Morris, too, in answer to his enquiries, said that he had been well looked after in the servants' quarters of the guest-house, and had had an entertaining supper with an agreeable Frenchman who, it seemed, had come with the Cluniac commissioners. Respect for his master and a sense of the ludicrous struggled in Mr. Morris's voice as he described the foreigner's pronunciation and his eloquent gestures.

"He's not like a man, sir," he said, and shook with reminiscent laughter.

*I*t was half an hour before Dom Anthony returned, and after hospitable enquiries, sat down by Chris again in the wide window-seat and began to talk.

He told him that guests were not expected to attend the night-offices, and that indeed he strongly recommended Chris doing nothing of the kind at any rate that night; that masses were said at all hours from five o'clock onwards; that prime was said at seven, and was followed by the *Missa familiaris* for the servants and work-people of the house. Breakfast would be ready in the guest-house at eight; the chapter-mass would be said at the half-hour and after the daily chapter which followed it had taken place, the Prior wished to see Christopher. The high mass was sung at ten, and dinner would be served at eleven. He directed his attention, too, to the card that hung by the door on which these hours were notified.

Christopher already knew that for the first three or four days he would have to remain in the guest-house before any formal step was taken with regard to him, but he said a word to Father Anthony about this.

"Yes," said the monk, "my Lord Prior will tell you about that. But you will be here as a guest until Sunday, and on that day you will come to the morning chapter to beg for admission. You will do that for three days, and then, please God, you will be clothed as a novice."

And once more he looked at him with deep smiling eyes.

Chris asked him a few more questions, and Dom Anthony told him what he wished to know, though protesting with monastic etiquette that it was not his province.

"Dom James Berkely is the novice-master," he said, "you will find him very holy and careful. The first matter you will have to learn is how to wear the habit, carry your hands, and to walk with gravity. Then you will learn how to bow, with the hands crossed on the knees, so —" and he illustrated it by a gesture — "if it is a profound inclination; and when and where the inclinations are to be made. Then you will learn of the custody of the eyes. It is these little things that help the soul at first, as you will find, like — like — the bindings of a peach tree, that it may learn how to grow and bear its fruit. And the Rule will be given you, and what a monk must have by rote, and how to sing. You will not be idle, Chris."

It was no surprise to Christopher to hear how much of the lessons at first were concerned with external behavior. In his visits to Lewes before, as well as from the books that Mr. Carleton had lent him, he had learnt that the perfection of the Religious Life depended to a considerable extent upon minutiæ that were both aids to, and the result of, a tranquil and recollected mind, the acquirement of which was part of the object of the monk's ambition. The ideal, he knew, was the perfect direction of every part of his being, of hands and eyes, as well as of the great powers of the soul; what God had joined together man must not put asunder, and the man who had every physical movement under control, and never erred through forgetfulness or impulse in these little matters, presumably also was master of his will, and retained internal as well as external equanimity.

The great bell began to toll presently for compline, and the guest-master rose in the midst of his explanations.

"My Lord Prior bade me thank you for the hares," he said. "Perhaps your servant will take the message back to Mr. Ralph tomorrow. Come."

They went down the stairs together and out into the summer twilight, the great strokes sounding overhead in the gloom as they walked. Over the high wall to the left shone a light or two from Lewes town, and beyond rose up the shadowy masses of the downs over which Christopher had ridden that afternoon. Over those hills, too, he knew, lay his old home. As they walked together in silence up the paved walk to the west end of the church, a vivid picture rose before the young man's eyes of the little parlor where he had sat last night — of his silent mother in her black satin; his father in the tall chair, Ralph in an unwontedly easy and genial mood lounging on the other side and telling stories of town, of the chaplain with his homely, pleasant face, slipping silently out at the door. That was the last time that all that was his, — that he had a right and a place there. If he ever saw it again it would be as a guest who had become the son of another home, with new rights and relations, and at the thought a pang of uncontrollable shrinking pricked at his heart.

But at the door of the church the monk drew his arm within his own for a moment and held it, and Chris saw the shadowed eyes under his brows rest on him tenderly.

"God bless you, Chris!" he said.

Chapter IV

A COMMISSION

*W*ithin a few days of Christopher's departure to Lewes, Ralph also
left Overfield and went back to London.

He was always a little intolerant at home, and generally appeared
there at his worst — caustic, silent, and unsympathetic. It seemed to him
that the simple country life was unbearably insipid; he found there
neither wit nor affairs: to see day after day the same faces, to listen to
the same talk either on country subjects that were distasteful to him, or,
out of compliment to himself, political subjects that were unfamiliar
to the conversationalists, was a very hard burden, and he counted such
things as the price he must pay for his occasional duty visits to his
parents. He could not help respecting the piety of his father, but he was
nonetheless bored by it; and the atmosphere of silent cynicism that
seemed to hang round his mother was his only relief. He thought he
understood her, and it pleased him sometimes to watch her, to calculate
how she would behave in any little domestic crisis or incident that
affected her, to notice the slight movement of her lips and her eyelids
gently lowering and rising again in movements of extreme annoyance.
But even this was not sufficient compensation for the other drawbacks
of life at Overfield Court, and it was with a very considerable relief that
he stepped into his carriage at last towards the end of July, nodded and
smiled once more to his father who was watching him from the terrace
steps with a wistful and puzzled face, anxious to please, and heard the
first crack of the whip of his return journey.

He had, indeed, a certain excuse for going, for a dispatch-rider had
come down from London with papers for him from Sir Thomas Cromwell, and it was not hard to assume a serious face and announce that

he was recalled by affairs; and there was sufficient truth in it, too, for one of the memoranda bore on the case of Elizabeth Barton, the holy maid of Kent, and announced her apprehension. Cromwell however, did not actually recall him, but mentioned the fact of her arrest, and asked if he had heard much said of her in the country, and what the opinion of her was in that district.

*T*he drive up to London seemed very short to him now; he went slowly through the bundle of papers on which he had to report, annotating them in order here and there, and staring out of the window now and again with unseeing eyes. There were a dozen cases on which he was engaged, which had been forwarded to him during his absence in the country — the priest at High Hatch was reported to have taken a wife, and Cromwell desired information about this; Ralph had ridden out there one day and gossiped a little outside the parsonage; an inn-keeper a few miles to the north of Cuckfield had talked against the divorce and the reigning Consort; a mistake had been made in the matter of a preaching license, and Cranmer had desired Cromwell to look into it; a house had been sold in Cheapside on which Ralph had been told to keep a suspicious eye, and he was asked his opinion on the matter; and such things as these occupied his time fully, until towards four o'clock in the afternoon his carriage rolled up to the horse-ferry at Lambeth, and he thrust the papers back into his bag before stepping out.

On arriving at his own little house in Westminster, the rent of which was paid by his master, he left his other servants to carry up the luggage, and set out himself again immediately with Morris in a hackney carriage for Chancery Lane.

As he went, he found himself for the hundredth time thinking of the history of the man to whom he was going.

Sir Thomas Cromwell was beginning to rise rapidly from a life of adventure and obscurity abroad. He had passed straight from the Cardinal's service to the King's three years before, and had since then been knighted, appointed privy-councilor, Master of the Jewel-house, and Clerk of the Hanaper in the Court of Chancery. At the same time he was actively engaged on his amazing system of espionage through which he was able to detect disaffection in all parts of the country, and thereby render himself invaluable to the King, who, like all the Tudors, while perfectly fearless in the face of open danger was pitiably terrified of secret schemes.

And it was to this man that he was confidential agent! Was there any limit to the possibilities of his future?

Ralph found a carriage drawn up at the door and, on enquiry, heard that his master was on the point of leaving; and even as he hesitated in the entrance, Cromwell shambled down the stairs with a few papers in his hand, his long sleeveless cloak flapping on each step behind him, and his felt plumed cap on his head in which shone a yellow jewel.

His large dull face, clean shaven like a priest's, lighted up briskly as he saw Ralph standing there, and he thrust his arm pleasantly through his agent's.

"Come home to supper," he said, and the two wheeled round and went out and into the carriage. Mr. Morris handed the bag through the window to his master, and stood bare-headed as the carriage moved off over the newly laid road.

It would have been a very surprising sight to Sir James Torridon to see his impassive son's attitude towards Cromwell. He was deferential, eager to please, nervous of rebuke, and almost servile, for he had found his hero in that tremendous personality. He pulled out his papers now, shook them out briskly, and was soon explaining, marking and erasing. Cromwell leaned back in his corner and listened, putting in a word of comment now and again, or dotting down a note on the back of a letter, and watching Ralph with a pleasant, oblique look, for he liked to see his people alert and busy. But he knew very well what his demeanor was like at other times, and had at first indeed been drawn to the young man by his surprising insolence of manner and impressive observant silences.

"That is very well, Mr. Torridon," he said. "I will see to the license. Put them all away."

Ralph obeyed, and then sat back too, silent indeed, but with a kind of side-long readiness for the next subject; but Cromwell spoke no more of business for the present, only uttering short sentences about current affairs, and telling his friend the news.

"Frith has been burned," he said. "Perhaps you knew it. He was obstinate to the end, my Lord Bishop reported. He threw Saint Chrysostom and Saint Augustine back into their teeth. He gave great occasion to the funny fellows. There was one who said that since Frith would have no purgatory, he was sent there by my Lord to find out for himself whether there be such a place or not. There was a word more about his manner of going there, 'Frith frieth,' but 'twas not good. Those funny fellows overreach themselves. Hewet went with him to Smithfield and hell."

Ralph smiled, and asked how they took it.

"Oh, very well. A priest bade the folk pray no more for Frith than for a dog, but Frith smiled on him and begged the Lord to forgive him his unkind words."

He was going on to tell him a little more about the talk of the Court, when the carriage drove up to the house in Throgmorton Street, near Austin Friars, which Cromwell had lately built for himself.

"My wife and children are at Hackney," he said as he stepped out. "We shall sup alone."

It was a great house, built out of an older one, superbly furnished with Italian things, and had a large garden at the back on to which looked the windows of the hall. Supper was brought up almost immediately — a couple of woodcocks and a salad — and the two sat down, with a pair of servants in blue and silver to wait on them. Cromwell spoke no more word of business until the bottle of wine had been set on the table, and the servants were gone. And then he began again, immediately.

"And what of the country?" he said. "What do they say there?" He took a peach from the carved roundel in the center of the table, and seemed absorbed in its contemplation.

Ralph had had some scruples at first about reporting private conversations, but Cromwell had quieted them long since, chiefly by the force of his personality, and partly by the argument that a man's duty to the State overrode his duty to his friends, and that since only talk that was treasonable would be punished, it was simpler to report all conversations in general that had any suspicious bearing, and that he himself was most competent to judge whether or no they should be followed up. Ralph, too, had become completely reassured by now that no injury would be done to his own status among his friends, since his master had never yet made direct use of any of his information in such a manner as that it was necessary for Ralph to appear as a public witness. And again, too, he had pointed out that the work had to be done, and that was better for the cause of justice and mercy that it should be done by conscientious rather than by unscrupulous persons.

He talked to him now very freely about the conversations in his father's house, knowing that Cromwell did not want more than a general specimen sketch of public feeling in matters at issue.

"They have great faith in the Maid of Kent, sir," he said. "My brother-in-law, Nicholas, spoke of her prophecy of his Grace's death. It is the devout that believe in her; the ungodly know her for a fool or a knave."

"*Filii hujus saeculi prudentiores sunt,*" — quoted Cromwell gravely. "Your brother-in-law, I should think, was a child of light."

"He is, sir."

"I should have thought so. And what else did you hear?"

"There is a good deal of memory of the Lady Katharine, sir. I heard the foresters talking one day."

"What of the Religious houses?"

Ralph hesitated.

"My brother Christopher has just gone to Lewes," he said. "So I heard more of the favorable side, but I heard a good deal against them, too. There was a secular priest talking against them one day, with our chaplain, who is a defender of them."

"Who was he?" asked Cromwell, with the same sharp, oblique glance.

"A man of no importance, sir; the parson of Great Keynes."

"The Holy Maid is in trouble," went on the other after a minute's silence. "She is in my Lord of Canterbury's hands, and we can leave her there. I suppose she will be hanged."

Ralph waited. He knew it was no good asking too much.

"What she said of the King's death and the pestilence is enough to cast her," went on Cromwell presently. "And Bocking and Hadleigh will be in his hands soon, too. They do not know their peril yet."

They went on to talk of the friars, and of the disfavor that they were in with the King after the unfortunate occurrences of the previous spring, when Father Peto had preached at Greenwich before Henry on the subject of Naboth's vineyard and the end of Ahab the oppressor. There had been a dramatic scene, Cromwell said, when on the following Sunday a canon of Hereford, Dr. Curwin, had preached against Peto from the same pulpit, and had been rebuked from the rood-loft by another of the brethren, Father Elstow, who had continued declaiming until the King himself had fiercely intervened from the royal pew and bade him be silent.

"The two are banished," said Cromwell, "but that is not the end of it. Their brethren will hear of it again. I have never seen the King so wrathful. I suppose it was partly because the Lady Katharine so cosseted them. She was always in the church at the night-office when the Court was at Greenwich, and Friar Forrest, you know, was her confessor. There is a rod in pickle."

Ralph listened with all his ears. Cromwell was not very communicative on the subject of the Religious houses, but Ralph had gathered from hints of this kind that something was preparing.

When supper was over and the servants were clearing away, Cromwell went to the window where the glass glowed overhead with his new arms and scrolls — a blue coat with Cornish choughs and a rose on a fess between three rampant lions — and stood there, a steady formidable figure, with his cropped head and great jowl, looking out on to the garden.

When the men had gone he turned again to Ralph.

"I have something for you," he said, "but it is greater than those other matters — a fool could not do it. Sit down."

He came across the room to the fireplace, as Ralph sat down, and himself took a chair by the table, lifting the baudkin cushion and settling it again comfortably behind him.

"It is this," he said abruptly. "You know that Master More has been in trouble. There was the matter of the gilt flagon which Powell said he had taken as a bribe, and the gloves lined with forty pound. Well, he disproved that, and I am glad of it, glad of it," he repeated steadily, looking down at his ring and turning it to catch the light. "But there is now another matter — I hear he has been practicing with the Holy Maid and hearkening to her ravings, and that my Lord of Rochester is in it too. But I am not sure of it."

Cromwell stopped, glanced up at Ralph a moment, and then down again.

"I am not sure of it," he said again, "and I wish to be. And I think you can help me."

Ralph waited patiently, his heart beginning to quicken. This was a great matter.

"I wish you to go to him," said his master, "and to get him into talk. But I do not see how it can be managed."

"He knows I am in your service, sir," suggested Ralph.

"Yes, yes," said Cromwell a little impatiently, "that is it. He is no fool, and will not talk. This is what I thought of. That you should go to him from me, and feign that you are on his side in the matter. But will he believe that?" he ended gloomily, looking at the other curiously.

There was silence for a minute, while Cromwell drummed his fingers softly on the table. Then presently Ralph spoke.

"There is this, sir," he said. "I might speak to him about my brother Chris who, as I told you, has gone to Lewes at the Maid's advice, and then see what Master More has to say."

Cromwell still looked at him.

"Yes," he said, "that seems reasonable. And for the rest — well, I will leave that in your hands."

They talked a few minutes longer about Sir Thomas More, and Cromwell told the other what a quiet life the ex-Chancellor had led since his resignation of office, of his house at Chelsea, and the like, and of the decision that he had apparently come to not to mix any further in public affairs.

"There is thunder in the air," he said, "as you know very well, and Master More is no mean weather-prophet. He misliked the matter of the Lady Katharine, and Queen Anne is no friend of his. I think he is wise to be quiet."

Ralph knew perfectly well that this tolerant language did not represent Cromwell's true attitude towards the man of whom they were speaking, but he assented to all that was said, and added a word or two about Sir Thomas More's learning, and of the pleasant manner in which he himself had been received when he had once had had occasion to see him before.

"He was throwing Horace at me," said the other, with a touch of bitterness, "the last time that I was there. I do not know which he loves best, that or his prayers."

Again Ralph recognized an animus. Cromwell had suffered somewhat from lack of a classical education.

"But it is a good thing to love the classics and devotion," he went on presently with a sententious air, "they are solaces in time of trouble. I have found that myself."

He glanced up at the other and down again.

"I was caught saying our Lady matins one day," he said, "when the Cardinal was in trouble. I remember I was very devout that morning."

He went on to talk of Wolsey and of his relations with him, and Ralph watched that heavy smooth face become reminiscent and almost sentimental.

"If he had but been wiser;" he said. "I have noticed again and again the folly of wise men. There is always clay mixed with gold. I suppose nothing but the fire that Fryth denied can purge it out; and my lord's was ambition."

He wagged his head in solemn reprobation, and Ralph did not know whether to laugh or to look grave. Then there fell a long silence, and Cromwell again fell to fingering his signet-ring, taking it off his thumb and rolling it on the smooth oak, and at last stood up with a brisker air.

"Welt," he said, "I have a thousand affairs, and my son Gregory is coming here soon. Then you will see about that matter. Remember I wish to know what Master More thinks of her, that — that I may know what to think."

Ralph understood sufficiently clearly, as he walked home in the evening light, what it was that his master wanted. It was no less than to catch some handle against the ex-chancellor, though he had carefully abstained from saying so. Ralph recognized the adroitness, and saw that while the directions had been plain and easy to understand, yet that not one word had been spoken that could by any means be used as a handle against Cromwell. If anyone in England at that time knew how to wield speech it was his master; it was by that weapon that he had prevailed with the King, and still kept him in check; it was that weapon rashly used by his enemies that he was continually turning against them, and under his tutoring Ralph himself had begun to be practiced in the same art.

Among other causes, too, of his admiration for Cromwell, was the latter's extraordinary business capacity. There was hardly an affair of any importance in which he did not have a finger at least, and most of them he held in the palm of his hand, and that, not only in the mass but in their minutest details. Ralph had marveled more than once at the minutiæ that he had seen dotted down on the backs of old letters lying on his master's table. Matters of Church and State, inextricably confused to other eyes, was simple to this man; he understood intuitively where the key of each situation lay, and dealt with them one after another briefly and effectively. And yet with all this no man wore an appearance of greater leisure; he would gossip harmlessly for an hour, and yet by the end had said all that he wished to say, and generally learnt, too, from his companion whoever he might be, all he wished to learn. Ralph had watched him more than once at this business; had seen delicate subjects introduced in a deft unsuspicious sentence that roused no alarm, and had marveled at his power to play with men without their dreaming of what was going forward.

And now it was Master More that was threatened. Ralph knew well that there was far more behind the scenes than he could understand or even perceive, and recognized that the position of Sir Thomas was more significant than would appear, and that developments might be expected to follow soon.

For himself he had no shrinking from his task. He understood that government was carried on by such methods, and that More himself would be the first to acknowledge that in war many things were permissible that would be outrageous in times of peace, and that these were times of war. To call upon a friend, to eat his bread and salt, and talk familiarly with him, and to be on the watch all the while for a weak spot through which that friend might be wounded, seemed to Ralph, trained now and perfected in Cromwell's school, a perfectly legitimate policy, and he walked homewards this summer evening, pleased with this new mark of confidence, and anxious to acquit himself well in his task.

*T*he house that Ralph occupied in Westminster was in a street to the west of the Abbey, and stood back a little between its neighbors. It was a very small one, of only two rooms in width and one in depth, and three stories high; but it had been well furnished, chiefly with things brought up from Overfield Court, to which Ralph had taken a fancy, and which his father had not denied him. He lived almost entirely in the first floor, his bedroom and sitting room being divided by the narrow landing at the head of the stairs that led up to the storey above, which was occupied by Mr. Morris and a couple of other servants. The lower storey Ralph used chiefly for purposes of business, and for interviews which were sufficiently numerous for one engaged in so many affairs. Cromwell had learnt by now that he could be trusted to say little and to learn much, and the early acts of many little dramas that had ended in tragedy had been performed in the two gravely-furnished rooms on the ground floor. A good deal of the law-business, in its early stages, connected with the annulling of the King's marriage with Queen Katharine had been done there; a great canonist from a foreign university had explained there his views in broken English, helped out with Latin, to a couple of shrewd-faced men, while Ralph watched the case for his master; and Cromwell himself had found the little retired house a convenience for meeting with persons whom he did not wish to frighten over much, while Ralph and Mr. Morris sat alert and expectant on the other side of the hall, with the door open, listening for raised voices or other signs of a quarrel.

The rooms upstairs had been furnished with considerable care. The floors of both were matted, for the plan involved less trouble than the continual laying of clean rushes. The sitting room was paneled up six feet from the floor, and the three feet of wall above were covered with really beautiful tapestry that Ralph had brought up from Overfield. There was a great table in the center, along one side of which rested a set of drawers with brass handles, and in the center of the table was a deep well, covered by a flap that lay level with the rest of the top. Another table stood against the wall, on which his meals were served, and the door of a cupboard in which his plate and knives were kept opened immediately above it, designed in the thickness of the wall. There were half-a-dozen chairs, two or three other pieces of furniture, a backed settle by the fire and a row of bookshelves opposite the windows; and over the mantelpiece, against the tapestry, hung a picture of Cromwell, painted by Holbein, and rejected by him before it was finished. Ralph had begged it from the artist who was on the point of destroying it. It represented the sitter's head and shoulders in three-quarter face, showing his short hair, his shrewd heavy face, with its double chin, and the furred gown below.

Mr. Morris was ready for his master and opened the door to him.

"There are some letters come, Mr. Ralph, sir," he said. "I have laid them on your table."

Ralph nodded, slipped off his thin cloak into his servant's hands without speaking, laid down his cane and went upstairs.

The letters were very much what he expected, and dealt with cases on which he was engaged. There was an entreaty from a country squire near Epping Forest, whose hounds had got into trouble with the King's foresters that he would intercede for him to Cromwell. A begging letter from a monk who had been ejected from his monastery for repeated misconduct, and who represented himself as starving; Ralph lifted this to his nostrils and it smelt powerfully of spirits, and he laid it down again, smiling to himself. A torrent of explanation from a schoolmaster who had been reported for speaking against the sacrament of the altar, calling the saints to witness that he was no follower of Fryth in such detestable heresy. A dignified protest from a Justice of the Peace in Kent who had been reproved by Cromwell, through Ralph's agency, for acquitting a sturdy beggar, and who begged that he might in future deal with a responsible person; and this Ralph laid aside, smiling again and promising himself that he would have the pleasure of granting the request. An offer, written in a clerkly hand, from a fellow who could not sign his name but had appended a cross, to submit some important evidence of a treasonable plot, on the consideration of secrecy and a suitable reward.

A year ago such a budget would have given Ralph considerable pleasure, and a sense of his own importance; but business had been growing on him rapidly of late, as his master perceived his competence, and it gave him no thrill to docket this one, write a refusal to that, a guarded answer to another, and finally to open the well of his table and drop the bundle in.

Then he turned round his chair, blew out one candle carefully, and set to thinking about Master Thomas More.

Chapter V
MASTER MORE

*I*t was not until nearly a month later that Ralph made an opportunity to call upon Sir Thomas More. Cromwell had given him to understand that there was no immediate reason for haste; his own time was tolerably occupied, and he thought it as well not to make a show of overgreat hurry. He wrote to Sir Thomas, explaining that he wished to see him on a matter connected with his brother Christopher, and received a courteous reply begging him to come to dinner on the following Thursday, the octave of the Assumption, as Sir Thomas thought it proper to add.

*I*t was a wonderfully pleasant house, Ralph thought, as his wherry came up to the foot of the garden stairs that led down from the lawn to the river. It stood well back in its own grounds, divided from the river by a wall with a wicket gate in it. There was a little grove of trees on either side of it; a flock of pigeons were wheeling about the bell-turret that rose into the clear blue sky, and from which came a stroke or two, announcing the approach of dinner-time as he went up the steps.

There was a figure lying on its face in the shadow by the house, as Ralph came up the path, and a small dog, that seemed to be trying to dig the head out from the hands in which it was buried, ceased his excavations and set up a shrill barking. The figure rolled over, and sat up; the pleasant brown face was all creased with laughter; small pieces of grass were clinging to the long hair, and Ralph, to his amazement, recognized the ex-Lord Chancellor of England.

"I beg your pardon, sir," said More, rising and shaking himself. "I had no idea — you take me at a disadvantage; it is scarcely dignified" — and he stopped, smiling and holding out one hand, while he stretched the other deprecatingly, to quiet that insistent barking.

Ralph had a sensation of mingled contempt and sympathy as he took his hand.

"I had the honor of seeing you once before, Master More," he said.

"Why, yes," said More, "and I hope I cut a better figure last time, but Anubis would take no refusal. But I am ashamed, and beg you will not speak of it to Mrs. More. She is putting on a new coif in your honor."

"I will be discreet," said Ralph, smiling.

They went indoors almost immediately, when Sir Thomas had flicked the grass sufficiently off his gown to escape detection, and straight through to the hall where the table was laid, and three or four girls were waiting.

"Your mother is not here yet, I see," said Sir Thomas, when he had made Ralph known to his daughters, and the young man had kissed them deferentially, according to the proper etiquette — "I will tell you somewhat — hush —" and he broke off again sharply as the door from the stairs opened, and a stately lady, with a rather solemn and uninteresting face, sailed in, her silk skirts rustling behind her, and her fresh coif stiff and white on her head. A middle-aged man followed her in, looking a little dejected, and made straight across to where the ladies were standing with an eagerness that seemed to hint at a sense of escape.

"Mrs. Alice," said Sir Thomas, "this is Mr. Ralph Torridon, of whom you have heard me speak. I was fortunate enough to welcome him on the lawn just now."

"I saw you, Mr. More," said his wife with dignity, as she took Ralph's hand and said a word about the weather.

"Then I will confess," said Sir Thomas, smiling genially round, "I welcomed Mr. Torridon with the back of my head, and with Anubis biting my ears."

Ralph felt strangely drawn to this schoolboy kind of man, who romped with dogs and lay on his stomach, and was so charmingly afraid of his wife. His contempt began to melt as he looked at him and saw those wise twinkling eyes, and strong humorous mouth, and remembered once more who he was, and his reputation.

Sir Thomas said grace with great gravity and signed himself reverently before he sat down. There was a little reading first of the Scriptures and a commentary on it, and then as dinner went on Ralph began to attend less and less to his hostess, who, indeed appeared wholly absorbed in domestic details of the table and with whispering severely to the servants behind her hand, and to listen and look towards the further end where Sir Thomas sat in his tall chair, his flapped cap on his head, and talked to his daughters on either side. Mr. Roper, the man who had come in with Mrs. More, was sitting opposite Ralph, and seemed to be chiefly

occupied in listening too. A bright-looking tall girl, whom her father
had introduced by the name of Cecily, sat between Ralph and her father.

"Not at all," cried Sir Thomas, in answer to something that Ralph
did not catch, "nothing of the kind! It was Juno that screamed. Argus
would not condescend to it. He was occupied in dancing before the
bantams."

Ralph lost one of the few remarks that Mrs. More addressed to him,
in wondering what this meant, and the conversation at the other end
swept round a corner while he was apologizing. When he again caught
the current Sir Thomas was speaking of wherries.

"I would love to row a wherry," he said. "The fellows do not know
their fortune; they might lead such sweet meditative lives; they do not,
I am well aware, for I have never heard such blasphemy as I have heard
from wherrymen. But what opportunities are theirs! If I were not your
father, my darling, I would be a wherryman. *Si cognovisses et tu quae ad
pacem tibi!* Mr. Torridon, would you not be a wherryman if you were not
Mr. Torridon?"

"I thought not this morning," said Ralph, "as I came here. It seemed
hot rowing against the stream."

"It is part of the day's work," said More. "When I was Chancellor I
loved nothing more than a hot summer's day in Court, for I thought
of my cool garden where I should soon be walking. I must show you
the New Building after dinner, Mr. Torridon."

Cecily and Margaret presently had a short encounter across the table
on some subject that Ralph did not catch, but he saw Margaret on the
other side flush up and bring her lips sharply together. Sir Thomas leapt
into the breach.

"*Unde leves animae tanto caluere furore?*" he cried, and glanced up at
Ralph to see if he understood the quotation, as the two girls dropped
their eyes ashamed.

"*Pugnavare pares, succubuere pares,*" said Ralph by a flash of inspiration,
and looking at the girls.

Sir Thomas's eyes shone with pleasure.

"I did not know you were such a treasure, Mr. Torridon. Now, Master
Cromwell could not have done that."

There fell a silence as that name was spoken, and all at the table eyed
Ralph.

"He was saying as much to me the other day," went on Ralph, excited
by his success. "He told me you knew Horace too well."

"And that my morals were corrupted by him," went on More. "I know
he thinks that, but I had the honor of confuting him the other day with
regard to the flagon and gloves. Now, there is a subject for Martial, Mr.

Torridon. A corrupt statesman who has retired on his ill-gotten gains disproves an accusation of bribery. Let us call him Atticus 'Attice . . . Attice' . . . — We might say that he put on the gloves lest his forgers should be soiled while he drank from the flagon, or something of the kind."

Sir Thomas's eyes beamed with delight as he talked. To make an apt classical quotation was like wine to him, but to have it capped appropriately was like drunkenness. Ralph blessed his stars that he had been so lucky, for he was no great scholar, and he guessed he had won his host's confidence.

Dinner passed on quietly, and as they rose from table More came round and took his guest by the arm.

"You must come with me and see my New Building," he said, "you are worthy of it, Mr. Torridon."

He still held his arm affectionately as they walked out into the garden behind the house, and as he discoursed on the joys of a country life.

"What more can I ask of God?" he said. "He has given me means and tastes to correspond, and what man can say more. I see visions, and am able to make them realities. I dream of a dovecote with a tiled roof, and straightway build it; I picture a gallery and a chapel and a library away from the clack of tongues, and behold there it is. The eye cannot say to the hand, 'I have no need of thee.' To see and dream without the power of performance is heart-breaking. To perform without the gift of imagination is soul-slaying. The man is blessed that hath both eye and hand, tastes and means alike."

It was a very pleasant retreat that Sir Thomas More had built for himself at the end of his garden, where he might retire when he wanted solitude. There was a little entrance hall with a door at one corner into the chapel, and a long low gallery running out from it, lined with bookshelves on one side, and with an open space on the other lighted by square windows looking into the garden. The polished boards were bare, and there was a path marked on them by footsteps going from end to end.

"Here I walk," said More, "and my friends look at me from those shelves, ready to converse but never to interrupt. Shall we walk here, Mr. Torridon, while you tell me your business?"

Ralph had, indeed, a touch of scrupulousness as he thought of his host's confidence, but he had learnt the habit of silencing impulses and of only acting on plans deliberately formed; so he was soon laying bare his anxiety about Chris, and his fear that he had been misled by the Holy Maid.

"I am very willing, Mr. More," he said, "that my brother should be a monk if it is right, but I could not bear he should be so against God's leading. How am I to know whether the maid's words are of God or no?"

Sir Thomas was silent a moment.

"But he had thoughts of it before, I suppose," he said, "or he would not have gone to her. In fact, you said so."

Ralph acknowledged that this was so.

"— And for several years," went on the other.

Again Ralph assented.

"And his tastes and habits are those of a monk, I suppose. He is long at his prayers, given to silence, and of a tranquil spirit?"

"He is not always tranquil," said Ralph. "He is impertinent sometimes."

"Yes, yes; we all are that. I was very impertinent to you at dinner in trying to catch you with Martial his epigram, though I shall not offend again. But his humor may be generally tranquil in spite of it. Well, if that is so, I do not see why you need trouble about the Holy Maid. He would likely have been a monk without that. She only confirmed him."

"But," went on Ralph, fighting to get back to the point, "if I thought she was trustworthy I should be the more happy."

"There must always be doubtfulness," said More, "in such matters. That is why the novitiate is so severe; it is to show the young men the worst at once. I do not think you need be unhappy about your brother."

"And what is your view about the Holy Maid?" asked Ralph, suddenly delivering his point.

More stopped in his walk, cocked his head a little on one side like a clever dog, and looked at his companion with twinkling eyes.

"It is a delicate subject," he said, and went on again.

"That is what puzzles me," said Ralph. "Will you not tell me your opinion, Mr. More?"

There was again a silence, and they reached the further end of the gallery and turned again before Sir Thomas answered.

"If you had not answered me so briskly at dinner, Mr. Torridon, do you know that I should have suspected you of coming to search me out. But such a good head, I think, cannot be allied with a bad heart, and I will tell you."

Ralph felt a prick of triumph but none of remorse.

"I will tell you," went on More, "and I am sure you will keep it private. I think the Holy Maid is a good woman who has a maggot."

Ralph's spirits sank again. This was a very non-committing answer.

"I do not think her a knave as some do, but I think, to refer to what we said just now, that she has a large and luminous eye, and no hand worth mentioning. She sees many visions, but few facts. That tale about the Host being borne by angels from Calais to my mind is nonsense. Almighty God does not work miracles without reason, and there is none for that. The blessed sacrament is the same at Dover as at Calais. And a woman who can dream that can dream anything, for I am sure she did not invent it. On other matters, therefore, she may be dreaming too, and that is why once more I tell you that to my mind you can leave her out of your thoughts with regard to your brother. She is neither prophetess nor pythoness."

This was very unsatisfactory, and Ralph strove to remedy it.

"And in the matter of the King's death, Mr. More?" he said.

Again Sir Thomas stopped in his walk.

"Do you know, Mr. Torridon, I think we may leave that alone," he said a little abruptly. And Ralph sucked in his lip and bit it sharply at the consciousness of his own folly.

"I hope your brother will be very happy," went on the other after a moment, "and I am sure he will be, if his call is from God, as I think likely. I was with the Carthusians myself, you know, for four years, and sometimes I think I should have stayed there. It is a blessed life. I do not envy many folks, but I do those. To live in the daily companionship of our blessed Lord and of his saints as those do, and to know His secrets — *secreta Domini* — even the secrets of His Passion and its ineffable joys of pain — that is a very fortunate lot, Mr. Torridon. I sometimes think that as it was with Christ's natural body so it is with His mystical body: there be some members, His hands and feet and side, through which the nails are thrust, though indeed there is not one whole spot in His body — *inglorious erit inter viros aspectus ejus — nos putavimus eum quasi leprosum* — but those parts of His body that are especially pained are at once more honorable and more happy than those that are not. And the monks are those happy members."

He was speaking very solemnly, his voice a little tremulous, and his kindly eyes were cast down, and Ralph watched him sidelong with a little awe and pity mingled. He seemed so natural too, that Ralph thought that he must have overrated his own indiscretion.

A shadow fell across the door into the garden as they came near it, and one of the girls appeared in the opening.

"Why, Meg," cried her father, "what is it, my darling?"

"Beatrice has come, sir," said the girl. "I thought you would wish to know."

More put out his arm and laid it round his daughter's waist as she turned with him.

"Come, Mr. Torridon," he said, "if you have no more to say, let us go and see Beatrice."

There was a group on the lawn under one of the lime trees, two or three girls and Mr. Roper, who all rose to their feet as the three came up. More immediately sat down on the grass, putting his feet delicately together before him.

"Will, fetch this gentleman a chair. It is not fit for Master Cromwell's friend to sit on the grass like you and me."

Ralph threw himself down on the lawn instantly, entreating Mr. Roper not to move.

"Well, well," said Sir Thomas, "let be. Sit down too, Will, *et cubito remanete presso.* Mr. Torridon understands that, I know, even if Master Cromwell's friend does not. Why, tillie-vallie, as Mrs. More says, I have not said a word to Beatrice. Beatrice, this is Mr. Ralph Torridon, and this, Mr. Torridon, is Beatrice. Her other name is Atherton, but to me she is a feminine benediction, and naught else."

Ralph rose swiftly and looked across at a tall slender girl that was sitting contentedly on an outlying root of the lime tree, beside of Sir Thomas, and who rose with him.

"Mr. More cannot let my name alone, Mr. Torridon," she said tranquilly, as she drew back after the salute. "He made a play upon it the other day."

"And have been ashamed of it ever since," said More; "it was sacrilege with such a name. Now, I am plain Thomas, and more besides. Why did you send for me, Beatrice?"

"I have no defense," said the girl, "save that I wanted to see you."

"And that is the prettiest defense you could have made — if it does not amount to corruption. Mr. Torridon, what is the repartee to that?"

"I need no advocate," said the girl; "I can plead well enough."

Ralph looked up at her again with a certain interest. She seemed on marvelously good terms with the whole family, and had an air of being entirely at her ease. She had her black eyes bent down on to a piece of grass that she was twisting into a ring between her slender jeweled fingers, and her white teeth wore closed firmly on her lower lip as she worked. Her long silk skirts lay out unregarded on the grass, and her buckles gleamed beneath. Her voice was pleasant and rather deep, and Ralph found himself wondering who she was, and why he had not seen her before, for she evidently belonged to his class, and London was a small place.

"I see you are making one more chain to bind me to you," said More presently, watching her.

She held it up.

"A ring only," she said.

"Then it is not for me," said More, "for I do not hold with Dr. Melanchthon, nor yet Solomon in the matter of wives. Now, Mr. Torridon, tell us all some secrets. Betray your master. We are all agog. Leave off that ring, Beatrice, and attend."

"I am listening," said the girl as serenely as before, still intent on her weaving.

"The King breakfasted this morning at eight of the clock," said Ralph gravely. "It is an undoubted fact, I had it on the highest authority."

"This is excellent," said Sir Thomas. "Let us all talk treason. I can add to that. His Grace had a fall last night and lay senseless for several hours."

He spoke with such gravity that Ralph glanced up. At the same moment Beatrice looked up from her work and their eyes met.

"He fell asleep," added Sir Thomas.

*I*t was very pleasant to lie there in the shadow of the lime that afternoon, and listen to the mild fooling, and Ralph forgot his manners, and almost his errand too, and never offered to move. The grass began to turn golden as the sun slanted to the West, and the birds began to stir after the heat of the day, and to chirp from tree to tree. A hundred yards away the river twinkled in the sun, seen beyond the trees and the house, and the voices of the boatmen came, softened by distance and water, as they plied up and down the flowing highway. Once a barge went past under the Battersea bank, with music playing in the stern, and Ralph raised himself on his elbow to watch it as it went down the stream with flags flying behind, and the rhythmical throb of the row-locks sounding time to the dancing melody.

Ralph did his best to fall in with the humor of the day, and told a good story or two in his slow voice — among them one of his mother exercising her gift of impressive silence towards a tiresome chatterbox of a man, with such effect that the conversationalist's words died on his lips, after the third or fourth pause made for applause and comment. He told the story well, and Lady Torridon seemed to move among them, her skirts dragging majestically on the grass, and her steady, somber face looking down on them all beneath half-closed languid eye-lids.

"He has never been near us again," said Ralph, "but he never fails to ask after my mother's distressing illness when I meet him in town."

He was a little astonished at himself as he talked, for he was not accustomed to take such pains to please, but he was conscious that though he looked round at the faces, and addressed himself to More, he was really watching for the effect on the girl who sat behind. He was aware of every movement that she made; he knew when she tossed the ring on the little sleeping brown body of the dog that had barked at him earlier in the day, and set to work upon another. She slipped that on her finger when she had done, and turned her hand this way and that, her fingers bent back, a ruby catching the light as she did so, looking at the effect of the green circle against the whiteness. But he never looked at her again, except once when she asked him some question, and then he looked her straight in her black eyes as he answered.

A bell sounded out at last again from the tower, and startled him. He got up quickly.

"I am ashamed," he said smiling, "how dare I stay so long? It is your kindness, Mr. More."

"Nay, nay," said Sir Thomas, rising too and stretching himself. "You have helped us to lose another day in the pleasantest manner possible — you must come again, Mr. Torridon."

He walked down with Ralph to the garden steps, and stood by him talking, while the wherry that had been hailed from the other side made its way across.

"Beatrice is like one of my own daughters," he said, "and I cannot give her better praise than that. She is always here, and always as you saw her today. I think she is one of the strongest spirits I know. What did you think of her, Mr. Torridon?"

"She did not talk much," said Ralph.

"She talks when she has aught to say," went on More, "and otherwise is silent. It is a good rule, sir; I would I observed it myself."

"Who is she?" asked Ralph.

"She is the daughter of a friend I had, and she lives just now with my wife's sisters, Nan and Fan. She is often in town with one of them. I am astonished you have not met her before."

The wherry slid up to the steps and the man in his great boots slipped over the side to steady it.

"Now is the time to begin your philosophy," said More as Ralph stepped in, "and a Socrates is ready. Talk it over, Mr. Torridon."

Chapter VI

RALPH'S INTERCESSION

Ralph was astonished to find how the thought of the tall girl he had met at Sir Thomas More's house remained with him. He had reported the result of his interview with More himself to his master; and Cromwell had received it rather coldly. He had sniffed once or twice.

"That was not very well done, Mr. Torridon. I fear that you have frightened him, and gained nothing by it."

Ralph stood silent.

"But I see you make no excuses," went on Cromwell, "so I will make them for you. I daresay he was frightened already; and knew all about what had passed between her and the Archbishop. You must try again, sir."

Ralph felt his heart stir with pleasure.

"I may say I have made friends with Mr. More, sir," he said. "I had good fortune in the matter of a quotation, and he received me kindly. I can go there again without excusing my presence, as often as you will."

Cromwell looked at him.

"There is not much to be gained now," he said, "but you can go if you will; and you may perhaps pick up something here and there. The more friends you make the better."

Ralph went away delighted; he had not wholly failed then in his master's business, and he seemed to have set on foot a business of his own; and he contemplated with some excitement his future visits to Chelsea.

He had his first word with the King a couple of months later. He had often, of course, seen him before, once or twice in the House of Lords, formidable and frowning on his throne, his gross chin on his hand, barking out a word or two to his subjects, or instructing them in theology, for which indeed he was very competent; and several times in processions, riding among his gentlemen on his great horse, splendid in velvet and gems; and he had always wondered what it was that gave him his power. It could not be mere despotism, he thought, or his burly English nature; and it was not until he had seen him near at hand, and come within range of his personality that he understood why it was that men bore such things from him.

He was sent for one afternoon by Cromwell to bring a paper and was taken up at once by a servant into the gallery where the minister and the King were walking together. They were at the further end from that at which he entered, and he stood, a little nervous at his heart, but with his usual appearance of self-possession, watching the two great backs turned to him, and waiting to be called.

They turned again in a moment, and Cromwell saw him and beckoned, himself coming a few steps to meet him. The King waited, and Ralph was aware of, rather than saw, that wide, coarse, strong face, and the long narrow eyes, with the feathered cap atop, and the rich jeweled dress beneath. The King stood with his hands behind his back and his legs well apart.

Cromwell took the paper from Ralph, who stepped back, hesitating what to do.

"This is it, your Grace," said the minister going back again. "Your Grace will see that it is as I said."

Ralph perceived a new tone of deference in his master's voice that he had never noticed before, except once when Cromwell was ironically bullying a culprit who was giving trouble.

The King said nothing, took the paper and glanced over it, standing a little aside to let the light fall on it.

"Your Grace will understand —" began Cromwell again.

"Yes, yes, yes," said the harsh voice impatiently. "Let the fellow take it back," and he thrust the paper into Cromwell's hand, who turned once more to Ralph.

"Who is he?" said the King. "I have seen his face. Who are you?"

"This is Mr. Ralph Torridon," said Cromwell; "a very useful friend to me, your Grace."

"The Torridons of Overfield?" questioned Henry once more, who never forgot a face or a name.

"Yes, your Grace," said Cromwell.

"You are tall enough, sir," said the King, running his narrow eyes up and down Ralph's figure; — "a strong friend."

"I hope so, your Grace," said Ralph.

The King again looked at him, and Ralph dropped his eyes in the glare of that mighty personality. Then Henry abruptly thrust out his hand to be kissed, and as Ralph bent over it he was aware of the thick straight fingers, the creased wrist, and the growth of hair on the back of the hand.

*R*alph was astonished, and a little ashamed at his own excitement as he passed down the stairs again. It was so little that had happened; his own part had been so insignificant; and yet he was tingling from head to foot. He felt he knew now a little better how it was that the King's will, however outrageous in its purposes, was done so quickly. It was the sheer natural genius of authority and royalty that forced it through; he had felt himself dominated and subdued in those few moments, so that he was not his own master. As he went home through the street or two that separated the Palace gate from his own house, he found himself analyzing the effect of that presence, and, in spite of its repellence, its suggestion of coarseness, and its almost irritating imperiousness, he was conscious that there was a very strong element of attractiveness in it too. It seemed to him the kind of attractiveness that there is for a beaten dog in the chastising hand: the personality was so overwhelming that it compelled allegiance, and that not wholly one of fear. He found himself thinking of Queen Katharine and understanding a little better how it was that the refined, delicately nurtured and devout woman, so constant in her prayers, so full of the peculiar fineness of character that gentle birth and religion alone confer, could so cling to this fierce lord of hers, throw herself at his feet with tears before all the company, and entreat not to be separated from him, calling him her "dear lord," her "love," and her most "merciful and gracious prince."

*T*he transition from this train of thought to that bearing on Beatrice was not a difficult one; for the memory of the girl was continually in his mind. He had seen her half a dozen times now since their first meeting; for he had availed himself to the full of Cromwell's encouragement to make himself at home at Chelsea; and he found that his interest in her deepened every time. With a touch of amusement he found himself studying Horace and Terence again, not only for Sir Thomas More's benefit, but in order to win his approval and his good report to his household, among whom Beatrice was practically to be reckoned.

He was pleased too by More's account of Beatrice.

"She is nearly as good a scholar as my dear Meg," he had said one day. "Try her, Mr. Torridon."

Ralph had carefully prepared an apt quotation that day, and fired it off presently, not at Beatrice, but, as it were, across her; but there was not the faintest response or the quiver of an eyelid.

There was silence a moment; and then Sir Thomas burst out —

"You need not look so demure, my child; we all know that you understand."

Beatrice had given him a look of tranquil amusement in return.

"I will not be made a show of," she said.

Ralph went away that day more engrossed than ever. He began to ask himself where his interest in her would end; and wondered at its intensity.

As he questioned himself about it, it seemed that to him it was to a great extent her appearance of detached self-possession that attracted him. It was the quality that he most desired for himself, and one which he had in measure attained; but he was aware that in the presence of Cromwell at least it deserted him. He knew well that he had found his master there, and that he himself was nothing more than a hero-worshipper before a shrine; but it provoked him to feel that there was no one who seemed to occupy the place of a similar divinity with regard to this girl. Obviously she admired and loved Sir Thomas More — Ralph soon found out how deeply in the course of his visits — but she was not in the least afraid of her friend. She serenely contradicted him when she disagreed with what he said, would fail to keep her appointments at his house with the same equanimity, and in spite of Sir Thomas's personality never appeared to give him more than a friendly and affectionate homage. With regard to Ralph himself, it was the same. She was not in the least awed by him, or apparently impressed by his reputation which at this time was growing rapidly as that of a capable and daring agent of Cromwell's; and even once or twice when he condescended to hint at the vastness of the affairs on which he was engaged, in a desperate endeavor to rouse her admiration, she only looked at him steadily a moment with very penetrating eyes, and began to speak of something else. He began to feel discouraged.

*T*he first hint that Ralph had that he had been making a mistake in his estimate of her, came from Margaret Roper, who was still living at Chelsea with her husband Will.

Ralph had walked up to the house one bleak afternoon in early spring along the river-bank from Westminster, and had found Margaret alone in the dining-hall, seated by the window with her embroidery in her hand, and a Terence propped open on the sill to catch the last gleams of light from the darkening afternoon. She greeted Ralph warmly, for he was a very familiar figure to them all by now, and soon began to talk, when he had taken a seat by the wide open fireplace whence the flames flickered out, casting shadows and lights round the high room, across the high-hung tapestries and in the gloomy corners.

"Beatrice is here," she said presently, "upstairs with father. I think she is doing some copying for him."

"She is a great deal with him," observed Ralph.

"Why, yes; father thinks so much of her. He says that none can write so well as she, or has such a quick brain. And then she does not talk, he says, nor ask foolish woman-questions like the rest of us." And Margaret glanced up a moment, smiling.

"I suppose I must not go up," said Ralph, a little peevishly; for he was tired with his long day.

"Why, no, you must not," said Margaret, "but she will be down soon, Mr. Torridon."

There was silence for a moment or two; and then Margaret spoke again.

"Mr. Torridon," she said, "may I say something?" Ralph made a little sound of assent. The warmth of the fire was making him sleepy.

"Well, it is this," said Margaret slowly, "I think you believe that Beatrice does not like you. That is not true. She is very fond of you; she thinks a great deal of you," she added, rather hastily.

Ralph sat up; his drowsiness was gone.

"How do you know that, Mrs. Roper?" he asked. His voice sounded perfectly natural, and Margaret was reassured at the tone of it. She could not see Ralph well; it was getting dark now.

"I know it well," she said. "Of course we talk of you when you are gone."

"And does Mrs. Beatrice talk of me?"

"Not so much," said Margaret, "but she listens very closely; and asks us questions sometimes." The girl's heart was beating with excitement as she spoke; but she had made up her mind to seek this opportunity. It seemed a pity, she thought, that two friends of hers should so misunderstood one another.

"And what kind of questions?" asked Ralph again.

"She wonders — what you really think —" went on Margaret slowly, bending down over her embroidery, and punctuating her words with stitches — "about — about affairs — and — and she said one day that —"

"Well?" said Ralph in the same tone.

"That she thought you were not so severe as you seemed," ended Margaret, her voice a little tremulous with amusement.

Ralph sat perfectly still, staring at the great fire-plate on which a smoky Phoebus in relief drove the chariot of the sun behind the tall wavering flames that rose from the burning logs. He knew very well why Margaret had spoken, and that she would not speak without reason; but the fact revealed was so bewilderingly new to him that he could not take it in. Margaret looked at him once or twice a little uneasily; and at last sighed.

"It is too dark," she said, "I must fetch candles."

She slipped out of the side-door that led to the servants' quarters, and Ralph was left alone. All his weariness was gone now; the whirl of images and schemes with which his brain had been seething as he walked up the river-bank half-an-hour before, had receded into obscurity; and one dominating thought filled their place: What if Margaret were right? And what did he mean to do himself? Surely he was not —

The door from the entrance passage opened, and a tall slender figure stood there, now in light, now in shadow, as the flames rose and fell.

"Meg," said a voice.

Ralph sat still a moment longer.

"Meg," said Beatrice again, "how dark you are."

Ralph stood up.

"Mrs. Roper has just gone," he said, "you must put up with me, Mrs. Beatrice."

"Who is it?" said the girl advancing. "Mr. Torridon?"

She had a paper in her hand as she came across the floor, and Ralph drew out a chair for her on the other side of the hearth.

"Yes," he said. "Mrs. Roper has gone for lights. She will be back immediately."

Beatrice sat down.

"It is a troublesome word," she said. "Master More cannot read it himself, and has sent me to ask Meg. He says that every dutiful daughter should be able to read her father's hand."

And Ralph could see a faint amused smile in her black eyes, as the firelight shone on them.

"Master More always has an escape ready," he said, as he too sat down.

The girl's hand holding the paper suddenly dropped on to her knee, and the man saw she was looking at him oddly.

"Yes?" he said interrogatively; and then —

"Why do you look at me like that, Mrs. Beatrice?"

"It is what you said. Do you really think that, Mr. Torridon?"

Ralph was bewildered for a moment.

"I do not understand," he said.

"Do you truly think he always has an escape ready?" repeated the girl. Then Ralph understood.

"You mean he is in danger," he said steadily. "Well, of course he is. There is no great man that is not. But I do not see why he should not escape as he has always done."

"You think that, Mr. Torridon?"

"Why, yes;" went on Ralph, a little hastily. "You remember the matter of the bribe. See how he cleared himself. Surely, Mrs. Beatrice —"

"And you really think so," said the girl. "I know that you know what we do not; and I shall believe what you say."

"How can I tell?" remonstrated Ralph. "I can only tell you that in this matter I know nothing that you do not. Master More is under no suspicion."

Beatrice drew a breath of relief.

"I am glad I spoke to you, sir," she said. "It has been on my mind. And something that he said a few minutes ago frightened me."

"What did he say?" asked Ralph curiously.

"Ah! it was not much. It was that no man knew what might come next; that matters were very strange and dismaying — and — and that he wanted this paper copied quickly, for fear —"

The girl stopped again, abruptly.

"I know what you feel, Mrs. Beatrice," said Ralph gently. "I know how you love Master More, and how terrified we may become for our friends."

"What do you think yourself, Mr. Torridon," she said suddenly, almost interrupting him.

He looked at her doubtfully a moment, and half wished that Margaret would come back.

"That is a wide question," he said.

"Well, you know what I mean," she said coolly, completely herself again. She was sitting back in her chair now, drawing the paper serenely to and fro between her fingers; and he could see the firelight on her chin and brows, and those steady eyes watching him. He had an impulse of confidence.

"I do think changes are coming," he said. "I suppose we all do."

"And you approve?"

"Oh! how can I say off-hand? — But I think changes are needed."

She was looking down at the fire again now, and did not speak for a moment.

"Master More said you were of the new school," she said meditatively.

Ralph felt a curious thrill of exultation. Margaret was right then; this girl had been thinking about him.

"There is certainly a stirring," he said; and his voice was a little restrained.

"Oh, I am not blind or deaf," said the girl. "Of course, there is a stirring — but I wondered —"

Then Margaret came in with the candles.

Ralph went away that evening more excited than he liked. It seemed as if Mistress Roper's words had set light to a fire ready laid, and he could perceive the warmth beginning to move about his heart and odd wavering lights flickering on his circumstances and business that had not been there before.

*H*e received his first letter from Beatrice a few weeks later, and it threw him into a strait between his personal and official claims.

Cromwell at this time was exceedingly occupied with quelling the ardor of the House of Lords, who were requesting that the Holy Maid of Kent and her companions might have an opportunity of defending themselves before the Act of Attainder ordered by the King was passed against them; but he found time to tell his agent that trouble was impending over More and Fisher; and to request him to hand in any evidence that he might have against the former.

"I suppose we shall have to let the Bishop off with a fine," said the minister, "in regard to the Maid's affair; but we shall catch him presently over the Act; and Mr. More is clear of it. But we shall have him too in a few days. Put down what you have to say, Mr. Torridon, and let me have it this evening."

And then he rustled off down the staircase to where his carriage was waiting to take him to Westminster, where he proposed to tell the scrupulous peers that the King was not accustomed to command twice, and that to suspect his Grace of wishing them to do an injustice was a piece of insolence that neither himself nor his royal master had expected of them.

Ralph was actually engaged in putting down his very scanty accusations against Sir Thomas More when the letter from Beatrice was brought up to him. He read it through twice in silence; and then ordered the courier to wait below. When the servant had left the room, he read it through a third time.

It was not long; but it was pregnant.

"I entreat you, sir," wrote the girl, "for the love of Jesu, to let us know if anything is designed against our friend. Three weeks ago you told me it was not so; I pray God that may be true still. I know that you would not lift a finger against him yourself —" (Ralph glanced at his own neat little list at these words, and bit his pen) — "but I wish you to do what you can for him and for us all." Then followed an erasure.

Ralph carried the paper to the window, flattened it against the panes and read clearly the words, "If my" under the scratching lines, and smiled to himself as he guessed what the sentence was that she was beginning.

Then the letter continued.

"I hear on good authority that there is something against him. He will not escape; and will do nothing on such hearsay, but only tells us to trust God, and laughs at us all. Good Mr. Torridon, do what you can. Your loving friend, B.A."

Ralph went back from the window where he was still standing, and sat down again, bending his head into his hands. He had no sort of scruples against lying as such or betraying Mr. More's private conversation; his whole training was directed against such foolishness, and he had learnt at last from Cromwell's incessant precept and example that the good of the State overrode all private interests. But he had a disinclination to lie to Beatrice; and he felt simply unable to lose her friendship by telling her the truth.

As he sat there perfectly still, the servant peeped in once softly to see if the answer was ready, and noiselessly withdrew. Ralph did not stir; but still sat on, pressing his eyeballs till they ached and fiery rings twisted before him in the darkness. Then he abruptly sat up, blinked a moment or two, took up a pen, bit it again, and laid it down and sat eyeing the two papers that lay side by side on his desk.

He took up his own list, and read it through. After all, it was very insignificant, and contained no more than minute scraps of conversation that Sir Thomas More had let drop. He had called Queen Katharine "poor woman" three or four times; had expressed a reverence for the Pope of Rome half a dozen times, and had once called him the Vicar of Christ. He had been silent when someone had mentioned Anne Boleyn's name; he had praised the Carthusians and the Religious Life generally, at some length.

They were the kind of remarks that might mean nothing or a great deal; they were consistent with loyalty; they were not inconsistent with treason; in fact they were exactly the kind of material out of which serious accusations might be manufactured by a skilled hand, though as they stood they proved nothing.

A further consideration to Ralph was his duty to Cromwell; he scarcely felt it seemly to lie whole-heartedly to him; and on the other hand he felt now simply unable to lie to Beatrice. There was only one way out of it, — to prevaricate to them both.

He took up his own paper, glanced at it once more; and then with a slightly dramatic gesture tore it across and across, and threw it on the ground. Then he took up his pen and wrote to Beatrice.

"I have only had access to one paper against our friend — that I have destroyed, though I do not know what Master Cromwell will say. But I tell you this to show at what a price I value your friendship.

"Of course our friend is threatened. Who is not in these days? But I swear to you that I do not know what is the design."

He added a word or two more for politeness' sake, prayed that "God might have her in His keeping," and signed himself as she had done, her "loving friend."

Then he dried the ink with his pounce box, sealed the letter with great care, and took it down to the courier himself.

*H*e faced Cromwell in the evening with a good deal of terror, but with great adroitness; swore positively that More had said nothing actually treasonable, and had found, on putting pen to paper, that the accusations were flimsier than he thought.

"But it is your business to see that they be not so," stormed his master. Ralph paused a moment respectfully.

"I cannot make a purse out of a sow's ear, sir. I must have at least some sort of silk."

When Cromwell had ceased to walk up and down, Ralph pointed out with considerable shrewdness that he did not suppose that his evidence was going to form the main ground of the attack on More; and that it would merely weaken the position to bring such feeble arguments to bear.

"Why he would tear them to shreds, sir, in five minutes; he would make out that they were our principal grounds — he is a skilled lawyer. If I may dare to say so, Master Cromwell, let your words against Mr. More be few and choice."

This was bolder speaking than he had ever ventured on before; but Cromwell was in a good humor. The peers had proved tractable and had agreed to pass the attainder against Elizabeth Barton without anymore talk of justice and the accused's right of defense; and he looked now at Ralph with a grim approval.

"I believe you are right, Mr. Torridon. I will think, over it."

A week later the blow fell.

*C*romwell looked up at him one Sunday evening as he came into the room, with his papers, and without any greeting spoke at once.

"I wish you to go to Lambeth House tomorrow morning early, Mr. Torridon. Master More is to be there to have the Oath of Succession tendered to him with the others. Do your best to persuade him to take it; be his true friend."

A little grim amusement shone in his eyes as he spoke. Ralph looked at him a moment.

"I mean it, Mr. Torridon: do your best. I wish him to think you his friend."

*A*s Ralph went across the Thames in a wherry the following morning, he was still thinking out the situation. Apparently Cromwell wished to keep in friendly touch with More; and this now, of course, was only possible through Ralph, and would have been impossible if the latter's evidence had been used, or were going to be used. It was a relief to him to know that the consummation of his treachery was postponed at least for the present; (but he would not have called it treachery).

As Lambeth towers began to loom ahead, Ralph took out Beatrice's letter that had come in answer to his own a few days before, and ran his eyes over it. It was a line of passionate thanks and blessing. Surely he had reached her hidden heart at last. He put the letter back in his inner pocket, just before he stepped ashore. It no doubt would be a useful evidence of his own sincerity in his interview with More.

There was a great crowd in the court as he passed through, for many were being called to take the oath, which, however, was not made strictly legal until the following Second Act in the autumn. Several carriages were drawn up near the house door, and among them Ralph recognized the liveries of his master and of Lord Chancellor Audley. A number of horses and mules too were tethered to rings in the wall on the other side with grooms beside them, and ecclesiastics and secretaries were coming and going, disputing in groups, calling to one another, in the pleasant April sunshine.

On enquiry he found that the Commissioners were sitting in one of the downstairs parlors; but one of Cromwell's servants at the door told him that he was not to go in there, but that Mr. More was upstairs by himself, and that if he pleased he would show him the way.

It was an old room looking on to the garden, scantily furnished, with a patch of carpet by the window and a table and chair set upon it. More turned round from the window-seat on which he was kneeling to look out, and smiled genially as Ralph heard the servant close the door.

"Why, Mr. Torridon, are you in trouble too? This is the detention-room whither I am sent to consider myself."

He led Ralph, still holding his hand, to the window-seat, where he leaned again looking eagerly into the garden.

"There go the good boys," he said, "to and fro in the playground; and here sit I. I suppose I have nothing but the rod to look for."

Ralph felt a little awkward in the presence of this gaiety; and for a minute or two leaned out beside More, staring mechanically at the figures that passed up and down. He had expected almost to find him at his prayers, or at least thoughtfully considering himself.

More commented agreeably on the passers-by.

"Dr. Wilson was here a moment ago; but he is off now, with a man on either side. He too is a naughty fellow like myself, and will not listen to reason. There is the Vicar of Croydon, good man, coming out of the buttery wiping his mouth."

Ralph looked down at the priest's flushed excited face; he was talking with a kind of reckless gaiety to a friend who walked beside him.

"He was sad enough just now," went on the other, "while he was still obstinate; but his master hath patted him on the head now and given him cake and wine. He was calling out for a drink just now (which he hath got, I see) either for gladness or for dryness, or else that we might know *quod ille notus erat pontifici.*"

Dr. Latimer passed presently, his arms on either side flung round a priest's neck; he too was talking volubly and laughing; and the skirts of his habit wagged behind him.

"He is in high feather," said More, "and I have no doubt that his conscience is as clear as his eyes. Come, Mr. Torridon; sit you down. What have you come for?"

Ralph sat back on the window-seat with his back to the light, and his hat between his knees.

"I came to see you, sir; I have not been to the Commissioners. I heard you were here."

"Why, yes," said More, "here I am."

"I came to see if I could be of any use to you, Master More; I know a friend's face is a good councilor sometimes, even though that friend be a fool."

More patted him softly on the knee.

"No fool," he said, "far from it."

He looked at him so oddly that Ralph feared that he suspected him; so he made haste to bring out Beatrice's letter.

"Mistress Atherton has written me this," he said. "I was able to do her a little service — at least I thought it so then."

More took the letter and glanced at it.

"A very pretty letter," he said, "and why do you show it me?"

Ralph looked at him steadily.

"Because I am Master Cromwell's servant; and you never forget it."

More burst into a fit of laughter; and then took Ralph kindly by the hand.

"You are either very innocent or very deep," he said. "And what have you come to ask me?"

"I have come to ask nothing, Master More," said Ralph indignantly, withdrawing his hand — "except to be of service to you."

"To talk about the oath," corrected the other placidly. "Very well then. Do you begin, Mr. Torridon."

Ralph made a great effort, for he was sorely perplexed by Sir Thomas' attitude, and began to talk, putting all the reasons forward that he could think of for the accepting of the oath. He pointed out that government and allegiance would be impossible things if every man had to examine for himself the claims of his rulers; when vexed and elaborate questions arose — and this certainly was one such — was it not safer to follow the decrees of the King and Parliament, rather than to take up a position of private judgment, and decide upon details of which a subject could have no knowledge? How, too, could More, under the circumstances, take upon himself to condemn those who had subscribed the oath? — he named a few eminent prelates, the Abbot of Westminster and others.

"I do not condemn them," put in More, who was looking interested.

"Then you are uncertain of the matter?" went on Ralph who had thought out his line of argument with some care.

More assented.

"But your duty to the King's grace is certain; therefore it should outweigh a thing that is doubtful."

Sir Thomas sucked in his lower lip, and stared gravely on the young man.

"You are very shrewd, sir," he said. "I do not know how to answer that at this moment; but I have no reasonable doubt but that there is an answer."

Ralph was delighted with his advantage, and pursued it eagerly; and after a few minutes had won from More an acknowledgment that he might be willing to consider the taking of the oath itself; it was the other clauses that touched his conscience more. He could swear to be loyal to Anne's children; but he could not assent to the denunciation of the Pope contained in the preamble of the Act, and the oath would commit him to that.

"But you will tell that to the Commissioners, sir?" asked Ralph eagerly.

"I will tell them all that I have told you," said More smiling.

Ralph himself was somewhat doubtful as to whether the concession would be accepted; but he professed great confidence, and secretly congratulated himself with having made so much way. But presently a remark of More's showed that he appreciated the situation.

"I am very grateful to you, Mr. Torridon, for coming and talking to me; and I shall tell my wife and children so. But it is of no use. They are resolved to catch me. First there was the bribe; then the matter of the Maid; then this; and if I took a hundred oaths they would find one more that I could not, without losing my soul; and that indeed I do not propose to do. *Quid enim proficit homo?*"

There was a knock at the door a moment later, and a servant came in to beg Mr. More to come downstairs again; the Commissioners were ready for him.

"Then good-day, Mr. Torridon. You will come and see me sometimes, even if not at Chelsea. Wherever I may be it will be as nigh heaven as Chelsea."

Ralph went down with him, and parted from him at the door of the Commissioner's room; and half-an-hour later a message was sent out to him by Cromwell that he need wait no longer; Mr. More had refused the oath, and had been handed over to the custody of the Abbot of Westminster.

Chapter VII
A MERRY PRISONER

*T*he arrest of Sir Thomas More and Bishop Fisher and their committal to the Tower a few days later caused nothing less than consternation in England and of furious indignation on the Continent. It was evident that greatness would save no man; the best hope lay in obscurity, and men who had been loud in self-assertion now grew timorous and silent.

Ralph was now in the thick of events. Besides his connection with More, he had been present at one of the examinations of the Maid of Kent and her admirers; had formed one of the congregation at Paul's Cross when the confession drawn up for her had been read aloud in her name by Dr. Capon, who from the pulpit opposite the platform where the penitents were set, preached a vigorous sermon against credulity and superstition. Ralph had read the confession over a couple of days before in Cromwell's room, and had suggested a few verbal alterations; and he had been finally present, a few days after More's arrest, at the last scene of the drama, when Elizabeth Barton, with six priests, suffered, under the provisions of an act of attainder, on Tyburn gallows.

All these events were indications of the course that things were taking in regard to greater matters. Parliament had now advanced further than ever in the direction of a breach with Rome, and had transferred the power of nomination to bishoprics from the Holy See to the Crown, and, what was as least as significant, had dealt in a similar manner with the authority over Religious houses.

On the other side, Rome had declared definitely against the annulling of Queen Katharine's marriage, and to this the King had retorted by turning the pulpits against the Pope, and in the course of this had found himself compelled to deal sharply with the Franciscans, who were at the same time the most popular and the most papal of all preachers. In the following out of this policy, first several notable friars were imprisoned, and next a couple of subservient Religious, a Dominican and an Augustinian, were appointed grand visitors of the rebellious Order.

A cloud of terror now began to brood over the Religious houses in England, as the news of these proceedings became known, and Ralph had a piteous letter from his father, entreating him to give some explanation of the course of affairs so far as was compatible with loyalty to his master, and at least his advice as to Christopher's profession.

"We hear sad tales, dear son," wrote Sir James, "on all sides are fears, and no man knows what the end will be. Some even say that the Orders will be reduced in number. And who knows what may be toward now that the Bishop and Mr. More are in trouble. I know not what is all this that Parliament has been doing about the Holy Father his authority; but I am sure that it cannot be more than what other reigns have brought about in declaring that the Prince is temporal lord of his land. But, however that may be, what do you advise that your brother should do? He is to be professed in August, unless it is prevented, and I dare not put out my hand to hinder it, until I know more. I do not ask you, dear son, to tell me what you should not; I know my duty and yours too well for that. But I entreat you to tell me what you can, that I may not consent to your brother's profession if it is better that it should not take place until affairs are quieter. Your mother would send you her dear love, I know, if she knew I were writing, but she is in her chamber, and the messenger must go with this. Jesu have you in His blessed keeping!"

Ralph wrote back that he knew no reason against Christopher's profession, except what might arise from the exposure of the Holy Maid on whose advice he had gone to Lewes, and that if his father and brother were satisfied on that score, he hoped that Christopher would follow God's leading.

At the same time that he wrote this he was engaged, under Cromwell's directions, in sifting the evidence offered by the grand visitors to show that the friars refused to accept the new enactments on the subject of the papal jurisdiction.

O n the other hand, the Carthusians in London had proved more submissive. There had been a struggle at first when the oath of the succession had been tendered to them, and Prior Houghton, with the Procurator, Humphrey Middlemore, had been committed to the Tower. The oath affirmed the nullity of Queen Katharine's marriage with the King on the alleged ground of her consummated marriage with Henry's elder brother, and involved, though the Carthusians did not clearly understand it so at the time, a rejection of the Pope's authority as connected with the dispensation for Katharine's union with Henry. In May their scruples were removed by the efforts of some who had influence with them, and the whole community took the oath as required of them, though with the pathetic addition of a clause that they only submitted "so far as it was lawful for them so to do." This actual submission, to Cromwell's mind and therefore to Ralph's, was at first of more significance than was the uneasy temper of the community, as reported to them, which followed their compliance; but as the autumn drew on this opinion was modified.

It was in connection with this that Ralph became aware for the first time of what was finally impending with regard to the King's supremacy over the Church.

He had been sitting in Cromwell's room in the Chancery all through one morning, working at the evidence that was flowing in from all sides of disaffection to Henry's policy, sifting out worthless and frivolous charges from serious ones. Every day a flood of such testimony poured in from the spies in all parts of the country, relating to the deepening dissatisfaction with the method of government; and Cromwell, as the King's adviser, came in for much abuse. Every kind of manifestation of this was reported, the talk in the ale-houses and at gentlemen's tables alike, words dropped in the hunting-field or over a game of cards; and the offenders were dealt with in various ways, some by a sharp rebuke or warning, others by a sudden visit of a pursuivant and his men.

Ralph made his report as usual at the end of the morning, and was on the point of leaving, when his master called him back from the door.

"A moment," he said, "I have something to say. Sit down."

When Ralph had taken the chair again that he had just left, Cromwell took up a pen, and began to play with it delicately as he talked.

"You will have noticed," he began, "how hot the feeling runs in the country, and I am sure you will also have understood why it is so. It is not so much what has happened, — I mean in the matter of the marriage and of the friars, — but what folk fear is going to happen. It seems to the people that security is disappearing; they do not understand that their best security lies in obedience. And, above all, they think that matters are dangerous with regard to the Church. They know now that the Pope has spoken, and that the King pays no heed, but, on the other hand, waxes more bold. And that because his conscience bids him. Remember that, sir, when you have to do with his Highness."

He glanced at Ralph again, but there was no mockery in his solemn eyes. Then he went on.

"I am going to tell you, Mr. Torridon, that these folks are partly right, and that his Grace has not yet done all that he intends. There is yet one more step to take — and that is to declare the King supreme over the Church of England."

Ralph felt those strong eyes bent upon him, and he nodded, making no sign of approval or otherwise.

"This is no new thing, Mr. Torridon," went on Cromwell, after a moment's silence. "The King of England has always been supreme, though I will acknowledge that this has become obscured of late. But it is time that it be re-affirmed. The Popes have waxed presumptuous, and have laid claim to titles that Christ never gave them, and it is time that they be reminded that England is free, and will not suffer their domination. As for the unity of the Catholic Church, that can be attended to later on, and on firmer ground; when the Pope has been taught not to wax so proud. There will be an Act passed by Parliament presently, perhaps next year, to do this business, and then we shall know better what to do. Until that, it is very necessary, as you have already seen, to keep the folks quiet, and not to suffer any contradiction of his Grace's rights. Do you understand me, Mr. Torridon?"

Cromwell laid the pen clown and leaned back in his chair, with his fingers together.

"I understand, sir," said Ralph, in a perfectly even tone.

"Well, that is all that I have to say," ended his master, still watching him. "I need not tell you how necessary secrecy is in the matter."

Ralph was considerably startled as he went home, and realized better what it was that he had heard. While prudent persons were already trembling at the King's effrontery and daring in the past, Henry was meditating a yet further step. He began to see now that the instinct of the country was, as always, sharper than that of the individual, and that these uneasy strivings everywhere rose from a very definite perception of danger. The idea of the King's supremacy, as represented by Cromwell, would not seem to be a very startling departure; similar protests of freedom had been made in previous reigns, but now, following as it did upon overt acts of disobedience to the Sovereign Pontiff, and of disregard of his authority in matters of church-law and even of the status of Religious houses, it seemed to have a significance that previous protests had lacked.

And behind it all was the King's conscience! This was a new thought to Ralph, but the more he considered it the more it convinced him. It was a curious conscience, but a mighty one, and it was backed by an indomitable will. For the first time there opened out to Ralph's mind a glimpse of the possibility that he had scarcely dreamed of hitherto —

of a Nationalism in Church affairs that was a reality rather than a theory
— in which the Bishop of Rome while yet the foremost bishop of
Christendom and endowed with special prerogatives, yet should have
no finger in national affairs, which should be settled by the home
authorities without reference to him. No doubt, he told himself, a
readjustment was needed — visions and fancies had encrusted themselves
so quickly round the religion credible by a practical man that a scouring
was called for. How if this should be the method by which not only
such accretions should be done away, but yet more practical matters
should be arranged, and steps taken to amend the unwarranted inter-
ferences and pecuniary demands of this foreign bishop?

He had had more than one interview with Sir Thomas More in the
Tower, and once was able to take him news of his own household at
Chelsea. For a month none of his own people, except his servant, was
allowed to visit him, and Ralph, calling on him about three weeks after
the beginning of his imprisonment, found him eager for news.

He was in a sufficiently pleasant cell in the Beauchamp Tower,
furnished with straw mats underfoot, and straw hangings in place of a
wainscot; his bed stood in one corner, with his crucifix and beads on a
little table beside it, and his narrow window looked out through eleven
feet of wall towards the Court and the White Tower. His books, too,
which his servant, John Wood, had brought from Chelsea, and which
had not yet been taken from him, stood about the room, and several
lay on the table among his papers, at which he was writing when Ralph
was admitted by the warder.

"I am very glad to see you, Mr. Torridon," he said, "I knew you would
not forget an old friend, even though he could not take your counsel.
I daresay you have come to give it me again, however."

"If I thought you would take it," began Ralph.

"But I will not," said More smiling, "no more than before. Sit down,
Mr. Torridon."

Ralph had come at Cromwell's suggestion, and with a very great
willingness of his own, too. He knew he could not please Beatrice more
than by visiting her friend, and he himself was pleased and amused to
think that he could serve his master's interests from one side and his
own from another by one action.

He talked a little about the oath again, and mentioned how many
had taken it during the last week or two.

"I am pleased that they can do it with a good conscience," observed
More. "And now let us talk of other matters. If I would not do it for
my daughter's sake, who begged me, I would not do it for the sake of

both the Houses of Parliament, nor even, dear Mr. Torridon, for yours and Master Cromwell's."

Ralph saw that it was of no use, and began to speak of other things. He gave him news of Chelsea.

"They are not very merry there," he said, "and I hardly suppose you would wish them to be."

"Why not?" cried More, with a beaming face, "I am merry enough. I would not be a monk; so God hath compelled me to be one, and treats me as one of His own spoilt children. He setteth me on His lap and dandleth me. I have never been so happy."

He told Ralph presently that his chief sorrow was that he could not go to mass or receive the sacraments. The Lieutenant, Sir Edward Walsingham, who had been his friend, had told him that he would very gladly have given him liberties of this kind, but that he dared not, for fear of the King's displeasure.

"But I told him," said More, "not to trouble himself that I liked his cheer well enough as it was, and if ever I did not he was to put me out of his doors."

After a little more talk he showed Ralph what he was writing. It was a treatise called a "Dialogue of Comfort against Tribulation."

"It is to persuade myself," he said, "that I am no more a prisoner than I was before; I know I am, but sometimes forget it. We are all God's prisoners."

Ralph glanced down the page just written and was astonished at its good humor.

"Some prisoner of another jail," he read, "singeth, danceth in his two fetters, and feareth not his feet for stumbling at a stone; while God's prisoner, that hath but his one foot fettered by the gout, lieth groaning on a couch, and quaketh and crieth out if he fear there would fall on his foot no more than a cushion."

Ralph went straight up the river from the Tower to Chelsea to take them news of the prisoner, and was silent and moody as he went. He had been half touched and half enraged by More's bearing — touched by his simplicity and cheerfulness and enraged by his confidence in a bad cause.

Mrs. Alice More behaved as usual when he got there: she had a genius for the obvious; commented on the weariness of living in one room, the distress at the thought that one was fastened in at the will of another; deplored the plainness of the prison fare, and the folly of her husband in refusing an oath that she herself and her children and the vast majority of the prominent persons in England had found so simple in accepting. She left nothing unsaid.

Finally, she apologized for the plainness of her dress.

"You must think me a slattern, Mr. Torridon, but I cannot help it. I have not the heart nor the means, now that my man is in prison, to do better."

And her solemn eyes filled with tears.

When he had given the news to the family he went aside from the group in the garden to where Beatrice Atherton was sitting below the Jesu tree, with work on her lap.

He had noticed as he talked that she was sitting there, and had raised his voice for her benefit. He fancied, and with a pleasure at the delicate instinct, that she did not wish to appear as intimately interested in the news from the Tower as those who had a better right to be. He was always detecting now faint shades in her character, as he knew her better, that charmed and delighted him.

She was doing some mending, and only glanced up and down again without ceasing or moving, as Ralph stood by her.

"I thought you never used the needle," he began in a moment.

"It is never too late to mend," she said, without the faintest movement.

Ralph felt again an odd prick of happiness. It gave him a distinct thrill of delight that she would make such an answer and so swiftly; and at such a time, when tragedy was round her and in her heart, for he knew how much she loved the man from whom he had just come.

He sat down on the garden chair opposite, and watched her fingers and the movements of her wrist as she passed the needle in and out, and neither spoke again till the others had dispersed.

"You heard all I said?" said Ralph at last.

She bowed her head without answering.

"Shall I go and bring you news again presently?"

"If you please," she said.

"I hope to be able to do some little things for him," went on Ralph, dropping his eyes, and he was conscious that she momentarily looked up.

— "But I am afraid there is not much. I shall speak for him to Master Cromwell and the Lieutenant."

The needle paused and then went on again.

Ralph was conscious of an extraordinary momentousness in every word that he said. He was well aware that this girl was not to be wooed by violence, but that he must insinuate his mind and sympathies delicately with hers, watching for every movement and ripple of thought. He had known ever since his talk with Margaret Roper that Beatrice was, as it were, turned towards him and scrutinizing him, and that any mistake on his part, however slight, might finally alienate her. Even his gestures, the tones of his voice, his manner of walking, were important elements. He knew now that he was the kind of person who might be acceptable to her — or rather that his personality contained one facet that pleased her, and that he must be careful now to keep that facet turned towards her continually at such an angle that she caught the flash. He had sufficient sense, not to act a part, for that, he knew, she would soon discover, but to be natural in his best way, and to use the fine instincts that he was aware of possessing to tell him exactly how she would wish him to express himself. It would be a long time yet, he recognized, before he could attain his final object; in fact he was not perfectly certain what he wanted; but meanwhile he availed himself of every possible opportunity to get nearer, and was content with his progress.

He was sorely tempted now to discuss Sir Thomas's position and to describe his own, but he perceived from her own aloofness just now that it would seem a profanity, so he preserved silence instead, knowing that it would be eloquent to her. At last she spoke again, and there was a suggestion of a tremor in her voice.

"I suppose you can do nothing for him really? He must stay in the Tower?"

Ralph threw out his hands, silently, expostulating.

"Nothing?" she said again, bending over her work.

Ralph stood up, looking down at her, but made no answer.

"I — I would do anything," she said deliberately, "anything, I think, for the man —" and then broke off abruptly.

Ralph went away from Chelsea that afternoon with a whirling head and dancing heart. She had said no more than that, but he knew what she had meant, and knew, too that she would not have said as much to anyone to whom she was indifferent. Of course, it was hopeless to think of bringing about More's release, but he could at least pretend to try, and Ralph was aware that to chivalrous souls a pathetic failure often appeals more than an excellent success.

Folks turned to look after him more than once as he strode home.

Chapter VIII
A HIGHER STEP

*A*s Chris, on the eve of his profession, looked back over the year that had passed since his reception at the guest-house, he scarcely knew whether it seemed like a week or a century. At times it appeared as if the old life in the world were a kind of faraway picture in which he saw himself as one detached from his present personality, moving among curious scenes in which now he had no part; at other times the familiar past rushed on him fiercely, deafened him with its appeal, and claimed him as its own. In such moods the monastery was an intolerable prison, the day's round an empty heart-breaking formality in which his soul was being stifled, and even his habit, which he had once touched so reverently, the badge of a fool.

The life of the world at such times seemed to him the only sanity; these men used the powers that God had given them, were content with simple and unostentatious doings and interests, reached the higher vocation by their very naïveté, and did not seek to fly on wings that were not meant to bear them. How sensible, Christopher told himself, was Ralph's ideal! God had made the world, so Ralph lived in it — a world in which great and small affairs were carried on, and in which he interested himself. God had made horses and hawks, had provided materials for carriages and fine clothes and crossbows, had formed the sexes and allowed for love and domestic matters, had created brains with their capacities of passion and intellect; and so Ralph had taken these things as he found them, hunted, dressed, lived, managed and mixed with men. At times in his cell Chris saw that imposing figure in all its quiet bravery of dress, that sane, clever face, those pitying and contemptuous eyes looking at him, and heard the well-bred voice asking and commenting and wondering at the misguided zeal of a brother who could give all this up, and seek to live a life that was built on and sustained by illusions.

One event during his first six months of the novitiate helped to solemnize him and to clear the confusion.

Old Dom Augustine was taken sick and died, and Chris for the first time in his life watched the melting tragedy of death. The old monk had been moved from the dortor to the sick-room when the end seemed imminent, and one afternoon Chris noticed the little table set outside the door, with its candles and crucifix, the basin of cotton-wool, and the other signs that the last sacraments were to be administered. He knew little of the old man, except his bleared face and shaking hands as he had seen them in choir, and had never been greatly impressed by him; but it was another matter when in the evening of the same day, at his master's order he passed into the cell and knelt down with the others to see the end.

The old monk was lying now on the cross of ashes that had been spread on the floor; his features looked pinched and white in the candlelight; his old mouth moved incessantly, and opened now and again to gasp; but there was an august dignity on his face that Chris had never seen there before.

Outside the night was still and frosty; only now and again the heavy stroke of the bell told the town that a soul was passing.

Dom Augustine had received Viaticum an hour before. Chris had heard the steady tinkle of the bell, like the sound of Aaron's garments, as the priest who had brought him Communion passed back with his sacred burden, and Chris had fallen on his knees where he stood as he caught a glimpse of the white procession passing back to the church, their frosty breath going up together in the winter night air, the wheeling shadows, and the glare of the torches giving a pleasant warm light in the dull cloister.

But all that was over now, and the end was at hand.

As Chris knelt there, mechanically responding to the prayers on which the monk's soul was beginning to lift itself and flutter for escape, there fell a great solemnity on his spirit. The thought, as old as death, made itself real to him, that this was the end of every man and of himself too. Where Dom Augustine lay, he would lie, with his past behind him, of which every detail would be instinct with eternal import. All the tiny things of the monastic life — the rising in time for the night office, attention during it, the responses to grace, the little movements prescribed by etiquette, the invisible motions of a soul that had or had not acted for the love of God, those stirrings, falls, aspirations, that incessant activity of eighty years — all so incredibly minute from one point of view, so incredibly weighty from another — the account of all those things was to be handed in now, and an eternal judgment given.

He looked at the wearied, pained old face again, at the tight-shut eyes, the jerking movements of the unshaven lips, and wondered what was passing behind; — what strange colloquy of the soul with itself or its Master or great personages of the Court of Heaven. And all was set in this little bare setting of white walls, a tumbled bed, a shuttered window, a guttering candle or two, a cross of ashes on boards, a ring of faces, and a murmur of prayers!

The solemnity rose and fell in Chris's soul like a deep organ-note sounding and waning. How homely and tender were these last rites, this accompaniment of the departing soul to the edge of eternity with all that was dear and familiar to it — the drops of holy water, the mellow light of candles, and the sonorous soothing Latin! And yet — and yet — how powerless to save a soul that had not troubled to make the necessary efforts during life, and had lost the power of making them now!

*W*hen all was over he went out of the cell with an indescribable gravity at his heart.

*W*hen the great events in the spring of '34 began to take place, Chris was in a period of abstracted peace, and the rumors of them came to him as cries from another planet.

Dom Anthony Marks came into the cloister one day from the guest-house with a great excitement in his face,

"Here is news!" he said, joining himself to Chris and another young monk with whom the lonely novice was sometimes allowed to walk. "Master Humphreys, from London, tells me they are all in a ferment there."

Chris looked at him with a deferential coldness, and waited for more.

"They say that Master More hath refused the oath, and that he is lodged in the Tower, and my Lord of Rochester too."

The young monk burst into exclamations and questions, but Chris was silent. It was sad enough, but what did it matter to him? What did it really matter to anyone? God was King.

Dom Anthony was in a hurry, and scuffled off presently to tell the Prior, and in an hour or two there was an air of excitement through the house. Chris, however, heard nothing more except the little that the novice-master chose to tell him, and felt a certain contempt for the anxious-eyed monks who broke the silence by whispers behind doors, and the peace of the monastery by their perturbed looks.

*E*ven when a little later in the summer the commissioner came down
to tender the oath of succession Chris heard little and cared less. He
was aware of a fine gentleman striding through the cloister, lolling in
the garth, and occupying a prominent seat in the church; he noticed
that his master was long in coming to him after the protracted chapter-
meetings, but it appeared to him all rather an irrelevant matter. These
things were surely quite apart from the business for which they were all
gathered in the house — the *opus Dei* and the salvation of souls; this or
that legal document did not seriously affect such high matters.

The novice-master told him presently that the community had signed
the oath, as all others were doing, and that there was no need for anxiety:
they were in the hands of their Religious Superiors.

"I was not anxious," said Chris abruptly, and Dom James hastened
to snub him, and to tell him that he ought to have been, but that novices
always thought they knew everything, and were the chief troubles that
Religious houses had to put up with.

Chris courteously begged pardon, and went to his lessons wondering
what in the world all the pother was about.

But such moods of detachment were not continuous they visited him
for weeks at a time, when his soul was full of consolation, and he was
amazed that any other life seemed possible to anyone. He seemed to
himself to have reached the very heart and secret of existence — surely
it was plain enough; God and eternity were the only things worth
considering; a life passed in an ecstasy, if such were possible, was surely
more consonant with reality than one of ordinary activities. Activities
were, after all, but concessions to human weakness and desire for variety;
contemplation was the simple and natural attitude of a soul that knew
herself and God.

But he was a man as well as a novice, and when these moods ebbed
from his soul they left him strangely bitter and dry: the clouds would
gather; the wind of discontent would begin to shrill about the angles of
his spirit, and presently the storm of desolation would be up.

He had one such tempestuous mood immediately before his profession.

During its stress he had received a letter from his father which he was
allowed to read, in which Sir James half hinted at the advisability of
postponing the irrevocable step until things were quieter, and his heart
had leaped at the possibility of escape. He did not know till then how
strong had grown the motive of appearing well in the eyes of his relatives
and of fearing to lose their respect by drawing back; and now that his
father, too, seemed to suggest that he had better re-consider himself, it

appeared that a door was opened in the high monastery wall through which he might go through and take his honor with him.

He passed through a terrible struggle that night.

Never had the night-office seemed so wearisomely barren. The glamour that had lighted those dark walls and the double row of cowls and down-bent faces, the mystical beauty of the single flames here and there that threw patches of light on the carving of the stalls and the somber habits, and gave visibility and significance to what without them was obscure, the strange suggestiveness of the high-groined roof and the higher vault glimmering through the summer darkness — all this had faded and left him, as it seemed, sane and perceptive of facts at last. Out there through those transepts lay the town where reasonable folk slept, husband and wife together, and the children in the great bed next door, with the tranquil ordinary day behind them and its fellow before; there were the streets, still now and dark and empty but for the sleeping dogs, where the signs swung and the upper stories leaned together, and where the common life had been transacted since the birth of the town and would continue till its decay. And beyond lay the cool round hills, with their dark dewy slopes, over which he had ridden a year ago, and all England beyond them again, with its human life and affairs and interests; and over all hung the serene stars whence God looked down well pleased with all that He had made.

And, meanwhile, here he stood in his stall in his night shoes and black habit and cropped head, propped on his misericorde, with the great pages open before him, thumbed and greasy at their corners, from which he was repeating in a loud monotone formula after formula that had had time to grow familiar from repetition, but not yet sweet from associations — here he stood with heavy eyelids after his short sleep, his feet aching and hot, and his whole soul rebellious.

*H*e was sent by his novice-master next day to the Prior, with his father's letter in his hand, and stood humbly by the door while the Prior read it. Chris watched him under half-raised eye-lids; saw the clean-cut profile with its delicate mouth bent over the paper, and the hand with the enameled ring turn the page. Prior Crowham was a cultivated, well-bred man, not over strong-willed, but courteous and sympathetic. He turned a little to Chris in his carved chair, as he laid the letter down.

"Well," he said, smiling, "it is for you to choose whether you will offer yourself. Of course, there is uneasiness abroad, as this letter says, but what then?"

He smiled pleasantly at the young man, and Chris felt a little ashamed. There was silence for a moment.

"It is for you to choose," said the Prior again, "you have been happy with us, I think?"

Chris pressed his lips together and looked down.

"Of course Satan will not leave you alone," went on the monk presently. "He will suggest many reasons against your profession. If he did not, I should be afraid that you had no vocation."

Again he waited for an answer, and again Chris was silent. His soul was so desolate that he could not trust himself to say all that he felt.

"You must wait a little," went on the Prior, "recommend yourself to our Lady and our Patron, and then leave yourself in their hands. You will know better when you have had a few days. Will you do this, and then come to me again?"

"Yes, my Lord Prior," said Chris, and he took up the letter, bowed, and went out.

*W*ithin the week relief and knowledge came to him. He had done what the monk had told him, and it had been followed by a curious sense of relief at the thought suggested to him that the responsibility of decision did not rest on him but on his heavenly helpers. And then as he served mass the answer came.

It was in the chapel of the Blessed Virgin, a little building entered from the north transept, with its windows opening directly on to the road leading up into the town; there was no one there but the two. It was about seven o'clock on the feast of the Seven Martyrs, and the chapel was full of a diffused tender morning light, for the chapel was sheltered from the direct sunshine by the tall church on its south.

As they went up to the altar the bell sounded for the Elevation at the high-altar of the church, at the *missa familiaris*, and the footstep of someone passing through the north transept ceased instantly at the sound. The priest ascended the steps, set down the vessels, spread the corporal, opened the book, and came down again for the preparation. There was no one else in the chapel, and the peace of the place in the summer light, only vitalized by the brisk chirping of a sparrow under the eaves, entered into Christopher's soul.

As the mass went on it seemed as if a veil were lifting from his spirit, and leaving it free and sensible again. The things around him fell into their proper relationships, and there was no doubt in his mind that this newly restored significance of theirs was their true interpretation. They seemed penetrated and suffused by the light of the inner world; the red-brocaded chasuble moving on a level with his eyes, stirring with the shifting of the priest's elbows, was more than a piece of rich stuff, the white alb beneath more than mere linen, the hood thrown back in the amice a sacramental thing. He looked up at the smoky yellow flames against the painted woodwork at the back of the altar, at the discolored stones beside the grey window-moldings still with the slanting marks of the chisel upon them, at the black rafters overhead, and last out through the shafted window at the heavy July foliage of the elm that stood by the road and the brilliant morning sky beyond; and once more he saw what these things meant and conveyed to an immortal soul. The words that he had said during these last weeks so mechanically were now rich and alive again, and as he answered the priest he perceived the spiritual vibration of them in the inner world of which his own soul was but a part. And then the climax was reached, and he lifted the skirt of the vestment with his left hand and shook the bell in his right; the last shreds of confusion were gone, and his spirit basked tranquil and content and certain again in the light that was newly risen on him.

He went to the novice-master after the morning-chapter, and told him that he had made up his mind to offer himself for profession if it was thought advisable by the authorities.

*T*owards the end of August he presented himself once more before the chapter to make his solemn demand; his petition was granted, and a day appointed for his profession.

Then he withdrew into yet stricter seclusion to prepare for the step.

Chapter IX
LIFE AT LEWES

Under the direction of the junior-master who overlooked the young monks for some years after their profession, Chris continued his work of illumination, for which he had shown great aptitude during his year of noviceship.

The art was beginning to disappear, since the introduction of printing had superseded the need of manuscript, but in some Religious Houses it was still thought a suitable exercise during the hours appointed for manual labor.

It was soon after the beginning of the new year that Chris was entrusted with a printed antiphonary that had its borders and initials left white; and he carried the great loose sheets with a great deal of pride to the little carrel or wooden stall assigned to him in the northern cloister.

It was a tiny room, scarcely six feet square, lighted by the window into the cloister-garth, and was almost entirely filled by the chair, the sloping desk against the wall, and the table where the pigments and brushes lay ready to the hand. The door opened on to the cloister itself where the professed monks were at liberty to walk, and on the opposite side stood the broad aumbries that held the library of the house; and it was from the books here that Chris was allowed to draw ideas for his designs. It was a great step in that life of minute details when now for the first time he was permitted to follow his own views, instead of merely filling in with color outlines already drawn for him; and he found his scheme for the decoration a serious temptation to distraction during the office. As he stood among the professed monks, in his own stall at last, he found his eyes wandering away to the capitals of the round pillars, the stone foliage and fruit that burst out of the slender shafts, the grim heads that strained forward in miter and crown overhead, and even the living faces of his brethren and superiors, clear against the dark woodwork. When he bent his eyes resolutely on his book he found his mind still intent on his more secular business; he mentally corrected this awkward curve of the initial, substituted an oak spray with acorns for that stiff monstrosity, and set my Lord Prior's face grinning among griffins at the foot of the page where humor was more readily admitted.

It was an immense joy when he closed his carrel-door, after his hour's siesta in the dormitory, and sat down to his work. He was still warm with sleep, and the piercing cold of the unwarmed cloister did not affect him, but he set his feet on the sloping wooden footstool that rested on the straw for fear they should get cold, and turned smiling to his side-table.

There were all the precious things laid out; the crow's quills sharpened to an almost invisible point for the finer lines, the two sets of pencils, one of silver-point that left a faint grey line, and the other of haematite for the burnishing of the gold, the badger and minever brushes, the sponge and pumice-stone for erasures; the horns for black and red ink lay with the scissors and rulers on the little upper shelf of his desk. There were the pigments also there, which he had learnt to grind and prepare, the crushed lapis lazuli first calcined by heat according to the modern degenerate practice, with the cheap German blue beside it, and the indigo beyond; the prasinum; the vermilion and red lead ready mixed, and the rubrica beside it; the yellow orpiment, and, most important of all, the white pigments, powdered chalk and egg shells, lying by the biacca. In a separate compartment covered carefully from chance drafts or dust lay the precious gold leaf, and a little vessel of the inferior fluid gold used for narrow lines.

*H*is first business was to rule the thick red lines down the side of the text, using a special metal pen for it; and then to begin to sketch in his initials and decorations. For this latter part of the work he had decided to follow the lines of Foucquet from a Book of the Hours that he had taken out of its aumbry; a mass of delicate foliage and leaves, with medallions set in it united by twisted thorn-branches twining upwards through the broad border. These medallions on the first sheet he purposed to fill with miniatures of the famous relics kept at Lewes, the hanging sleeve of the Blessed Virgin in its crystal case, the drinking-cup of Cana, the rod of Moses, and the Magdalene's box of ointment. In the later pages which would be less elaborate he would introduce the other relics, and allow his humor free play in designing for the scrolls at the foot tiny portraits of his brethren; the Prior should be in a miter and have the legs and tail of a lion, the novice-master, with a fox's brush emerging from his flying cowl, should be running from a hound who carried a discipline in his near paw. But there was time yet to think of these things; it would be weeks before that page could be reached, and meanwhile there was the foliage to be done, and the rose leaf that lay on his desk to be copied minutely from a hundred angles.

*H*is distractions at mass and office were worse than ever now that the great work was begun, and week after week in confession there was the same tale. The mere process was so absorbing, apart from the joy of creation and design. More than once he woke from a sweating nightmare in the long dormitory, believing that he had laid on gold-leaf without first painting the surface with the necessary mordant, or had run his stilus through his most delicate miniature. But he made extraordinary progress in the art; and the Prior more than once stepped into his carrel and looked over his shoulder, watching the slender fingers with the bone pen between them polishing the gold till it shone like a mirror, or the steady lead pencil moving over the white page in faultless curve. Then he would pat him on the shoulder, and go out in approving silence.

*C*hris was supremely content that he had done right in asking for profession. It appeared to him that he had found a life that was above all others worthy of an immortal soul. The whole day's routine was directed to one end, the performance of the *Opus Dei*, the uttering of praises to Him who had made and was sustaining and would receive again all things to Himself.

They rose at midnight for the night-office that the sleeping world might not be wholly dumb to God; went to rest again; rose once more with the world, and set about a yet sublimer worship. A stream of sacrifice poured up to the Throne through the mellow summer morning, or the cold winter darkness and gloom, from altar after altar in the great church. Christopher remembered pleasantly a morning soon after the beginning of his novitiate when he had been in the church as a set of priests came in and began mass simultaneously; the mystical fancy suggested itself as the hum of voices began that he was in a garden, warm and bright with grace, and that bees were about him making honey — that fragrant sweetness of which it had been said long ago that God should eat — and as the tinkle of the Elevation sounded out here and there, it seemed to him as a signal that the mysterious confection was done, and that every altar sprang into perfume from those silver vessels set with jewel and crystal.

When the first masses were over, there was a pause in which the *mixtum* was taken — bread and wine or beer — standing in the refectory, after a short prayer that the Giver of all good gifts might bless the food and drink of His servants, and was closed again by another prayer said privately for all benefactors. Meanwhile the bell was ringing for the Lady mass, to remind the monks that the interval was only as it were a parenthetical concession; and after Terce and the Lady Mass followed the Chapter, in which faults were confessed and penances inflicted, and the living instruments of God's work were examined and scoured for use. The martyrology was read at this time, as well as some morning prayers, to keep before the monks' minds the remembrance of those great vessels of God's household called to so high an employment. It was then, too, that other business of the house was done, and the seal affixed to any necessary documents. Christopher had an opportunity once of examining this seal when it had been given him to clean, and he looked with awe on the figures of his four new patrons, St. Peter, St. Pancras, St. Paul and Our Lady, set in niches above a cliff with the running water of the Ouse beneath, and read the petition that ran round the circle —

"Dulcis agonista tibi convertit domus ista Pancrati memorum precibus memor esto tuorum."

When the chapter was over, and the deaths of any brethren of the order had been announced, and their souls prayed for, there was a pause for recreation in the cloister and the finishing of further business before they assembled again in time to go into church for the high mass, at which the work and prayers of the day were gathered up and consecrated in a supreme offering. Even the dinner that followed was a religious ceremony; it began by a salutation of the Christ in glory that was on the wall over the Prior's table, and then a long grace was sung before they took their seats. The reader in the stone-pulpit on the south wall of the refectory began his business on the sounding of a bell; and at a second stroke there was a hum and clash of dishes from the kitchen end, and the aproned servers entered in line bearing the dishes. Immediately the meal was begun the drink destined for the poor at the gate was set aside, and a little later a representative of them was brought into the refectory to receive his portion; at the close again what was left over was collected for charity; while the community after singing part of the grace after meat went to finish it in the church.

Chris learned to love the quiet religious graciousness of the refectory. The taking of food here was a consecrated action; it seemed a sacramental thing. He loved the restraint and preciseness of it, ensured by the solemn crucifix over the door with its pathetic inscription "SITIO," the polished oak tables, solid and narrow, the shining pewter dishes, the folded napkins, the cleanly-served plentiful food, to each man his portion, the indescribable dignity of the prior's little table, the bowing of the servers before it, the mellow grace ringing out in its monotone that broke into minor thirds and octaves of melody, like a grave line of woodwork on the paneling bursting into a stiff leaf or two at its ends. There was a strange and wonderful romance it about on early autumn evenings as the light died out behind the stained windows and the reader's face glowed homely and strong between his two candles on the pulpit. And surely these tales of saints, the extract from the Rule, these portions of Scripture sung with long pauses and on a monotone for fear that the reader's personality should obscure the message of what he read — surely this was a better accompaniment to the taking of food, in itself so gross a thing, than the feverish chatter of a secular hall and the bustling and officiousness of paid servants.

After a general washing of hands the monks dispersed to their work, and the novices to bowls or other games; the Prior first distributing the garden instruments, and then beginning the labor with a commendation of it to God; and after finishing the manual work and a short time of study, they re-assembled in the cloister to go to Vespers. This, like the high mass, was performed with the ceremonial proper to the day, and was followed by supper, at which the same kind of ceremonies were observed as at dinner. When this was over, after a further short interval the evening reading or Collation took place in the chapter-house, after which the monks were at liberty to go and warm themselves at the one great fire kept up for the purpose in the calefactory; and then compline was sung, followed by Our Lady's Anthem.

This for Chris was one of the climaxes of the day's emotions. He was always tired out by now with the day's work, and longing for bed, and this approach to the great Mother of Monks soothed and quieted him. It was sung in almost complete darkness, except for a light or two in the long nave where a dark figure or two would be kneeling, and the pleasant familiar melody, accompanied softly by the organ overhead after the bare singing of Compline, seemed like a kind of good-night kiss. The infinite pathos of the words never failed to touch him, the cry of the banished children of Eve, weeping and mourning in this vale of tears to Mary whose obedience had restored what Eve's self-will had ruined, and the last threefold sob of endearment to the "kindly, loving, sweet, Virgin Mary." After the high agonizings and aspirations of the day's prayer, the awfulness of the holy Sacrifice, the tramping monotony of the Psalter, the sting of the discipline, the aches and sweats of the manual labor, the intent strain of the illuminating, this song to Mary was a running into Mother's arms and finding compensation there for all toils and burdens.

Finally in complete silence the monks passed along the dark cloister, sprinkled with holy water as they left the church, up to the dormitory which ran over the whole length of the chapter house, the bridges and other offices, to sleep till midnight.

*T*he effect of this life, unbroken by external distractions, was to make Chris's soul alert and perceptive to the inner world, and careless or even contemptuous of the ordinary world of men. This spiritual realm began for the first time to disclose its details to him, and to show itself to some extent a replica of nature. It too had its varying climate, its long summer of warmth and light, its winter of dark discontent, its strange and bewildering sunrises of Christ upon the soul, when He rose and went about His garden with perfume and music, or stayed and greeted His creature with the message of His eyes. Chris began to learn that these spiritual changes were in a sense independent of him, that they were not in his soul, but rather that his soul was in them. He could be happy and content when the winds of God were cold and His light darkened, or sad and comfortless when the flowers of grace were apparent and the river of life bright and shining.

And meanwhile the ordinary world went on, but far away and dimly heard and seen; as when one looks down from a castle-garden on to humming streets five hundred feet below; and the old life at Overfield, and Ralph's doings in London seemed unreal and fantastic activities, purposeless and empty.

Little by little, however, as the point of view shifted, Chris began to find that the external world could not be banished, and that the annoyances from the clash of characters discordant with his own were as positive as those which had distressed him before. Dom Anselm Bowden's way of walking and the patch of grease at the shoulder of his cowl, never removed, and visible as he went before him into the church was as distractingly irritating as Ralph's contempt; the buzz in the voice of a cantor who seemed always to sing on great days was as distressing as his own dog's perversity at Overfield, or the snapping of a bow-string.

When *accidie* fell upon Chris it seemed as if this particular house was entirely ruined by such incidents; the Prior was finickin, the junior-master tyrannical, the paints for illumination inferior in quality, the straw of his bed peculiarly sharp, the chapter-house unnecessarily drafty. And until he learnt from his confessor that this spiritual ailment was a perfectly familiar one, and that its symptoms and effects had been diagnosed centuries before, and had taken him at his word and practiced the remedies he enjoined, Chris suffered considerably from discontent and despair alternately. At times others were intolerable, at times he was intolerable to himself, reproaching himself for having attempted so high a life, criticizing his fellows for so lowering it to a poor standard.

*T*he first time that he was accused in chapter of a fault against the Rule was a very great and shocking humiliation.

He had accused himself as usual on his knees of his own remissions, of making an unnecessarily loud noise in drinking, of intoning a wrong antiphon as cantor, of spilling crumbs in the refectory; and then leaned back on his heels well content with the insignificance of his list, to listen with a discreet complacency to old Dom Adrian, who had overslept himself once, spilled his beer twice, criticized his superior, and talked aloud to himself four times during the Greater Silence, and who now mumbled out his crimes hastily and unconcernedly.

When the self-accusations were done, the others began, and to his horror Chris heard his own name spoken.

"I accuse Dom Christopher Torridon of not keeping the guard of the eyes at Terce this morning."

It was perfectly true; Chris had been so much absorbed in noticing an effect of shade thrown by a corbel, and in plans for incorporating it into his illumination that he had let a verse pass as far as the star that marked the pause. He felt his heart leap with resentment. Then a flash of retort came to him, and he waited his turn.

"I accuse Dom Bernard Parr of not keeping the guard of the eyes at Terce this morning. He was observing me."

Just the faintest ripple passed round the line; and then the Prior spoke with a tinge of sharpness, inflicting the penances, and giving Chris a heavy sentence of twenty strokes with the discipline.

When Chris's turn came he threw back his habit petulantly, and administered his own punishment as the custom was, with angry fervor.

As he was going out the Prior made him a sign, and took him through into his own cell.

"Counter-accusations are contrary to the Rule," he said. "It must not happen again," and dismissed him sternly.

And then Chris for a couple of days had a fierce struggle against uncharitableness, asking himself whether he had not eyed Dom Bernard with resentment, and then eyeing him again. It seemed too as if a fiend suggested bitter sentences of reproach, that he rehearsed to himself, and then repented. But on the third morning there came one of those strange breezes of grace that he was beginning to experience more and more frequently, and his sore soul grew warm and peaceful again.

*I*t was in those kinds of temptation now that he found his warfare to lie; internal assaults so fierce that it was terribly difficult to know whether he had yielded or not, sudden images of pride and anger and lust that presented themselves so vividly and attractively that it seemed he must have willed them; it was not often that he was tempted to sin in word or deed — such, when they came, rushed on him suddenly; but in the realm of thought and imagination and motive he would often find himself, as it were, entering a swarm of such things, that hovered round him, impeding his prayer, blinding his insight, and seeking to sting the very heart of his spiritual life. Then once more he would fight himself free by despising and rejecting them, or would emerge without conscious will of his own into clearness and serenity.

But as he looked back he regretted nothing. It was true that the warfare was more subtle and internal, but it was more honorable too; for to conquer a motive or tame an imagination was at once more arduous and more far-reaching in its effects than a victory in merely outward matters, and he seldom failed to thank God half-a-dozen times a day for having given him the vocation of a monk.

There was one danger, however, that he did not realize, and his confessor failed to point it out to him; and that was the danger of the wrong kind of detachment. As has been already seen the theory of the Religious Life was that men sought it not merely for the salvation of their own souls, but for that of the world. A monastery was a place where in a special sense the spiritual commerce of the world was carried on: as a workman's shed is the place deputed and used by the world for the manufacture of certain articles. It was the manufactory of grace where skilled persons were at work, busy at a task of prayer and sacrament which was to be at other men's service. If the father of a family had a piece of spiritual work to be done, he went to the monastery and arranged for it, and paid a fee for the sustenance of those he employed, as he might go to a merchant's to order a cargo and settle for its delivery.

Since this was so then, it was necessary that the spiritual workmen should be in a certain touch with those for whom they worked. It was true that they must be out of the world, undominated by its principles and out of love with its spirit; but in another sense they must live in its heart. To use another analogy they were as windmills, lifted up from the earth into the high airs of grace, but their base must be on the ground or their labor would be ill-spent. They must be mystically one with the world that they had resigned.

Chris forgot this; and labored, and to a large extent succeeded, in detaching himself wholly; and symptoms of this mistake showed themselves in such things as tending to despise secular life, feeling impatient with the poor to whom he had to minister, in sneering in his heart at least at anxious fussy men who came to arrange for masses, at troublesome women who haunted the sacristy door in a passion of elaborateness, and at comfortable families who stamped into high mass and filled a seat and a half, but who had yet their spiritual burdens and their claims to honor.

But he was to be brought rudely down to facts again. He was beginning to forget that England was about him and stirring in her agony; and he was reminded of it with some force in the winter after his profession.

*H*e was going out to the gate-house one day on an errand from the junior-master when he became aware of an unusual stir in the court. There were a couple of palfreys there, and half-a-dozen mules behind, whilst three or four strange monks with a servant or two stood at their bridles.

Chris stopped to consider, for he had no business with guests; and as he hesitated the door of the guest-house opened, and two prelates came out with Dom Anthony behind them — tall, stately men in monks' habits with furred cloaks and crosses. Chris slipped back at once into the cloister from which he had just come out, and watched them go past to the Prior's lodging.

They appeared at Vespers that afternoon again, sitting in the first returned stalls near the Prior, and Chris recognized one of them as the great Abbot of Colchester. He looked at him now and again during Vespers with a reverential awe, for the Abbot was a great man, a spiritual peer of immense influence and reputation, and watched that fatherly face, his dignified bows and stately movements, and the great sapphire that shone on his hand as he turned the leaves of his illuminated book.

The two prelates were at supper, sitting on either side of the Prior on the dais; and afterwards the monks were called earlier than usual from recreation into the chapter-house.

The Prior made them a little speech saying that the Abbot had something to say to them, and then sat down; his troubled eyes ran over the faces of his subjects, and his fingers twitched and fidgeted on his knees.

The Abbot did not make them a long discourse; but told them briefly that there was trouble coming; he spoke in veiled terms of the Act of Supremacy, and the serious prayer that was needed; he said that a time of testing was close at hand, and that every man must scrutinize his own conscience and examine his motives; and that the unlearned had better follow the advice and example of their superiors.

It was all very vague and unsatisfactory; but Chris became aware of three things. First, that the world was very much alive and could not be dismissed by a pious aspiration or two; second, that the world was about to make some demand that would have to be seriously dealt with, and third, that there was nothing really to fear so long as their souls were clean and courageous. The Abbot was a melting speaker, full at once of a fatherly tenderness and vehemence, and as Chris looked at him he felt that indeed there was nothing to fear so long as monks had such representatives and protectors as these, and that the world had better look to itself for fear it should dash itself to ruin against such rocks of faith and holiness.

But as the spring drew on, an air of suspense and anxiety made itself evident in the house. News came down that More and Fisher were still in prison, that the oath was being administered right and left, that the King had thrown aside all restraints, and that the civil breach with Rome seemed in no prospect of healing. As for the spiritual breach the monks did not seriously consider it yet; they regarded themselves as still in union with the Holy See whatever their rulers might say or do, and only prayed for the time when things might be as before and there should be no longer any doubt or hesitation in the minds of weak brethren.

But the Prior's face grew more white and troubled, and his temper uncertain.

Now and again he would make them speeches assuring them fiercely that all was well, and that all they had to do was to be quiet and obedient; and now he would give way to a kind of angry despair, tell them that all was lost, that every man would have to save himself; and then for days after such an exhibition he would be silent and morose, rapping his fingers softly as he sat at his little raised table in the refectory, walking with downcast eyes up and down the cloister muttering and staring.

Towards the end of April he sent abruptly for Chris, told him that he had news from London that made his presence there necessary, and ordered him to be ready to ride with him in a week or two.

Chapter X

THE ARENA

*I*t was in the evening of a warm May day that the Prior and Chris arrived at the hostelry in Southwark, which belonged to Lewes Priory.

It was on the south side of Kater Lane, opposite St. Olave's church, a great house built of stone with arched gates, with a large porch opening straight into the hall, which was high and vaulted with a frieze of grotesque animals and foliage running round it. There were a few servants there, and one or two friends of the Prior waiting at the porch as they arrived; and one of them, a monk himself from the cell at Farley, stepped up to the Prior's stirrup and whispered to him.

Chris heard an exclamation and a sharp indrawing of breath, but was too well trained to ask; so he too dismounted and followed the others into the hall, leaving his beast in the hands of a servant.

The Prior was already standing by the monk at the upper end, questioning him closely, and glancing nervously this way and that.

"Today?" he asked sharply, and looked at the other horrified.

The monk nodded, pale-faced and anxious, his lower lip sucked in.

The Prior turned to Chris.

"They have suffered today," he said.

News had reached Lewes nearly a week before that the Carthusians had been condemned, for refusing to acknowledge the King as head of the English Church, but it had been scarcely possible to believe that the sentence would be carried out, and Chris felt the blood beat in his temples and his lips turn suddenly dry as he heard the news.

"I was there, my Lord Prior," said the monk.

He was a middle-aged man, genial and plump, but his face was white and anxious now, and his mouth worked. "They were hanged in their habits," he went on. "Prior Houghton was the first dispatched;" and he added a terrible detail or two.

"Will you see the place, my Lord Prior?" he said, "You can ride there. Your palfrey is still at the door."

Prior Robert Crowham looked at him a moment with pursed lips; and then shook his head violently.

"No, no," he said. "I – I must see to the house." The monk looked at Chris.

"May I go, my Lord Prior?" he asked.

The Prior stared at him a moment, in a desperate effort to fix his attention; then nodded sharply and wheeled round to the door that led to the upper rooms.

"Mother of God!" he said. "Mother of God!" and went out.

Chris went through with the strange priest, down the hall and out into the porch again. The others were standing there, fearful and whispering, and opened out to let the two monks pass through.

Chris had been tired and hot when he arrived, but he was conscious now of no sensation but of an overmastering desire to see the place; he passed straight by his horse that still stood with a servant at his head, and turned up instinctively toward the river.

The monk called after him.

"There, there," he cried, "not so fast – we have plenty of time."

They took a wherry at the stairs and pushed out with the stream. The waterman was a merry-looking man who spoke no word but whistled to himself cheerfully as he laid himself to the oars, and the boat began to move slantingly across the flowing tide. He looked at the monks now and again; but Chris was seated, staring out with eyes that saw nothing down the broad stream away to where the cathedral rose gigantic and graceful on the other side. It was the first time he had been in London since a couple of years before his profession, but the splendor and strength of the city was nothing to him now. It only had one significance to his mind, and that that it had been this day the scene of a martyrdom. His mind that had so long lived in the inner world, moving among supernatural things, was struggling desperately to adjust itself.

Once or twice his lips moved, and his hands clenched themselves under his scapular; but he saw and heard nothing; and did not even turn his head when a barge swept past them, and a richly dressed man leaned from the stem and shouted something mockingly. The other monk looked nervously and deprecatingly up, for he heard the taunting threat across the water that the Carthusians were a good riddance, and that there would be more to follow.

They landed at the Blackfriars stairs, paid the man, who was still whistling as he took the money, and passed up by the little stream that flowed into the river, striking off to the left presently, and leaving the city behind them. They were soon out again on the long straight road that led to Tyburn, for Chris walked desperately fast, paying little heed to his companion except at the corners when he had to wait to know the way; and presently Tyburn-gate began to raise its head high against the sky.

Once the strange monk, whose name Chris had not even troubled to ask, plucked him by his hanging sleeve.

"The hurdles came along here," he said; and Chris looked at him vacantly as if he did not understand.

Then they were under Tyburn-gate, and the clump of elms stood before them.

*I*t was a wide open space, dusty now and trampled.

What grass there had been in patches by the two little streams that flowed together here, was crushed and flat under foot. The elms cast long shadows from the west, and birds were chirping in the branches; there was a group or two of people here and there looking curiously about them. A man's voice came across the open space, explaining; and his arm rose and wheeled and pointed and paused — three or four children hung together, frightened and interested.

But Chris saw little of all this. He had no eyes for the passing details; they were fixed on the low mound that rose fifty yards away, and the three tall posts, placed in a triangle and united by crossbeams, that stood on it, gaunt against the sky.

As he came nearer to it, walking as one in a dream across the dusty ground and trampled grass, and paying no heed to the priest behind him who whispered with an angry nervousness, he was aware of the ends of three or four ropes that hung motionless from the beams in the still evening air; and with his eyes fixed on these in exaltation and terror he stumbled up the sloping ground and came beneath them.

There was a great peace round him as he stood there, stroking one of the uprights with a kind of mechanical tenderness; the men were silent as they saw the two monks there, and watched to see what they would do.

The towers of Tyburn-gate rose a hundred yards away, empty now, but crowded this morning; and behind them the long road with the fields and great mansions on this side and that, leading down to the city in front and Westminster on the right, those two dens of the tiger that had snarled so fiercely a few hours before, as she licked her lips red with martyrs' blood. It was indescribably peaceful now; there was no sound but the birds overhead, and the soft breeze in the young leaves, and the trickle of the streams defiled today, but running clean and guiltless now; and the level sunlight lay across the wide flat ground and threw the shadow of the mound and gallows nearly to the foot of the gate.

But to Chris the place was alive with phantoms; the empty space had vanished, and a sea of faces seemed turned up to him; he fancied that there were figures about him, watching him too, brushing his sleeve, faces looking into his eyes, waiting for some action or word from him. For a moment his sense of identity was lost; the violence of the associations, and perhaps even the power of the emotions that had been wrought there that day, crushed out his personality; it was surely he who was here to suffer; all else was a dream and an illusion. From his very effort of living in eternity, a habit had been formed that now asserted itself; the laws of time and space and circumstance for the moment ceased to exist; and he found himself for an eternal instant facing his own agony and death.

*T*hen with a rush facts re-asserted themselves, and he started and looked round as the monk touched him on the arm.

"You have seen it," he said in a sharp undertone, "it is enough. We shall be attacked." Chris paid him no heed beyond a look, and turned once more.

It was here that they had suffered, these gallant knights of God; they had stood below these beams, their feet on the cart that was their chariot of glory, their necks in the rope that would be their heavenly badge; they had looked out where he was looking as they made their little speeches, over the faces to Tyburn-gate, with the same sun that was now behind him, shining into their eyes.

He still stroked the rough beam; and as the details came home, and he remembered that it was this that had borne their weight, he leaned and kissed it; and a flood of tears blinded him.

Again the priest pulled his sleeve sharply.

"For God's sake, brother!" he said.

Chris turned to him.

"The cauldron," he said; "where was that?"

The priest made an impatient movement, but pointed to one side, away from where the men were standing still watching them; and Chris saw below, by the side of one of the streams a great blackened patch of ground, and a heap of ashes.

The two went down there, for the other monk was thankful to get to any less conspicuous place; and Chris presently found himself standing on the edge of the black patch, with the trampled mud and grass beyond it beside the stream. The grey wood ashes had drifted by now far across the ground, but the heavy logs still lay there, charred and smoked, that had blazed beneath the cauldron where the limbs of the monks had been seethed; and he stared down at them, numbed and fascinated by the horror of the thought. His mind, now in a violent reaction, seemed unable to cope with its own knowledge, crushed beneath its weight; and his friend heard him repeating with a low monotonous insistence —

"Here it was," he said, "here; here was the cauldron; it was here."

Then he turned and looked into his friend's eyes.

"It was here," he said; "are you sure it was here?"

The other made an impatient sound.

"Where else?" he said sharply. "Come, brother, you have seen enough."

*H*e told him more details as they walked home; as to what each had said, and how each had borne himself. Father Reynolds, the Syon monk, had looked gaily about him, it seemed, as he walked up from the hurdle; the secular priest had turned pale and shut his eyes more than once; the three Carthusian priors had been unmoved throughout, showing neither carelessness nor fear; Prior Houghton's arm had been taken off to the London Charterhouse as a terror to the others; their heads, he had heard, were on London Bridge.

Chris walked slowly as he listened, holding tight under his scapular the scrap of rough white cloth he had picked up near the cauldron, drinking in every detail, and painting it into the mental picture that was forming in his mind; but there was much more in the picture than the other guessed.

The priest was a plain man, with a talent for the practical, and knew nothing of the vision that the young monk beside him was seeing — of the air about the gallows crowded with the angels of the Agony and Passion, waiting to bear off the straggling souls in their tender experienced hands; of the celestial faces looking down, the scarred and glorious arms stretched out in welcome; of Mary with her mother's eyes, and her virgins about her — all ring above ring in deepening splendor up to the white blinding light above, where the Everlasting Trinity lay poised in love and glory to receive and crown the stalwart soldiers of God.

Chapter XI

A CLOSING-IN

*R*alph kept his resolution to pretend to try and save Sir Thomas More, and salved his own conscience by protesting to Beatrice that his efforts were bound to fail, and that he had no influence such as she imagined. He did certainly more than once remark to Cromwell that Sir Thomas was a pleasant and learned man, and had treated him kindly, and once had gone so far as to say that he did not see that any good would be served by his death; but he had been sharply rebuked, and told to mind his own business; then, softening, Cromwell had explained that there was no question of death for the present; but that More's persistent refusal to yield to the pressure of events was a standing peril to the King's policy.

This policy had now shaped itself more clearly. In the autumn of '34 the bill for the King's supremacy over the Church of England began to take form; and Ralph had several sights of the documents as all business of this kind now flowed through Cromwell's hands, and he was filled with admiration and at the same time with perplexity at the adroitness of the wording. It was very short, and affected to assume rather than to enact its object.

"Albeit the King's Majesty justly and rightfully is and ought to be," it began, "the supreme head of the Church of England, and so is recognized by the clergy of this realm in their Convocations, yet, nevertheless, for corroboration and confirmation thereof . . . and to repress and extirp all errors, heresies and other enormities . . . be it enacted by authority of this present Parliament that the King our sovereign lord . . . shall be taken, accepted, and reputed the only supreme head in earth of the Church of England, called *Anglicans Ecclesia.*" The bill then proceeded to confer on him a plenitude of authority over both temporal and spiritual causes.

There was here considerable skill in the manner of its drawing up, which it owed chiefly to Cromwell; for it professed only to re-state a matter that had slipped out of notice, and appealed to the authority of Convocation which had, truly, under Warham allowed a resolution to the same effect, though qualified by the clause, "as far as God's law permits," to pass in silence.

Ralph was puzzled by it: he was led to believe that it could contain no very radical change from the old belief, since the clergy had in a sense already submitted to it; and, on the other hand, the word "the only supreme head in earth" seemed not only to assert the Crown's civil authority over the temporalities of the Church, but to exclude definitely all jurisdiction on the part of the Pope.

"It is the assertion of a principle," Cromwell said to him when he asked one day for an explanation; "a principle that has always been held in England; it is not intended to be precise or detailed: that will follow later."

Ralph was no theologian, and did not greatly care what the bill did or did not involve. He was, too, in that temper of inchoate agnosticism that was sweeping England at the time, and any scruples that he had in his more superstitious moments were lulled by the knowledge that the clergy had acquiesced. What appeared more important to him than any hair-splittings on the exact provinces of the various authorities in question, was the necessity of some step towards the crippling of the spiritual empire whose hands were so heavy, and whose demands so imperious. He felt, as an Englishman, resentful of the leading strings in which, so it seemed to him, Rome wished to fetter his country.

The bill passed through parliament on November the eighteenth.

*R*alph lost no opportunity of impressing upon Beatrice how much he had risked for the sake of her friend in the Tower, and drew very moving sketches of his own peril.

The two were sitting together in the hall at Chelsea one winters evening soon after Christmas. The high paneling was relieved by lines of greenery, with red berries here and there; a bunch of mistletoe leaned forward over the sloping mantelpiece, and there was an acrid smell of holly and laurel in the air. It was a little piteous, Ralph thought, under the circumstances.

Another stage had been passed in More's journey towards death, in the previous month, when he had been attainted of misprision of treason by an act designed to make good the illegality of his former conviction, and the end was beginning to loom clear.

"I said it would be no use, Mistress Beatrice, and it is none — Master Cromwell will not hear a word."

Beatrice looked up at Ralph, and down again, as her manner was. Her hands were lying on her lap perfectly still as she sat upright in her tall chair.

"You have done what you could, I know," she said, softly.

"Master Cromwell did not take it very well," went on Ralph with an appearance of resolute composure, "but that was to be expected."

Again she looked up, and Ralph once more was seized with the desire to precipitate matters and tell her what was in his heart, but he repressed it, knowing it was useless to speak yet.

It was a very stately and slow wooing, like the movement of a minuet; each postured to each, not from any insincerity, except perhaps a little now and then on Ralph's side, but because for both it was a natural mode of self-expression. It was an age of dignity abruptly broken here and there by violence. There were slow and gorgeous pageants followed by brutal and bestial scenes, like the life of a peacock who paces composedly in the sun and then scuttles and screams in the evening. But with these two at present there was no occasion for abruptness, and Ralph, at any rate, contemplated with complacency his own graciousness and grandeur, and the skillfully posed tableaux in which he took such a sedate part.

As the spring drew on and the crocuses began to star the grass along the river and the sun to wheel wider and wider, the chill and the darkness began to fall more heavily on the household at Chelsea. They were growing very poor by now; most of Sir Thomas's possessions elsewhere had been confiscated by the King, though by his clemency Chelsea was still left to Mrs. Alice for the present; and one by one the precious things began to disappear from the house as they were sold to obtain necessaries. All the private fortune of Mrs. More had gone by the end of the winter, and her son still owed great sums to the Government on behalf of his father.

At the beginning of May she told Ralph that she was making another appeal to Cromwell for help, and begged him to forward her petition.

"My silks are all gone," she said, "and the little gold chain and cross that you may remember, Mr. Torridon, went last month, too — I cannot tell what we shall do. Mr. More is so obstinate" — and her eyes filled with tears — "and we have to pay fifteen shillings every week for him and John a' Wood."

She looked so helpless and feeble as she sat in the window seat, stripped now of its tapestry cushions, with the roofs of the New Building rising among its trees at the back, where her husband had walked a year ago with such delight, that Ralph felt a touch of compunction, and promised to do his best.

He said a word to Cromwell that evening as he supped with him at Hackney, and his master looked at him curiously, sitting forward in the carved chair he had had from Wolsey, in his satin gown, twisting the stem of his German glass in his ringed fingers.

"And what do you wish me to do, sir?" he asked Ralph with a kind of pungent irony.

Ralph explained that he scarcely knew himself; perhaps a word to his Grace —

"I will tell you what it is, Mr. Torridon," broke in his master, "you have made another mistake. I did not intend you to be their friend, but to seem so."

"I can scarcely seem so," said Ralph quietly, but with a certain indignation at his heart, "unless I do them little favors sometimes."

"You need not seem so any longer," said Cromwell dryly, "the time is past."

And he set his glass down and sat back.

Yet Ralph's respect and admiration for his master became no less. He had the attractiveness of extreme and unscrupulous capability. It gave Ralph the same joy to watch him as he found in looking on at an expert fencer; he was so adroit and strong and ready; mighty and patient in defense, watchful for opportunities of attack and merciless when they came. His admirers scarcely gave a thought to the piteousness of the adversary; they were absorbed in the scheme and proud to be included in it; and men of heart and sensibility were as hard as their master when they carried out his plans.

*T*he fate of the Carthusians would have touched Ralph if he had been a mere onlooker, as it touched so many others, but he had to play his part in the tragedy, and was astonished at the quick perceptions of Cromwell and his determined brutality towards these peaceful contemplatives whom he recognized as a danger-center against the King's policy.

He was present first in Cromwell's house when the three Carthusian priors of Beauvale, Axholme and London called upon him of their own accord to put their questions on the meaning of the King's supremacy: but their first question, as to how was it possible for a layman to hold the keys of the kingdom of heaven was enough, and without any further evidence they were sent to the Tower.

Then, again, he was present in the Court of the Rolls a few days later when Dom Laurence, of Beauvale, and Dom Webster, of Axholme, were examined once more. There were seven or eight others present, laymen and ecclesiastics, and the priors were once more sent back to the Tower.

And so examination after examination went on, and no answer could be got out of the monks, but that they could never reconcile it with their conscience to accept the King to be what the Act of Supremacy declared that he was.

Ralph's curiosity took him down to the Charterhouse one day shortly before the execution of the priors; he had with him an order from Cromwell that carried him everywhere he wished to go; but he did not penetrate too deeply. He was astonished at the impression that the place made on him.

As he passed up the Great Cloister there was no sound but from a bird or two singing in the afternoon sunlight of the garth; each cell-door, with its hatch for the passage of food, was closed and silent; and Ralph felt a curious quickening of his heart as he thought of the human life passed in the little houses, each with its tiny garden, its workshop, its two rooms, and its paved ambulatory, in which each solitary lived. How strangely apart this place was from the buzz of business from which he had come! And yet he knew very well that the whole was as good as condemned already.

He wondered to himself how they had taken the news of the tragedy that was beginning — those white, demure men with shaved heads and faces, and downcast eyes. He reflected what the effect of that news must be; as it penetrated each day, like a stone dropped softly into a pool, leaving no ripple. There, behind each brown door, he fancied to himself, a strange alchemy was proceeding, in which each new terror and threat from outside was received into the crucible of a beating heart and transmuted by prayer and welcome into some wonderful jewel of glory — at least so these poor men believed; and Ralph indignantly told himself it was nonsense; they were idlers and dreamers. He reminded himself of a sneer he had heard against the barrels of Spanish wine that were taken in week by week at the monastery door; if these men ate no flesh too, at least they had excellent omelets.

But as he passed at last through the lay-brothers' choir and stood looking through the gates of the Fathers' choir up to the rich altar with its hangings and its posts on either side crowned with gilded angels bearing candles, to the splendid window overhead, against which, as in a glory, hung the motionless silk-draped pyx, the awe fell on him again.

This was the place where they met, these strange, silent men; every panel and stone was saturated with the prayers of experts, offered three times a day — in the night-office of two or three hours when the world was asleep; at the chapter-mass; and at Vespers in the afternoon.

His heart again stirred a little, superstitiously he angrily told himself, at the memory of the stories that were whispered about in town.

Two years ago, men said, a comet had been seen shining over the house. As the monks went back from matins, each with his lantern in his hand, along the dark cloister, a ray had shot out from the comet, had glowed upon the church and bell-tower, and died again into darkness. Again, a little later, two monks, one in his cell-garden and the other in the cemetery, had seen a blood-red globe, high and menacing, hanging in the air over the house.

Lastly, at Pentecost, at the mass of the Holy Ghost, offered at the end of a triduum with the intention of winning grace to meet any sacrifice that might be demanded, not one nor two, but the whole community, including the lay-brothers outside the Fathers' Choir, had perceived a soft whisper of music of inexpressible sweetness that came and went overhead at the Elevation. The celebrant bowed forward in silence over the altar, unable to continue the mass, the monks remained petrified with joy and awe in their stalls.

Ralph stared once more at the altar as he remembered this tale; at the row of stalls on either side, the dark roof overhead, the glowing glass on either side and in front — and asked himself whether it was true, whether God had spoken, whether a chink of the heavenly gate had been opened here to let the music escape.

It was not true, he told himself; it was the dream of a man mad with sleeplessness, foolish with fasting and discipline and vigils: one had dreamed it and babbled of it to the rest and none had liked to be less spiritual or perceptive of divine manifestations.

A brown figure was by the altar now to light the candles for Vespers; a taper was in his hand, and the spot of light at the end moved like a star against the gilding and carving. Ralph turned and went out.

Then on the fourth of May he was present at the execution of the three priors and the two other priests at Tyburn. There was an immense

crowd there, nearly the whole Court being present; and it was reported
here and there afterwards that the King himself was there in a group of
five horsemen, who came in the accoutrements of Borderers, vizored
and armed, and took up their position close to the scaffold. There fell
a terrible silence as the monks were dragged up on the hurdles, in their
habits, all three together behind one horse. They were cut down almost
at once, and the butchery was performed on them while they were still
alive.

Ralph went home in a glow of resolution against them. A tragedy
such as that which he had seen was of necessity a violent motive one
way or the other, and it found him determined that the sufferers were
in the wrong, and left him confirmed in his determination. Their very
passivity enraged him.

Meanwhile, he had of course heard nothing of his brother's presence
in London, and it was with something of a shock that on the next
afternoon he heard the news from Mr. Morris that Mr. Christopher was
below and waiting for him in the parlor.

As he went down he wondered what Chris was doing in London, and
what he himself could say to him. He was expecting Beatrice, too, to
call upon him presently with her maid to give him a message and a
bundle of letters which he had promised to convey to Sir Thomas More.
But he was determined to be kind to his brother.

Chris was standing in his black monk's habit on the other side of
the walnut table, beside the fireplace, and made no movement as Ralph
came forward smiling and composed. His face was thinner than his
brother remembered it, clean-shaven now, with hollows in the checks,
and his eyes were strangely light.

"Why, Chris!" said Ralph, and stopped, astonished at the other's
motionlessness.

Then Chris came round the table with a couple of swift steps, his
hands raised a little from the wide, drooping sleeves.

"Ah! brother," he said, "I have come to bring you away: this is a
wicked place."

Ralph was so amazed that he fell back a step.

"Are you mad?" he said coldly enough, but he felt a twitch of
superstitious fear at his heart.

Chris seized the rich silk sleeve in both his hands, and Ralph felt
them trembling and nervous.

"You must come away," he said, "for Jesu's sake, brother! You must
not lose your soul."

Ralph felt the old contempt surge up and drown his fear. The
familiarity of his brother's presence weighed down the religious sugges-

tion of his habit and office. This is what he had feared and almost expected; — that the cloister would make a fanatic of this fantastic brother of his.

He glanced round at the door that he had left open, but the house was silent. Then he turned again.

"Sit down, Chris," he said, with a strong effort at self-command, and he pulled his sleeve away, went back and shut the door, and then came forward past where his brother was standing, to the chair that stood with its back to the window.

"You must not be fond and wild," he said decidedly. "Sit down, Chris."

The monk came past him to the other side of the hearth, and faced him again, but did not sit down. He remained standing by the fireplace, looking down at Ralph, who was in his chair with crossed legs.

"What is this folly?" said Ralph again.

Chris stared down at him a moment in silence.

"Why, why —" he began, and ceased.

Ralph felt himself the master of the situation, and determined to be paternal.

"My dear lad," he said, "you have dreamed yourself mad at Lewes. When did you come to London?"

"Yesterday," said Chris, still with that strange stare.

"Why, then —" began Ralph.

"Yes — you think I was too late, but I saw it," said Chris; "I was there in the evening and saw it all again."

All his nervous tension seemed relaxed by the warm common-sense atmosphere of this trim little room, and his brother's composure. His lips were beginning to tremble, and he half turned and gripped the mantel-shelf with his right hand. Ralph noticed with a kind of contemptuous pity how the heavy girded folds of the frock seemed to contain nothing, and that the wrist from which the sleeve had fallen back was slender as a reed. Ralph felt himself so infinitely his brother's superior that he could afford to be generous and kindly.

"Dear Chris," he said, smiling, "you look starved and miserable. Shall I tell Morris to bring you something? I thought you monks fared better than that."

In a moment Chris was on his knees on the rushes; his hands gripped his brother's arms, and his wild eyes were staring up with a fanatical fire of entreaty in them. His words broke out like a torrent.

"Ralph," he said, "dear brother! for Jesu's sake, come away! I have heard everything. I know that these streets are red with blood, and that your hands have been dipped in it. You must not lose your soul. I know everything; you must come away. For Jesu's sake!"

Ralph tore himself free and stood up, pushing back his chair.

"Godbody!" he said, "I have a fool for a brother. Stand up, sir. I will have no mumming in my house."

He rapped his foot fiercely on the floor, staring down at Chris who had thrown himself back on his heels.

"Stand up, sir," he said again.

"Will you hear me, brother?"

Ralph hesitated.

"I will hear you if you will talk reason. I think you are mad."

Chris got up again. He was trembling violently, and his hands twitched and clenched by his sides.

"Then you shall hear me," he said, and his voice shook as he spoke. "It is this —"

"You must sit down," interrupted Ralph, and he pointed to the chair behind.

Chris went to it and sat down. Ralph took a step across to the door and opened it.

"Morris," he called, and came back to his chair.

There was silence a moment or two, till the servant's step sounded in the hall, and the door opened. Mr. Morris's discreet face looked steadily and composedly at his master.

"Bring the pasty," said Ralph, "and the wine."

He gave the servant a sharp look, seemed to glance out across the hall for a moment and back again. There was no answering look on Mr. Morris's face, but he slipped out softly, leaving the door just ajar.

Then Ralph turned to Chris again.

Chris had had time to recover himself by now, and was sitting very pale and composed after his dramatic outburst, his hands hidden under his scapular, and his fingers gripped together.

"Now tell me," said Ralph, with his former kindly contempt. He had begun to understand now what his brother had come about, and was determined to be at once fatherly and decisive. This young fool must be taught his place.

"It is this," said Chris, still in a trembling voice, but it grew steadier as he went on. "God's people are being persecuted — there is no longer any doubt. They were saints who died yesterday, and Master Cromwell is behind it all; and — and you serve him."

Ralph jerked his head to speak, but his brother went on.

"I know you think me a fool, and I daresay you an right. But this I know, I would sooner be a fool than — than —"

— "than a knave" ended Ralph. "I thank you for your good opinion, my brother. However, let that pass. You have come to teach me my business, then?"

"I have come to save your soul," said Chris, grasping the arms of his chair, and eyeing him steadily.

"You are very good to me," said Ralph bitterly. "Now, I do not want anymore play-acting —" He broke off suddenly as the door opened. "And here is the food. Chris, you are not yourself" — he gave a swift look at his servant again — "and I suppose you have had no food today."

Again he glanced out through the open door as Mr. Morris turned to go.

Chris paid no sort of attention to the food. He seemed not to have seen the servant's entrance and departure.

"I tell you," he said again steadily, with his wide bright eyes fixed on his brother, "I tell you, you are persecuting God's people, and I am come, not as your brother only, but as a monk, to warn you."

Ralph waved his hand, smiling, towards the dish and the bottle. It seemed to sting Chris with a kind of fury, for his eyes blazed and his mouth tightened as he stood up abruptly.

"I tell you that if I were starving I would not break bread in this house: it is the house of God's enemy."

He dashed out his left hand nervously, and struck the bottle spinning across the table; it crashed over on to the floor, and the red wine poured on to the boards.

"Why, there is blood before your eyes," he screamed, mad with hunger and sleeplessness, and the horrors he had seen; "the ground cries out."

Ralph had sprung up as the bottle fell, and stood trembling and glaring across at the monk; the door opened softly, and Mr. Morris stood alert and discreet on the threshold, but neither saw him.

"And if you were ten times my brother," cried Chris, "I would not touch your hand."

There came a knocking at the door, and the servant disappeared.

"Let him come, if it be the King himself," shouted the monk, "and hear the truth for once."

The servant was pushed aside protesting, and Beatrice came straight forward into the room.

Chapter XII
A RECOVERY

*T*here was a moment of intense silence, only emphasized by the settling rustle of the girl's dress. The door had closed softly, and Mr. Morris stood within, in the shadow by the window, ready to give help if it were needed. Beatrice remained a yard inside the room, very upright and dignified, a little pale, looking from one to the other of the two brothers, who stared back at her as at a ghost.

Ralph spoke first, swallowing once or twice in his throat before speaking, and trying to smile.

"It is you then," he said.

Beatrice moved a step nearer, looking at Chris, who stood white and tense, his eyes wide and burning.

"Mr. Torridon," said Beatrice softly, "I have brought the bundle. My woman has it."

Still she looked, as she spoke, questioningly at Chris.

"Oh! this is my brother, the monk," snapped Ralph bitterly, glancing at him. "Indeed, he is."

Then Chris lost his self-control again.

"And this is my brother, the murderer; indeed, he is."

Beatrice's lips parted, and her eyes winced. She put out her hand hesitatingly towards Ralph, and dropped it again as he moved a little towards her.

"You hear him?" said Ralph.

"I do not understand," said the girl, "your brother —"

"Yes, I am his brother, God help me," snarled Chris.

Beatrice's lips closed again, and a look of contempt came into her face.

"I have heard enough, Mr. Torridon. Will you come with me?"

Chris moved forward a step.

"I do not know who you are, madam," he said, "but do you understand what this gentleman is? Do you know that he is a creature of Master Cromwell's?"

"I know everything," said Beatrice.

"And you were at Tyburn, too?" questioned Chris bitterly, "perhaps with this brother of mine?"

Beatrice faced him defiantly.

"What have you to say against him, sir?"

Ralph made a movement to speak, but the girl checked him.

"I wish to hear it. What have you to say?"

"He is a creature of Cromwell's who plotted the death of God's saints. This brother of mine was at the examinations, I hear, and at the scaffold. Is that enough?"

Chris had himself under control again by now, but his words seemed to burn with vitriol. His lips writhed as he spoke.

"Well?" said Beatrice.

"Well, if that is not enough; how of More and my Lord of Rochester?"

"He has been a good friend to Mr. More," said Beatrice, "that I know."

"He will get him the martyr's crown, surely," sneered Chris.

"And you have no more to say?" asked the girl quietly.

A shudder ran over the monk's body; his mouth opened and closed, and the fire in his eyes flared up and died; his clenched hands rose and fell. Then he spoke quietly.

"I have no more to say, madam."

Beatrice moved across to Ralph, and put her hand on his arm, looking steadily at Chris. Ralph laid his other hand on hers a moment, then raised it, and made an abrupt motion towards the door.

Chris went round the table; Mr. Morris opened the door with an impassive face, and followed him out, leaving Beatrice and Ralph alone.

*C*hris had come back the previous evening from Tyburn distracted almost to madness. He had sat heavily all the evening by himself, brooding and miserable, and had not slept all night, but waking visions had moved continually before his eyes, as he turned to and fro on his narrow bed in the unfamiliar room. Again and again Tyburn was before him, peopled with phantoms; he had seen the thick ropes, and heard their creaking, and the murmur of the multitude; had smelt the pungent wood-smoke and the thick drifting vapor from the cauldron. Once it seemed to him that the very room was full of figures, white-clad and silent, who watched him with impassive pale faces, remote and unconcerned. He had flung himself on his knees again and again, had lashed himself with the discipline that he, too, might taste of pain; but all the serenity of divine things was gone. There was no heaven, no Savior, no love. He was bound down here, crushed and stifled in this apostate city whose sounds and cries came up into his cell. He had lost the fiery vision of the conqueror's welcome; it was like a tale heard long ago. Now he was beaten down by physical facts, by the gross details of the tragedy, the strangling, the blood, the smoke, the acrid smell of the crowd, and heaven was darkened by the vapor.

It was not until the next day, as he sat with the Prior and a stranger or two, and heard the tale once more, and the predictions about More and Fisher, that the significance of Ralph's position appeared to him clearly. He knew no more than before, but he suddenly understood what he knew.

A monk had said a word of Cromwell's share in the matters, and the Prior had glanced moodily at Chris for a moment, turning his eyes only as he sat with his chin in his hand; and in a moment Chris understood.

This was the work that his brother was doing. He sat now more distracted than ever: mental pictures moved before him of strange council-rooms with great men in silk on raised seats, and Ralph was among them. He seemed to hear his bitter questions that pierced to the root of the faith of the accused, and exposed it to the world, of their adherence to the Vicar of Christ, their uncompromising convictions.

He had sat through dinner with burning eyes, but the Prior noticed nothing, for he himself was in a passion of absorption, and gave Chris a hasty leave as he rose from table to go and see his brother if he wished.

Chris had walked up and down his room that afternoon, framing sentences of appeal and pity and terror, but it was useless: he could not fix his mind; and he had gone off at last to Westminster at once terrified for Ralph's soul, and blazing with indignation against him.

And now he was walking down to the river again, in the cool of the evening, knowing that he had ruined his own cause and his right to speak by his intemperate fury.

It was another strange evening that he passed in the Prior's chamber after supper. The same monk, Dom Odo, who had taken him to Tyburn the day before, was there again; and Chris sat in a corner, with the reaction of his fury on him, spent and feverish, now rehearsing the scene he had gone through with Ralph, and framing new sentences that he might have used, now listening to the talk, and vaguely gathering its meaning.

It seemed that the tale of blood was only begun.

Bedale, the Archdeacon of Cornwall, had gone that day to the Charterhouse; he had been seen driving there, and getting out at the door with a bundle of books under his arm, and he had passed in through the gate over which Prior Houghton's arm had been hung on the previous evening. It was expected that some more arrests would be made immediately.

"As for my Lord of Rochester," said the monk, who seemed to revel in the business of bearing bad news, "and Master More, I make no doubt they will be cast. They are utterly fixed in their opinions. I hear that my lord is very sick, and I pray that God may take him to Himself. He is made Cardinal in Rome, I hear; but his Grace has sworn that he shall have no head to wear the hat upon."

Then he went off into talk upon the bishop, describing his sufferings in the Tower, for he was over eighty years old, and had scarcely sufficient clothes to cover him.

Now and again Chris looked across at his Superior. The Prior sat there in his great chair, his head on his hand, silent and absorbed; it was only when Dom Odo stopped for a moment that he glanced up impatiently and nodded for him to go on. It seemed as if he could not hear enough, and yet Chris saw him wince, and heard him breathe sharply as each new detail came out.

The monk told them, too, of Prior Houghton's speech upon the cart.

"They asked him whether even then he would submit to the King's laws, and he called God to witness that it was not for obstinacy or perversity that he refused, but that the King and the Parliament had decreed otherwise than our Holy Mother enjoins; and that for himself he would sooner suffer every kind of pain than deny a doctrine of the Church. And when he had prayed from the thirtieth Psalm, he was turned off."

The Prior stared almost vacantly at the monk who told his story with a kind of terrified gusto, and once or twice his lips moved to speak; but he was silent, and dropped his chin upon his hand again when the other had done.

Chris scarcely knew how the days passed away that followed his arrival in London. He spent them for the most part within doors, writing for the Prior in the mornings, or keeping watch over the door as his Superior talked with prelates and churchmen within, for ecclesiastical London was as busy as a broken anthill, and men came and went continually — scared, furtive monks, who looked this way and that, an abbot or two up for the House of Lords, priors and procurators on business. There were continual communications going to and fro among the religious houses, for the prince of them, the contemplative Carthusian, had been struck at, and no one knew where the assault would end.

Meanwhile, Chris had heard no further news from Ralph.' He thought of writing to him, and even of visiting him again, but his heart sickened at the thought of it. It was impossible, he told himself, that any communication should pass between them until his brother had forsaken his horrible business; the first sign of regret must come from the one who had sinned. He wondered sometimes who the girl was, and, as a hotheaded monk, suspected the worst. A man who could live as Ralph was living could have no morals left. She had been so friendly with him, so ready to defend him, so impatient, Chris thought, of any possibility of wrong. No doubt she, too, was one of the corrupt band, one of the great ladies that buzzed round the Court, and sucked the blood of God's people.

His own interior life, however, so roughly broken by his new experiences, began to mend slowly as the days went on.

He had begun, like a cat in a new house, to make himself slowly at home in the hostel, and to set up that relation between outward objects and his own self that is so necessary to interior souls not yet living in detachment. He arranged his little room next the Prior's to be as much as possible like his cell, got rid of one or two pieces of furniture that distracted him, set his bed in another corner, and hung up his beads in the same position that they used to occupy at Lewes. Each morning he served the Prior's mass in the tiny chapel attached to the house, and did his best both then and at his meditation to draw in the torn fibers of his spirit. At moments of worship the supernatural world began to appear again, like points of living rock emerging through sand, detached and half stifled by external details, but real and abiding. Little by little his serenity came back, and the old atmosphere reasserted itself. After all, God was here as there; grace, penance, the guardianship of the angels and the sacrament of the altar was the same at Southwark as at Lewes. These things remained; while all else was accidental — the different height of his room, the unfamiliar angles in the passages, the new noises of London, the street cries, the clash of music, the disordered routine of dally life.

Halfway through June, after a long morning's conversation with a stranger, the Prior sent for him.

He was standing by the tall carved fireplace with his back to the door, his head and one hand leaning against the stone, and he turned round despondently as Chris came in. Chris could see he was deadly pale and that his lips twitched with nervousness.

"Brother," he said, "I have a perilous matter to go through, and you must come with me."

Chris felt his heart begin to labor with heavy sick beats.

"I am to see my Lord of Rochester. A friend hath obtained the order. We are to go at five o'clock. See that you be ready. We shall take boat at the stairs."

Chris waited, with his eyes deferentially cast down.

"He is to be tried again on Thursday," went on the Prior, "and my friends wish me to see him, God knows —"

He stopped abruptly, made a sign with his hand, and as Chris left the room he saw that he was leaning once more against the stone-work, and that his head was buried in his arms.

Three more Carthusians had been condemned in the previous week, but the Bishop's trial, though his name was in the first indictment, was postponed a few days.

He too, like Sir Thomas More, had been over a year in the Tower; he had been deprived of his see by an Act of Parliament, his palace had been broken into and spoiled, and he himself, it was reported, was being treated with the greatest rigor in the Tower.

Chris was overcome with excitement at the thought that he was to see this man. He had heard of his learning, his holiness, and his austerities on all hands since his coming to London. When the bishop had left Rochester at his summons to London a year before there had been a wonderful scene of farewell, of which the story was still told in town. The streets had been thronged with a vast crowd weeping and praying, as he rode among them bare-headed, giving his blessing as he went. He had checked his horse by the city-gate, and with a loud voice had bidden them all stand by the old religion, and let no man take it from them. And now here he lay himself in prison for the Faith, a Cardinal of the Holy Roman Church, with scarcely clothes to cover him or food to eat. At the sacking of his palace, too, as the men ran from room to room tearing down the tapestries, and piling the plate together, a monk had found a great iron box hidden in a corner. They cried to one another that it held gold "for the bloody Pope"; and burst it open to find a hair shirt, and a pair of disciplines.

*I*t was a long row down to the Tower from Southwark against the in-flowing tide. As they passed beneath the bridge Chris stared up at the crowding houses, the great gates at either end, and the faces craning down; and he caught one glimpse as they shot through the narrow passage between the piers, of the tall wall above the gate, the poles rising from it, and the severed heads that crowned them. Somewhere among that forest of grim stems the Carthusian priors looked down.

As he turned in his seat he saw the boatman grinning to himself, and following his eyes observed the Prior beside him with a white fixed face looking steadily downwards towards his feet.

They found no difficulty when they landed at the stairs, and showed the order at the gate. The warder called to a man within the guardroom who came out and went before them along the walled way that led to the inner ward. They turned up to the left presently and found themselves in the great court that surrounded the White Tower.

The Prior walked heavily with his face downcast as if he wished to avoid notice, and Chris saw that he paid no attention to the men-at-arms and other persons here and there who saluted his prelate's insignia. There were plenty of people going about in the evening sunshine, soldiers and attendants, and here and there at the foot of a tower stood a halberdier in his buff jacket leaning on his weapon. There were many distinguished persons in the Tower now, both ecclesiastics and laymen who had refused to take one or both of the oaths, and Chris eyed the windows wonderingly, picturing to himself where each lay, and with what courage.

But more and more as he went he wondered why the Prior and he were here, and who had obtained the order of admittance, for he had not had a sight of it.

When they reached the foot of the prison-tower the warder said a word to the sentry, and took the two monks straight past, preceding them up the narrow stairs that wound into darkness. There were windows here and there, slits in the heavy masonry, through which Chris caught glimpses, now of the moat on the west, now of the inner ward with the White Tower huge and massive on the east.

The Prior, who went behind the warder and in front of Chris, stopped suddenly, and Chris could hear him whispering to himself; and at the same time there sounded the creaking of a key in front.

As the young monk stood there waiting, grasping the stone-work on his right, again the excitement surged up; and with it was mingled something of terror. It had been a formidable experience even to walk those few hundred yards from the outer gate, and the obvious apprehensiveness of the Prior who had spoken no audible word since they had landed, was far from reassuring.

Here he stood now for the first time in his life within those terrible walls; he had seen the low Traitor's Gate on his way that was for so many the gate of death. Even now as he gripped the stone he could see out to the left through the narrow slit a streak of open land beyond the moat and the wall, and somewhere there he knew lay the little rising ground, that reddened week after week in an ooze of blood and slime. And now he was at the door of one who without doubt would die there soon for the Faith that they both professed.

The Prior turned sharply round.

"You!" he said, "I had forgotten: you must wait here till I call you in."

There was a sounding of an opening door above; the Prior went up and forward, leaving him standing there; the door closed, but not before Chris had caught a glimpse of a vaulted roof; and then the warder stood by him again, waiting with his keys in his hand.

Chapter XIII

PRISONER AND PRINCE

*T*he sun sank lower and had begun to throw long shadows before the door opened again and the Prior beckoned. As Chris had stood there staring out of the window at the green water of the moat and the shadowed wall beyond, with the warder standing a few steps below, now sighing at the delay, now humming a line or two, he had heard voices now and again from the room above, but it had been no more than a murmur that died once more into silence.

*C*hris was aware of a dusty room as he stepped over the threshold, bare walls, one or two solid pieces of furniture, and of the Prior's figure very upright in the light from the tiny window at one side; and then he forgot everything as he looked at the man that was standing smiling by the table.

It was a very tall slender figure, dressed in a ragged black gown turning green with age; a little bent now, but still dignified; the face was incredibly lean, with great brown eyes surrounded by wrinkles, and a little white hair, ragged, too, and long, hung down under the old flapped cap. The hand that Chris kissed seemed a bundle of reeds bound with parchment, and above the wrist bones the arm grew thinner still under the loose, torn sleeve.

Then the monk stood up and saw those kindly proud eyes looking into his own.

The Prior made a deferential movement and said a word or two, and the bishop answered him.

"Yes, yes, my Lord Prior; I understand — God bless you, my son."

The bishop moved across to the chair, and sat down, panting a little, for he was torn by sickness and deprivation, and laid his long hands together.

"Sit down, brother," he said, "and you too, my Lord Prior."

Chris saw the Prior move across to an old broken stool, but he himself remained standing, awed and almost terrified at that worn face in which the eyes alone seemed living; so thin that the cheekbones stood out hideously, and the line of the square jaw. But the voice was wonderfully sweet and penetrating.

"My Lord Prior and I have been talking of the times, and what is best to be done, and how we must all be faithful. You will be faithful, brother?"

Chris made an effort against the absorbing fascination of that face and voice.

"I will, my lord."

"That is good; you must follow your prior and be obedient to him. You will find him wise and courageous."

The bishop nodded gently towards the Prior, and Chris heard a sobbing indrawn breath from the corner where the broken stool stood.

"It is a time of great moment," went on the bishop; "much hangs on how we carry ourselves. His Grace has evil counselors about him."

There was silence for a moment or two; Chris could not take his eyes from the bishop's face. The frightful framework of skin and bones seemed luminous from within, and there was an extraordinary sweetness on those tightly drawn lips, and in the large bright eyes.

"His Grace has been to the Tower lately, I hear, and once to the Marshalsea, to see Dom Sebastian Newdegate, who, as you know, was

at Court for many years till he entered the Charterhouse; but I have had
no visit from him, nor yet, I should think, Master More — you must
not judge his Grace too hardly, my son; he was a good lad, as I knew
very well — a very gallant and brave lad. A Frenchman said that he
seemed to have come down from heaven. And he has always had a great
faith and devotion, and a very strange and delicate conscience that has
cost him much pain. But he has been counseled evilly."

Chris remembered as in a dream that the bishop had been the King's
tutor years before.

"He is a good theologian too," went on the bishop, "and that is his
misfortune now, though I never thought to say such a thing. Perhaps
he will become a better one still, if God has mercy on him, and he will
come back to his first faith. But we must be good Catholics ourselves,
and be ready to die for our Religion, before we can teach him."

Again, after another silence, he went on.

"You are to be a priest, I hear, my son, and to take Christ's yoke more
closely upon you. It is no easy one in these days, though love will make
it so, as Himself said. I suppose it will be soon now?"

"We are to get a dispensation, my lord, for the interstices," said the
Prior.

Chris had heard that this would be done, before he left Lewes, and
he was astonished now, not at the news, but at the strange softness of
the Prior's voice.

"That is very well," went on the bishop. "We want all the faithful
priests possible. There is a great darkness in the land, and we need lights
to lighten it. You have a brother in Master Cromwell's service, sir, I
hear?"

Chris was silent.

"You must not grieve too much. God Almighty can set all right. It
may be he thinks he is serving Him. We are not here to judge, but to
give our own account."

The bishop went on presently to ask a few questions and to talk of
Master More, saying that he had managed to correspond with him for
a while, but that now all the means for doing so had been taken away
from them both, as well as his own books.

"It is a great grief to me that I cannot say my office, nor say nor hear
mass: I must trust now to the Holy Sacrifice offered by others."

He spoke so tenderly and tranquilly that Chris was hardly able to
keep back his tears. It seemed that the soul still kept its serene poise in
that wasted body, and was independent of it. There was no weakness
nor peevishness anywhere. The very room with its rough walls, its
cobwebbed roof, its uneven flooring, its dreadful chill and gloom,

seemed alive with a warm, redolent, spiritual atmosphere generated by this keen, pure soul. Chris had never been near so real a sanctity before.

"You have seen nothing of my Rochester folk, I suppose?" went on the bishop to the Prior.

The Prior shook his head.

"I am very downcast about them sometimes; I saw many of them at the court the other day. I forget that the Good Shepherd can guard His own sheep. And they were so faithful to me that I know they will be faithful to Him."

*T*here came a sound of a key being knocked upon the door outside, and the bishop stood up, slowly and painfully.

"That will be Mr. Giles," he said, "hungry for supper."

The two monks sank down on their knees, and as Chris closed his eyes he heard a soft murmur of blessing over his head.

Then each kissed his hand and Chris went to the door, half blind with tears.

He heard a whisper from the bishop to the Prior, who still lingered a moment, and a half sob —

"God helping me!" — said the Prior.

There was no more spoken, and the two went down the stairs together into the golden sunshine with the warder behind them.

Chris dared not look at the other. He had had a glimpse of his face as he stood aside on the stairs to let him pass, and what he saw there told him enough.

*T*here were plenty of boats rocking on the tide at the foot of the river stairs outside the Tower, and they stepped into one, telling the man to row to Southwark.

It was a glorious summer evening now. The river lay bathed in the level sunshine that turned it to molten gold, and it was covered with boats plying in all directions. There were single wherries going to and from the stairs that led down on all sides into the water, and barges here and there, of the great merchants or nobles going home to supper, with a line of oars on each side, and a glow of color gilding in the stem and prow, were moving up stream towards the City. London Bridge stood out before them presently, like a palace in a fairy-tale, blue and romantic against the western glow, and above it and beyond rose up the tall spire of the Cathedral. On the other side a fringe of houses began a little to the east of the bridge, and ran up to the spires of Southwark on the other side, and on them lay a glory of sunset with deep shadows barring them where the alleys ran down to the water's edge. Here and there behind rose up the heavy masses of the June foliage. A troop of swans, white patches on the splendor, were breasting up against the out-flowing tide.

The air was full of sound; the rattle and dash of oars, men's voices coming clear and minute across the water; and as they got out near mid-stream the bell of St. Paul's boomed far from away, indescribably solemn and melodious; another church took it up, and a chorus of mellow voices tolled out the Angelus.

Chris was half through saying it to himself, when across the soft murmur sounded the clash of brass far away beyond the bridge.

The boatman paused at his oars, turned round a moment, grasping them in one hand, and stared up-stream under the other. Chris could see a movement among the boats higher up, and there seemed to break out a commotion at the foot of the houses on London Bridge, and then far away came the sound of cheering.

"What is it?" asked the Prior sharply, lifting his head, as the boatman gave an exclamation and laid furiously to his oars again.

The man jerked his head backwards.

"The King's Grace," he said.

*F*or a minute or two nothing more was to be seen. A boat or two near them was seen making off to the side from mid-stream, to leave a clear passage, and there were cries from the direction of the bridge where someone seemed to be in difficulties with the strong stream and the piers. A wherry that was directly between them and the bridge moved off, and the shining water-way was left for the King's Grace to come down.

Then, again, the brass horns sounded nearer.

Chris was conscious of an immense excitement. The dramatic contrast of the scene he had just left with that which he was witnessing overpowered him. He had seen one end of the chain of life, the dying bishop in the Tower, in his rags; now he was to see the other end, the Sovereign at whose will he was there, in all the magnificence of a pageant. The Prior was sitting bolt upright on the seat beside him; one hand lay on his knee, the knuckles white with clenching, the other gripped the side of the boat.

Then, again, the fierce music sounded, and the first boat appeared under one of the wider spans of the bridge, a couple of hundred yards away.

The stream was running out strongly by now, and the boatman tugged to get out of it into the quieter water at the side, and as he pulled an oar snapped. The Prior half started up as the man burst out into an exclamation, and began to paddle furiously with the other oar, but the boat revolved helplessly, and he was forced to change it to the opposite side.

Meanwhile the boats were beginning to stream under the bridge, and Chris, seeing that the boat in which he sat was sufficiently out of the way to allow a clear passage in mid-stream even if not far enough removed for proper deference, gave himself up to watching the splendid sight.

The sun had now dropped behind the high houses by the bridge, and a shadow lay across the water, but nearer at hand the way was clear, and in a moment more the leading boat had entered the sunlight.

There was no possibility of mistake as to whether this were the royal barge or no. It was a great craft, seventy feet from prow to stem at the very least, and magnificent with color. As it burst out into the sun, it blazed blindingly with gold; the prow shone with blue and crimson; the stern, roofed in with a crimson canopy with flying tassels, trailed brilliant coarse tapestries on either side; and the Royal Standard streamed out behind.

Chris tried to count the oars, as they swept into the water with a rhythmical throb and out again, flashing a fringe of drops and showing a coat painted on each blade. There seemed to be eight or ten a side. A couple of trumpeters stood in the bows, behind the gilded carved figurehead, their trumpets held out symmetrically with the square hangings flapping as they came.

He could see now the heads of the watermen who rowed, with the caps of the royal livery moving together like clockwork at the swing of the oars.

Behind followed the other boats, some half dozen in all; and as each pair burst out into the level sunlight with a splendor of gold and color, and the roar from London Bridge swelled louder and louder, for a moment the young monk forgot the bitter underlying tragedy of all that he had seen and knew — forgot oozy Tower-hill and trampled Tyburn and the loaded gallows — forgot even the grim heads that stared out with dead tortured eyes from the sheaves of pikes rising high above him at this moment against the rosy sky — forgot the monks of the Charterhouse and their mourning hearts; the insulted queen, repudiated and declared a concubine — forgot all that made life so hard to live and understand at this time — as this splendid vision of the lust of the eyes broke out in pulsating sound and color before him.

But it was only for a moment.

There was a group of half-a-dozen persons under the canopy of the seat-of-state of the leading boat; the splendid center of the splendid show, brilliant in crimson and gold and jewels.

On the further side sat two men. Chris did not know their faces, but as his eyes rested on them a moment he noticed that one was burly and clean-shaven, and wore some insignia across his shoulders. At the near side were the backs of two ladies, silken clad and slashed with crimson, their white jeweled necks visible under their coiled hair and tight square cut caps. And in the center sat a pair, a man and a woman; and on these he fixed his eyes as the boat swept up not twenty yards away, for he knew who they must be.

The man was leaning back, looking gigantic in his puffed sleeves and wide mantle; one great arm was flung along the back of the tapestried seat, and his large head, capped with purple and feathers, was bending towards the woman who sat beyond. Chris could make out a fringe of reddish hair beneath his ear and at the back of the flat head between the high collar and the cap. He caught a glimpse, too, of a sedate face beyond, set on a slender neck, with downcast eyes and red lips. And then as the boat came opposite, and the trumpeters sent out a brazen crash from the trumpets at their lips, the man turned his head and stared straight at the boat.

It was an immensely wide face, fringed with reddish hair, scanty about the lips and more full below; and it looked the wider from the narrow drooping eyes set near together and the small pursed mouth. Below, his chin swelled down fold after fold into his collar, and the cheeks were wide and heavy on either side.

It was the most powerful face that Chris had ever seen or dreamed of — the animal brooded in every line and curve of it — it would have been brutish but for the steady pale stare of the eyes and the tight little lips. It fascinated and terrified him.

The flourish ended, the roar of the rowlocks sounded out again like the beating of a furious heart; the King turned his head again and said something, and the boat swept past.

Chris found that he had started to his feet, and sat down again, breathing quickly and heavily, with a kind of indignant loathing that was new to him.

This then was the master of England, the heart of all their troubles — that gorgeous fat man with the broad pulpy face, in his crimson and jewels; and that was his concubine who sat demure beside him, with her white folded ringed hands on her lap, her beautiful eyes cast down, and her lord's hot breath in her ear! It was these that were purifying the Church of God of such men as the Cardinal-bishop in the Tower, and the witty holy lawyer! It was by the will of such as these that the heads of the Carthusian Fathers, bound brow and chin with linen, stared up and down with dead eyes from the pikes overhead.

He sat panting and unseeing as the other boats swept past, full of the King's friends all going down to Greenwich.

There broke out a roar from the Tower behind, and he started and turned round to see the white smoke eddying up from the edge of the wall beside the Traitor's gate; a shrill cheer or two, far away and thin, sounded from the figures on the wharf and the boatmen about the stairs.

The wherryman sat down again and put on his cap.

"Body of God!" he said, "there was but just time."

And he began to pull again with his single oar towards the shore.

Chris looked at the Prior a moment and down again. He was sitting with tight lips, and hands clasped in his lap, and his eyes were wild and piteous.

They borrowed an oar presently from another boat, and went on up towards Southwark. The wherryman pawed once to spit on his hands as they neared the rush of the current below the bridge.

"That was Master Cromwell with His Grace," he said.

Chris looked at him questioningly.

"Him with the gold collar," he added, "and that was Audley by him."

The Prior had glanced at Chris as Cromwell's name was mentioned; but said nothing for the present. And Chris himself was lost again in musing. That was Ralph's master then, the King's right-hand man, feared next in England after the King himself — and Chancellor Audley, too, and Anne, all in one wooden boat. How easy for God to put out His hand and finish them! And then he was ashamed at his own thought, so faithless and timid; and he remembered Fisher once more and his gallant spirit in that broken body.

A minute or two later they had landed at the stairs, and were making their way up to the hostel.

The Prior put out his hand and checked him as he stepped ahead to knock.

"Wait," he said. "Do you know who signed the order we used at the Tower?"

Chris shook his head.

"Master Cromwell," said the Prior. "And do you know by whose hand it came?"

Chris stared in astonishment.

"It was by your brother," he said.

Chapter XIV

THE SACRED PURPLE

*I*t was a bright morning a few days later when the Bishop of Rochester suffered on Tower Hill.

Chris was there early, and took up his position at the outskirts of the little crowd, facing towards the Tower itself; and for a couple of hours watched the shadows creep round the piles of masonry, and the light deepen and mellow between him and the great mass of the White Tower a few hundred yards away. There was a large crowd there a good while before nine o'clock, and Chris found himself at the hour no longer on the outskirts but in the center of the people.

He had served the Prior's mass at six o'clock, and had obtained leave from him the night before to be present at the execution; but the Prior himself had given no suggestion of coming. Chris had begun to see that his superior was going through a conflict, and that he wished to spare himself any further motives of terror; he began too to understand that the visit to the bishop had had the effect of strengthening the Prior's courage, whatever had been the intention on the part of the authorities in allowing him to go. He was still wondering why Ralph had lent himself to the scheme; but had not dared to press his superior further.

*T*he bishop had made a magnificent speech at his trial, and had protested with an extraordinary pathos, that called out a demonstration from the crowd in court, against Master Rich's betrayal of his confidence. Under promise of the King that nothing that he said to his friend should be used against him, the bishop had shown his mind in a private conversation on the subject of the Supremacy Act, and now this had been brought against him by Rich himself at the trial.

"Seeing it pleased the King's Highness," said the bishop, "to send to me thus secretly to know my poor advice and opinion, which I most gladly was, and ever will be, ready to offer to him when so commanded, methinks it very hard to allow the same as sufficient testimony against me, to prove me guilty of high treason."

Rich excused himself by affirming that he said or did nothing more than what the King commanded him to do; and the trial ended by the bishop's condemnation.

As Chris waited by the scaffold he prayed almost incessantly. There was sufficient spur for prayer in the menacing fortress before him with its hundred tiny windows, and the new scaffold, some five or six feet high, that stood in the foreground. He wondered how the bishop was passing his time and thought he knew. The long grey wall beyond the moat, and the towers that rose above it, were suggestive in their silent strength. From where he stood too he could catch a glimpse of the shining reaches of the river with the green slopes on the further side; and the freedom and beauty of the sight, the delicate haze that hung over the water, the birds winging their way across, the boats plying to and fro, struck a vivid contrast to the grim fatality of the prison and the scaffold.

A bell sounded out somewhere from the Tower, and a ripple ran through the crowd. There was an immensely tall man a few yards from Chris, and Chris could see his face turn suddenly towards the lower ground by the river where the gateway rose up dark against the bright water. The man's face suddenly lighted with interest, and Chris saw his lips move and his eyes become intent. Then a surging movement began, and the monk was swept away to the left by the packed crowd round him. There were faces lining the wall and opposite, and all were turned one way. A great murmur began to swell up, and a woman beside him turned white and began to sob quietly.

His eyes caught a bright point of light that died again, flashed out, and resolved itself into a gleaming line of halberds, moving on towards the right above the heads, up the slope to the scaffold. He saw a horse toss his head; and then a feathered cap or two swaying behind.

Then for one instant between the shifting heads in front he caught sight of a lean face framed in a flapped cap swaying rhythmically as if borne on a chair. It vanished again.

The flashing line of halberds elongated itself, divided, and came between the scaffold and him; and the murmur of the crowd died to a heart-shaking silence. A solemn bell clanged out again from the interior of the prison, and Chris, his wet hands knit together, began to count the strokes mechanically, staring at the narrow rail of the scaffold, and waiting for the sight that he knew would come. Then again he was swept along a yard or two to the right, and when he had recovered his feet a man was on the scaffold, bending forwards and gesticulating. Another head rose into the line of vision, and this man too turned towards the steps up which he had come, and stood, one hand outstretched.

Again a murmur and movement began; Chris had to look to his foothold, and when he raised his head again a solemn low roar was rising up and swelling, of pity and excitement, for, silhouetted against the sunlit Tower behind, stood the man for whose sake all were there.

He was in a black gown and tippet, and carried his two hands clasped to his breast; and in them was a book and a crucifix. His cap was on his head, and the white face, incredibly thin, looked out over the heads of the crowd.

Chris hardly noticed that the scaffold was filling with people, until a figure came forward, in black, with a masked face, and bowed deferentially to the bishop; and in an instant silence fell again.

He saw the bishop turn and bow slightly in return, and in the stillness that wonderful voice sounded out, with the clear minuteness of words spoken in the open air, clear and penetrating over the whole ground.

"I forgive you very heartily; and I hope you will see me overcome this storm lustily."

The black figure fell back, and the bishop stood hesitating, looking this way and that as if for direction.

The Lieutenant of the Tower came forward; but Chris could only see his lips move, as a murmur had broken out again at the bishop's answer; but he signed with his hand and stepped behind the prisoner.

The bishop nodded, lifted his hand and took off his cap; and his white hair appeared; then he fumbled at his throat, holding the book and crucifix in his other hand; and, with the Lieutenant's help, slipped off his tippet and loose gown; and as he freed himself, and stood in his doublet and hose, a great sobbing cry of horror and compassion rose from the straining faces, for he seemed scarcely to be a living man, so dreadful was his emaciation. Above that lean figure of death looked out the worn old face, serene and confident. He was again holding the book and crucifix clasped to his breast, as he stepped to the edge of the scaffold.

The cry died to a murmur and ceased abruptly as he began his speech, every word of which was audible.

"Christian people," he began, "I am come hither to die for the faith of Christ's holy Catholic Church." He raised his voice a little, and it rang out confidently. "And I thank God that hitherto my stomach hath served me very well thereunto, so that yet I have not feared death. Wherefore I desire you all to help and assist with your prayers, that at the very point and instant of death's stroke I may in that very moment stand steadfast, without fainting in any one point of the Catholic Faith, free from any fear."

He paused again; his hands closed one on the other. He glanced up.

"And I beseech the Almighty God of His infinite goodness and mercy, to save the King and this realm; and that it may please Him to hold His hand over it, and send the King's Highness good counsel."

He ceased abruptly; and dropped his head.

A gentle groan ran through the crowd.

Chris felt his throat contract, and a mist blinded his eyes for a moment.

Then he saw the bishop slip the crucifix into his other hand, and open the book, apparently at random. His lean finger dropped upon the page; and he read aloud softly, as if to himself.

"This is life eternal, that they might know Thee, the one true God, and Jesus Christ whom Thou hast sent. I have glorified Thee on the earth; I have finished the work which Thou gavest me to do."

Again there was silence, for it seemed as if he was going to make a sermon, but he looked down at the book a moment or two. Then he closed it gently.

"Here is learning enough for me," he said, "to my life's end."

There was a movement among the silent figures at the back of the scaffold; and the Lieutenant stepped forward once more. The bishop turned to meet him and nodded; handing him the book; and then with the crucifix still in his hands, and with the officers help, sank on to his knees.

*I*t seemed to Chris as if he waited an eternity; but he could not take his eyes off him. Round about was the breathing mass of the crowd, overhead the clear summer sky; up from the river came the sounds of cries and the pulse of oars, and from the Tower now and again the call of a horn and the stroke of a bell; but all this was external, and seemed to have no effect upon the intense silence of the heart that radiated from the scaffold, and in which the monk felt himself enveloped. The space between himself and the bishop seemed annihilated; and Chris found himself in company with a thousand others close beside the man's soul that was to leave the world so soon. He could not pray; but he had the sensation of gripping that imploring spirit, pulsating with it, furthering with his own strained will that stream of effort that he knew was going forth.

Meanwhile his eyes stared at him; and saw without seeing how the old man now leaned back with closed eyes and moving lips; now he bent forward, and looked at the crucified figure that he held between his hands, now lifted it and lingeringly kissed the pierced feet. Behind stood the stiff line of officers, and in front below the rail rose the glitter of the halberds.

The minutes went by and there was no change. The world seemed to have grown rigid with expectancy; it was as if time stood still. There fell upon the monk's soul, not suddenly but imperceptibly, something of that sense of the unseen that he had experienced at Tyburn. For a certain space all sorrow and terror left him; he knew tangibly now that to which at other times his mere faith assented; he knew that the world of spirit was the real one; that the Tower, the axe, the imminent shadow of death, were little more than illusions; they were part of the staging, significant and necessary, but with no substance of reality. The eternal world in which God was all, alone was a fact. He felt no longer pity or regret. Nothing but the sheer existence of a Being of which all persons there were sharers, poised in an eternal instant, remained with him.

This strange sensation was scarcely disturbed by the rising of the lean black figure from its knees; Chris watched him as he might have watched the inevitable movement of an actor performing his pre-arranged part. The bishop turned eastward, to where the sun was now high above the Tower gate, and spoke once more.

"Accedite ad eum, et illuminamini; et facies vestræ non confundentur."

Then once more in the deathly stillness he turned round; and his eyes ran over the countless faces turned up to his own. But there was a certain tranquil severity in his face — the severity of one who has taken a bitter cup firmly into his hand; his lips were tightly compressed, and his eyes were deep and steady.

Then very slowly he lifted his right hand, touched his forehead, and enveloped himself in a great sign of the cross, still looking out unwaveringly over the faces; and immediately, without any hesitation, sank down on his knees, put his hands before him on to the scaffold, and stretched himself flat.

He was now invisible to Chris; for the low block on which he had laid his neck was only a few inches high.

There was again a surge and a murmur as the headsman stepped forward with the huge-headed axe over his shoulder, and stood waiting.

Then again the moments began to pass.

Chris lost all consciousness of his own being; he was aware of nothing but the objective presence of the scaffold, of an overpowering expectancy. It seemed as if something were stretched taut in his brain, at breaking point; as if some vast thing were on the point of revelation. All else had vanished, — the scene round him, the sense of the invisible; there was but the point of space left, waiting for an explosion.

There was a sense of wrenching torture as the headsman lifted the axe, bringing it high round behind him; the motion seemed shockingly slow, and to wring the strained nerves to agony. . . .

Then in a blinding climax the axe fell.

Chapter XV
THE KING'S FRIEND

Overfield Court was mildly stirred at the news that Master Christopher would stay there a few days on his way back from London to Lewes. It was not so exciting as when Master Ralph was to come, as the latter made more demands than a mere monk; for the one the horses must be in the pink of condition, the game neither too wild nor too tame, his rooms must be speckless, neither too full nor too empty of furniture; for the other it did not matter so much, for he was now not only a younger brother, but a monk, and therefore accustomed to contradiction and desirous to acquiesce in arrangements.

Lady Torridon indeed took no steps at all when she heard that Chris was coming, beyond expressing a desire that she might not be called upon to discuss the ecclesiastical situation at every meal; and when Chris finally arrived a week after Bishop Fisher's execution, having parted with the Prior at Cuckfield, she was walking in her private garden beyond the moat.

Sir James was in a very different state. He had caused two rooms to be prepared, that his son might take his choice, one next to Mr. Carleton's and therefore close to the chapel, and the other the old chamber that Chris had occupied before he went to Lewes; and when the monk at last rode up on alone on his tired mule with his little bag strapped to the crupper, an hour before sunset, his father was out at the gatehouse to meet him, and walked up beside him to the house, with his hand laid on his son's knee.

They hardly spoke a word as they went; Sir James had looked up at Chris's white strained face, and had put one question; and the other had nodded; and the hearts of both were full as they went together to the house.

The father and son supped together alone that night in the private parlor, for no one had dared to ask Lady Torridon to postpone her usual supper hour; and as soon as that was over and Chris had told what he had seen, with many silences, they went into the oak-room where Lady Torridon and Mr. Carleton were awaiting them by the hearth with the Flemish tiles.

The mother was sitting as usual in her tall chair, with her beautiful hands on her lap, and smiled with a genial contempt as she ran her eyes up and down her son's figure.

"The habit suits you very well, my son — in every way," she added, looking at him curiously.

Chris had greeted her an hour before at his arrival, so there was no ceremony of salute to be gone through now. He sat down by his father.

"You have seen Ralph, I hear," observed Lady Torridon.

Chris did not know how much she knew, and simply assented. He had told his father everything.

"I have some news," she went on in an unusually talkative mood, "for you both. Ralph is to marry Beatrice Atherton — the girl you saw in his rooms, Christopher."

Sir James gave an exclamation and leant forward; and Chris tightened his lips.

"She is a friend of Mr. More's," went on Lady Torridon, apparently unconscious of the sensation she was making, "but that is Ralph's business, I suppose."

"Why did Ralph not write to me?" asked his father, with a touch of sternness.

Lady Torridon answered him by a short pregnant silence, and then went on —

"I suppose he wished me to break it to you. It will not be for two or three years. She says she cannot leave Mrs. More for the present."

Chris's brain was confused by the news, and yet it all seemed external to him. As he had ridden up to the house in the evening he had recognized for the first time how he no longer belonged to the place; his two years at Lewes had done their work, and he came to his home now not as a son but as a guest. He had even begun to perceive the difference after his quarrel with Ralph, for he had not been conscious of the same personal sting at his brother's sins that he would have felt five years ago. And now this news, while it affected him, did not penetrate to the still sanctuary that he had hewn out of his heart during those months of discipline.

But his father was roused.

"He should have written to me," he said sternly. "And, my wife, I will beg you to remember that I have a right to my son's business."

Lady Torridon did not move or answer. He leaned back again, and passed his hand tenderly through Chris's arm.

*I*t was very strange to the younger son to find himself a few minutes later up again in the west gallery of the chapel, where he had knelt two years before; and for a few moments he almost felt himself at home. But the mechanical shifting of his scapular aside as he sat down for the psalms, recalled facts. Then he had been in his silk suit, his hands had been rough with his crossbow, his beard had been soft on his chin, and the blood hot in his cheeks. Now he was in his habit, smooth-faced and shaven, tired and oppressed, still weak from the pangs of soul-birth. He was further from human love, but nearer the Divine, he thought.

He sat with his father a few minutes after compline; and Sir James spoke more frankly of the news that they had heard.

"If she is really a friend of Mr. More's," he said, "she may be his salvation. I am sorely disappointed in him. I did not know Master Cromwell when I sent him to him, as I do now. Is it my fault, Chris?"

Chris told his father presently of what the Prior had said as to Ralph's assistance in the matter of the visit that the two monks had paid to the Tower; and asked an interpretation.

Sir James sat quiet a minute or two, stroking his pointed grey beard softly, and looking into the hearth.

"God forgive me if I am wrong, my son," he said at last, "but I wonder whether they let the my Lord Prior go to the Tower in order to shake the confidence of both. Do you think so, Chris?"

Chris too was silent a moment; he knew he must not speak evil of dignities.

"It may be so. I know that my Lord Prior —"

"Well, my son?"

"My Lord Prior has been very anxious —"

Sir James patted his son on the knee, and reassured him.

"Prior Crowham is a very holy man, I think; but — but somewhat delicate. However their designs have come to nothing. The bishop is in glory; and the other more courageous than he was."

Chris also had a few words with Mr. Carleton before he went to bed, sitting where he had sat in the moonlight two years before.

"If they have done so much," said the priest, "they will do more. When a man has slipped over a precipice he cannot save his fall. Master More will be the next to go; I make no doubt of that. You are to be a priest soon, Chris?"

"They have applied for leave," said the monk shortly. "In two years I shall be a priest, no doubt, if God wills."

"You are happy?" asked the other.

Chris made a little gesture.

"I do not know what that means," he said, "but I know I have done right. I feel nothing. God's ways and His world are too strange."

The priest looked at him oddly, without speaking.

"Well, father?" asked Chris, smiling.

"You are right," said the chaplain brusquely. "You have done well. You have crossed the border."

Chris felt the blood surge in his temples.

"The border?" he asked.

"The border of dreams. They surround the Religious Life; and you have passed through them."

Chris still looked at him with parted lips. This praise was sweet, after the bitterness of his failure with Ralph. The priest seemed to know what was passing in his mind.

"Oh! you will fail sometimes," he said, "but not finally. You are a monk, my son, and a man."

*L*ady Torridon retired into her impregnable silence again after her sallies of speech on the previous evening; but as the few days went on that Chris had been allowed to spend with his parents he was nonetheless aware that her attitude towards him was one of contempt. She showed it in a hundred ways — by not appearing to see him, by refusing to modify her habits in the smallest particular for his convenience, by a rigid silence on the subject that was in the hearts of both him and his father. She performed her duties as punctually and efficiently as ever, dealt dispassionately and justly with an old servant who had been troublesome, and with regard to whom her husband was both afraid and tender; but never asked for confidences or manifested the minutest detail of her own accord.

*O*n the fourth day after Chris's arrival news came that Sir Thomas More had been condemned, but it roused no more excitement than the fall of a threatening rod. It had been known to be inevitable. And then on Chris's last evening at home came the last details.

*S*ir James and Chris had been out for a long ride up the estate, talking but little, for each knew what was in the heart of the other; and they were just dismounting at the terrace-steps when there was a sound of furious galloping; and a couple of riders burst through the gateway a hundred yards away.

Chris felt his heart leap and hammer in his throat, but stood passively awaiting what he knew was coming; and a few seconds later, Nicholas Maxwell checked his horse passionately at the steps.

"God damn them!" he cried, with a crimson quivering face.

Sir James stepped up at once and took him by the arm.

"Nick," he said, and glanced at the staring grooms.

Nicholas showed his teeth like a dog.

"God damn them!" he said again.

The other rider had come up by now; he was dusty and seemed spent. He was a stranger to the father and son who waited on the steps; but he looked like a groom, and slipped off his horse deftly and took Sir Nicholas's bridle.

"Come in Nick," said Sir James. "We can talk in the house."

As the three went up together, with the strange rider at a respectful distance behind, Nicholas broke out again in one sentence.

"They have done it," he said, "he is dead. Mother of God!"

His whip twitched in his clenching hand. He turned and jerked his head beckoningly to the man who followed; and the four went on together, through the hall and into Sir James's parlor. Sir James shut the door.

"Tell us, Nick."

Nicholas stood at the hearth, glaring and shifting.

"This fellow knows — he saw it; tell them, Dick."

The man gave his account. He was one of the servants of Sir Nicholas' younger brother, who lived in town, and had been sent down to Great Keynes immediately after the execution that had taken place that morning. He was a man of tolerable education, and told his story well.

Sir James sat as he listened, with his hand shading his eyes; Nicholas was fidgeting at the hearth, interrupting the servant now and again with questions and reminders; and Chris leaned in the dark corner by the window. There floated vividly before his mind as he listened the setting of the scene that he had looked upon a few days ago, though there were new actors in it now.

"It was this morning, sir, on Tower Hill. There was a great company there long before the time. He came out bravely enough, walking with the Lieutenant that was his friend, and with a red cross in his hand."

"You were close by," put in Nicholas

"Yes, sir; I was beside the stairs. They shook as he went up; they were crazy steps, and he told the Lieutenant to have a care to him."

"The words, man, the words!"

"I am not sure, sir; but they were after this fashion: 'See me safe up, Master Lieutenant; I will shift for myself at the coming down.' So he got up safe, and stamped once or twice merrily to see if all were firm. Then he made a speech, sir, and begged all there to pray for him. He told them that he was to die for the faith of the Catholic Church, as my Lord of Rochester did."

"Have you heard of my lord's head being taken to Nan Boleyn?" put in Nicholas fiercely.

Sir James looked up.

"Presently, Nick," he said.

The man went on.

"Master More kneeled down presently at his prayers; and all the folk kept very quiet. There was not one that cried against him. Then he stood up again, put off his gown, so that his neck was bare; and passed his hand over it smiling. Then he told the headsman that it was but a short one, and bade him be brave and strike straight, lest his good name should suffer. Then he laid himself down to the block, and put his neck on it; but he moved again before he gave the sign, and put his beard out in front — for he had grown one in prison" —

"Give us the words," snarled Nicholas.

"He said, sir, that his beard had done no treason, and need not therefore suffer as he had to do. And then he thrust out his hand for a sign — and 'twas done at a stroke."

"God damn them!" hissed Nicholas again as a kind of Amen, turning swiftly to the fireplace so that his face could not be seen.

There was complete silence for a few seconds. The groom had his eyes cast down, and stood there — then again he spoke.

"As to my Lord of Rochester's head, that was taken off to the — the Queen, they say, in a white bag, and she struck it on the mouth."

Nicholas dropped his head against his hand that rested on the wood-work.

"And the body rested naked all day on the scaffold, with the halberd-men drinking round about; and 'twas tumbled into a hole in Barking Churchyard that night."

"At whose orders?"

"At Master Cromwell's, sir."

Again there was silence; and again the groom broke it.

"There was more said, sir —" and hesitated.

The old man signed to him to go on.

"They say that my lord's head shone with light each night on the bridge," said the man reverently; "there was a great press there, I know, all day, so that the streets were blocked, and none could come or go. And so they tumbled that into the river at last; at least 'tis supposed so — for 'twas gone when I looked."

Nicholas turned round; and his eyes were bright and his face fiery and discolored.

Sir James stood up, and his voice was broken as he spoke.

"Thank you, my man. You have told your story well."

*A*s the groom turned to go out, Sir Nicholas wheeled round swiftly to the hearth, and buried his face on his arm; and Chris saw a great heaving begin to shake his broad shoulders.

BOOK II

THE KING'S TRIUMPH

PART I

THE SMALLER HOUSES

Chapter I

AN ACT OF FAITH

*T*owards the end of August Beatrice Atherton was walking up the north bank of the river from Charing to Westminster to announce to Ralph her arrival in town on the previous night.

*S*he had gone through horrors since the June day on which she had seen the two brothers together. With Margaret beside her she had watched Master More in court, in his frieze gown, leaning on his stick, bent and grey with imprisonment, had heard his clear answers, his searching questions, and his merry conclusion after sentence had been pronounced; she had stayed at home with the stricken family on the morning of the sixth of July, kneeling with them at her prayers in the chapel of the New Building, during the hours until Mr. Roper looked in grey-faced and trembling, and they knew that all was over. She went with them to the burial in St. Peter's Chapel in the Tower; and last, which was the most dreadful ordeal of all, she had stood in the summer darkness by the wicket-gate, had heard the cautious stroke of oars, and the footsteps coming up the path, and had let Margaret in bearing her precious burden robbed from the spike on London Bridge.

Then for a while she had gone down to the country with Mrs. More and her daughters; and now she was back once more, in a kind of psychical convalescence, at her aunt's new house on the river-bank at Charing.

*H*er face was a little paler than it used to be, but there was a quickening brightness in her eyes as she swept along in her blue mantle, with her maid beside her, in the rear of the liveried servant, who carried a silver-headed wand a few yards in front.

She was rehearsing to herself the scene in which Ralph had asked her to be his wife.

Where Chris had left the room the two had remained perfectly still until the street-door had closed; and then Ralph had turned to her with a question in his steady eyes.

She had told him then that she did not believe one word of what the monk had insinuated; but she had been conscious even at the time that she was making what theologians call an act of faith. It was not that there were not difficulties to her in Ralph's position — there were plenty — but she had determined by a final and swift decision to disregard them and believe in him. It was a last step in a process that continued ever since she had become interested by this strong brusque man; and it had been precipitated by the fanatical attack to which she had just been a witness. The discord, as she thought it, of Ralph's character and actions had not been resolved; yet she had decided in that moment that it need not be; that her data as concerned those actions were insufficient; and that if she could not explain, at least she could trust.

Ralph had been very honest, she told herself now. He had reminded her that he was a servant of Cromwell's whom many believed to be an enemy of Church and State. She had nodded back to him steadily and silently, knowing what would follow from the paleness of his face, and his bright eyes beneath their wide lids. She had felt her own breast rise and fall and a pulse begin to hammer at the spring of her throat. Even now as she thought of it her heart quickened, and her hands clenched themselves.

And then in one swift moment it had come. She had found her hands caught fiercely, and her eyes imprisoned by his; and then all was over, and she had given him an answer in a word.

It had not been easy even after that. Cecily had questioned her more than once. Mrs. More had said a few indiscreet things that had been hard to bear; her own aunt had received the news in silence.

But that was over now. The necessary consent on both sides had been given; and here she was once more walking up the road to Westminster with Ralph's image before her eyes, and Ralph himself a hundred yards away.

*S*he turned the last corner from the alley, passed up the little street, and turned again across the little cobbled yard that lay before the house.

Mr. Morris was at the door as she came up, and he now stood aside. He seemed doubtful.

"Mr. Torridon has gentlemen with him, madam."

"Then I will wait," said Beatrice serenely, and made a motion to come in. The servant still half-hesitating opened the door wider; and Beatrice and her maid went through into the little parlor on the right.

As she passed in she heard voices from the other door. Mr. Morris's footsteps went down the passage.

She had not very long to wait. There was the sound of a carriage driving up to the door presently, and her maid who sat in view of the window glanced out. Her face grew solemn.

"It is Master Cromwell's carriage," she said.

Beatrice was conscious of a vague discomfort; Master Cromwell, in spite of her efforts, was the shadowed side of Ralph's life.

"Is he coming in?" she said.

The maid peeped again.

"No, madam."

The door of the room they were in was not quite shut, and there was still a faint murmur of voices from across the hall; but almost immediately there was the sound of a lifted latch, and then Ralph's voice clear and distinct.

"I will see to it, my lord."

Beatrice stood up, feeling a little uneasy. She fancied that perhaps she ought not to be here; she remembered now the servant's slight air of unwillingness to let her in. There was a footfall in the hall, and the sound of talking; and as Mr. Morris's hasty step came up the passage, the door was pushed abruptly open, and Ralph was looking into the room, with one or two others beyond him.

"I did not know," he began, and flushed a little, smiling and making as if to close the door. But Cromwell's face, with its long upper lip and close-set grey eyes, appeared over his shoulder, and Ralph turned round, almost deprecatingly.

"I beg your pardon, sir; this is Mistress Atherton, and her woman."

Cromwell came forward into the room, with a kind of keen smile, in his rich dress and chain.

"Mistress Beatrice Atherton?" he said with a questioning deference; and Ralph introduced them to one another. Beatrice was conscious of a good deal of awkwardness. It was uncomfortable to be caught here, as if she had come to spy out something. She felt herself flushing as she explained that she had had no idea who was there.

Cromwell looked at her very pleasantly.

"There is nothing to ask pardon for, Mistress," he said. "I knew you were a friend of Mr. Torridon. He has told me everything."

Ralph seemed strangely ill-at-case, Beatrice thought, as Cromwell congratulated them both with a very kindly air, and then turned towards the hall again.

"My lord," he called, "my lord —"

Then Beatrice saw a tall ecclesiastic, clean-shaven, with a strangely insignificant but kindly face, with square drooping lip and narrow hazel eyes, come forward in his prelate's dress; and at the sight of him her eyes grew hard and her lips tight.

"My lord," said Cromwell, "this is Mistress Beatrice Torridon."

The prelate put out his hand, smiling faintly, with the ring uppermost to be kissed. Beatrice stood perfectly still. She could see Ralph at an angle looking at her imploringly.

"You know my Lord of Canterbury," said Cromwell, in an explanatory voice.

"I know my Lord of Canterbury," said Beatrice.

There was a dead silence for a moment, and then a faint whimper from the maid.

Cranmer dropped his hand, but still smiled, turning to Ralph.

"We must be gone, Mr. Torridon. Master Cromwell has very kindly —"

Cromwell who had stood amazed for a moment, turned round at his name.

"Yes," he said to Ralph, "my lord is to come with me. And you will be at my house tomorrow."

He said good-day to the girl, looking at her with an amused interest that made her flush; and as Dr. Cranmer passed out of the street-door to the carriage with Ralph bare-headed beside him, he spoke very softly.

"You are like the others, mistress," he said; and shook his heavy head at her like an indulgent father. Then he too turned and went out.

*B*eatrice went across at once to the other room, leaving her maid behind, and stood by the hearth as Ralph came in. She heard the door close and his footstep come across the floor beside her.

"Beatrice," said Ralph.

She turned round and looked at him.

"You must not scold me," she said with great serenity. "You must leave me my conscience." Ralph's face cleared instantly.

"No, no," he said. "I feared it would be the other way."

"A married priest, they say!" remarked the girl, but without bitterness.

"I daresay, my darling, — but — but I have more tenderness for marriage than I had."

Beatrice's black eyes just flickered with amusement.

"Yes; but priests!" she said.

"Yes — even priests —" said Ralph, smiling back.

Beatrice turned to a chair and sat down.

"I suppose I must not ask any questions," she said, glancing up for a moment at Ralph's steady eyes. She thought he looked a little uneasy still.

"Oh! I scarcely know," said Ralph; and he took a turn across the room and came back. She waited, knowing that she had already put her question, and secretly pleased that he knew it, and was perplexed by it.

"I scarcely know," he said again, standing opposite her. "Well, — yes — all will know it soon."

"Oh! I can wait till then," said Beatrice quickly, not sure whether she were annoyed or not by being told a secret of such a common nature. Ralph glanced at her, not sure either.

"I am afraid —" he began.

"No — no," she said, ashamed of her doubt. "I do not wish to know; I can wait."

"I will tell you," said Ralph. He went and sat down in the chair opposite, crossing his legs.

"It is about the Visitation of the Religious Houses. I am to go with the Visitors in September."

Beatrice felt a sudden and rather distressed interest; but she showed no sign of it.

"Ah, yes!" she said softly, "and what will be your work?"

Ralph was reassured by her tone.

"We are to go to the southern province. I am with Dr. Layton's party. We shall make enquiries of the state of Religion, how it is observed and so forth; and report to Master Cromwell."

Beatrice looked down in a slightly side-long way.

"I know what you are thinking," said Ralph, his tone a mixture of amusement and pride. She looked up silently.

"Yes I knew it was so," he went on, smiling straight at her. "You are wondering what in the world I know about Religious Houses. But I have a brother —"

A shadow went over her face; Ralph saw she did not like the allusion.

"Besides," he went on again, "they need intelligent men, not ecclesiastics, for this business."

"But Dr. Layton?" questioned Beatrice.

"Well, you might call him an ecclesiastic; but you would scarcely guess it from himself. And no man could call him a partisan on that side."

"He would do better in one of his rectories, I should think," said Beatrice.

"Well, that is not my business," observed Ralph.

"And what is your business?"

"Well, to ride round the country; examine the Religious, and make enquiries of the country folk."

Beatrice began to tap her foot very softly. Ralph glanced down at the bright buckle and smiled in spite of himself.

The girl went on.

"And by whose authority?"

"By his Grace's authority."

"And Dr. Cranmer's?"

"Well, yes; so far as he has any."

"I see," said Beatrice; and cast her eyes down again.

There was silence for a moment or two.

"You see too that I cannot withdraw," explained Ralph, a little distressed at her air. "It is part of my duty."

"Oh! I understand that," said Beatrice.

"And so long as I act justly, there is no harm done."

The girl was silent.

"You understand that?" he asked.

"I suppose I do," said Beatrice slowly.

Ralph made a slight impatient movement.

"No — wait," said the girl, "I do understand. If I cannot trust you, I had better never have known you. I do understand that I can trust you; though I cannot understand how you can do such work."

She raised her eyes slowly to his; and Ralph as he looked into them saw that she was perfectly sincere, and speaking without bitterness.

"Sweetheart," he said. "I could not have taken that from any but you; but I know that you are true, and mean no more nor less than your words. You do trust me?"

"Why, yes," said the girl; and smiled at him as he took her in his arms.

When she had gone again Ralph had a difficult quarter of an hour.

He knew that she trusted him, but was it not simply because she did not know? He sat and pondered the talk he had had with Cromwell and the Archbishop. Neither had expressly said that what was wanted was adverse testimony against the Religious Houses; but that, Ralph knew very well, was what was asked of him. They had talked a great deal about the corruptions that the Visitors would no doubt find, and Cranmer had told a story or two, with an appearance of great distress, of scandalous cases that had come under his own notice. Cromwell too had pointed out that such corruptions did incalculable evil; and that an immoral monk did far more harm in a countryside than his holy brethren could do of good. Both had said a word too about the luxury and riches to be found in the houses of those who professed poverty, and of the injury done to Christ's holy religion by such insincere pretences.

Ralph knew too, from previous meetings with the other Visitors, the kind of work for which such men would be likely to be selected.

There was Dr. Richard Layton first, whom Ralph was to join in Sussex at the end of September, a priest who had two or three preferments and notoriously neglected them; Ralph had taken a serious dislike to him. He was a coarse man who knew how to cringe effectively; and Ralph had listened to him talking to Cromwell, with some dismay. But he would be to a large extent independent of him, and only in his company at some of the larger houses that needed more than one Visitor. Thomas Legh, too, a young doctor of civil law, was scarcely more attractive. He was a man of an extraordinary arrogance, carrying his head high, and looking about him with insolently drooping eyes. Ralph had been at once amused and angry to see him go out into the street after his interview with Cromwell, where his horse and half-a-dozen footmen awaited him, and to watch him ride off with the airs of a vulgar prince. The Welshman Ap Rice too, and the red-faced bully, Dr. London, were hardly persons whom he desired as associates, and the others were not much better; and Ralph found himself feeling a little thankful that none of these men had been in his house just now, when Cromwell and the Archbishop had called in the former's carriage, and when Beatrice had met them there.

*R*alph had a moment, ten minutes after Beatrice had left, when he was inclined to snatch up his hat and go after Cromwell to tell him to do his own dirty work; but his training had told, and he had laughed at the folly of the thought. Why, of course, the work had to be done! England was rotten with dreams and superstition. Ecclesiasticism had corrupted genuine human life, and national sanity could not be restored except by a violent process. Innocent persons would no doubt suffer — innocent according to conscience, but guilty against the common-wealth. Every great movement towards good was bound to be attended by individual catastrophes; but it was the part of a strong man to carry out principles and despise details.

The work had to be done; it was better then that there should be at least one respectable workman. Of course such a work needed coarse men to carry it out; it was bound to be accompanied by some brutality; and his own presence there might do something to keep the brutality within limits.

*A*nd as for Beatrice — well, Beatrice did not yet understand. If she understood all as he did, she would sympathize, for she was strong too. Besides — he had held her in his arms just now, and he knew that love was king.

But he sat for ten minutes more in silence, staring with unseeing eyes at the huddled roofs opposite and the clear sky over them; and the point of the quill in his fingers was split and cracked when Mr. Morris looked in to see if his master wanted anything.

Chapter II

THE BEGINNING OF THE VISITATION

*I*t was on a wet foggy morning in October that Ralph set out with Mr. Morris and a couple more servants to join Dr. Layton in the Sussex visitation. He rode alone in front; and considered as he went.

*T*he Visitation itself, Cromwell had told him almost explicitly, was in pursuance of the King's policy to get the Religious Houses, which were considered to be the strongholds of the papal power in England, under the authority of the Crown; and also to obtain from them reinforcements of the royal funds which were running sorely low. The crops were most disappointing this year, and the King's tenants were wholly unable to pay their rents; and it had been thought wiser to make up the deficit from ecclesiastical wealth rather than to exasperate the Commons by a direct call upon their resources.

So far, he knew very well, the attempt to get the Religious Houses into the King's power had only partially succeeded. Bishop Fisher's influence had availed to stave off the fulfillment of the royal intentions up to the present; and the oath of supremacy, in which to a large extent the key of the situation lay, had been by no means universally accepted. Now, however, the scheme was to be pushed forward; and as a preparation for it, it was proposed to visit every monastery and convent in the kingdom, and to render account first of the temporal wealth of each, and then of the submissiveness of its inmates; and, as Cromwell had hinted to Ralph, anything that could damage the character of the Religious would not be unacceptable evidence.

Ralph was aware that the scheme in which he was engaged was supported in two ways; first, by the suspension of episcopal authority during the course of the visitation, and secondly by the vast powers committed to the visitors. In one of the saddle-bags strapped on to Mr. Morris's horse was a sheaf of papers, containing eighty-six articles of enquiry, and twenty-five injunctions, as well as certificates from the King endowing Ralph with what was practically papal jurisdiction. He was authorized to release from their vows all Religious who desired it, and ordered to dismiss all who had been professed under twenty years of age, or who were at the present date under twenty-four years old. Besides this he was commissioned to enforce the enclosure with the utmost rigor, to set porters at the doors to see that it was observed, and to encourage all who had any grievance against their superiors to forward complaints through himself to Cromwell.

Ralph understood well enough the first object of these regulations, namely to make monastic life impossible. It was pretty evident that a rigorous confinement would breed discontent; which in its turn would be bound to escape through the vent-hole which the power of appeal provided; thus bringing about a state of anarchy within the house, and the tightening of the hold of the civil authority upon the Religious.

Lastly the Visitors were authorized to seize any church furniture or jewels that they might judge would be better in secular custody.

Once more, he had learned both from Cromwell, and from his own experience at Paul's Cross, how the laity itself was being carefully prepared for the blow that was impending, by an army of selected preachers who could be trusted to say what they were told. Only a few days before Ralph had halted his horse at the outskirts of a huge crowd gathered round Paul's Cross, and had listened to a torrent of vituperation poured out by a famous orator against the mendicant friars; and from the faces and exclamations of the people round him he had learned once more that greed was awake in England.

*I*t was a somewhat dismal ride that he had this day. The sky was heavy and overcast, it rained constantly, and the roads were in a more dreary condition even than usual. He splashed along through the mud with his servants behind him, wrapped in his cloak; and his own thoughts were not of a sufficient cheerfulness to compensate for the external discomforts. His political plane of thought was shot by a personal idea. He guessed that he would have to commit himself in a manner that he had never done before; and was not wholly confident that he would be able to explain matters satisfactorily to Beatrice. Besides, the particular district to which he was appointed included first Lewes, where Chris would have an eye on his doings, and secondly the little Benedictine house of Rusper, where his sister Margaret had been lately professed; and he wondered what exactly would be his relation with his own family when his work was done.

But for the main object of his visitation he had little but sympathy. It was good, he thought, that a scouring should be made of these idle houses, and their inmates made more profitable to the commonwealth. And lastly, whether or no he sympathized, it would be fatal to his career to refuse the work offered to him.

As he did not feel very confident at first, he had arranged to meet with Dr. Layton's party at the Premonstratension Abbey of Durford, situated at the borders of Sussex and Hampshire, and there learn the exact methods to be employed in the visitation; but it was a long ride, and he took two days over it, sleeping on the way at Waverly in the Cistercian House. This had not yet been visited, as Dr. Layton was riding up gradually from the west country, but the rumor of his intentions had already reached there, and Ralph was received with a pathetic deference as one of the representatives of the Royal Commission.

The Abbot was a kindly nervous man, and welcomed Ralph with every sign of respect at the gate of the abbey, giving contradictory orders about the horses and the entertainment of the guests to his servants who seemed in very little awe of him.

After mass and breakfast on the following morning the Abbot came into the guest-house and begged for a short interview.

*H*e apologized first for the poorness of the entertainment, saying that he had done his best. Ralph answered courteously; and the other went on immediately, standing deferentially before the chair where Ralph was seated, and fingering his cross.

"I hope, Mr. Torridon, that it will be you who will visit us; you have found us all unprepared, and you know that we are doing our best to keep our Rule. I hope you found nothing that was not to your liking."

Ralph bowed and smiled.

"I would sooner that it were you," went on the Abbot, "and not another that visited us. Dr. Layton —"

He stopped abruptly, embarrassed.

"You have heard something of him?" questioned Ralph.

"I know nothing against him," said the other hastily, "except that they say that he is sharp with us poor monks. I fear he would find a great deal here not to his taste. My authority has been so much weakened

of late; I have some discontented brethren — not more than one or two,
Mr. Torridon — and they have learned that they will be able to appeal
now to the King's Grace, and get themselves set free; and they have
ruined the discipline of the house. I do not wish to hide anything, sir,
you see; but I am terribly afraid that Dr. Layton may be displeased."

"I am very sorry, my lord," said Ralph, "but I fear I shall not be
coming here again."

The Abbot's face fell.

"But you will speak for us, sir, to Dr. Layton? I heard you say you
would be seeing him tonight."

Ralph promised to do his best, and was overwhelmed with thanks.

He could not help realizing some of the pathos of the situation as
he rode on through the rain to Durford. It was plain that a wave of
terror and apprehensiveness was running through the Religious Houses,
and that it brought with it inevitable disorder. Lives that would have
been serene and contented under other circumstances were thrown off
their balance by the rumors of disturbance, and authority was weakened.
If the Rule was hard of observance in tranquil times, it was infinitely
harder when doors of escape presented themselves on all sides.

And yet he was impatient too. Passive or wavering characters irritated
his own strong temperament, and he felt a kind of anger against the
Abbot and his feeble appeal. Surely men who had nothing else to do
might manage to keep their own subjects in order, and a weak crying
for pity was in itself an argument against their competence. And meanwhile, if he had known it, he would have been still more incensed, for
as he rode on down towards the southwest, the Abbot and his monks
in the house he had left were prostrate before the high altar in the dark
church, each in his stall, praying for mercy.

"O God, the heathens are come into thine inheritance," they murmured, "they have defiled thy holy temple."

*I*t was not until the sun was going down in the stormy west that Ralph
rode up to Durford abbey. The rain had ceased an hour before sunset,
and the wet roofs shone in the evening light.

There were certain signs of stir as he came up. One or two idlers were
standing outside the gate-house; the door was wide open, and a couple
of horses were being led away round the corner.

Inside the court as he rode through he saw further signs of confusion.
Half a dozen packhorses were waiting with hanging heads outside the
stable door, and an agitated lay brother was explaining to a canon in

his white habit, rochet and cap, that there was no more room. He threw out his hands with a gesture of despair towards Ralph as he came in.

"Mother of God!" he said, "here is another of them."

The priest frowned at him, and hurried up to Ralph.

"Yes, father," said Ralph, "I am another of them."

The canon explained that the stable was full, that they were exceedingly sorry, but that they were but a poor house; and that he was glad to say there was an outhouse round the corner outside where the beasts could be lodged.

"But as for yourself, sir," he said, "I know not what to do. We have every room full. You are a friend of Dr. Layton's, sir?"

"I am one of the Visitors," said Ralph. "You must make room."

The priest sucked his lips in.

"I see nothing for it," he said, "Dr. Layton and you, sir, must share a room."

Ralph threw a leg over the saddle and slipped to the ground.

"Where is he?" he asked.

"He is with my Lord Abbot, sir," he said. "Will you come with me?"

The canon led the way across the court, his white fur tails swinging as he went, and took Ralph through the cloister into one of the parlors. There was a sound of a high scolding voice as he threw open the door.

"What in God's name are ye for then, if ye have not hospitality?"

Dr. Layton turned round as Ralph came in. He was flushed with passion; his mouth worked, and his eyes were brutal.

"See this, Mr. Torridon," he said. "There is neither room for man or beast in this damned abbey. The guest house has no more than half a dozen rooms, and the stable — why, it is not fit for pigs, let alone the horses of the King's Visitors."

The Abbot, a young man with a delicate face, very pale now and trembling, broke in deprecatingly.

"I am very sorry, gentlemen," he said, looking from one to the other, "but it is not my fault. It is in better repair than when I came to it. I have done my best with my Lord Abbot of Welbeck; but we are very poor, and he can give me no more."

Layton growled at him.

"I don't say it's you, man; we shall know better when we have looked into your accounts; but I'll have a word to say at Welbeck."

"We are to share a room, Dr. Layton," put in Ralph "At least —"

The doctor turned round again at that, and stormed once more.

"I cannot help it, gentlemen," retorted the Abbot desperately. "I have given up my own chamber already. I can but do my best."

Ralph hastened to interpose. His mind revolted at this coarse bully-ing, in spite of his contempt at this patient tolerance on the part of the Abbot.

"I shall do very well, my Lord Abbot," he said. "I shall give no trouble. You may put me where you please."

The young prelate looked at him gratefully.

"We will do our best, sir," he said. "Will you come, gentlemen, and see your chambers?"

Layton explained to Ralph as they went along the poor little cloister that he himself had only arrived an hour before.

"I had a rare time among the monks," he whispered, "and have some tales to make you laugh."

*H*e grew impatient again presently at the poor furnishing of the rooms, and kicked over a broken chair.

"I will have something better than that," he said. "Get me one from the church."

The young Abbot faced him.

"What do you want of us, Dr. Layton? Is it riches or poverty? Which think you that Religious ought to have?"

The priest gave a bark of laughter.

"You have me there, my lord," he said; and nudged Ralph.

They sat down to supper presently in the parlor downstairs, a couple of dishes of meat, and a bottle of Spanish wine. Dr. Layton grew voluble.

"I have a deal to tell you, Mr. Torridon," he said, "and not a few things to show you, — silver crosses and such like; but those we will look at tomorrow. I doubt whether we shall add much to it here, though there is a relic-case that would look well on Master Cromwell's table; it is all set with agates. But the tales you shall have now. My servant will be here directly with the papers."

A man came in presently with a bag of documents, and Layton seized them eagerly.

"See here, Mr. Torridon," he said, shaking the papers on to the table, "here is a story-box for the ladies. Draw your chair to the fire."

Ralph felt an increasing repugnance for the man; but he said nothing; and brought up his seat to the wide hearth on which the logs burned pleasantly in the cold little room.

The priest lifted the bundle on to his lap, crossed his legs comfortably, with a glass of wine at his elbow, and began to read.

*F*or a while Ralph wondered how the man could have the effrontery to call his notes by the name of evidence. They consisted of a string of obscene guesses, founded upon circumstances that were certainly compatible with guilt, but no less compatible with innocence. There was a quantity of gossip gathered from country-people and colored by the most flagrant animus, and even so the witnesses did not agree. Such sentences as "It is reported in the country round that the prior is a lewd man" were frequent in the course of the reading, and were often the chief evidence offered in a case.

In one of the most categorical stories, Ralph leaned forward and interrupted.

"Forgive me, Master Layton," he said, "but who is Master What's-his-name who says all this?"

The priest waved the paper in the air.

"A monk himself," he said, "a monk himself! That is the cream of it."

"A monk!" exclaimed Ralph.

"He was one till last year," explained the priest.

"And then?" said the other.

"He was expelled the monastery. He knew too much, you see."

Ralph leaned back.

*H*alf an hour later there was a change in his attitude: his doubts were almost gone; the flood of detail was too vast to be dismissed as wholly irrelevant; his imagination was affected by the evidence from without and his will from within, and he listened without hostility, telling himself that he desired only truth and justice.

There were at least half a dozen stories in the mass of filthy suspicion that the priest exultingly poured out which appeared convincing; particularly one about which Ralph put a number of questions.

In this there was first a quantity of vague evidence gathered from the country-folk, who were, unless Layton lied quite unrestrainedly, convinced of the immoral life of a certain monk. The report of his sin had penetrated ten miles from the house where he lived. There was besides definite testimony from one of his fellows, precise and detailed; and there was lastly a half admission from the culprit himself. All this was worked up with great skill — suggestive epithets were plastered over the weak spots in the evidence; clever theories put forward to account for certain incompatibilities; and to Ralph at least it was convincing.

He found himself growing hot with anger at the thought of the hypocrisy of this monk's life. Here the fellow had been living in gross sin month after month, and all the while standing at the altar morning by morning, and going about in the habit of a professed servant of Jesus Christ!

"But I have kept the cream till the last," put in Dr. Layton. And he read out a few more hideous sentences, that set Ralph's heart heaving with disgust.

He began now to feel the beginnings of that fury against whitewashed vice with which worldly souls are so quick to burn. He would have said that he himself professed no holiness beyond the average, and would have acknowledged privately at least that he was at any rate uncertain of the whole dogmatic scheme of religion; but that he could not tolerate a man whose whole life was on the outside confessedly devoted to both sides of religion, faith and morals, and who claimed the world's reverence for himself on the score of it. He knit his forehead in a righteous fury, and his fingers began to drum softly on his chair-arms.

Dr. Layton now began to recur to some of the first stories he had told, and to build up their weak places; and now that Ralph was roused his critical faculty subsided. They appeared more convincing than before in the light of this later evidence. *Ex pede Herculem* — from the fellow who had confessed he interpreted the guilt of those who had not. The seed of suspicion sprang quickly in the soil that hungered for it.

This then was the fair religious system that was dispersed over England; and this the interior life of those holy looking roofs and buildings surmounted by the sign of the Crucified, visible in every town to point men to God. When he saw a serene monk's face again he would know what kind of soul it covered; he would understand as never before how vice could wear a mask of virtue.

The whole of that flimsy evidence that he had heard before took a new color; those hints and suspicions and guesses grew from shadow to substance. Those dark spots were not casual filth dropped from above, they were the symptoms of a deep internal infection.

As Dr. Layton went on with his tales, gathered and garnered with devilish adroitness, and presented as convincingly as a clever brain could do it, the black certainty fell deeper and deeper on Ralph's soul, and by the time that the priest chuckled for the last time that evening, and gathered up his papers from the boards where they had fallen one by one, he had done his work in another soul.

Chapter III
A HOUSE OF LADIES

*T*hey parted the next day, Dr. Layton to Waverly, where he proposed to sleep on Saturday night, and Ralph to the convent at Rusper.

He had learnt now how the work was to be done; and he had been equipped for it in a way that not even Dr. Layton himself suspected; for he had been set aflame with that filth-fed fire with which so many hearts were burning at this time. He had all the saint's passion for purity, without the charity of his holiness.

He had learnt too the technical details of his work — those rough methods by which men might be coerced, and the high-sounding phrases with which to gild the coercion. All that morning he had sat side by side with Dr. Layton in the chapter-house, inspecting the books, comparing the possessions of the monastery with the inventories of them, examining witnesses as to the credibility of the lists offered, and making searching enquiries as to whether any land or plate had been sold. After that, when a silver relic-case had been added to Dr. Layton's collection, the Religious and servants and all else who cared to offer evidence on other matters, were questioned one by one and their answers entered in a book. Lastly, when the fees for the Visitation had been collected, arrangements had been made, which in the Visitors' opinion, would be most serviceable to the carrying out of the injunctions; fresh officials were appointed to various posts, and the Abbot himself ordered to go up to London and present himself to Master Cromwell; but he was furnished with a letter commending his zeal and discretion, for the Visitors had found that he had done his duty to the buildings and lands; and stated that they had nothing to complain of except the poverty of the house.

"And so much for Durford," said Layton genially, as he closed the last book just before dinner-time, "though it had been better called Dirtyford." And he chuckled at his humor.

After dinner he had gone out with Ralph to see him mount; had thanked him for his assistance, and had reminded him that they would meet again at Lewes in the course of a month or so.

"God speed you!" he cried as the party rode off.

*R*alph's fury had died to a glow, but it was red within him; the reading last night had done its work well, driven home by the shrewd conviction of a man of the world, experienced in the ways of vice. It had not died with the dark. He could not say that he was attracted to Dr. Layton; the priest's shocking familiarity with the more revolting forms of sin, as well as his under-breeding and brutality, made him a disagreeable character; but Ralph had very little doubt now that his judgment on the religious houses was a right one. Even the nunneries, it seemed, were not free from taint; there had been one or two terrible tales on the previous evening; and Ralph was determined to spare them nothing, and at any rate to remove his sister from their power. He remembered with satisfaction that she was below the age specified, and that he would have authority to dismiss her from the home.

He knew very little of Margaret; and had scarcely seen her once in two years. He had been already out in the world before she had ceased to be a child, and from what little he had seen of her he had thought of her but as little more than a milk-and-water creature, very delicate and shy, always at her prayers, or trailing about after nuns with a pale radiant face. She had been sent to Rusper for her education, and he never saw her except now and then when they chanced to be at home together for a few days. She used to look at him, he remembered, with awe-stricken eyes and parted lips, hardly daring to speak when he was in the room, continually to be met with going from or to the tall quiet chapel.

He had always supposed that she would be a nun, and had acquiesced in it in a cynical sort of way; but he was going to acquiesce no longer now. Of course she would sob, but equally of course she would not dare to resist.

He called Morris up to him presently as they emerged from one of the bridle paths on to a kind of lane where two could ride abreast. The servant had seemed oddly silent that morning.

"We are going to Rusper," said Ralph.

"Yes, sir."

"Mistress Margaret is there."

"Yes, sir."

"She will come away with us. I may have to send you on to Overfield with her. You must find a horse for her somehow."

"Yes, sir."

There was silence between the two for a minute or two. Mr. Morris had answered with as much composure as if he had been told to brush a coat. Ralph began to wonder what he really felt.

"What do you think of all this, Morris?" he asked in a moment or two.

The servant was silent, till Ralph glanced at him impatiently.

"It is not for me to have an opinion, sir," said Mr. Morris.

Ralph gave a very short laugh.

"You haven't heard what I have," he said, "or you would soon have an opinion."

"Yes, sir," said Morris as impassively as before.

"I tell you —" and then Ralph broke off, and rode on silent and moody. Mr. Morris gradually let his horse fall back behind his master.

*T*hey began to come towards Rusper as the evening drew in, by a bridle path that led from the west, and on arriving at the village found that they had overshot their mark, and ought to have turned sooner. The nunnery, a man told them, was a mile away to the southwest. Ralph made a few enquiries, and learnt that it was a smallish house, and that it was scarcely likely that room could be found for his party of four; so he left Morris to make enquiries for lodgings in the village, and himself rode on alone to the nunnery, past the church and the timberhouses.

It was a bad road, and his tired horse had to pick his way very slowly, so that it was nearly dark before he came to his destination, and the pointed roofs rose before him against the faintly luminous western sky. There were lights in one or two windows as he came up that looked warm and homely in the chill darkness; and as he sat on his horse listening to the jangle of the bell within, just a breath of doubtfulness touched his heart for a moment as he thought of the peaceful home-life that lay packed within those walls, and of the errand on which he had come.

But the memory of the tales he had heard, haunted him still; and he spoke in a harsh voice as the shutter slid back, and a little crisscrossed square of light appeared in the black doorway.

"I am one of the King's Visitors," he said. "Let my Lady Abbess know I am here. I must speak with her."

There was a stifled sound behind the grating; and Ralph caught a glimpse of a pair of eyes looking at him. Then the square grew dark again. It was a minute or two before anything further happened, and Ralph as he sat cold and hungry on his horse, began to grow impatient. His hand was on the twisted iron handle to ring again fiercely, when there was a step within, and a light once more shone out.

"Who is it?" said an old woman's voice, with a note of anxiety in it.

"I have sent word in," said Ralph peevishly, "that I am one of the King's Visitors. I should be obliged if I might not be kept here all night."

There was a moment's silence; the horse sighed sonorously.

"How am I to know, sir?" said the voice again.

"Because I tell you so," snapped Ralph. "And if more is wanted, my name is Torridon. You have a sister of mine in there."

There was an exclamation from within; and the sound of whispering; and then hasty footsteps went softly across the paved court inside.

The voice spoke again.

"I ask your pardon, sir; but have you any paper — or —"

Ralph snatched out a document of identification, and leaned forward from his horse to pass it through the opening. He felt trembling fingers take it from him; and a moment later heard returning footsteps.

There was a rustle of paper, and then a whisper within.

"Well, my dear?"

Something shifted in the bright square, and it grew gloomy as a face pressed up against the bars. Then again it shifted and the light shone out, and a flutter of whispers followed.

"Really, madam —" began Ralph; but there was the jingle of keys, and the sound of panting, and almost immediately a bolt shot back, followed by the noise of a key turning. A chorus of whispers broke out and a scurry of footsteps, and then the door opened inwards and a little old woman stood there in a black habit, her face swathed in white above and below. The others had vanished.

"I am very sorry, Mr. Torridon, to have kept you at the door; but we have to be very careful. Will you bring your horse in, sir?"

Ralph was a little abashed by the sudden development of the situation, and explained that he had only come to announce his arrival; he had supposed that there would not be room at the nunnery.

"But we have a little guest-house here," announced the old lady with a dignified air, "and room for your horse."

Ralph hesitated; but he was tired and hungry.

"Come in, Mr. Torridon. You had better dismount and lead your horse in. Sister Anne will see to it."

"Well, if you are sure —" began Ralph again, slipping a foot out of the stirrup.

"I am sure," said the Abbess; and stood aside for him and his beast to pass.

There was a little court, lighted by a single lamp burning within a window, with the nunnery itself on one side, and a small cottage on the other. Beyond the latter rose the roofs of an outhouse.

As Ralph came in, the door from the nunnery opened again, and a lay sister came out hastily; she moved straight across and took the horse by the bridle.

"Give him a good meal, sister," said the Abbess; and went past Ralph to the door of the guest-house.

"Come in, Mr. Torridon; there will be lights immediately."

*I*n half an hour Ralph found himself at supper in the guest-parlor; a bright fire crackled on the hearth, a couple of candles burned on the table, and a pair of old darned green curtains hung across the low window.

The Abbess came in when he had finished, dismissed the lay-sister who had waited on him, and sat down herself.

"You shall see your sister tomorrow, Mr. Torridon," she said, "it is a little late now. I have sent the boy up to the village for your servant; he can sleep in this room if you wish. I fear we have no room for more."

Ralph watched her as she talked. She was very old, with hanging cheeks, and solemn little short-sighted eyes, for she peered at him now and again across the candles. Her upper lip was covered with a slight growth of dark hair. She seemed strangely harmless; and Ralph had another prick of compunction as he thought of the news he had to give her on the morrow. He wondered how much she knew.

"We are so glad it is you, Mr. Torridon, that have come to visit us. We feared it might be Dr. Layton; we have heard sad stories of him."

Ralph hardened his heart.

"He has only done his duty, Reverend Mother," he said.

"Oh! but you cannot have heard," exclaimed the old lady. "He has robbed several of our houses we hear — even the altar itself. And he has turned away some of our nuns."

Ralph was silent; he thought he would at least leave the old lady in peace for this last night. She seemed to want no answer; but went on expatiating on the horrors that were happening round them, the wicked accusations brought against the Religious, and the Divine vengeance that would surely fall on those who were responsible.

Finally she turned and questioned him, with a mingling of deference and dignity.

"What do you wish from us. Mr. Torridon? You must tell me, that I may see that everything is in order."

Ralph was secretly amused by her air of innocent assurance.

"That is my business, Reverend Mother. I must ask for all the books of the house, with the account of any sales you may have effected, properly recorded. I must have a list of the inmates of the house, with a statement of any corrodies attached; and the names and ages and dates of profession of all the Religious."

The Abbess blinked for a moment.

"Yes, Mr. Torridon. You will allow me of course to see all your papers tomorrow; it is necessary for me to be certified that all your part is in order."

Ralph smiled a little grimly.

"You shall see all that," he said. "And then there is more that I must ask; but that will do for a beginning. When I have shown you my papers you will see what it is that I want."

There was a peal at the bell outside; the Abbess turned her head and waited till there was a noise of bolts and unlocking.

"That will be your man, sir. Will you have him in now, Mr. Torridon?"

Ralph assented.

"And then he must look at the horses to see that all is as you wish."

Mr. Morris came in a moment later, and bowed with great deference to the little old lady, who enquired his name.

"When you have finished with your man, Mr. Torridon, perhaps you will allow him to ring for me at the door opposite. I will go with him to see the horses."

Mr. Morris had brought with him the mass of his master's papers, and when he had set these out and prepared the bedroom that opened out of the guest-parlor, he asked leave to go across and fetch the Abbess.

Ralph busied himself for half-an-hour or so in running over the Articles and Injunctions once more, and satisfying himself that he was perfect in his business; and he was just beginning to wonder why his servant had not reappeared when the door opened once more, and Mr. Morris slipped in.

"My horse is a little lame, sir," he said. "I have been putting on a poultice."

Ralph glanced up.

"He will be fit to travel, I suppose?"

"In a day or two, Mr. Ralph."

"Well; that will do. We shall be here till Monday at least."

*R*alph could not sleep very well that night. The thought of his business troubled him a little. It would have been easier if the Abbess had been either more submissive or more defiant; but her air of mingled courtesy and dignity affected him. Her innocence too had something touching in it, and her apparent ignorance of what his visit meant. He had supped excellently at her expense, waited on by a cheerful sister, and well served from the kitchen and cellar; and the Reverend Mother herself had come in and talked sensibly and bravely. He pictured to himself what life must be like through the nunnery wall opposite — how brisk and punctual it must be, and at the same time homely and caressing.

And it was his hand that was to pull down the first prop. There would no doubt be three or four nuns below age who must be dismissed, and probably there would be a few treasures to be carried off, a processional crucifix perhaps, such as he had seen in Dr. Layton's collection, and a rich chalice or two, used on great days. His own sister too must be one of those who must go. How would the little old Abbess behave herself then? What would she say? Yet he comforted himself, as he lay there in the clean, low-ceilinged room, staring at the tiny crockery stoup gleaming against the doorpost, by recollecting the principle on which he had come. Possibly a few innocents would have to suffer, a few old hearts be broken; but it was for a man to take such things in his day's work.

And then as he remembered Dr. Layton's tales, his heart grew hot and hard again.

Chapter IV

AN UNEXPECTED MEETING

*T*he enquiry was to be made in the guest-parlor on the next morning.

*R*alph went to mass first at nine o'clock, which was said by a priest from the parish church who acted as chaplain to the convent; and had a chair set for him outside the nuns' choir from which he could see the altar and the tall pointed window; and then, after some refreshment in the guest-parlor, spread out his papers, and sat enthroned behind a couple of tables, as at a tribunal. Mr. Morris stood deferentially by his chair as the examination was conducted.

Ralph was a little taken aback by the bearing of the Abbess. In the course of the enquiry, when he was perplexed by one or two of the records, she rose from her chair before the table, and came round to his side, drawing up a seat as she did so; Ralph could hardly tell her to go back, but his magisterial air was a little affected by having one whom he almost considered as a culprit sitting judicially beside him.

"It is better for me to be here," she said. "I can explain more easily so."

*T*here was a little orchard that the nuns had sold in the previous year; and Ralph asked for an explanation.

"It came from the Kingsford family," she said serenely; "it was useless to us."

"But —" began the inquisitor.

"We needed some new vestments," she went on. "You will understand, Mr. Torridon, that it was necessary for for us to sell it. We are not rich at all."

There was nothing else that called for comment; except the manner in which the books were kept. Ralph suggested some other method.

"Dame Agnes has her own ways," said the old lady. "We must not disturb her."

And Dame Agnes assumed a profound and financial air on the other side of the table.

Presently Ralph put a mark in the inventory against a "cope of gold bawdekin," and requested that it might be brought.

The sister-sacristan rose at a word from the Abbess and went out, returning presently with the vestment. She unfolded the coverings and spread it out on the table before Ralph.

It was a magnificent piece of work, of shimmering gold, with orphreys embroidered with arms; and she stroked out its folds with obvious pride.

"These are Warham's arms," observed the Abbess. "You know them, Mr. Torridon? We worked these the month before his death."

Ralph nodded briskly.

"Will you kindly leave it here, Reverend Mother," he said. "I wish to see it again presently."

The Abbess gave no hint of discomposure, but signed to the sacristan to place it over a chair at one side.

There were a couple of other things that Ralph presently caused to be fetched and laid aside — a precious miter with a couple of cameos in front, and bordered with emeralds, and a censer with silver filigree work.

Then came a more difficult business.

"I wish to see the nuns one by one, Reverend Mother," he said. "I must ask you to withdraw."

The Abbess gave him a quick look, and then rose.

"Very well, sir, I will send them in." And she went out with Mr. Morris behind her.

They came in one by one, and sat down before the table, with downcast eyes, and hands hidden beneath their scapulars; and all told the same tale, except one. They had nothing to complain of; they were happy; the Rule was carefully observed; there were no scandals to be revealed; they asked nothing but to be left in peace. But there was one who came in nervously and anxiously towards the end, a woman with quick black eyes, who glanced up and down and at the door as she sat down. Ralph put the usual questions.

"I wish to be released, sir," she said. "I am weary of the life, and the —" she stopped and glanced swiftly up again at the commissioner.

"Well?" said Ralph.

"The papistical ways," she said.

Ralph felt a sudden distrust of the woman; but he hardened his heart. He set a mark opposite her name; she had been professed ten years, he saw by the list.

"Very well," he said; "I will tell my Lady Abbess." She still hesitated a moment.

"There will be a provision for me?" she asked

"There will be a provision," said Ralph a little grimly. He was authorized to offer in such cases a secular dress and a sum of five shillings.

Lastly came in Margaret herself.

Ralph hardly knew her. He had been unable to distinguish her at mass, and even now as she faced him in her black habit and white headdress it was hard to be certain of her identity. But memory and sight were gradually reconciled; he remembered her delicate eyebrows and thin straight lips; and when she spoke he knew her voice.

They talked a minute or two about their home; but Ralph did not dare to say too much, considering what he had yet to say.

"I must ask you the questions," he said at last, smiling at her.

She looked up at him nervously, and dropped her eyes once more.

She nodded or shook her head in silence at each enquiry, until at last one bearing upon the morals of the house came up; then she looked swiftly up once more, and Ralph saw that her grey eyes were terrified.

"You must tell me," he said; and put the question again.

"I do not know what you mean," she answered, staring at him bewildered.

Ralph went on immediately to the next.

At last he reached the crisis.

"Margaret," he said, "I have something to tell you." He stopped and began to play with his pen. He had seldom felt so embarrassed as now in the presence of this shy sister of his of whom he knew so little. He could not look at her.

"Margaret, you know, you — you are under age. The King's Grace has ordered that all under twenty years of age are to leave their convents."

There was a dead silence.

Ralph was enraged with his own weakness. He had begun the morning's work with such determination; but the strange sweet atmosphere of the house, the file of women coming in one by one with their air of innocence and defenselessness had affected him. In spite of himself his religious side had asserted itself, and he found himself almost tremulous now.

He made a great effort at self-repression, and looked up with hard bright eyes at his sister.

"There must be no crying or rebellion," he said. "You must come with me tomorrow. I shall send you to Overfield."

Still Margaret said nothing. She was staring at him now, white-faced with parted lips.

"You are the last?" he said with a touch of harshness, standing up with his hands on the table. "Tell the Reverend Mother I have done."

Then she rose too.

"Ralph," she cried, "my brother! For Jesu's sake —"

"Tell the Reverend Mother," he said again, his eyes hard with decision.

She turned and went out without a word.

*R*alph found the interview with the Abbess even more difficult than he had expected.

Once her face twitched with tears; but she drove them back bravely and faced him again.

"Do you mean to tell me, Mr. Torridon, that you intend to take your sister away?"

Ralph bowed.

"And that Dame Martha has asked to be released?"

Again he bowed.

"Are you not afraid, sir, to do such work?"

Ralph smiled bitterly.

"I am not, Reverend Mother," he said. "I know too much."

"From whom?"

"Oh! not from your nuns," he said sharply, "they of course know nothing, or at least will tell me nothing. It was from Dr. Layton."

"And what did Dr. Layton tell you?"

"I can hardly tell you that, Reverend Mother; it is not fit for your ears."

She looked at him steadily.

"And you believe it?"

Ralph smiled.

"That makes no difference," he said. "I am acting by his Grace's orders."

There was silence for a moment.

"Then may our Lord have mercy on you!" she said.

She turned to where the gold cope gleamed over the chair, with the miter and censer lying on its folds.

"And those too?" she asked.

"Those too," said Ralph.

She turned towards the door without a word.

"There are the fees as well," remarked Ralph. "We can arrange those this evening, Reverend Mother."

The little stiff figure turned and waited at the door. "And at what time will you dine, sir?"

"Immediately," said Ralph.

*H*e was served at dinner with the same courtesy as before; but the lay sister's eyes were red, and her hands shook as she shifted the plates. Neither spoke a word till towards the end of the meal.

"Where is my man?" asked Ralph, who had not seen him since he had gone out with the Abbess a couple of hours before.

The sister shook her head.

"Where is the Reverend Mother?"

Again she shook her head.

Ralph enquired the hour of Vespers, and when he had learnt it, took his cap and went out to look for Mr. Morris. He went first to the little dark outhouse, and peered in over the bottom half of the door, but there was no sign of him there. He could see a horse standing in a stall opposite, and tried to make out the second horse that he knew was there; but it was too dark, and he turned away.

It was a warm October afternoon as he went out through the gate-house, still and bright, with the mellow smell of dying leaves in the air; the fields stretched away beyond the road into the blue distance as he went along, and were backed by the thinning woods, still ruddy with the last flames of autumn. Overhead the blue sky, washed with recent rains, arched itself in a great transparent vault, and a stream of birds crossed it from east to west.

He went round the corner of the convent buildings and turned up into a meadow beside a thick privet hedge that divided it from the garden, and as he moved along he heard a low humming noise sounding from the other side.

There was a door in the hedge at the point, and at either side the growth was a little thin, and he could look through without being himself seen.

The grass was trim and smooth inside; there was a mass of autumn flowers, grown no doubt for the altar, running in a broad bed across the nearer side of the garden, and beyond it rose a grey dial, round which sat a circle of nuns.

Ralph pressed his face to the hedge and watched.

There they were, each with her wheel before her, spinning in silence. The Abbess sat in the center, immediately below the dial, with a book in her hand, and was turning the pages.

He could see a nun's face steadily bent on her wheel — that was Dame Agnes who had fetched the cope for him in the morning. She seemed perfectly quiet and unaffected, watching her thread, and putting out a deft hand now and again to the machinery. Beside her sat another, whose face he remembered well; she had stammered a little as she gave her answers in the morning, and even as he looked the face twitched suddenly, and broke into tears. He saw the Abbess turn from her book and lay her hand, with a kind of tender decision on the nun's arm, and saw her lips move, but the hum and rattle of the spinning-wheels was too loud to let him hear what she said; he saw now the other nun lift her face again from her hands, and wink away her tears as she laid hold of the thread once more.

*R*alph had a strange struggle with himself that afternoon as he walked on in the pleasant autumn weather through meadow and copse. The sight of the patient women had touched him profoundly. Surely it was almost too much to ask him to turn away his own sister from the place she loved! If he relented, it was certain that no other Visitor would come that way for the present; she might at least have another year or two of peace. Was it too late?

He reminded himself again how such things were bound to happen; how every change, however beneficial, must bring sorrow with it, and that to turn back on such work because a few women suffered was not worthy of a man. It was long before he could come to any decision, and the evening was drawing on, and the time for Vespers come and gone before he turned at last into the village to enquire for his servant.

The other men had seen nothing of Mr. Morris that day; he had not been back to the village.

A group or two stared awefully at the fine gentleman with the strong face and steady intolerant eyes, as he strode down the tiny street in his rich dress, swinging his long silver-headed cane. They had learnt who he was now, but were so overcome by seeing the King's Commissioner that they forgot to salute him. As he turned the corner again he looked round once more, and there they were still watching him. A few women had come to the doors as well, and dropped their arched hands hastily and disappeared as he turned.

The convent seemed all as he had left it earlier in the afternoon, as he came in sight of it again. The high chapel roof rose clear against the reddening sky, with the bell framed in its turret distinct as if carved out of cardboard against the splendor.

He was admitted instantly when he rang on the bell, but the portress seemed to look at him with a strange air of expectancy, and stood looking after him as he went across the paved court to the door of the guest-house.

There was a murmur of voices in the parlor as he paused in the entry, and he wondered who was within, but as his foot rang out the sound ceased.

He opened the door and went in; and then stopped bewildered.

In the dim light that passed through the window stood his father and Mary Maxwell, his sister.

Chapter V

FATHER AND SON

None of the three spoke for a moment.

Then Mary drew her breath sharply as she saw Ralph's face, for it had hardened during that moment into a kind of blind obstinacy which she had only seen once or twice in her life before.

As he stood there he seemed to stiffen into resistance. His eyelids drooped, and little lines showed themselves suddenly at either side of his thin mouth. His father saw it too, for the hand that he had lifted entreatingly sank again, and his voice was tremulous as he spoke.

"Ralph — Ralph, my son!" he said.

Still the man said nothing; but stood frozen, his face half-turned to the windows.

"Ralph, my son," said the other again, "you know why we have come."

"You have come to hinder my business."

His voice was thin and metallic, as rigid as steel.

"We have come to hinder a great sin against God," said Sir James.

Ralph opened his eyes wide with a sort of fury, and thrust his chin out.

"She should pack a thousand times more now than before," he said.

The father's face too deepened into strength now, and he drew himself up.

"Do you know what you are doing?" he said.

"I do, sir."

There was an extraordinary insolence in his voice, and Mary took a step forward.

"Oh! Ralph," she said, "at least do it like a gentleman!"

Ralph turned on her sharply, and the obstinacy vanished in anger.

"I will not be pushed like this," he snarled. "What right is it of yours to come between me and my work?"

Sir James made a quick imperious gesture, and his air of entreaty fell from him like a cloak.

"Sit down, sir," he said, and his voice rang strongly. "We have a right in Margaret's affairs. We will say what we wish."

Mary glanced at him: she had never seen her father like this before as he stood in three quarter profile, rigid with decision. When she looked at Ralph again, his face had tightened once more into obstinacy. He answered Sir James with a kind of silky deference.

"Of course, I will sit down, sir, and you shall say what you will."

He went across the room and drew out a couple of chairs before the cold hearth where the white ashes and logs of last night's fire still rested. Sir James sat down with his back to the window so that Mary could not see his face, and Ralph stood by the other chair a moment, facing her.

"Sit down, Mary," he said. "Wait, I will have candles."

He stepped back to the door and called to the portress, and then returned, and seated himself deliberately, setting his cane in the corner beside him.

None of the three spoke again until the nun had come in with a couple of candles that she set in the stands and lighted; then she went out without glancing at anyone. Mary was sitting in the window seat, so the curtains remained undrawn, and there was a mystical compound of twilight and candlelight in the room.

She had a flash of metaphor, and saw in it the meeting of the old and new religions; the type of these two men, of whom the light of one was fading, and the other waxing. The candlelight fell full on Ralph's face that stood out against the whitewashed wall behind.

Then she listened and watched with an intent interest.

"It is this," said Sir James, "we heard you were here —"

Ralph smiled with one side of his mouth, so that his father could see it.

"I do not wish to do anything I should not," went on the old man, "or to meddle in his Grace's matters —"

"And you wish me not to meddle either, sir," put in Ralph.

"Yes," said his father. "I am very willing to receive you and your wife at home; to make any suitable provision; to give you half the house if you wish for it; if you will only give up this accursed work."

He was speaking with a tranquil deliberation; all the emotion and passion seemed to have left his voice; but Mary, from behind, could see his right hand clenched like a vice upon the knob of his chair-arm. It seemed to her as if the two men had suddenly frozen into self-repression. Their air was one of two acquaintances talking, not of father and son.

"And if not, sir?" asked Ralph with the same courtesy.

"Wait," said his father, and he lifted his hand a moment and dropped it again. He was speaking in short, sharp sentences. "I know that you have great things before you, and that I am asking much from you. I do not wish you to think that I am ignorant of that. If nothing else will do I am willing to give up the house altogether to you and your wife. I do not know about your mother."

Mary drew her breath hard. The words were like an explosion in her soul, and opened up unsuspected gulfs. Things must be desperate if her father could speak like that. He had not hinted a word of this during that silent strenuous ride they had had together when he had called for her suddenly at Great Keynes earlier in the afternoon. She saw Ralph give a quick stare at his father, and drop his eyes again.

"You are very generous, sir," he said almost immediately, "but I do not ask for a bribe."

"You — you are unlike your master in that, then," said Sir James by an irresistible impulse.

Ralph's face stiffened yet more.

"Then that is all, sir?" he asked.

"I beg your pardon for saying that," added his father courteously. "It should not have been said. It is not a bribe, however; it is an offer to compensate for any loss you may incur."

"Have you finished, sir?"

"That is all I have to say on that point," said Sir James, "except —"

"Well, sir?"

"Except that I do not know how Mistress Atherton will take this story."

Ralph's face grew a shade paler yet. But his lips snapped together, though his eyes flinched.

"That is a threat, sir."

"That is as you please."

A little pulse beat sharply in Ralph's cheek. He was looking with a kind of steady fury at his father. But Mary thought she saw indecision too in his eye-lids, which were quivering almost imperceptibly.

"You have offered me a bribe and a threat, sir. Two insults. Have you a third ready?"

Mary heard a swift-drawn breath from her father, but he spoke quietly.

"I have no more to say on that point," he said.

"Then I must refuse," said Ralph instantly. "I see no reason to give up my work. I have very hearty sympathy with it."

The old man's hand twitched uncontrollably on his chair-arm for a moment; he half lifted his hand, but he dropped it again.

"Then as to Margaret," he went on in a moment. "I understand you had intended to dismiss her from the convent?"

Ralph bowed.

"And where do you suggest that she should go?"

"She must go home," said Ralph.

"To Overfield?"

Ralph assented.

"Then I will not receive her," said Sir James.

Mary started up.

"Nor will Mary receive her," he added, half turning towards her.

Mary Maxwell sat back at once. She thought she understood what he meant now.

Ralph stared at his father a moment before he too understood. Then he saw the point, and riposted deftly. He shrugged his shoulders ostentatiously as if to shake off responsibility.

"Well, then, that is not my business; I shall give her a gown and five shillings tomorrow, with the other one."

The extraordinary brutality of the words struck Mary like a whip, but Sir James met it.

"That is for you to settle then," he said. "Only you need not send her to Overfield or Great Keynes, for she will be sent back here at once."

Ralph smiled with an air of tolerant incredulity. Sir James rose briskly.

"Come, Mary," he said, and turned his back abruptly on Ralph, "we must find lodgings for tonight. The good nuns will not have room."

As Mary looked at his face in the candlelight she was astonished by its decision; there was not the smallest hint of yielding. It was very pale but absolutely determined, and for the fast time in her life she noticed how like it was to Ralph's. The line of the lips was identical, and his eyelids drooped now like his son's.

Ralph too rose and then on a sudden she saw the resolute obstinacy fade from his eyes and mouth. It was as if the spirit of one man had passed into the other.

"Father —" he said.

She expected a rush of emotion into the old man's face, but there was not a ripple. He paused a moment, but Ralph was silent.

"I have no more to say to you, sir. And I beg that you will not come home again."

As they passed out into the entrance passage she turned again and saw Ralph dazed and trembling at the table. Then they were out in the road through the open gate and a long moan broke from her father.

"Oh! God forgive me," he said, "have I failed?"

Chapter VI

A NUN'S DEFIANCE

*I*t was a very strange evening that Mary and her father passed in the little upstairs room looking on to the street at Rusper.

Sir James had hardly spoken, and after supper had sat near the window, with a curious alertness in his face. Mary knew that Chris was expected, and that Mr. Morris had ridden on to fetch him after he had called at Overfield, but from her short interview with Margaret she had seen that his presence would not be required. The young nun, though bewildered and stunned by the news that she must go, had not wavered for a moment as regards her intention to follow out her Religious vocation in some manner; and it was to confirm her in it, in case she hesitated, that Sir James had sent on the servant to fetch Chris.

It was all like a dreadful dream to Mary.

She had gone out from dinner at her own house into the pleasant October sunshine with her cheerful husband beside her, when her father had come out through the house with his riding-whip in his hand; and in a few seconds she had found herself plunged into new and passionate relations, first with him, for she had never seen him so stirred, and then with her brothers and sister. Ralph, that dignified man of affairs, suddenly stepped into her mind as a formidable enemy of God and man; Chris appeared as a spiritual power, and the quiet Margaret as the very center of the sudden storm.

She sat here now by the fire, shading her face with her hand and watching that familiar face set in hard and undreamed lines of passion and resolution and expectancy.

Once as footsteps came up the street he had started up and sat down trembling.

She waited till the steps went past, and then spoke.

"Chris will be riding, father."

He nodded abruptly, and she saw by his manner that it was not Chris he was expecting. She understood then that he still had hopes of his other son, but they sat on into the night in the deep stillness, till the fire burned low and red, and the stars she had seen at the horizon wheeled up and out of sight above the window-frame.

Then he suddenly turned to her.

"You must go to bed, Mary," he said. "I will wait for Chris."

She lay long awake in the tiny cupboard room that the laborer and his wife had given up to her, hearing the horses stamp in the cold shed at the back of the house, and the faces moved and turned like the colors of a kaleidoscope. Now her father's eyes and mouth hung like a mask before her, with that terrible look that had been on them as he faced Ralph at the end; now Ralph's own face, defiant, icy, melting in turns; now Margaret's with wide terrified eyes, as she had seen it in the parlor that afternoon; now her own husband's. And the sweet autumn woods and meadows lay before her as she had seen them during that silent ride; the convent, the village, her own home with its square windows and yew hedge — a hundred images.

*T*here was a talking when she awoke for the last time and through the crazy door glimmered a crack of grey dawn, and as she listened she knew that Chris was come.

It was a strange meeting when she came out a few minutes later. There was the monk, unshaven and pale under the eyes, with his thinned face that gave no smile as she came in; her father desperately white and resolved; Mr. Morris, spruce and grave as usual sitting with his hat between his knees behind the others; — he rose deferentially as she came in and remained standing.

Her father began abruptly as she appeared.

"He can do nothing," he said, "he can but turn her on to the road. And I do not think he will dare."

"Ah! Beatrice Atherton?" questioned Mary, who had a clearer view of the situation now.

"Yes — Beatrice Atherton. He fears that we shall tell her. He cannot send Margaret to Overfield or Great Keynes now."

"And if he turns her out after all?"

Sir James looked at her keenly.

"We must leave the rest to God," he said.

The village was well awake by the time that they had finished their talk and had had something to eat. The drama at the convent had leaked out through the boy who served the altar there, and a little group was assembled opposite the windows of the cottage to which the monk had been seen to ride up an hour or two before. It seemed strange that no priest had been near them, but it was fairly evident that the terror was too great.

As the four came out on to the road, a clerical cap peeped for a moment from the churchyard wall and disappeared again.

They went down towards the convent along the grey road, in the pale autumn morning air. Mary still seemed to herself to walk in a dream, with her father and brother on either side masquerading in strange character; the familiar atmosphere had been swept from them, the background of association was gone, and they moved now in a new scene with new parts to play that were bringing out powers which she had never suspected in them. It seemed as if their essential souls had been laid bare by a catastrophe, and that she had never known them before.

For herself, she felt helpless and dazed; her own independence seemed gone, and she was aware that her soul was leaning on those of the two who walked beside her, and who were masculine and capable beyond all her previous knowledge of them.

Behind she heard a murmur of voices and footsteps of three or four villagers who followed to see what would happen.

She had no idea of what her father meant to do; it was incredible that he should leave Margaret in the road with her gown and five shillings; but it was yet more incredible that all his threats should be idle. Only one thing emerged clearly, that he had thrown a heavier responsibility upon Ralph than the latter had foreseen. Perhaps the rest must indeed be left to God. She did not even know what he meant to do now, whether to make one last effort with Ralph, or to leave him to himself; and she had not dared to ask.

They passed straight down together in silence to the convent-gate; and were admitted immediately by the portress whose face was convulsed and swollen.

"They are to go," she sobbed.

Sir James made a gesture, and passed in to the tiny lodge on the left where the portress usually sat; Chris and Mary followed him in, and Mr. Morris went across to the guest-house.

The bell sounded out overhead for mass as they sat there in the dim morning light, twenty or thirty strokes, and ceased; but there was no movement from the little door of the guest-house across the court. The portress had disappeared through the second door that led from the tiny room in which they sat, into the precincts of the convent itself.

Mary looked distractedly round her; at the little hatch that gave on to the entrance gate, and the chain hanging by it that communicated with one of the bolts, at the little crucifix that hung beside it, the devotional book that lay on the shelf, the door into the convent with the title *"Clausura"* inscribed above it. She glanced at her father and brother.

Sir James was sitting with his grey head in his hands, motionless and soundless; Chris was standing upright and rigid, staring steadily out through the window into the court.

Then through the window she too saw Mr. Morris come out from the guest-house and pass along to the stable.

Again there was silence.

The minutes went by, and the Saunce bell sounded three strokes from the turret. Chris sank on to his knees, and a moment later Mary and her father followed his example, and so the three remained in the dark silent lodge, with no sound but their breathing, and once a sharp whispered word of prayer from the old man.

As the sacring bell sounded there was a sudden noise in the court, and Mary lifted her head.

From where she knelt she could see the two doors across the court, those of the guest-house and the stable beyond, and simultaneously, out of the one came Ralph, gloved and booted, with his cap on his head, and Mr. Morris leading his horse out of the other.

The servant lifted his cap at the sound of the bell, and dropped on to his knees, still holding the bridle; his master stood as he was, and looked at him. Mary could only see the latter's profile, but even that was scornful and hard.

Again the bell sounded; the mystery was done; and the servant stood up.

As her father and Chris rose, Mary rose with them; and the three remained in complete silence, watching the little scene in the court.

Ralph made a sign; and the servant attached the bridle of the horse to a ring beside the stable-door, and went past his master into the guest-house with a deferential stoop of the shoulders. Ralph stood a moment longer, and then followed him in.

Then again the minutes went by.

There was a sound of horse-hoofs on the road presently, and of talking that grew louder. The hoofs ceased; there was a sharp peal on the bell; and the talking began again.

Chris glanced across at his father; but the old man shook his head; and the three remained as they were, watching and listening. As the bell rang out again impatiently, the door behind opened, and the portress came swiftly through, followed by the Abbess.

"Come quickly," the old lady whispered. "Sister Susan is going to let them in."

She stood aside, and made a motion to them to come through, and a moment late the four were in the convent, and the door was shut behind them.

"They are Mr. Torridon's men," whispered the Abbess, her eyes round with excitement; "they are come to pack the things."

She led them on through the narrow passage, up a stone flight of stairs to the corridor that ran over the little cloister, and pushed open the door of a cell.

"Wait here," she said. "You can do no more. I will go down to them. You are in the enclosure, but I cannot help it."

And she had whisked out again, with an air of extraordinary composure, shutting the door behind her.

The three went across to the window, still speaking no word, and looked down.

The tiny court seemed half full of people now. There were three horses there, besides Ralph's own marked by its rich saddle, and still attached to the ring by the stable door, and a couple of men were busy loading one of them with bundles. From one of these, which was badly packed, a shimmering corner of gold cloth projected.

Ralph was standing by the door of the guest-house watching, and making a sign now and again with his whip. They could not see his face as he stood so directly below them, only his rich cap and feather, and his strong figure beneath. Mr. Morris was waiting now by his master's horse; the portress was by her door.

As they looked the little black and white figure of the Abbess came out beneath them, and stood by the portress.

The packing went on in silence. It was terrible to Mary to stand there and watch the dumb-show tragedy, the wrecking and robbing of this peaceful house; and yet there was nothing to be done. She knew that the issues were in stronger hands than hers; she glanced piteously at her father and brother on either side, but their faces were set and white, and they did not turn at her movement.

There was the sound of an opening door, and two women came out from the convent at one side and stood waiting. One was in secular dress; the other was still in her habit, but carried a long dark mantle across her arm, and Mary caught her breath and bit her lip fiercely as she recognized the second to be her sister.

She felt she must cry out, and denounce the sacrilege, and made an instinctive movement nearer the window, but in a moment her father's hand was on her arm.

"Be still, Mary: it is all well."

One of the horses was being led away by now through the open door; and the two others followed almost immediately; but the principal actors were still in their places; the Abbess and the portress together on this side; Ralph on that; and the two other women, a little apart from one another, at the further end of the court.

Then Ralph beckoned abruptly with his whip, and Mary saw her sister move out towards the gate; she caught a glance of her face, and saw that her lips were white and trembling, and her eyes full of agony. The other woman followed briskly, and the two disappeared through to the road outside.

Again Ralph beckoned, and Mr. Morris brought up the horse that he had now detached from the ring, and stood by its head, holding the off-stirrup for his master to mount. Ralph gathered the reins into his left hand, and for a moment they saw his face across the back of the horse fierce and white; then he was up, and settling his right foot into the stirrup.

Mr. Morris let go, and stood back; and simultaneously Ralph struck him with his riding-whip across the face, a furious back-handed slash.

Mary cried out uncontrollably and shrank back; and a moment later her father was leaning from the window, and she beside him.

"You damned coward!" he shouted. "Morris, you are my servant now."

Ralph did not turn his head an inch, and a moment later disappeared on horse-back through the gate, and the portress had closed it behind him.

The little court was silent now, and empty except for the Abbess' motionless figure behind, with Mr. Morris beside her, and the lay sister by the gate, her hand still on the key that she had turned, and her eyes intent and expectant fixed on her superior. Mr. Morris lifted a handkerchief now and again gently to his face, and Mary as she leaned half sobbing from above saw that there were spots of crimson on the white.

"Oh! Morris!" she whispered.

The servant looked up, with a great weal across one cheek, and bowed a little, but he could not speak yet. Outside they could hear the jingle of bridle-chains; and then a voice begin; but they could not distinguish the words.

It was Ralph speaking; but they could only guess what it was that he was saying. Overhead the autumn sky was a vault of pale blue; and a bird or two chirped briskly from the roof opposite.

The voice outside grew louder, and ceased, and the noise of horse hoofs broke out.

Still there was no movement from any within. The Abbess was standing now with one hand uplifted as if for silence, and Mary heard the hoofs sound fainter up the road; they grew louder again as they reached higher ground; and then ceased altogether.

The old man touched Mary on the arm, and the three went out along the little corridor, and down the stone stairs.

As they passed through the lodge and came into the court Mary saw that the Abbess had moved from her place, and was standing with the portress close by the gate; her face was towards them, a little on one side, and she seemed to be listening intently, her ear against the door, her lower lip sucked in, and her eyes bright and vacant; she still held one hand up for silence.

Then there came a tiny tapping on the wood-work, and she instantly turned and snatched at the key, and a moment later the door was wide.

"Come in, my poor child," she said.

Chapter VII
ST PANCRAS PRIORY

*I*t was a little more than a month later that Ralph met his fellow-Visitor at Lewes Priory.

He had left Rusper in a storm of angry obstinacy, compelled by sheer pride to do what he had not intended. The arrival of his father and Mary there had had exactly the opposite effect to that which they hoped, and Ralph had turned Margaret out of the convent simply because he could not bear that they should think that he could be frightened from his purpose.

As he had ridden off on that October morning, leaving Margaret standing outside with her cloak over her arm he had had a very sharp suspicion that she would be received back again; but he had not felt himself strong enough to take any further steps; so he contented himself with sending in his report to Dr. Layton, knowing well that heavy punishment would fall on the convent if it was discovered that the Abbess had disobeyed the Visitors' injunctions.

Then for a month or so he had ridden about the county, carrying off spoils, appointing new officials, and doing the other duties assigned to him; he was offered bribes again and again by superiors of Religious Houses, but unlike his fellow-Visitors always refused them, and fell the more hardly on those that offered them; he turned out numbers of young Religious and released elder ones who desired it, and by the time that he reached Lewes was fairly practiced in the duties of his position.

But the thought of the consequences of his action with regard to his future seldom left him. He had alienated his family, and perhaps Beatrice. As he rode once through Cuckfield, and caught a glimpse of the woods above Overfield, glorious in their autumn livery, he wondered whether he would ever find himself at home there again. It was a good deal to give up; but he comforted himself with the thought of his own career, and with the pleasant prospect of possessing some such house in his own right when the work that he now understood had been accomplished, and the monastic buildings were empty of occupants.

He had received one letter, to his surprise, from his mother; that was brought to him by a messenger in one of the houses where he stayed. It informed him that he had the writer's approval, and that she was thankful to have one son at least who was a man, and described further how his father and Mary had come back, and without Margaret, and that she supposed that the Abbess of Rusper had taken her back.

"Go on, my son," she ended, "it will be all well. You cannot come home, I know, while your father is in his present mind; but it is a dull place and you lose nothing. When you are married it will be different. Mr. Carleton is very tiresome, but it does not matter."

Ralph smiled to himself as he thought of the life that must now be proceeding at his home.

He had written once to Beatrice, in a rather tentative tone, assuring her that he was doing his best to be just and merciful, and professing to take it for granted that she knew how to discount any exaggerated stories of the Visitors' doings that might come to her ears. But he had received no answer, and indeed had told her that he did not expect one, for he was continually on the move and could give no fixed address.

As he came up over the downs above Lewes he was conscious of a keen excitement; this would be the biggest work he had undertaken, and it had the additional zest of being a means of annoying his brother who had provoked him so often. Since his quarrel with Chris in his own rooms in the summer he had retained an angry contempt towards him. Chris had been insolent and theatrical, he told himself, and had thrown off all claims to tenderness, and Ralph's feelings towards him were not improved by the information given him by one of his men that his brother had been present at the scene at Rusper, no doubt summoned there by Morris, who had proved such a desperate traitor to his master by slipping off to Overfield on the morning of the Sunday.

Ralph was very much puzzled at first by Morris's behavior; the man had always been respectful and obedient, but it was now evident to him that he had been half-hearted all along, and still retained a superstitious reverence for ecclesiastical things and persons; and although it was very inconvenient and tiresome to lose him, yet it was better to be inadequately than treacherously served.

*L*ewes Priory was a magnificent sight as Ralph came up on to the top of the last shoulder below Mount Harry. The town lay below him in the deep, cuplike hollow, piled house above house along the sides. Beyond it in the evening light, against the rich autumn fields and the gleam of water, towered up the tall church with the monastic buildings nestling behind.

The thought crossed his mind that it would do very well for himself; the town was conveniently placed between London and the sea, within a day's ride from either; there would be shops and company there, and the priory itself would be a dignified and suitable house, when it had been properly re-arranged. The only drawback would be Beatrice's scrupulousness; but he had little doubt that ultimately that could be overcome. It would be ridiculous for a single girl to set herself up against the conviction of a country, and refuse to avail herself of the advantages of a reform that was so sorely needed. She trusted him already; and it would not need much persuasion he thought to convince her mind as well as her heart.

Of course Lewes Priory would be a great prize, and there would be many applicants for it, and he realized that more than ever as he came up to its splendid gateway and saw the high tower overhead, and the long tiled roofs to the right; but his own relations with Cromwell were of the best, and he decided that at least no harm could result from asking.

It was with considerable excitement that he dismounted in the court, and saw the throng of Dr. Layton's men going to and fro. As at Durford, so here, his superior had arrived before him, and the place was already astir. The riding-horses had been bestowed in the stables, and the baggage-beasts were being now unloaded before the door of the guest-house; there were servants going to and fro in Dr. Layton's livery, with an anxious-faced monk or two here and there among them, and a buzz and clatter rose on all sides. One of Dr. Layton's secretaries who had been at Durford, recognized Ralph and came up immediately, saluting him deferentially.

"The doctor is with the Sub-Prior, sir," he said. "He gave orders that you were to be brought to him as soon as you arrived, Mr. Torridon."

Ralph followed him into the guest-house, and up the stairs up which Chris had come at his first arrival, and was shown into the parlor. There was a sound of voices as they approached the door, and as Ralph entered he saw at once that Dr. Layton was busy at his work.

"Come in, sir," he cried cheerfully from behind the table at which he sat. "Here is desperate work for you and me. No less than rank treason, Mr. Torridon."

A monk was standing before the table, who turned nervously as Ralph came in; he was a middle-aged man, grey-haired and brown-faced like a

foreigner, but his eyes were full of terror now, and his lips trembling
piteously.

Ralph greeted Dr. Layton shortly, and sat down beside him.

"Now, sir," went on the other, "your only hope is to submit yourself
to the King's clemency. You have confessed yourself to treason in your
preaching, and even if you did not, it would not signify, for I have the
accusation from the young man at Farley in my bag. You tell me you
did not know it was treason; but are you ready, sir, to tell the King's
Grace that?"

The monk's eyes glanced from one to the other anxiously. Ralph
could see that he was desperately afraid.

"Tell me that, sir," cried the doctor again, rapping the table with his
open hand.

"I — I — what shall I do, sir?" stammered the monk.

"You must throw yourself on the King's mercy, reverend father. And
as a beginning you must throw yourself on mine and Mr. Torridon's
here. Now, listen to this."

Dr. Layton lifted one of the papers that lay before him and rend it
aloud, looking severely at the monk over the top of it between the
sentences. It was in the form of a confession, and declared that on such
a date in the Priory Church of St Pancras at Lewes the undersigned had
preached treason, although ignorant that it was so, in the presence of
the Prior and community; and that the Prior, although he knew what
was to be said, and had heard the sermon in question, had neither
forbidden it beforehand nor denounced it afterwards, and that the
undersigned entreated the King's clemency for the fault and submitted
himself entirely to his Grace's judgment.

"I — I dare not accuse my superior," stammered the monk.

Dr. Layton glared at him, laying the paper down.

"The question is," he cried, "which would you sooner offend — your
Prior, who will be prior no longer presently, or the King's Grace, who
will remain the King's Grace for many years yet, by the favor of God,
and who has moreover supreme rights of life and death. That is your
choice, reverend father." — He lifted the paper by the corners. — "You
have only to say the word, sir, and I tear up this paper, and write my
own report of the matter."

The monk again glanced helplessly at the two men. Ralph had a touch
of contentment at the thought that this was Christopher's superior,
ranged like a naughty boy at the table, and looked at him coldly. Dr.
Layton made a swift gesture as if to tear the paper, and the Sub-Prior
threw out his hands.

"I will sign it, sir," he said, "I will sign it."

When the monk had left the room, leaving his signed confession behind him, Dr. Layton turned beaming to Ralph.

"Thank God!" he said piously. "I do not know what we should have done if he had refused; but now we hold him and his prior too. How have you fared, Mr. Torridon?"

Ralph told him a little of his experiences since his last report, of a nunnery where all but three had been either dismissed or released; of a monastery where he had actually caught a drunken cellarer unconscious by a barrel, and of another where he had reason to fear even worse crimes.

"Write it all down, Mr. Torridon," cried the priest, "and do not spare the adjectives. I have some fine tales for you myself. But we must dispatch this place first. We shall have grand sport in the chapter-house tomorrow. This prior is a poor timid fellow, and we can do what we will with him. Concealed treason is a sharp sword to threaten him with."

Ralph remarked presently that he had a brother a monk here.

"But you can do what you like to him," he said. "I have no love for him. He is an insolent fellow."

Dr. Layton smiled pleasantly.

"We will see what can be done," he said.

Ralph slept that night in the guest-house, in the same room that Chris had occupied on his first coming. He awoke once at the sound of the great bell from the tower calling the monks to the night-office, and smiled at the fantastic folly of it all. His work during the last month had erased the last remnants of superstitious fear, and to him now more than ever the Religious Houses were but noisy rookeries, clamant with bells and chanting, and foul with the refuse of idleness. The sooner they were silenced and purged the better.

He did not trouble to go to mass in the morning, but lay awake in the whitewashed room, hearing footsteps and voices below, and watching the morning light brighten on the wall. He found himself wondering once or twice what Chris was doing, and how he felt; he did not rise till one of his men looked in to tell him that Dr. Layton would be ready for him in half-an-hour, if he pleased.

The chapter-house was a strange sight as he entered it from the cloister. It was a high oblong chamber some fifty feet long, with arched roof like a chapel, and a paved floor. On a dozen stones or so were cut inscriptions recording the presence of bodies entombed below, among them those of Earl William de Warenne and Gundrada, his wife, founders of the priory five centuries ago. Ralph caught sight of the names as he strode through the silent monks at the door and entered the chamber, talking loudly with his fellow-Visitor. The tall vaulted room looked bare and severe; the seats ran round it, raised on a step, and before the Prior's chair beneath the crucifix stood a large table covered with papers. Beneath it, and emerging on to the floor lay a great heap of vestments and precious things which Dr. Layton had ordered to be piled there for his inspection, and on the table itself for greater dignity burned two tapers in massive silver candlesticks.

"Sit here, Mr. Torridon," said the priest, himself taking the Prior's chair, "we represent the supreme head of the Church of England now, you must remember."

And he smiled at the other with a solemn joy.

He glanced over his papers, settled himself judicially, and then signed to one of his men to call the monks in. His two secretaries seated themselves at either end of the table that stood before their master.

Then the two lines began to file in, in reverse order, as the doctor had commanded; black silent figures with bowed heads buried in their hoods, and their hands invisible in the great sleeves of their cowls.

Ralph ran his eyes over them; there were men of all ages there, old wrinkled faces, and smooth ones; but it was not until they were all standing in their places that he recognized Chris.

There stood the young man, at a stall near the door, his eyes bent down, and his face deadly pale, his figure thin and rigid against the pale oak paneling that rose up some eight feet from the floor. Ralph's heart quickened with triumph. Ah! it was good to be here as judge, with that brother of his as culprit!

The Prior and Sub-prior, whose places were occupied, stood together in the center of the room, as the doctor had ordered. It was their case that was to come first.

There was an impressive silence; the two Visitors sat motionless, looking severely round them; the secretaries had their clean paper before them, and their pens, ready dipped, poised in their fingers.

Then Dr. Layton began.

*I*t was an inexpressibly painful task, he said, that he had before him; the monks were not to think that he gloried in it, or loved to find fault and impose punishments; and, in fact, nothing but the knowledge that he was there as the representative of the supreme authority in Church and State could have supplied to him the fortitude necessary for the performance of so sad a task.

Ralph marveled at him as he listened. There was a solemn sound in the man's face and voice, and dignity in his few and impressive gestures. It could hardly be believed that he was not in earnest; and yet Ralph remembered too the relish with which the man had dispersed his foul tales the evening before, and the cackling laughter with which their recital was accompanied. But it was all very wholesome for Chris, he thought.

"And now," said Dr. Layton, "I must lay before you this grievous matter. It is one of whose end I dare not think, if it should come before the King's Grace; and yet so it must come. It is no less a matter than treason."

His voice rang out with a melancholy triumph, and Ralph, looking at the two monks who stood in the center of the room, saw that they were both as white as paper. The lips of the Prior were moving in a kind of agonized entreaty, and his eyes rolled round.

"You, sir," cried the doctor, glaring at the Sub-Prior, who dropped his beseeching eyes at the fierce look, "you, sir, have committed the crime — in ignorance, you tell me — but at least the crime of preaching in this priory-church in the presence of his Grace's faithful subjects a sermon attacking the King's most certain prerogatives. I can make perhaps allowances for this — though I do not know whether his Grace will do so — but I can make allowances for one so foolish as yourself carried away by the drunkenness of words; but I can make none — none —" he shouted, crashing his hand upon the table, "none for your superior who stands beside you, and who forbore either to protest at the treason at the time or to rebuke it afterwards."

The Prior's hands rose and clasped themselves convulsively, but he made no answer.

Dr. Layton proceeded to read out the confession that he had wrung from the monk the night before, down to the signature; then he called upon him to come up.

"Is this your name, sir?" he asked slowly.

The Sub-Prior took the paper in his trembling hands.

"It is sir," he said.

"You hear it," cried the doctor, staring fiercely round the faces, "he tells you he has subscribed it himself. Go back to your place, reverend father, and thank our Lord that you had courage to do so.

"And now, you, sir, Master Prior, what have you to say?"

Dr. Layton dropped his voice as he spoke, and laid his fat hands together on the table. The Prior looked up with the same dreadful entreaty as before; his lips moved, but no sound came from them. The monks round were deadly still; Ralph saw a swift glance or two exchanged beneath the shrouding hoods, but no one moved.

"I am waiting, my Lord Prior," cried Layton in a loud terrible voice. Again the Prior writhed his lips to speak.

Dr. Layton rose abruptly and made a violent gesture.

"Down on your knees, Master Prior, if you need mercy."

There was a quick murmur and ripple along the two lines as the Prior dropped suddenly on to his knees and covered his face with his hands.

Dr. Layton threw out his hand with a passionate gesture and began to speak —.

"There, reverend fathers and brethren," he cried, "you see how low sin brings a man. This fellow who calls himself prior was bold enough, I daresay, in the church when treason was preached; and, I doubt not, has been bold enough in private too when he thought none heard him but his friends. But you see how treachery, — heinous treachery, — plucks the spirit from him, and how lowly he carries himself when he knows that true men are sitting in judgment over him. Take example from that, you who have served him in the past; you need never fear him more now."

Dr. Layton dropped his hand and sat down. For one moment Ralph saw the kneeling man lift that white face again, but the doctor was at him instantly.

"Do not dare to rise, sir, till I give you leave," he roared. "You had best be a penitent. Now tell me, sir, what you have to say. It shall not be said that we condemned a man unheard. Eh! Mr. Torridon?"

Ralph nodded sharply, and glanced at Chris; but his brother was staring at the Prior.

"Now then, sir," cried the doctor again.

"I entreat you, Master Layton —"

The Prior's voice was convulsed with terror as he cried this with outstretched hands.

"Yes, sir, I will hear you."

"I entreat you, sir, not to tell his Grace. Indeed I am innocent" — his voice rose thin and high in his panic — "indeed, I did not know it was treason that was preached."

"Did not know?" sneered the doctor, leaning forward over the table. "Why, you know your Faith, man —"

"Master Layton, Master Layton; there be so many changes in these days —"

"Changes!" shouted the priest; "there be no changes, except of such knaves as you, Master-Prior; it is the old Faith now as ever. Do you dare to call his Grace a heretic? Must that too go down in the charges?"

"No, no, Master Layton," screamed the Prior, with his hands strained forward and twitching fingers. "I did not mean that — Christ is my witness!"

"Is it not the same Faith, sir?"

"Yes, Master Layton — yes — indeed, it is. But I did not know — how could I know?"

"Then why are you Prior," cried the doctor with a dramatic gesture, "if it is not to keep your subjects true and obedient? Do you mean to tell me — ?"

"I entreat you, sir, for the love of Mary, not to tell his Grace —"

"Bah!" shouted Dr. Layton, "you may keep your breath till you tell his Grace that himself. There is enough of this." Again he rose, and swept his eyes round the white-faced monks. "I am weary of this work. The fellow has not a word to say —"

"Master Layton, Master Layton," cried the kneeling man once more, lifting his hands on one of which gleamed the prelatical ring.

"Silence, sir," roared the doctor. "It is I who am speaking now. We have had enough of this work. It seems that there be no true men left, except in the world; these houses are rotten with crime. Is it not so, Master Torridon? — rotten with crime! But of all the knaves that I did ever meet, and they are many and strong ones, I do believe Master Prior, that you are the worst. Here is my sentence, and see that it be carried out. You, Master Prior, and you Master Sub-Prior, are to appear before Master Cromwell in his court on All-Hallows' Eve, and tell your tales to him. You shall see if he be so soft as I; it may be that he will send you before the King's Grace — that I know not — but at least he will know how to get the truth out of you, if I cannot —"

Once more the Prior broke in, in an agony of terror; but the doctor silenced him in a moment.

"Have I not given my sentence, sir? How dare you speak?"

A murmur again ran round the room, and he lifted his hand furiously.

"Silence," he shouted, "not one word from a mother's son of you. I have had enough of sedition already. Clear the room, officer, and let not one shaveling monk put his nose within again, until I send for him. I am weary of them all — weary and broken-hearted."

The doctor dropped back into his seat, with a face of profound disgust, and passed his hand over his forehead.

The monks turned at the signal from the door, and Ralph watched the black lines once more file out.

"There, Mr. Torridon," whispered the doctor behind his hand. "Did I not tell you so? Master Cromwell will be able to do what he will with him."

Chapter VIII

RALPH'S RETURN

The Visitation of Lewes Priory occupied a couple of days, as the estates were so vast, and the account-books so numerous.

In the afternoon following the scene in the chapter-house, Dr. Layton and Ralph rode out to inspect some of the farms that were at hand, leaving orders that the stock was to be driven up into the court the next day, and did not return till dusk. The excitement in the town was tremendous as they rode back through the ill-lighted streets, and as the rumor ran along who the great gentlemen were that went along so gaily with their servants behind them; and by the time that they reached the priory-gate there was a considerable mob following in their train, singing and shouting, in the highest spirits at the thought of the plunder that would probably fall into their hands.

Layton turned in his saddle at the door, and made them a little speech, telling them how he was there with the authority of the King's Grace, and would soon make a sweep of the place.

"And there will be pickings," he cried, "pickings for us all! The widow and the orphan have been robbed long enough; it is time to spoil the fathers."

There was a roar of amusement from the mob; and a shout or two was raised for the King's Grace.

"You must be patient," cried Dr. Layton, "and then no more taxes. You can trust us, gentlemen, to do the King's work as it should be done."

As he passed in through the lamp-lit entrance he turned to Ralph again.

"You see, Mr. Torridon, we have the country behind us."

*I*t was that evening that Ralph for the first time since the quarrel met his brother face to face.

He was passing through the cloister on his way to Dr. Layton's room, and came past the refectory door just as the monks were gathering for supper. He glanced in as he went, and had a glimpse of the clean solemn hall, lighted with candles along the paneling, the long bare tables laid ready, the Prior's chair and table at the further end and the great fresco over it. A lay brother or two in aprons were going about their business silently, and three or four black figures, who had already entered, stood motionless along the raised dais on which the tables stood.

The monks had all stopped instantly as Ralph came among them, and had lowered their hoods with their accustomed courtly deference to a guest; and as he turned from his momentary pause at the refectory door in the full blaze of light that shone from it, he met Chris face to face.

The young monk had come up that instant, not noticing who was there, and his hood was still over his head. There was a second's pause, and then he lifted his hand and threw the hood back in salutation; and as Ralph bowed and passed on he had a moment's sight of that thin face and the large grey eyes in which there was not the faintest sign of recognition.

Ralph's heart was hot with mingled emotion as he went up the cloister. He was more disturbed by the sudden meeting, the act of courtesy, and the cold steady eyes of this young fool of a brother than he cared to recognize.

He saw no more of him, except in the distance among his fellows; and he left the house the next day when the business was done.

*M*atters in the rest of England were going forward with the same promptitude as in Sussex. Dr. Layton himself had visited the West earlier in the autumn, and the other Visitors were busy in other parts of the country. The report was current now that the resources of all the Religious Houses were to be certainly confiscated, and that those of the inmates who still persisted in their vocation would have to do so under the most rigorous conditions imaginable. The results were to be seen in the enormous increase of beggars, deprived now of the hospitality they were accustomed to receive; and the roads everywhere were thronged with those who had been holders of corrodies, or daily sustenance in the houses; as well as with the evicted Religious, some of whom, dismissed against their will, were on their way to the universities, where, in spite of the Visitation, it was thought that support was still to be had; and others, less reputable, who preferred freedom to monastic discipline. Yet others were to be met with, though not many in number, who were on their way to London to lay complaints of various kinds against their superiors.

From these and like events the whole country was astir. Men gathered in groups outside the village inns and discussed the situation, and feeling ran high on the movements of the day. What chiefly encouraged the malcontents was the fact that the benefits to be gained by the dissolution of the monasteries were evident and present, while the ill-results lay in the future. The great Religious Houses, their farms and stock, the jewels of the treasury, were visible objects; men actually laid eyes on them as they went to and from their work or knelt at mass on Sundays; it was all so much wealth that did not belong to them, and that might do so, while the corrodies, the daily hospitality, the employment of labor, and such things, lay either out of sight, or affected only certain individuals. Characters too that were chiefly stirred by such arguments, were those of the noisy and self-assertive faction; while those who saw a little deeper into things, and understood the enormous charities of the Religious Houses and the manner in which extreme poverty was kept in check by them, — even more, those who valued the spiritual benefits that flowed from the fact of their existence, and saw how life was kindled and inspired by these vast homes of prayer — such, then as always, were those who would not voluntarily put themselves forward in debate, or be able, when they did so, to use arguments that would appeal to the village gatherings. Their natural leaders too, the country clergy, who alone might have pointed out effectively the considerations that lay beneath the surface had been skillfully and peremptorily silenced by the episcopal withdrawing of all preaching licenses.

*I*n the course of Ralph's travels he came across, more than once, a hot scene in the village inn, and was able to use his own personality and prestige as a King's Visitor in the direction that he wished.

He came for example one Saturday night to the little village of Maresfield, near Fletching, and after seeing his horses and servants bestowed, came into the parlor, where the magnates were assembled. There were half a dozen there, sitting round the fire, who rose respectfully as the great gentleman strode in, and eyed him with a sudden awe as they realized from the landlord's winks and whispers that he was of a very considerable importance.

From the nature of his training Ralph had learnt how to deal with all conditions of men; and by the time that he had finished supper, and drawn his chair to the fire, they were talking freely again, as indeed he had encouraged them to do, for they did not of course, anymore than the landlord, guess at his identity or his business there.

Ralph soon brought the talk round again to the old subject, and asked the opinions of the company as to the King's policy in the visitation of the Religious Houses There was a general silence when he first opened the debate, for they were dangerous times; but the gentleman's own imperturbable air, his evident importance, and his friendliness, conspired with the strong beer to open their mouths, and in five minutes they were at it.

One, a little old man in the corner who sat with crossed legs, nursing his mug, declared that to his mind the whole thing was sacrilege; the houses, he said, had been endowed to God's glory and service, and that to turn them to other uses must bring a curse on the country. He went on to remark — for Ralph deftly silenced the chorus of protest — that his own people had been buried in the church of the Dominican friars at Arundel for three generations, and that he was sorry for the man who laid hands on the tomb of his grandfather — known as Uncle John — for the old man had been a desperate churchman in his day, and would undoubtedly revenge himself for any indignity offered to his bones.

Ralph pointed out, with a considerate self-repression, that the illustration was scarcely to the point, for the King's Grace had no intention, he believed, of disturbing anyone's bones; the question at issue rather regarded flesh and blood. Then a chorus broke out, and the hunt was up.

One, the butcher, with many blessings invoked on King Harry's head, declared that the country was being sucked dry by these rapacious ecclesiastics; that the monks encroached every year on the common land, absorbed the little farms, paid inadequate wages, and — which appeared his principal grievance — killed their own meat.

Ralph, with praiseworthy tolerance, pushed this last argument aside, but appeared to reflect on the others as if they were new to him, though he had heard them a hundred times, and used them fifty; and while he weighed them, another took up the tale; told a scandalous story or two, and asked how men who lived such lives as these which he related, could be examples of chastity.

Once more the little old man burst into the fray, and waving his pot in an access of religious enthusiasm, rebuked the last speaker for his readiness to pick up dirt, and himself instanced five or six Religious known to him, whose lives were no less spotless than his own.

Again Ralph interposed in his slow voice, and told them that that too was not the point at issue. The question was not as to whether here and there monks lived good lives or bad, for no one was compelled to imitate either, but as to whether on the whole the existence of the Religious Houses was profitable in such practical matters as agriculture, trade, and the relief of the destitute.

And so it went on, and Ralph began to grow weary of the inconsequence of the debaters, and their entire inability to hold to the salient points; but he still kept his hand on the rudder of the discussion, avoided the fogs of the supernatural and religious on the one side towards which the little old man persisted in pushing, and, on the other, the blunt views of the butcher and the man who had told the foul stories; and contented himself with watching and learning the opinion of the company rather than contributing his own.

Towards the end of the evening he observed two of his men, who had slipped in and were sitting at the back of the little stifling room, hugely enjoying the irony of the situation, and determined on ending the discussion with an announcement of his own identity.

Presently an opportunity occurred. The little old man had shown a dangerous tendency to discourse on the suffering souls in purgatory, and on the miseries inflicted on them by the cessation of masses and suffrages for their welfare; and an uncomfortable awe-stricken silence had fallen on the others.

Ralph stood up abruptly, and began to speak, his bright tired eyes shining down on the solemn faces, and his mouth set and precise.

"Well, gentlemen," he said, "your talk has pleased me very much. I have learned a great deal, and I hope shall profit by it. Some of you have talked a quantity of nonsense; and you, Mr. Miggers, have talked the most, about your uncle John's soul and bones."

A deadly silence fell as these startling words were pronounced; for his manner up to now had been conciliatory and almost apologetic. But he went on imperturbably.

"I am quite sure that Almighty God knows His business better than you or I, Mr. Miggers; and if He cannot take care of Uncle John without the aid of masses or dirges sung by fat-bellied monks —"

He stopped abruptly, and a squirt of laughter burst from the butcher.

"Well, this is my opinion," went on Ralph, "if you wish to know it. I do not think, or suspect, as some of you do – but I *know* – as you will allow presently that I do, when I tell you who I am – I *know* that these houses of which we have been speaking, are nothing better than wasps'-nests. The fellows look holy enough in their liveries, they make a deal of buzz, they go to and fro as if on business; but they make no honey that is worth your while or mine to take. There is but one thing that they have in their holes that is worth anything: and that is their jewels and their gold, and the lead on their churches and the bells in their towers. And all that, by the Grace of God we will soon have out of them."

There was a faint murmur of mingled applause and dissent. Mr. Miggers stared vacant-faced at this preposterous stranger, and set his mug resolutely down as a preparation for addressing him, but he had no opportunity. Ralph was warmed now by his own eloquence, and swept on.

"You think I do not know of what I am speaking? Well, I have a brother a monk at Lewes, and a sister a nun at Rusper; and I have been brought up in this religion until I am weary of it. My sister – well, she is like other maidens of her kind – not a word to speak of any matter but our Lady and the Saints and how many candles Saint Christopher likes. And my brother! – Well, we can leave that.

"I know these houses as none of you know them; I know how much wine they drink, how much they charge for their masses, how much treasonable chatter they carry on in private – I know their lives as I know my own; and I know that they are rotten and useless altogether. They may give a plateful or two in charity and a mug of beer; they gorge ten dishes themselves, and swill a hogshead. They give a penny to the poor man, and keep twenty nobles for themselves. They take field after field, house after house; turn the farmer into the beggar, and the beggar into their bedesman. And, by God! I say that the sooner King Henry gets rid of the crew, the better for you and me!"

Ralph snapped out the last words, and stared insolently down on the gaping faces. Then he finished, standing by the door as he did so, with his hand on the latch.

"If you would know how I know all this, I will tell you. My name is Torridon, of Overfield; and I am one of the King's Visitors. Good-night, gentlemen."

There was the silence of the grave within, as Ralph went upstairs smiling to himself.

*R*alph had intended returning home a week or two after the Lewes visitation, but there was a good deal to be done, and Layton had pointed out to him that even if some houses were visited twice over it would do no harm to the rich monks to pay double fees; so it was not till Christmas was a week away that he rode at last up to his house-door at Westminster.

His train had swelled to near a dozen men and horses by now, for he had accumulated a good deal of treasure beside that which he had left in Layton's hands, and it would not have been safe to travel with a smaller escort; so it was a gay and imposing cavalcade that clattered through the narrow streets. Ralph himself rode in front, in solitary dignity, his weapon jingling at his stirrup, his feather spruce and bright above his spare keen face; a couple of servants rode behind, fully armed and formidable looking, and then the train came behind — beasts piled with bundles that rustled and clinked suggestively, and the men who guarded them gay with scraps of embroidery and a cheap jewel or two here and there in their dress.

But Ralph did not feel so gallant as he looked. During these long country rides he had had too much time to think, and the thought of Beatrice and of what she would say seldom left him. The very harshness of his experiences, the rough faces round him, the dialect of the stable and the inn, the coarse conversation — all served to make her image the more gracious and alluring. It was a kind of worship, shot with passion, that he felt for her. Her grave silences coincided with his own, her tenderness yielded deliciously to his strength.

As he sat over his fire with his men whispering behind him, planning as they thought new assaults on the rich nests that they all hated and coveted together, again and again it was Beatrice's face, and not that of a shrewd or anxious monk, that burned in the red heart of the hearth. He had seen it with downcast eyes, with the long lashes lying on the cheek, and the curved red lips discreetly shut beneath; the masses of black hair shadowed the forehead and darkened the secret that he wished to read. Or he had watched her, like a jewel in a pig-sty, looking across the foul-littered farm where he had had to sleep more than once with his men about him; her black eyes looking into his own with tender gravity, and her mouth trembling with speech. Or best of all, as he rode along the bitter cold lanes at the fall of the day, the crowding yews above him had parted and let her stand there, with her long skirts rustling in the dry leaves, her slender figure blending with the darkness, and her sweet face trusting and loving him out of the gloom.

And then again, like the prick of a wound, the question had touched him, how would she receive him when he came back with the monastic spoils on his beasts' shoulders, and the wail of the nuns shrilling like the wind behind?

But by the time that he came back to London he had thought out his method of meeting her. Probably she had had news of the doings of the Visitors, perhaps of his own in particular; it was hardly possible that his father had not written; she would ask for an explanation, and she should have instead an appeal to her confidence. He would tell her that sad things had indeed happened, that he had been forced to be present at and even to carry out incidents which he deplored; but that he had done his utmost to be merciful. It was rough work, he would say; but it was work that had to be done; and since that was so — and this was Cromwell's teaching — it was better that honorable gentlemen should do it. He had not been able always to restrain the violence of his men — and for that he needed forgiveness from her dear lips; and it would be easy enough to tell stories against him that it would be hard to disprove; but if she loved and trusted him, and he knew that she did, let her take his word for it that no injustice had been deliberately done, that on the other hand he had been the means under God of restraining many such acts, and that his conscience was clear.

It was a moving appeal, Ralph thought, and it almost convinced himself. He was not conscious of any gross insincerity in the defense; of course it was shaded artistically, and the more brutal details kept out of sight, but in the main it was surely true. And, as he rehearsed its points to himself once more in the streets of Westminster, he felt that though there might be a painful moment or two, yet it would do his work.

*H*e had sent a message home that he was coming, and the door of his home was wide as he dismounted, and the pleasant light of candles shone out, for the evening was smoldering to dark in the west.

A crowd had collected as he went along; from every window faces were leaning; and as he stood on the steps directing the removal of the treasure into the house, he saw that the mob filled the tiny street, and the cobbled space, from side to side. They were chiefly of the idling class, folks who had little to do but to follow up excitements and shout; and there were a good many cries raised for the King's Grace and his Visitors, for such people as these were greedy for any movement that might bring them gain, and the Religious Houses were beginning to be more unpopular in town than ever.

One of the bundles slipped as it was shifted, the cord came off, and in a moment the little space beyond the mule before the door was covered with gleaming stuff and jewels.

There was a fierce scuffle and a cry, and Ralph was in a moment beyond the mule with his sword out. He said nothing but stood there fierce and alert as the crowd sucked back, and the servant gathered up the things. There was no more trouble, for it had only been a spasmodic snatch at the wealth, and a cheer or two was raised again among the grimy faces that stared at the fine gentleman and the shining treasure.

Ralph thought it better, however, to say a conciliatory word when the things had been bestowed in the house, and the mules led away; and he stood on the steps a moment alone before entering himself.

The crowd listened complacently enough to the statements which they had begun to believe from the fact of the incessant dinning of them into their ears by the selected preachers at Paul's Cross and elsewhere; and there was loud groan at the Pope's name.

Ralph was ending with an incise peroration that he had delivered more than once before.

"You know all this, good people; and you shall know it better when the work is done. Instead of the rich friars and monks we will have godly citizens, each with his house and land. The King's Grace has promised it, and you know that he keeps his word. We have had enough of the jackdaws and their stolen goods; we will have honest birds instead. Only be patient a little longer —"

The listening silence was broken by a loud cry —

"You damned plundering hound —"

A stone suddenly out of the gloom whizzed past Ralph and crashed through the window behind. A great roaring rose in a moment, and the crowd swayed and turned.

Ralph felt his heart suddenly quicken, and his hand flew to his hilt again, but there was no need for him to act. There were terrible screams already rising from the seething twilight in front, as the stone-thrower was seized and trampled. He stayed a moment longer, dropped his hilt and went into the house.

Chapter IX

RALPH'S WELCOME

"You will show Mistress Atherton into the room below," said Ralph to his man, "as soon as she comes."

He was sitting on the morning following his arrival in his own chamber upstairs. His table was a mass of papers, account-books, reckonings, reports bearing on his Visitation journey, and he had been working at them ever since he was dressed; for he had to present himself before Cromwell in the course of a day or two, and the labor would be enormous.

The room below, opposite that in which he intended to see Beatrice and where she had waited herself a few months before while he talked with Cromwell and the Archbishop, was now occupied by his collection of plate and vestments, and the key was in his own pocket.

He had heard from his housekeeper on the previous evening that Beatrice had called at the house during the afternoon, and had seemed surprised to hear that he was to return that night; but she had said very little, it appeared, and had only begged the woman to inform her master that she would present herself at his house the next morning.

And now Ralph was waiting for her.

He was more ill-at-ease than he had expected to be. The events of the evening before had given him a curious shock; and he cursed the whole business — the snapping of the cord round the bundle, his own action and words, the outrage that followed, and the death of the fellow that had thrown the stone — for the body had been rescued by the watch a few minutes later, a tattered crushed thing, beaten out of all likeness to a man. One of the watch had stepped in to see Ralph as he sat at supper, and had gone again saying the dog deserved it for daring to lift his voice against the King and his will.

But above all Ralph repented of his own words. There was no harm in saying such things in the country; but it was foolish and rash to do so in town. Cromwell's men should be silent and discreet, he knew, not street-orators; and if he had had time to think he would not have spoken. However the crowd was with him; there was plainly no one of any importance there; it was unlikely that Cromwell himself would hear of the incident; and perhaps after all no harm was done.

Meanwhile there was Beatrice to reckon with, and Ralph laid down his pen a dozen times that morning and rehearsed once more what he would have to say to her.

He was shrewd enough to know that it was his personality and not his virtues or his views that had laid hold of this girl's soul. As it was with him, so it was with her; each was far enough apart from the other in all external matters; such things had been left behind a year ago; it was not an affair of consonant tastes, but of passion. From each there had looked deep inner eyes; there had been on either side a steady and fearless scrutiny, and then the two souls had leapt together in a bright flame of desire, knowing that each was made for the other. There had been so little love-making, so few speeches after the first meeting or two, so few letters exchanged, and fewer embraces. The last veils had fallen at the fury of Chris's intervention, and they had known then what had been inevitable all along.

Ralph smiled to himself as he remembered how little he had said or she had answered; there had been no need to say anything. And then his eyes grew wide and passionate, and his hands gripped one another fiercely, as the memory died, and the burning flame of desire flared within him again from the deep well he bore in his heart. The world of affairs and explanations and evasions faded into twilight, and there was but one thing left, his love and hers. It was to that that he would appeal.

He sat so a moment longer, and then took up his pen again, though it shook in his hand, and went on with his reckonings.

*H*e was perfectly composed half an hour later as he went downstairs to meet her. He had finished his line of figures sedately when the man looked in to say that she was below; and had sat yet a moment longer, trying to remember mechanically what it was he had determined to tell her. Bah! it was trifling and unimportant; words did not affect the question; all the wrecked convents in the world could not touch the one fact that lay in fire at his heart. He would say nothing; she would understand.

In the tiny entrance hall there was a whiff of fragrance where she had passed through; and his heart stirred in answer. Then he opened the door, stepped through and closed it behind him.

She was standing upright by the hearth, and faced him as he entered. He was aware of her blue mantle, her white, jeweled headdress, one hand gripping the mantel-shelf, her pale steady face and bright eyes. Behind there was the warm rich paneling, and the leaping glow of the wood fire.

She made no movement.

Outside the lane was filled with street noises, the cries of children, the voices of men who went by talking, the rumble of a wagon coming with the crack of whips and jingle of bells from the river. The wheels came up and went past into silence again before either spoke or moved.

Then Ralph lifted his hands a little and let them drop, as he stared at her face. From her eyes looked out her will, tense as steel; and his own shook to meet it.

"Well?" she said at last; and her voice was perfectly steady.

"Beatrice," cried Ralph; and the agony of it tore his heart.

She dropped her hand to her side and still looked at him without flinching.

"Beatrice," cried Ralph once more.

"Then you have no more to say — after last night?"

A torrent of thoughts broke loose in his brain, and he tried to snatch one as they fled past — to say one word. His excuses went by him like phantoms; they bewildered and dazed him. Why, there were a thousand things to say, and each was convincing if he could but say it. The cloud passed and there were her eyes watching him still.

"Then that is all?" she said.

Again the cloud fell on him; little scenes piteously clear rose before him, of the road by Rusper convent, Layton's leering face, a stripped altar; and for each there was a tale if he could but tell it. And still the bright eyes never flinched.

It seemed to him as if she was watching him curiously; her lips were parted, and her head was a little on one side; her face interested and impersonal.

"Why, Beatrice —" he cried again.

Then her love shook her like a storm; he had never dreamed she could look like that; her mouth shook; he could see her white teeth clenched; and a shiver went over her. He took one step forward, but stopped again, for the black eyes shone through the passion that swayed her, as keen and remorseless as ever.

He dropped on to his knees at the table and buried his face in his hands. He knew nothing now but that he had lost her.

That was her voice speaking now, as steady as her eyes; but he did not hear a word she said. Words were nothing; they were not so much as those cries from the street, that shrill boy's voice over the way; not so much as the sighing crackle from the hearth where he had caused a fire to be lighted lest she should feel cold.

She was still speaking, but her voice had moved; she was no longer by the fire. He could feel the warmth of the fire now on his hands. But he dared not move nor look up; there was but one thing left for him — that he had lost her!

That was her hand on the latch; a breath of cold air stirred his hair; and still she was speaking. He understood a little more now; she knew it all — his doings — what he had said last night — and there was not one word to say in answer. Her short lashing sentences fell on his defenseless soul, but all sense was dead, and he watched with a dazed impersonalness how each stroke went home, and yet he felt no pain or shame.

She was going now; a picture stirred on the wall by the fire as the wind rushed in through the open street door.

*T*hen the door closed.

PART II

THE FALL OF LEWES

Chapter I

INTERNAL DISSENSION

*T*he peace was gone from Lewes Priory. A wave had broken in through the high wall from the world outside with the coming of the Visitors, and had left wreckage behind, and swept out security as it went. The monks knew now that their old privileges were gone with the treasures that Layton had taken with him, and that although the wave had recoiled, it would return again and sweep them all away.

Upon none of them had the blow fallen more fiercely than on Chris; he had tried to find peace, and instead was in the midst of storm. The high barriers had gone, and with them the security of his own soul, and the world that he thought he had left was grinning at the breach.

It was piteous to him to see the Prior — that delicate, quiet prelate who had held himself aloof in his dignities — now humbled by the shame of his exposure in the chapter-house. The courage that Bishop Fisher had restored to him in some measure was gone again; and it was miserable to look at that white downcast face in the church and refectory, and to recognize that all self-respect was gone. After his return from his appearance before Cromwell he was more wretched than ever; it was known that he had been sent back in contemptuous disgrace; but it was not known how much he had promised in his terror for life.

The house had lost too some half-dozen of its inmates. Two had petitioned for release; three professed monks had been dismissed, and a recent novice had been sent back to his home. Their places in the stately choir were empty, and eloquent with warning; and in their stead was a fantastic secular priest, appointed by the Visitors' authority, who seldom said mass, and never attended choir; but was regular in the refectory, and the chapter-house where he thundered St. Paul's epistles at the monks, and commentaries of his own, in the hopes of turning them from papistry to a purer faith.

The news from outside echoed their own misery. Week after week the tales poured in, of young and old dismissed back to the world whose ways they had forgotten, of the rape of treasures priceless not only for their intrinsic worth but for the love that had given and consecrated them through years of devout service. There was not a house that had not lost something; the King himself had sanctioned the work by taking precious horns and a jeweled cross from Winchester. And worse than all that had gone was the terror of what was yet to come. The world, which had been creeping nearer, pausing and creeping on again, had at last passed the boundaries and leapt to sacrilege.

It was this terror that poisoned life. The sacristan who polished the jewels that were left, handled them doubtfully now; the monk who superintended the farm sickened as he made his plans for another year; the scribe who sat in the carrel lost enthusiasm for his work; for the jewels in a few months might be on royal fingers, the beasts in strangers' sheds, and the illuminated leaves blowing over the cobbled court, or wrapped round grocers' stores.

Dom Anthony preached a sermon on patience one day in Christmastide, telling his fellows that a man's life, and still less a monk's, consisted not in the abundance of things that he possessed; and that corporate, as well as individual, poverty, had been the ideal of the monastic houses in earlier days. He was no great preacher, but the people loved to hear his homely remarks, and there was a murmur of sympathy as he pointed with a clumsy gesture to the lighted Crib that had been erected at the foot of one of the great pillars in the nave.

"Our Lady wore no cloth of gold," he said, "nor Saint Joseph a precious miter; and the blessed Redeemer Himself who made all things had but straw to His bed. And if our new cope is gone, we can make our processions in the old one, and please God no less. Nay, we may please Him more perhaps, for He knows that it is by no will of ours that we do so."

But there had been a dismal scene at the chapter next morning. The Prior had made them a speech, with a passionate white face and hands that shook, and declared that the sermon would be their ruin yet if the King's Grace heard of it.

"There was a fellow that went out halfway through," he cried in panic, "how do we know whether he is not talking with his Grace even now? I will not have such sermons; and you shall be my witnesses that I said so."

The monks eyed one another miserably. How could they prosper under such a prior as this?

But worse was to follow, though it did not directly affect this house. The bill, so long threatened, dissolving the smaller houses, was passed in February by a Parliament carefully packed to carry out the King's wishes, and from which the spiritual peers were excluded by his "permission to them to absent themselves." Lewes Priory, of course, exceeded the limit of revenue under which other houses were suppressed, and even received one monk who had obtained permission to go there when his community fell; but in spite of the apparent encouragement from the preamble of the bill which stated that "in the great solemn monasteries . . . religion was right well kept," it was felt that this act was but the herald of another which should make an end of Religious Houses altogether.

But there was a breath of better news later on, when tidings came in the early summer that Anne was in disgrace. It was well known that it was her influence that egged the King on, and that there was none so fierce against the old ways. Was it not possible that Henry might even yet repent himself, if she were out of the way?

Then the tidings were confirmed, and for a while there was hope.

Sir Nicholas Maxwell rode over to see Chris, and was admitted into one of the parlors to talk with him.

He seemed furiously excited, and hardly saluted his brother-in-law.

"Chris," he said, "I have come straight from London with great news. The King's harlot is fallen."

Chris stared.

"Dead?" he said.

"Dead in a day or two, thank God!"

He spat furiously.

"God strike her!" he cried. "She has wrought all the mischief, I believe. They told me so a year back, but I did not believe it."

"And where is she?"

Then Nicholas told his story, his ruddy comely face bright with exultation, for he had no room for pity left. The rumors that had come to Lewes were true. Anne had been arrested suddenly at Greenwich during the sports, and had been sent straight to the Tower. The King was weary of her, though she had borne him a child; and did not scruple to bring the most odious charges against her. She had denied, and denied; but it was useless. She had wept and laughed in prison, and called on God to vindicate her; but the process went on nonetheless. The marriage had been declared null and void by Dr. Cranmer who had blessed it; and now she was condemned for sinning against it.

"But she is either his wife," said Chris amazed, "or else she is not guilty of adultery."

Nicholas chuckled.

"God save us, Chris; do you think Henry can't manage it?"

Then he grew white with passion, and beat the table and damned the King and Anne and Cranmer to hell together.

Chris glanced up, drumming his fingers softly on the table.

"Nick," he said, "there is no use in that. When is she to die?"

The knight's face flushed again with pleasure, and he showed his teeth set together.

"Two days," he said, "please God, or three at the most. And she will not meet those she has sent before her, or John Fisher whose head she had brought to her — the bloody Herodias!"

"Pray God that she will!" said Chris softly. "They will pray for her at least."

"Pah!" shouted Nicholas, "an eye for an eye for me!"

Chris said nothing. He was thinking of all that this might mean. Who could know what might not happen? Nicholas broke in again presently.

"I heard a fine tale," he said, "do you know that the woman is in the very room where she slept the night before the crowning? Last time it was for the crown to be put on; now it is for the head to be taken off. And it is true that she weeps and laughs. They can hear her laugh two storeys away, I hear."

"Nick," said Chris suddenly, "I am weary of that. Let her alone. Pray God she may turn!"

Nicholas stared astonished, and a little awed too. Chris used not to be like this; he seemed quieter and stronger; he had never dared to speak so before.

"Yes; I am weary of this," said Chris again. "I stormed once at Ralph, and gained nothing. We do not win by those weapons. Where is Ralph?"

Nicholas knit his lips to keep in the fury that urged him.

"He is with Cromwell still," he said venomously, "and very busy, I hear. They will be making him a lord soon — but there will be no lady."

Chris had heard of Beatrice's rejection of Ralph.

"He is still busy?"

"Why, yes; he worked long at this bill, I hear."

Chris asked a few more questions, and learned that Ralph seemed fiercer than ever since the Visitation. He was well-known at Court; had been seen riding with the King; and it was supposed that he was rising rapidly in favor every day.

"God help him!" sighed Chris.

The change that had come over Chris was very much marked. Neither a life in the world would have done it, nor one in the peace of the cloister; but an alternation of the two. He had been melted by the fire of the inner life, and braced by the external bitterness of adversity. Ralph's visit to the priory, culminating in the passionless salutation of him in the cloister as being a guest and therefore a representative of Christ, had ended that stage in the development of the monk's character. Chris was disappointed in his brother, fearful for him and stern in his attitude towards him; but he was not resentful. He was sincere when he prayed God to help him.

When Nicholas had eaten and gone, carrying messages to Mary, Chris told the others, and there was a revival of hope in the house.

Then a few days later came the news of Anne's death and of the marriage of the King with Jane Seymour on the following day. At least Jane was a lawful wife and queen in the Catholics' eyes, for Katharine too was dead.

*C*hris had now passed through the minor orders, the sub-diaconate and the diaconate, and was looking forward to priesthood. It had been thought advisable by his superiors, in view of the troubled state of the times, to apply for the necessary dispensations, and they had been granted without difficulty. So many monks who were not priests had been turned into the world resourceless, since they could not be appointed to benefices, that it was thought only fair to one who was already bound by vows of religion and sacred orders not to hold him back from an opportunity to make his living, should affairs be pushed further in the direction of dissolution.

He was looking forward with an extraordinary zeal to the crown of priesthood. It seemed to him a possession that would compensate for all other losses. If he could but make the Body of the Lord, lift It before the Throne, and hold It in his hands, all else was trifling.

There were waves of ecstatic peace again breaking over his soul as he thought of it; as he moved behind the celebrant at high mass, lifted the pall of the chalice, and sang the exultant *Ite missa est* when all was done. What a power would be his on that day! He would have his finger then on the huge engine of grace, and could turn it whither he would, spraying infinite force on this and that soul, on Ralph stubbornly fighting against God in London, on his mother silent and bitter at home, on his father anxious and courageous, waiting for disaster, on Margaret trembling in Rusper nunnery as she contemplated the defiance she had flung in the King's face.

The Prior had given him but little encouragement; he had sent for him one day, and told him that he might prepare himself for priesthood by Michaelmas, for a foreign bishop was coming to them, and leave would be obtained for him to administer the rite. But he had not said a word of counsel or congratulation; but had nodded to the young monk, and turned his sickly face to the papers again on his table.

Dom Anthony, the pleasant stout guest-master, who had preached the sermon in Christmastide, said a word of comfort, as they walked in the cloister together.

"You must not take it amiss, brother," he said, "my Lord Prior is beside himself with terror. He does not know how to act."

Chris asked whether there were any new reason for alarm.

"Oh, no!" said the monk, "but the people are getting cold towards us here. You have seen how few come to mass here now, or to confession. They are going to the secular priests instead."

Chris remembered one or two other instances of this growing coldness. The poor folks who came for food complained of its quality two or three times; and one fellow, an old pensioner of the house, who had lost a leg, threw his portion down on the doorstep.

"I will have better than that some day," he had said, as he limped off. Chris had gathered up the cold lentils patiently and carried them back to the kitchen.

On another day a farmer had flatly refused a favor to the monk who superintended the priory-farm.

"I will not have your beasts in my orchard," he had said roughly. "You are not my masters."

The congregations too were visibly declining, as the guest-master had said. The great nave beyond the screen looked desolate in the summer-mornings, as the sunlight lay in colored patches on the wide empty pavement between the few faithful gathered in front, and the half dozen loungers who leaned in the shadow of the west wall — men who fulfilled their obligation of hearing mass, with a determination to do so with the least inconvenience to themselves, and who scuffled out before the blessing.

It was evident that the tide of faith and reverence was beginning to ebb even in the quiet country towns.

As the summer drew on the wider world too had its storms. A fierce sermon was preached at the opening of Convocation, by Dr. Latimer, now Bishop of Worcester, at the express desire of the Archbishop, that scourged not only the regular but the secular clergy as well. The sermon too was more furiously Protestant than any previously preached on such an occasion; pilgrimages, the stipends for masses, image-worship, and the use of an unknown tongue in divine service, were alike denounced as contrary to the "pure gospel." The phrases of Luther were abundantly used in the discourse; and it was evident, from the fact that no public censure fell upon the preacher, that Henry's own religious views had developed since the day that he had published his attack on the foreign reformers.

The proceedings of Convocation confirmed the suspicion that the sermon aroused. With an astonishing compliance the clergy first ratified the decree of nullity in the matter of Anne's marriage with the King, disclaimed obedience to Rome, and presented a list of matters for which they requested reform. In answer to this last point the King, assisted by a couple of bishops, sent down to the houses, a month later, a paper of articles to which the clergy instantly agreed. These articles proceeded in the direction of Protestantism through omission rather than affirmation. Baptism, Penance and the Sacrament of the Altar were spoken of in Catholic terms; the other four sacraments were omitted altogether; on the other hand, again, devotion to saints, image-worship, and prayers for the departed were enjoined with important qualifications.

Finally it was agreed to support the King in his refusal to be represented at the proposed General Council at Mantua.

*T*he tidings of all this, filtering in to the house at Lewes by priests and Religious who stayed there from time to time, did not tend to reassure those who looked for peace. The assault was not going to stop at matters of discipline; it was dogma that was aimed at, and, worse even than that, the foundation on which dogma rested. It was not an affair of Religious Houses, or even of morality; there was concerned the very Rock itself on which Christendom based all faith and morals. If it was once admitted that a National Church, apart from the See of Rome, could in the smallest degree adjudicate on a point of doctrine, the unity of the Catholic Church as understood by every monk in the house, was immediately ruptured.

Again and again in chapter there were terrible scenes. The Prior raved weakly, crying that it was not the part of a good Catholic to resist his prince, that the Apostle himself enjoined obedience to those in authority; that the new light of learning had illuminated perplexing problems; and that in the uncertainty it was safer to follow the certain duty of civil obedience. Dom Anthony answered that a greater than St. Paul had bidden His followers to render to God the things that were God's; that St. Peter was crucified sooner than obey Nero — and the Prior cried out for silence; and that he could not hear his Christian King likened to the heathen emperor. Monk after monk would rise; one following his Prior, and disclaiming personal learning and responsibility; another with ironic deference saying that a man's soul was his own, and that not even a Religious Superior could release from the biddings of conscience; another would balance himself between the parties, declaring that the distinction of duties was insoluble; that in such a case as this it was impossible to know what was due to God and what to man. Yet another voice would rise from time to time declaring that the tales that they heard were incredible; that it was impossible that the King should intend such evil against the Church; he still heard his three masses a day as he had always done; there was no more ardent defender of the Sacrament of the Altar.

Chris used to steady himself in this storm of words as well as he could, by reflecting that he probably would not have to make a decision, for it would be done for him, at least as regarded his life in the convent or out, by his superiors. Or again he would fix his mind resolutely on his approaching priesthood; while the Prior sat gnawing his lips, playing with his cross and rapping his foot, before bursting out again and bidding them all be silent, for they knew not what they were meddling with.

The misery rose to its climax when the Injunctions arrived; and the chapter sat far into the morning, meeting again after dinner to consider them.

These were directions, issued to the clergy throughout the country, by the authority of the King alone; and this very fact was significant of what the Royal Supremacy meant. Some of them did not touch the Religious, and were intended only for parish-priests; but others were bitterly hard to receive.

The community was informed that in future, once in every quarter, a sermon was to be preached against the Bishop of Rome's usurped power; the Ten Articles, previously issued, were to be brought before the notice of the congregation; and careful instructions were to be given as regards superstition in the matter of praying to the saints. It was the first of these that caused the most strife.

Dom Anthony, who was becoming more and more the leader of the conservative party, pointed out that the See of Peter was to every Catholic the root of authority and unity, and that Christianity itself was imperiled if this rock were touched.

The Prior angrily retorted that it was not the Holy See that was to be assaulted, but the erection falsely raised upon it; it was the abuse of power, not the use of it that had to be denounced.

Dom Anthony requested the Prior to inform him where the line of distinction lay; and the Prior in answer burst into angry explanations, instancing the pecuniary demands of the Pope, the appointment of foreigners to English benefices, and all the rest of the accusations that were playing such a part now in the religious controversy of the country.

Dom Anthony replied that those were not the matters principally aimed at by the Injunction; it concerned rather the whole constitution of Christ's Church, and was a question of the Pope's or the King's supremacy over that part of it that lay in England.

Finally the debate was ended by the Prior's declaration that he could trust no one to preach the enjoined sermon but himself, and that he would see to it on his own responsibility.

It was scarcely an inspiring atmosphere for one who was preparing to take on him the burden of priesthood in the Catholic Church.

Chapter II
SACERDOS IN AETERNUM

*I*t was a day of wonderful autumn peace when Chris first sang mass in the presence of the Community.

The previous day he had received priesthood from the hands of the little old French bishop in the priory church; one by one strange mystical ceremonies had been performed; the stole had been shifted and crossed on the breast, the token of Christ's yoke; the chasuble had been placed over his head, looped behind; then the rolling cry to the Spirit of God who alone seals to salvation and office had pealed round the high roof and down the long nave that stretched away westwards in sunlit gloom; while across the outstretched hands of the monk had been streaked the sacred oil, giving him the power to bless the things of God. The hands were bound up, as if to heal the indelible wound of love that had been inflicted on them; and, before they were unbound, into the hampered fingers were slid the sacred vessels of the altar, occupied now by the elements of bread and wine; while the awful power to offer sacrifice for the quick and the dead was committed to him in one tremendous phrase.

Then the mass went on; and the new priest, kneeling with Dom Anthony at a little bench set at the foot of the altar steps, repeated aloud with the bishop the words of the liturgy from the great painted missal lying before him.

How strange it had been too when all was over! He stood by a pillar in the nave, beneath St. Pancras's image, while all came to receive his blessing. First, the Prior, pale and sullen, as always now; then the Community, some smiling and looking into his eyes before they knelt, some perfunctory, some solemn and sedate with downcast faces; each kissed the fragrant hands, and stood aside, while the laity came up; and first among them his father and Mary.

His place too in the refectory had a flower or two laid beside it; and the day had gone by in a bewildering dream. He had walked with his father and sister a little, and had found himself smiling and silent in their company.

In the evening he had once more gone through the ceremonies of mass, Dom Anthony stood by, and watched and reminded and criticized. And now the morning was come, and he stood at the altar.

*T*he little wind had dropped last night, and the hills round Lewes stood in mellow sunlight; the atmosphere was full of light and warmth, that tender glow that falls on autumn days; the trees in the court outside stood, poised on the brink of sleep, with a yellow pallor tinging their leaves; the thousand pigeons exulted and wheeled in the intoxicating air.

The shadowy church was alight with sunshine that streamed through the clerestory windows on to the heavy pillars, the unevenly paved floor, and crept down the recumbent figures of noble and bishop from head to foot. There were a few people present beyond the screen, Sir James and his daughter in front, watching with a tender reverence the harvesting of the new priest, as he prepared to gather under his hands the mystical wheat and grapes of God.

Chris was perfectly practiced in his ceremonies; and there was no anxiety to dissipate the overpowering awe that lay on his soul. He felt at once natural and unreal; it was supremely natural that he should be here; he could not conceive being other than a priest; there was in him a sense of a relaxed rather than an intensified strain; and yet the whole matter was strange and intangible, as he felt the supernatural forces gathering round, and surging through his soul.

He was aware of a dusky sunlit space about him, of the glimmer of the high candles; and nearer of the white cloth, the shining vessels, the gorgeous missal, and the rustle of the ministers' vestments. But the whole was shot with an inner life, each detail was significant and sacramental; and he wondered sometimes at the inaudible vibration that stirred the silent air round him, as he spoke the familiar words to which he had listened so often.

He kept his eyes resolutely down as he turned from time to time, spreading his hands to the people, and was only partly conscious of the faces watching him from the dark stalls in front and the sunlit nave beyond. Even the sacred ministers, Dom Anthony and another, seemed to be little more than crimson impersonal figures that moved and went about their stately business with deft and gracious hands.

As he began to penetrate more nearly to the heart of the mystery, and the angels' song before the throne rolled up from the choir, there was an experience of a yet further retirement from the things of sense. Even the glittering halpas, and the gleams of light above it where the five chapels branched behind — even these things became shrouded; there was just a sheet of white beneath him, the glow of a chalice, and the pale disc of the sacrificial bread.

Then, as he paused, with hands together — *"famulorum famularumque tuarum"* — there opened out the world where his spirit was bending its intention. Figure after figure came up and passed before his closed eyes, and on each he turned the beam of God's grace. First Ralph, sneering and aloof in his rich dress, intent on some Satanic business; — Chris seized as it were the power of God, and enveloped and penetrated him with it. Then Margaret, waiting terrified on the divine will; his mother in her complacent bitterness; Mary; his father — and as he thought of him it seemed as if all God's blessings were not too great; Nicholas; his own brethren in religion, his Prior, contracted and paralyzed with terror; Dom Anthony, with his pathetic geniality. . . .

Ah! how short was the time; and yet so long that the Prior looked up sharply, and the deacon shifted in his rustling silk.

Then again the hands opened, and the stately flood of petition poured on, as through open gates to the boundless sea that awaited it, where the very heart of God was to absorb it into Itself.

The great names began to flit past, like palaces on a river-brink, their bases washed by the pouring liturgy — Peter and Paul, Simon and Thaddeus, Cosmas and Damian — vast pleasure houses alight with God, while near at hand now gleamed the line of the infinite ocean.

The hands came together, arched in blessing; and it marked the first sting of the healing water, as the Divine Essence pushed forward to meet man's need.

"Hanc igitur oblatianem . . ."

Then followed the swift silent signs, as if the pilot were ordering sails out to meet the breeze.

The muttering voice sank to a deliberate whisper, the ripples ceased to leap as the river widened, and Chris was delicately fingering the white linen before taking the Host into his hands.

There was a swift glance up, as to the great Sun that burned overhead, one more noiseless sign, and he sank forward in unutterable awe, with his arms on the altar, and the white disc, hovering on the brink of non-existence, beneath his eyes.

*T*he faintest whisper rose from behind as the people shifted their constrained attitudes. Sir James glanced up, his eyes full of tears, at the distant crimson figure beneath the steady row of lights, motionless with outspread hands, poised over the bosom of God's Love.

The first murmured words broke the silence; as if next to the Infinite Pity rose up the infinite need of man — *Nobis quoque peccatoribus* — and sank to silence again.

Then loud and clear rang out *Per omnia saecula saeculorum;* and the choir of monks sang *Amen.*

So the great mystery moved on, but upborne now by the very Presence itself that sustained all things. From the limitless sea of mercy, the children cried through the priest's lips to their Father who was in heaven, and entreated the Lamb of God who takes away sin to have mercy on them and give them peace.

Then from far beyond the screen Mary could see how the priest leaning a little forward towards That which he bore in his hands, looked on what he bore in them; and she whispered softly with him the words that he was speaking. *Ave in aeternum sanctissima caro Christi . . .*

Again she hid her face; and when she raised it once, all was over, and the Lord had entered and sanctified the body and soul of the man at whose words He had entered the creature of bread.

The father and daughter stood together silently in the sunshine outside the west end of the church, waiting for Chris. He had promised to come to them there for a moment when his thanksgiving was done.

Beyond the wall, and the guest-house where the Visitors had lived those two disastrous days, rose up the far sunlit downs, shadowed here and there with cuplike hollows, standing like the walls about Jerusalem.

As they turned, on the right above the red roofs of the town, rose the downs again, vast slopes and shoulders, over which Chris had ridden so short a while ago bearded and brown with hunting. It was over there that Ralph had come, through that dip, which seemed against the skyline a breach in a high wall.

Ah! surely God would spare this place; so stately and quiet, so graciously sheltered by the defenses that He Himself had raised! If all England tottered and fell, this at least might stand, this vast home of prayer that stirred day and night with the praises of the Eternal and the petitions of the mortal — this glorious house where a priest so dear to them had brought forth from his mystical paternity the very Son of God!

The door opened behind them, and Chris came out pale and smiling with a little anxious-eyed monk beside him. His eyes lightened as he saw them standing there; but he turned again for a moment.

"Yes — father," he said. "What was it?"

"You stayed too long," said the other, "at the *famularumque tuarum*; the rubric says *nullus nimis immoretur*, you know; — *nimis immoretur.*"

"Yes," said Chris.

Chapter III
THE NORTHERN RISING

A few of the smaller Religious houses had surrendered themselves to the King before the passing of the bill in the early spring; and the rest of them were gradually yielded up after its enactment during the summer of the same year; and among them was Rusper. Chris heard that his sister Margaret had returned to Overfield, and would stay there for the present.

Throughout the whole of England there were the same scenes to be witnessed. A troop of men, headed by a Commissioner, would ride up one evening to some village where a little convent stood, demand entrance at the gate, pass through, and disappear from the eyes of the watching crowd. Then the next day the work would begin; the lead would be stripped from the church and buildings; the treasures corded in bundles; the woodwork of the interior put up to auction on the village green; and a few days later the troop would disappear again, heavily laden, leaving behind roofless walls, and bewildered Religious in their new secular dress with a few shillings in their pockets, staring after the rich cavalcade and wondering what was best to do.

It had been hoped that the King would stay his hand at the death of Anne, and even yet return to the obedience of the Holy See. The Pope was encouraged to think so by the authorities on the continent, and in

England itself there prevailed even confidence that a return to the old ways would be effected. But Henry had gone too far; he had drunk too deeply of the wealth that lay waiting for him in the treasuries of the Religious houses, and after a pause of expectation he set his hand to the cup again. It was but natural too, and for more noble motives, to such a character as his. As he had aimed in his youth at nothing less than supremacy in tennis, hunting and tourney, and later in architecture, music and theological reputation; as, for the same reason Wolsey had fallen, when the King looked away from girls and sports to the fiercer game of politics; so now it was intolerable to Henry that there should be even the shadow of a spiritual independence within his domain.

A glow of resentful disappointment swept through the North of England at the news. It burst out into flame in Lincolnshire, and was not finally quenched until the early summer of the following year.

*T*he news that reached Lewes from time to time during the winter and spring sent the hearts of all that heard it through the whole gamut of emotions. At one time fierce hope, then despair, then rising confidence, then again blank hopelessness — each in turn tore the souls of the monks; and misery reached its climax in the summer at the news of the execution at Tyburn of the Abbots of Jervaulx and Fountains, with other monks and gentlemen.

The final recital of the whole tragedy was delivered to them at the mouth of a Religious from the Benedictine cell at Middlesborough who had been released by the Visitors at his own request, but who had afterwards repented and joined the rising soon after the outset; he had been through most of the incidents, and then when failure was assured had fled south in terror for his life, and was now on his way to the Continent to take up his monastic vocation once more.

The Prior was away on one of the journeys that he so frequently undertook at this time, no man knew whither, or the ex-monk and rebel would have been refused admittance; but the sub-Prior was persuaded to take him in for a night, and he sat long in one of the parlors that evening telling his story.

Chris leaned against the wall and watched him as he talked with the candlelight on his face. He was a stout middle-aged man in layman's dress, for he was not yet out of peril; he sat forward in his chair, making preacher's gestures as he spoke, and using well-chosen vivid words.

"They were gathered already when I joined them on their way to York; there were nearly ten thousand of them on the road, with Aske at their head. I have never set eyes on such a company! There was a troop of gentlemen and their sons riding with Aske in front, all in armor; and then the rabble behind with gentlemen again to their officers. The common folk had pikes and hooks only; and some were in leather harness, and some without; but they marched well and kept good order. They were of all sorts: hairy men and boys; and miners from the North. There were monks, too, and friars, I know not how many, that went with the army to encourage them; and everywhere we went the women ran out of their homes with food and drink, and prayed God to bless us; and the bells were rung in the village churches. We slept as we could, some in houses, some in churchyards and by the wayside, and as many of us as could get into the churches heard mass each day. As many too as could make them, wore the Five Wounds on a piece of stuff sewn on the arm. You would have said that none could stand against us, so eager we were and full of faith."

"There was a song, was there not?" began one of the monks.

"Yes, father. We sang it as we went.

"Christ crucified!
  For thy wounds wide
  Us commons guide
    Which pilgrims be!
  Through God his grace
  For to purchase
  Old wealth and peace
    Of the spiritualty!

"You could hear it up and down the lines, sung with weeping and shouting."

He described how they came to York, and how the Mayor was forced to admit them. They stayed there a couple of days; and Aske published his directions for all the ejected Religious to return to their houses.

"I went to a little cell near by — I forget its name — to help some canons to settle in again, whose friendship I had made. I had told them then that my mind was to enter Religion once more, and they took me very willingly. We got there at night. The roof was gone from the dormitory, but we slept there for all that — such of us as could sleep — for I heard one of them sobbing for joy as he lay there in his old corner under the stars; and we sang mass in the morning, as well as we could. The priest had an old tattered vestment that hardly hung on his shoulders; and there was no cross but one that came from a pair of beads, and that we hung over the altar. When I left them again, they were at their office as before, and busy roofing the house with old timbers; for my lord Cromwell had all the lead. And all their garden was trampled; but they said they would do very well. The village-folk were their good friends, and would bring them what they needed."

He described his journey to Doncaster; the furious excitement of the villages he passed through, and the news that reached him hour after hour as to the growing vastness of Aske's forces.

"There were thirty thousand, I heard, on the banks of the Don on one side; for my lords Nevill and Lumley and others had ridden in with St. Cuthbert his banner and arms, and five thousand men, besides those that came in from all the country. And on the further side was my Lord Shrewsbury for the King, with the Duke and his men. Master Aske had all he could do to keep his men back from being at them. Some of the young sparks were as terriers at a rat-hole. There was a parley held on the bridge, for Norfolk knew well that he must gain time; and Aske sent his demands to his Grace, and that was the mistake —"

The man beat one hand into the other and looked round with a kindling force —

"That was the mistake! He was too loyal for such work, and did not guess at their craft. Well, while we waited there, our men began to make off; their farms were wanting them, and their wives and the rest, and we melted. Master Aske had to be everywhere at once, it was no fault of his. My Lord Derby was marching up upon the houses again, and seeking to drive the monks out once more. But there was not an act of violence done by our men; not a penny-piece taken or a house burned. They were peaceable folk, and asked no more than that their old religion should be given back to them, and that they might worship God as they had always done."

He went on to explain how the time had been wasted in those fruitless negotiations, and how the force dwindled day by day. Various answers were attempted by the King, containing both threats and promises, and in these, as in all else the hand of Cromwell was evident. Finally, towards the end of November, the insurgents gathered again for another meeting with the King's representatives at Doncaster, summoned by beacons on the top of the high Yorkshire moors, and by the reversed pealing of the church bells.

"We had a parley among ourselves at Pomfret first, and had a great to-do, though I saw little of it; and drew up our demands; and then set out for Doncaster again. The duke was there, with the King's pardon in his hand, in the Whitefriars; and a promise that all should be as we asked. So we went back to Pomfret, well-pleased, and the next day on St. Thomas' hill the herald read the pardon to us all; and we, poor fools, thought that his Grace meant to keep his word —"

The monk looked bitterly round, sneering with his white strong teeth set together like a savage dog's; and there was silence for a moment. The Sub-Prior looked nervously round the faces of his subjects, for this was treasonable talk to hear.

Then the man went on. He himself it seemed had retired again to the little cell where he had seen the canons settled in a few weeks previously; and heard nothing of what was going forward; except that the heralds were going about the country, publishing the King's pardon to all who had taken part in the Rebellion, and affixing it to the market-cross in each town and village, with touching messages from the King relating to the grief which he had felt on hearing that his dear children believed such tales about him.

Little by little, however, the discontent began to smolder once more, for the King's pledges of restoration were not fulfilled; and Cromwell, who was now recognized to be the inspirer of all the evil done against Religion, remained as high as ever in the royal favor. Aske, who had been to the King in person, and given him an account of all that had taken place, now wrote to him that there was a danger of a further rising if the delay continued, for there were no signs yet of the promised free parliament being called at York.

Then again disturbances had broken out.

"I was at Hull," said the monk, "with Sir Francis Bygod in January; but we did nothing, and only lost our leader, and all the while Norfolk was creeping up with his army. It was piteous to think what might not have been done if we had not trusted his Grace; but 'twas no good, and I was back again in the dales here and there, hiding for my life by April. Everywhere 'twas the same; the monks were haled out again from their houses, and men were hanged by the score. I cut down four myself near Meux, and gave them Christian burial at night. One was a monk, and hanged in his habit. But the worst of all was at York."

The man's face twitched with emotion, and he passed his hand over his mouth once or twice before continuing.

"I did not dare to go into the court for fear I should be known; but I stood outside in the crowd and watched them go in. There was a fellow riding with Norfolk — a false knave of a man whom we had all learnt to hate at Doncaster — for he was always jeering at us secretly and making mischief when he could. I saw him with the duke before, when we went into the Whitefriars for the pardon; and he stood there behind with the look of a devil on his face; and now here he was again —"

"His name, sir?" put in Dom Adrian.

"Torridon, father, Torridon! He was a —"

There was a sharp movement in the room, so that the monk stopped and looked round him amazed. Chris felt the blood ebb from his heart and din in his ears, and he swayed a little as he leaned against the wall. He saw Dom Anthony lean forward and whisper to the stranger; and through the haze that was before his eyes saw the other look at him sharply, with a fallen jaw.

Then the monk rose and made a little stiff inclination to Chris, deferential and courteous, but with a kind of determined dignity in it too.

When Chris had recovered himself, the monk was deep in his story, but Ralph had fallen out of it.

"You would not believe it," he was saying, "but on the very jury that was to try Master Aske and Constable, there were empanelled their own blood-relations; and that by the express intention of Norfolk. John Aske was one of them, and some others who had to wives the sons of my Lord Darcy and Sir Robert Constable. You see how it would be. If the prisoners were found guilty, men would say that it must be so, for that their own kin had condemned them; and if they were to be acquitted, then these men themselves would be cast."

There again broke out a murmur from the listening faces, as the man paused.

"Well, they were cast, as you know, for not taking the King to be the supreme head of the Church, and for endeavoring to force the King to hold a parliament that he willed not. And I was at York again when Master Aske was brought back from London to be hanged, and I saw it!"

Again an uncontrollable emotion shook him; and he propped his face on his hand as he ended his tale.

"There were many of his friends there in the crowd, and scarcely one dared to cry out, God save you, sir. . . . I dared not. . . ."

He gave one rending sob, and Chris felt his eyes prick with tears at the sight of so much sorrow. It was piteous to see a brave man thinking himself a coward.

Dom Anthony leaned forward.

"Thank you, father," he said, though his voice was a little husky, "and thank God that he died well. You have touched all our hearts."

"I was a hound," sobbed the man, "a hound, that I did not cry out to him and tell him that I loved him."

"No, no, father," said the other tenderly, "you must not think so. You must serve God well now, and pray for his soul."

The bell sounded out for Compline as he spoke, and the monks rose. "You will come into choir, father," said the Sub-Prior.

The man nodded, stood up, and followed him out.

Chris was in a strange ferment as he stood in his stall that night. It had been sad enough to hear of that gallant attempt to win back the old liberties and the old Faith — that attempt that had been a success except for the insurgents' trust in their King — and of the death of the leaders.

But across the misery had pierced a more poignant grief, as he had learnt how Ralph's hand was in this too and had taken once more the wrong side in God's quarrel. But still he had no resentment; the conflict had passed out of the personal plane into an higher, and he thought of his brother as God's enemy rather than his own. Would his prayers then never prevail — the prayers that he speeded up in the smoke of the great Sacrifice morning by morning for that zealous mistaken soul? Or was it perhaps that that brother of his must go deeper yet, before coming out to knowledge and pardon?

Chapter IV

THE DESTRUCTION OF THE SEAL

*T*he autumn drew in swiftly. The wet southwest wind blew over the downs that lay between Lewes and the sea, and beat down the loose browning leaves of the trees about the Priory. The grass in the cloister-garth grew rank and dark with the constant rain that drove and dropped over the high roofs.

And meanwhile the tidings grew heavier still.

After Michaelmas the King set to work in earnest. He had been checked by the northern risings, and still paused to see whether the embers had been wholly quenched; and then when it was evident that the North was as submissive as the South, began again his business of gathering in the wealth that was waiting.

He started first in the North, under show of inflicting punishment for the encouragement that the Religious had given to the late rebellions; and one by one the great abbeys were tottering. Furness and Sawley had already fallen, with Jervaulx and the other houses, and Holme Cultram was placed under the care of a superior who could be trusted to hand over his charge when called upon.

But up to the present not many great houses had actually fallen, except those which were supposed to have taken a share in the revolt; and owing to the pains taken by the Visitors to contradict the report that the King intended to lay his hands on the whole monastic property of England, it was even hoped by a few sanguine souls that the large houses might yet survive.

There were hot discussions in the chapter at Lewes from time to time during the year. The "Bishops' Book," issued by a committee of divines and approved by the King, and containing a digest of the new Faith that was being promulgated, arrived during the summer and was fiercely debated; but so high ran the feeling that the Prior dropped the matter, and the book was put away with other papers of the kind on an honorable but little-used shelf.

The acrimony in domestic affairs began to reach its climax in October, when the prospects of the Priory's own policy came up for discussion.

Some maintained that they were safe, and that quietness and confidence were their best security, and these had the support of the Prior; others declared that the best hope lay in selling the possessions of the house at a low price to some trustworthy man who would undertake to sell then back again at only a small profit to himself when the storm was passed.

The Prior rose in wrath when this suggestion was made.

"Would you have me betray my King?" he cried. "I tell you I will have none of it. It is not worthy of a monk to have such thoughts."

And he sat down and would hear no more, nor speak.

There were whispered conferences after that among the others, as to what his words meant. Surely there was nothing dishonorable in the device; they only sought to save what was their own! And how would the King be "betrayed" by such an action?

They had an answer a fortnight later; and it took them wholly by surprise.

During the second week in November the Prior had held himself more aloof than ever; only three or four of the monks, with the Sub-Prior among them, were admitted to his cell, and they were there at all hours. Two or three strangers too arrived on horseback, and were entertained by the Prior in a private parlor. And then on the morning of the fourteenth the explanation came.

When the usual business of the chapter was done, the faults confessed and penances given, and one or two small matters settled, the Prior, instead of rising to give the signal to go, remained in his chair, his head bent on to his hand.

It was a dark morning, heavy and lowering; and from where Chris sat at the lower end of the great chamber he could scarcely make out the features of those who sat under the high window at the east; but as soon as the Prior lifted his face and spoke, he knew by that tense strain of the voice that something impended.

"There is another matter," said the Prior; and paused again.

For a moment there was complete silence. The Sub-Prior leant a little forward and was on the point of speaking, when his superior lifted his head again and straightened himself in his chair.

"It is this," he said, and his voice rang hard and defiant, "it is this. It is useless to think we can save ourselves. We are under suspicion, and worse than suspicion. I have hoped, and prayed, and striven to know God's will; and I have talked with my Lord Cromwell not once or twice, but often. And it is useless to resist any further."

His voice cracked with misery; but Chris saw him grip the bosses of his chair-arms in an effort for self-control. His own heart began to sicken; this was not frightened raving such as he had listened to before; it was the speech of one who had been driven into decision, as a rat into a corner.

"I have talked with the Sub-Prior, and others; and they think with me in this. I have kept it back from the rest, that they might serve God in peace so long as was possible. But now I must tell you all, my sons, that we must leave this place."

There was a hush of terrible tension. The monks had known that they were threatened; they could not think otherwise with the news that came from all parts, but they had not known that catastrophe was so imminent. An old monk opposite Chris began to moan and mutter; but the Prior went on immediately.

"At least I think that we must leave. It may be otherwise, if God has pity on us; I do not know; but we must be ready to leave, if it be His will, and, — and to say so."

He was speaking in abrupt sentences, with pauses between, in which he appeared to summon his resolution to speak again, and force out his tale. There was plainly more behind too; and his ill-ease seemed to deepen on him.

"I wish no one to speak now," he said, "Instead of the Lady-mass tomorrow we shall sing mass of the Holy Ghost; and afterwards I shall have more to say to you again. I do not desire any to hold speech with any other, but to look into their own hearts and seek counsel of God there."

He still sat a moment silent, then rose and gave the signal.

*I*t was a strange day for Chris. He did not know what to think, but he was certain that they had not yet been told all. The Prior's silences had been as pregnant as his words. There was something very close now that would be revealed immediately, and meanwhile he must think out how to meet it.

The atmosphere seemed charged all day; the very buildings wore a strange air, unfamiliar and menacing. The intimate bond between his soul and them, knit by associations of prayer and effort, appeared unreal and flimsy. He was tormented by doubtfulness; he could not understand on the one side how it was possible to yield to the King, on the other how it was possible to resist. No final decision could be made by him until he had heard the minds of his fellows; and fortunately they would all speak before him. He busied himself then with disentangling the strands of motive, desire, fear and hope, and waited for the shaking loose of the knot until he knew more.

Mass of the Holy Ghost was sung next morning by the Prior himself in red vestments; and Chris waited with expectant awe, remembering how the Carthusians under like circumstances had been visited by God; but the Host was uplifted and the bell rang; and there was nothing but the candle-lit gloom of the choir about the altar, and the sigh of the wind in the chapels behind.

Then in the chapter-meeting the Prior told them all.

*H*e reminded them how they had prayed that morning for guidance, and that they must be fearless now in following it out. It was easy to be reckless and call it faith, but prudence and reasonable common-sense were attributes of the Christian no less than trust in God. They had not to consider now what they would wish for themselves, but what God intended for them so far as they could read it in the signs of the times.

"For myself," he cried, — and Chris almost thought him sincere as he spoke, so kindled was his face — "for myself I should ask no more than to live and die in this place, as I had hoped. Every stone here is as dear to me as to you, and I think more dear, for I have been in a special sense the lord of it all; but I dare not think of that. We must be ready to leave all willingly if God wills. We thought that we had yielded all to follow Christ when we first set our necks here under His sweet yoke; but I think He asks of us even more now; and that we should go out from here even as we went out from our homes ten or twenty years ago. We shall be no further from our God outside this place; and we may be even nearer if we go out according to His will."

He seemed on fire with zeal and truth. His timid peevish air was gone, and his delicate scholarly face was flushed as he spoke. Chris was astonished, and more perplexed than ever. Was it then possible that God's will might lie in the direction he feared?

"Now this is the matter which we have to consider," went on the Prior more quietly. "His Grace has sent to ask, through a private messenger from my Lord Cromwell, whether we will yield up the priory. There is no compulsion in the matter —" he paused significantly — "and his Grace desires each to act according to his judgment and conscience, of — of his own free will."

There was a dead silence.

The news was almost expected by now. Through the months of anxiety each monk had faced the probability of such tidings coming to him sooner or later; and the last few days had brought expectation to its climax. Yet it was hard to see the enemy face to face, and to know that there was no possibility of resisting him finally.

The Sub-Prior rose to his feet and began to speak, glancing as if for corroboration to his superior from time to time. His mouth worked a little at the close of each sentence.

"My Lord Prior has shown us his own mind, and I am with him in the matter. His Grace treats us like his own children; he wishes us to be loving and obedient. But, as a father too, he has authority behind to compel us to his will if we will not submit. And, as my Lord Prior said yesterday, we do not know whether or no his Grace will not permit us to remain here after all, if we are docile; or perhaps refound the priory out of his own bounty. There is talk of the Chertsey monks going to the London Charterhouse from Bisham where the King set them last year. But we may be sure he will not do so with us if we resist his will now. I on my part then am in favor of yielding up the house willingly, and trusting ourselves to his Grace's clemency."

There was again silence as he sat down; and a pause of a minute or two before Dom Anthony rose. His ruddy face was troubled and perplexed; but he spoke resolutely enough.

He said that he could not understand why the matter had not been laid before them earlier, that they might have had time to consider it. The question was an extremely difficult one to the consciences of some of them. On the one hand there was the peril of acquiescing in sacrilege — the Prior twisted in his seat as he heard this — and on the other of willfully and petulantly throwing away their only opportunity of saving their priory. He asked for time.

Several more made speeches, some in favor of the proposal, and some asking, as Dom Anthony had done, for further tine for consideration. They had no precedents, they said, on which to decide such a question, for they understood that it was not on account of treason that they were required to surrender the house and property.

The Prior rose with a white face.

"No, no," he cried. "God forbid! That is over and done with. I — we have made our peace with my Lord Cromwell in that affair."

"Then why," asked Dom Anthony, "are we required to yield it?"

The Prior glanced helplessly at him.

"I — it is as a sign that the King is temporal lord of the land."

"We do not deny that," said the other.

"Some do," said the Prior feebly.

There was a little more discussion. Dom Anthony remarked that it was not a matter of temporal but spiritual headship that was in question. To meddle with the Religious Orders was to meddle with the Vicar of Christ under whose special protection they were; and it seemed to him at least a probable opinion, so far as he had had time to consider it, that to yield, even in the hopes of saving their property ultimately, was to acquiesce in the repudiation of the authority of Rome.

And so it went on for an hour; and then as it grew late, the Prior rose once more, and asked if anyone had a word to say who had not yet spoken.

Chris had intended to speak, but all that he wished to ask had already been stated by others; and he sat now silent, staring up at the Prior, and down at the smooth boarded floor at his feet. He had not an idea what to do. He was no theologian.

Then the Prior unmasked his last gun.

"As regards the matter of time for consideration, that is now passed. In spite of what some have said we have had sufficient warning. All here must have known that the choice would be laid before them, for months past; it is now an answer that is required of us."

He paused a moment longer. His lips began to tremble, but he made a strong effort and finished.

"Master Petre will be here tonight, as my lord Cromwell's representative, and will sit in the chapter-house tomorrow to receive the surrender."

Dom Anthony started to his feet. The Prior made a violent gesture for silence, and then gave the signal to break up.

*A*gain the bewildering day went past. The very discipline of the house was a weakness in the defense of the surprised party. It was impossible for them to meet and discuss the situation as they wished; and even the small times of leisure seemed unusually occupied. Dom Anthony was busy at the guest-house; one of the others who had spoken against the proposal was sent off on a message by the Prior, and another was ordered to assist the sacristan to clean the treasures in view of the Visitor's coming.

Chris was not able to ask a word of advice from any of those whom he thought to be in sympathy with him.

He sat all day over his antiphonary, in the little carrel off the cloister, and as he worked his mind toiled like a mill.

He had progressed a long way with the work now, and was engaged on the pages that contained the antiphons for Lent. The design was soberer here; the angels that had rested among the green branches and early roses of Septuagesima, thrusting here a trumpet and there a harp among the leaves, had taken flight, and grave menacing creatures were in their place. A jackal looked from behind the leafless trunk, a lion lifted his toothed mouth to roar from a thicket of thorns, as they had lurked and bellowed in the bleak wilderness above the Jordan fifteen hundred years ago. They were gravely significant now, he thought; and scarcely knowing what he did he set narrow human eyes in the lion's face (for he knew no better) and broadened the hanging jaws with a delicate line or two.

Then with a fierce impulse he crowned him, and surmounted the crown with a cross.

And all the while his mind toiled at the problem. There were three things open to him on the morrow. Either he might refuse to sign the surrender, and take whatever consequences might follow; or he might sign it; and there were two processes of thought by which he might take that action. By the first he would simply make an act of faith in his superiors, and do what they did because they did it; by the second he would sign it of his own responsibility because he decided to think that by doing so he would be taking the best action for securing his own monastic life.

He considered these three. To refuse to sign almost inevitably involved his ruin, and that not only, and not necessarily, in the worldly sense; about that he sincerely believed he did not care; but it would mean his exclusion from any concession that the King might afterwards make. He certainly would not be allowed under any circumstances, to remain in the home of his profession; and if the community was shifted he would not be allowed to go with them. As regards the second alternative he wondered whether it was possible to shift responsibility in that manner; as regards the third, he knew that he had very little capability in any case of foreseeing the course that events would take.

Then he turned it all over again, and considered the arguments for each course. His superiors were set over him by God; it was rash to set himself against them except in matters of the plainest conscience. Again it was cowardly to shelter himself behind this plea and so avoid responsibility. Lastly, he was bound to judge for himself.

The arguments twisted and turned as bewilderingly as the twining branches of his design; and behind each by which he might climb to decision lurked a beast. He felt helpless and dazed by the storm of conflicting motives.

As he bent over his work he prayed for light, but the question seemed more tangled than before; the hours were creeping in; by tomorrow he must decide.

Then the memory of the Prior's advice to him once before came back to his mind; this was the kind of thing, he told himself, that he must leave to God, his own judgment was too coarse an instrument; he must wait for a clear supernatural impulse; and as he thought of it he laid his pencil down, dropped on to his knees, and commended it all to God, to the Mother of God, St. Pancras, St. Peter and St. Paul. Even as he did it, the burden lifted and he knew that he would know, when the time came.

*D*r. Petre came that night, but Chris saw no more of him than his back as he went up the cloister with Dom Anthony to the Prior's chamber. The Prior was not at supper, and his seat was empty in the dim refectory.

Neither was he at Compline; and it was with the knowledge that Cromwell's man and their own Superior were together in conference, that the monks went up the dormitory stairs that night.

But he was in his place at the chapter-mass next morning, though he spoke to no one, and disappeared immediately afterwards.

Then at the appointed time the monks assembled in the chapter-house.

*A*s Chris came in he lifted his eyes, and saw that the room was arrayed much as it had been at the visit of Dr. Layton and Ralph. A great table, heaped with books and papers, stood at the upper end immediately below the dais, and a couple of secretaries were there, sharp-looking men, seated at either end and busy with documents.

The Prior was in his place in the shadow and was leaning over and talking to a man who sat beside him. Chris could make out little of the latter except that he seemed to be a sort of lawyer or clerk, and was dressed in a dark gown and cap. He was turning over the leaves of a book as the Prior talked, and nodded his head assentingly from time to time.

When all the monks were seated, there was still a pause. It was strangely unlike the scene of a tragedy, there in that dark grave room with the quiet faces downcast round the walls, and the hands hidden in the cowl-sleeves. And even on the deeper plane it all seemed very correct and legal. There was the representative of the King, a capable learned man, with all the indications of law and order round him, and his two secretaries to endorse or check his actions. There too was the Community, gathered to do business in the manner prescribed by the Rule, with the deeds of foundation before their eyes, and the great brass convent seal on the table. There was not a hint of bullying or compulsion; these monks were asked merely to sign a paper if they so desired it. Each was to act for himself; there was to be no overriding of individual privileges, or signing away another's conscience.

Nothing could have been arranged more peaceably.

And yet to every man's mind that was present the sedate room was black with horror. The majesty and terror of the King's will brooded in the air; nameless dangers looked in at the high windows and into every man's face; the quiet lawyerlike men were ministers of fearful vengeance; the very pens, ink and paper that lay there so innocently were sacraments of death or life.

The Prior ceased his whispering presently, glanced round to see if all were in their places, and then stood up.

His voice was perfectly natural as he told them that this was Dr. Petre, come down from Lord Cromwell to offer them an opportunity of showing their trust and love towards their King by surrendering to his discretion the buildings and property that they held. No man was to be compelled to sign; it must be perfectly voluntary on their part; his Grace wished to force no conscience to do that which it repudiated. For his own part, he said, he was going to sign with a glad heart. The King had shown his clemency in a hundred ways, and to that clemency he trusted.

Then he sat down; and Chris marveled at his self-control.

Dr. Petre stood up, and looked round for a moment before opening his mouth; then he put his two hands on the table before him, dropped his eyes and began his speech.

He endorsed first what the Prior had said, and congratulated all there on possessing such a superior. It was a great happiness, he said, to deal with men who showed themselves so reasonable and so loyal. Some he had had to do with had not been so — and — and of course their stubbornness had brought its own penalty. But of that he did not wish to speak. On the other hand those who had shown themselves true subjects of his Grace had already found their reward. He had great pleasure in announcing to them that what the Prior had said to them a day or two before was true; and that their brethren in religion of Chertsey Abbey, who had been moved to Bisham last year, were to go to the London Charterhouse in less than a month. The papers were made out; he had assisted in their drawing up.

He spoke in a quiet restrained voice, and with an appearance of great deference; there was not the shadow of a bluster even when he referred to the penalties of stubbornness; it was very unlike the hot bullying arrogance of Dr. Layton. Then he ended —

"And so, reverend fathers, the choice is in your hands. His Grace will use no compulsion. You will hear presently that the terms of surrender are explicit in that point. He will not force one man to sign who is not convinced that he can best serve his King and himself by doing so. It would go sorely against his heart if he thought that he had been the means of making the lowest of his subjects to act contrary to the conscience that God has given him. My Lord Prior, I will beg of you to read the terms of surrender."

The paper was read, and it was as it had been described. Again and again it was repeated in various phrases that the property was yielded of free-will. It was impossible to find in it even the hint of a threat. The properties in question were enumerated in the minutest manner, and the list included all the rights of the priory over the Cluniac cell of Castleacre.

The Prior laid the paper down, and looked at Dr. Petre.

The Commissioner rose from his seat, taking the paper as he did so, and so stood a moment.

"You see, reverend fathers, that it is as I told you. I understand that you have already considered the matter, so that there is no more to be said."

He stepped down from the dais and passed round to the further side of the table. One of the secretaries pushed an inkhorn and a couple of quills across to him.

"My Lord Prior," said Dr. Petre, with a slight bow. "If you are willing to sign this, I will beg of you to do so; and after that to call up your subjects."

He laid the paper down. The Prior stepped briskly out of his seat, and passed round the table.

Chris watched his back, the thin lawyer beside him indicating the place for the name; and listened as in a dream to the scratching of the pen. He himself still did not know what he would do. If all signed — ?

The Prior stepped back, and Chris caught a glimpse of a white face that smiled terribly.

The Sub-Prior stepped down at a sign from his Superior; and then one by one the monks came out.

Chris's heart sickened as he watched; and then stood still on a sudden in desperate hope, for opposite to him Dom Anthony sat steady, his head on his hand, and made no movement when it was his turn to come out. Chris saw the Prior look at the monk, and a spasm of emotion went over his face.

"Dom Anthony," he said.

The monk lifted his face, and it was smiling too.

"I cannot sign, My Lord Prior."

Then the veils fell, and decision flashed on Chris' soul.

He heard the pulse drumming in his ears, and his wet hands slipped one in the other as he gripped them together, but he made no sign till all the others had gone up. Then he looked up at the Prior.

It seemed an eternity before the Prior looked at him and nodded; and he could make no answering sign.

Then he heard his name called, and with a great effort he answered; his voice seemed not his own in his ears. He repeated Dom Anthony's words.

"I cannot sign, My Lord Prior."

Then he sat back with closed eyes and waited.

He heard movements about him, steps, the crackle of parchment, and at last Dr. Petre's voice; but he scarcely understood what was said. There was but one thought dinning in his brain, and that was that he had refused, and thrown his defiance down before the King — that terrible man whom he had seen in his barge on the river, with the narrow eyes, the pursed mouth and the great jowl, as he sat by the woman he called his wife — that woman who now —

Chris shivered, opened his eyes, and sense came back.

Dr. Petre was just ending his speech. He was congratulating the Community on their reasonableness and loyalty. By an overwhelming majority they had decided to trust the King, and they would not find his grace unmindful of that. As for those who had not signed he could say nothing but that they had used the liberty that his Grace had given them. Whether they had used it rightly was no business of his.

Then he turned to the Prior.

"The seal then, My Lord Prior. I think that is the next matter."

The Prior rose and lifted it from the table. Chris caught the gleam of the brass and silver of the ponderous precious thing in his hand — the symbol of their corporate existence — engraved, as he knew, with the four patrons of the house, the cliff, the running water of the Ouse, and the rhyming prayer to St. Pancras.

The Prior handed it to the Commissioner, who took it, and stood there a moment weighing it in his hand.

"A hammer," he said.

One of the secretaries rose, and drew from beneath the table a sheet of metal and a sharp hammer; he handed both to Dr. Petre.

Chris watched, fascinated with something very like terror, his throat contracted in a sudden spasm, as he saw the Commissioner place the metal in the solid table before him, and then, holding the seal sideways, lift the hammer in his right hand.

Then blow after blow began to echo in the rafters overhead.

Chapter V

THE SINKING SHIP

*D*r. Petre had come and gone, and to all appearance the priory was as before. He had not taken a jewel or a fragment of stuff; he had congratulated the sacristan on the beauty and order of his treasures, and had bidden him guard them carefully, for that there were knaves abroad who professed themselves as authorized by the King to seize monastic possessions, which they sold for their own profit. The offices continued to be sung day and night, and the masses every morning; and the poor were fed regularly at the gate.

But across the corporate life had passed a subtle change, analogous to that which comes to the body of a man. Legal death had taken place already; the unity of life and consciousness existed no more; the seal was defaced; they could no longer sign a document except as individuals. Now the *rigor mortis* would set in little by little until somatic death too had been consummated, and the units which had made up the organism had ceased to bear any relation one to the other.

But until after Christmas there was no further development; and the Feast was observed as usual, and with the full complement of monks. At the midnight mass there was a larger congregation than for many months, and the confessions and communions also slightly increased. It was a symptom, as Chris very plainly perceived, of the manner in which the shadow of the King reached even to the remotest details of the life of the country. The priory was now, as it were, enveloped in the royal protection, and the people responded accordingly.

There had come no hint from headquarters as to the ultimate fate of the house; and some even began to hope that the half-promise of a re-foundation would be fulfilled. Neither had any mark of disapproval arrived as to the refusal to sign on the part of the two monks; but although nothing further was said in conversation or at chapter, there was a consciousness in the minds of both Dom Anthony and Chris that a wall had arisen between them and the rest. Talk in the cloister was apt to flag when either approached; and the Prior never spoke a word to them beyond what was absolutely necessary.

Then, about the middle of January the last process began to be enacted.

One morning the Prior's place in church was empty.

He was accustomed to disappear silently, and no astonishment was caused on this occasion; but at Compline the same night the Sub-Prior too was gone.

This was an unheard-of state of things, but all except the guest-master and Chris seemed to take it as a matter of course; and no word was spoken.

After the chapter on the next morning Dom Anthony made a sign to Chris as he passed him in the cloister, and the two went out together into the clear morning-sunshine of the outer court.

Dom Anthony glanced behind him to see that no one was following, and then turned to the other.

"They are both gone," he said, "and others are going. Dom Bernard is getting his things together. I saw them under his bed last night."

Chris stared at him, mute and terrified.

"What are we to do, Dom Anthony?"

"We can do nothing. We must stay. Remember that we are the only two who have any rights here now, before God."

There was silence a moment. Chris glanced at the other, and was reassured by the steady look on his ruddy face.

"I will stay, Dom Anthony," he said softly.

The other looked at him tenderly.

"God bless you, brother!" he said.

That night Dom Bernard and another were gone. And still the others made no sign or comment; and it was not until yet another pair had gone that Dom Anthony spoke plainly.

He was now the senior monk in the house; and it was his place to direct the business of the chapter. When the formal proceedings were over he stood up fearlessly.

"You cannot hide it longer," he said. "I have known for some while what was impending." He glanced round at the empty stalls, and his face flushed with sudden anger: "For God's sake, get you gone, you who mean to go; and let us who are steadfast serve our Lord in peace."

Chris looked along the few faces that were left; but they were downcast and sedate, and showed no sign of emotion.

Dom Anthony waited a moment longer, and then gave the signal to depart. By a week later the two were left alone.

*I*t was very strange to be there, in the vast house and church, and to live the old life now stripped of three-fourths of its meaning; but they did not allow one detail to suffer that it was possible to preserve. The *opus Dei* was punctually done, and God was served in psalmody. At the proper hours the two priests met in the cloister, cowled and in their choir-shoes, and walked through to the empty stalls; and there, one on either side, each answered the other, bowed together at the *Gloria,* confessed and absolved alternately. Two masses were said each day in the huge lonely church, one at the high altar and the other at our Lady's, and each monk served the other. In the refectory one read from the pulpit as the other sat at the table; and the usual forms were observed with the minutest care. In the chapter each morning they met for mutual confession and accusation; and in the times between the exercises and meals each worked feverishly at the details that alone made the life possible.

They were assisted in this by two paid servants, who were sent to them by Chris's father, for both the lay-brothers and the servants had gone with the rest; and the treasurer had disappeared with the money.

Chris had written to Sir James the day that the last monk had gone, telling him the state of affairs, and how the larder was almost empty; and by the next evening the servants had arrived with money and provisions; and a letter from Sir James written from a sick-bed, saying that he was unable to come for the present, for he had taken the fever, and that Morris would not leave him, but expressing a hope that he would come soon in person, and that Morris should be sent in a few days. The latter ended with passionate approval of his son's action.

"God bless and reward you, dear lad!" he had written. "I cannot tell you the joy that it is to my heart to know that you are faithful. It cannot be for long; but whether it is for long and short, you shall have my prayers and blessings; and please God, my poor presence too after a few days. May our Lady and your holy patron intercede for you both who are so worthy of their protection!"

*A*t the end of the second week in March Mr. Morris arrived.

Chris was taking the air in the court shortly before sunset, after a hard day's work in church. The land was beginning to stir with the resurrection-life of spring; and the hills set round the town had that faint flush of indescribable color that tinges slopes of grass as the sleeping sap begins to stir. The elm trees in the court were hazy with growth as the buds fattened at the end of every twig, and a group of daffodils here and there were beginning to burst their sheaths of gold. There on the little lawn before the guest-house were half a dozen white and lavender patches of color that showed where the crocuses would star the grass presently; and from the high west front of the immense church, and from beneath the eaves of the offices to the right the birds were practicing the snatches of song that would break out with full melody a month or two later.

In spite of all that threatened, Chris was in an ecstasy of happiness. It rushed down on him, overwhelmed and enveloped him; for he knew now that he had been faithful. The flood of praise in the church had dwindled to a thread; but it was still the *opus Dei*, though it flowed but from two hearts; and the pulse of the heavenly sacrifice still throbbed morning by morning, and the Divine Presence still burned as unceasingly as the lamp that beaconed it, in the church that was now all but empty of its ministers. There were times when the joy that was in his heart trembled into tears, as when last night he and his friend had sung the song to Mary; and the contrast between the two poor voices, and the roar of petition that had filled the great vaulting a year before, had suddenly torn his heart in two.

But now the poignant sorrow had gone again; and as he walked here alone on this March evening, with the steady hills about him and the flushing sky overhead, and the sweet life quickening in the grass at his feet, an extraordinary peace flooded his soul.

There came a knocking at the gate, and the jangle of a bell; and he went across quickly and unbarred the door.

Mr. Morris was there on horseback, a couple of saddlebags strapped to his beast; and a little group of loungers stood behind.

Chris smiled with delight, and threw the door wide.

The servant saluted him and then turned to the group behind.

"You have no authority," he said, "as to my going in."

Then he rode through; and Chris barred the gate behind him, glancing as he did so at the curious faces that stared silently.

Mr. Morris said nothing till he had led his horse into the stable. Then he explained.

"One of the fellows told me, sir, that this was the King's house now; and that I had no business here."

Chris smiled again.

"I know we are watched," he said, "the servants are questioned each time they set foot outside."

Mr. Morris pursed his lips.

"How long shall you be here, sir?" he asked.

"Until we are turned out," said Chris.

*I*t was true, as he had said, that the house was watched. Ever since the last monk had left there had been a man or two at the gate, another outside the church-door that opened towards the town; and another yet again beyond the stream to the south of the priory-buildings. Dom Anthony had told him what it meant. It was that the authorities had no objection to the two monks keeping the place until it could be dealt with, but were determined that nothing should pass out. It had not been worthwhile to send in a caretaker, for all the valuables had been removed either by the Visitors or by the Prior when he went at night. There were only two sets of second-best altar vessels left, and a few other comparatively worthless utensils for the use of the church and kitchen. The great relics and the jeweled treasures had gone long before. Chris had wondered a little at the house being disregarded for so long; but the other monk had reminded him that such things as lead and brass and bells were beyond the power of two men to move, and could keep very well until other more pressing business had been dispatched elsewhere.

Mr. Morris gave him news of his father. It had not been the true fever after all, and he would soon be here; in at any rate a week or two. As regarded other news, there was no tidings of Mr. Ralph except that he was very busy. Mistress Margaret was at home; no notice seemed to have been taken of her when she had been turned out with the rest at the dissolution of her convent.

It was very pleasant to see that familiar face about the cloister and refectory; or now and again, when work was done, looking up from beyond the screen as the monks came in by the sacristy door. Once or twice on dark evenings when terror began to push through the rampart of the will that Chris had raised up, it was reassuring too to know that Morris was there, for he bore with him, as old servants do, an atmosphere of home and security, and he carried himself as well with a wonderful naturalness, as if the relief of beleaguered monks were as ordinary a duty as the cleaning of plate.

March was half over now; and still no sign had come from the world outside. There were no guests either to bring tidings, for the priory was a marked place and it was well not to show or receive kindliness in its regard.

Within, the tension of nerves grew acute. Chris was conscious of a deepening exaltation, but it was backed by horror. He found himself now smiling with an irrepressible internal joy, now twitching with apprehension, starting at sudden noises, and terrified at loneliness. Dom Anthony too grew graver still; and would take his arm sometimes and walk with him, and tell him tales, and watch him with tender eyes. But in him, as in the younger monk, the strain tightened every day.

*T*hey were singing Compline together one evening with tired, over-strained voices, for they had determined not to relax any of the chant until it was necessary. Mr. Morris was behind them at a chair set beyond the screen; and there were no others present in church.

The choir was perfectly dark (for they knew the office by heart) except for a glimmer from the sacristy door where a lamp burned within to light them to bed. Chris's thoughts had fled back to that summer evening long ago when he had knelt far down in the nave and watched the serried line of the black-hooded soldiers of God, and listened to the tramp of the psalmody, and longed to be of their company. Now the gallant regiment had dwindled to two, of which he was one, and the guest-master that had received him and encouraged him, the other.

Dom Anthony was the officiant this evening, and had just sung lustily out in the dark that God was about them with His shield, that they need fear no nightly terror.

The movement flagged for a moment, for Chris was not attending; Mr. Morris's voice began alone, *A sagitta volante* — and then stopped abruptly as he realized that he was singing by himself; and simultane-ously came a sharp little crash from the dark altar that rose up in the gloom in front.

A sort of sobbing breath broke from Chris at the sudden noise, and he gripped his hands together.

In a moment Dom Anthony had taken up the verse.

A sagitta volante — "From the arrow that flieth by day, from the thing that walketh in darkness —" Chris recovered himself; and the office passed on.

As the two passed out together towards the door, Dom Anthony went forward up the steps; and Chris waited, and watched him stoop and pass his hands over the floor. Then he straightened himself, came down the steps and went before Chris into the sacristy.

Under the lamp he stopped, and lifted what he carried to the light. It was the little ivory crucifix that he had hung there a few weeks ago when the last cross of precious metal had disappeared with the Sub-Prior. It was cracked across the body of the figure now, and one of the arms was detached at the shoulder and swung free on the nail through the hand.

Dom Anthony looked at it, turned and looked at Chris; and without a word the two passed out into the cloister and turned up the dormitory stairs. To both of them it was a sign that the end was at hand.

O n the following afternoon Mr. Morris ran in to Chris's carrel, and found him putting the antiphonary and his implements up into a parcel.

"Master Christopher," he said, "Sir James and Sir Nicholas are come."

As he hurried out of the cloister he saw the horses standing there, spent with fast traveling, and the two riders at their heads, with the dust on their boots, and their clothes disordered. They remained motionless as the monk came towards them; but he saw that his father's face was working and that his eyes were wide and anxious.

"Thank God," said the old man softly. "I am in time. They are coming tonight, Chris." But there was a questioning look on his face.

Chris looked at him.

"Will you take the horses?" said his father again. "Nick and I are safe."

Chris still stared bewildered. Then he understood; and with understanding came decision.

"No, father," he said.

The old man's face broke up into lines of emotion.

"Are you sure, my son?"

Chris nodded steadily.

"Then we will all be together," said Sir James; and he turned to lead his horse to the stable.

T here was a little council held in the guest-house a few minutes later. Dom Anthony hurried to it, his habit splashed with whitewash, for he had been cleaning the dormitory, and the four sat down together.

It seemed that Nicholas had ridden over from Great Keynes to Overfield earlier in the afternoon, and had brought the news that a company of men had passed through the village an hour before, and that one of them had asked which turn to take to Lewes. Sir Nicholas had ridden after them and enquired their business, and had gathered that they were bound for the priory, and he then turned his horse and made off to Overfield. His horse was spent when he arrived there; but he had changed horses and came on immediately with Sir James, to warn the monks of the approach of the men, and to give them an opportunity of making their escape if they thought it necessary.

"Who were the leaders?" asked the elder monk.

Nicholas shook his head.

"They were in front; I dared not ride up."

But his sturdy face looked troubled as he answered, and Chris saw his father's lips tighten. Dom Anthony drummed softly on the table.

"There is nothing to be done," he said. "We wait till we are cast out."

"You cannot refuse admittance?" questioned Sir James.

"But we shall do so," said the other tranquilly; "at least we shall not open."

"But they will batter the door down."

"Certainly," said the monk.

"And then?"

He shrugged his shoulders.

"I suppose they will put us out."

There was absolutely nothing to be done. It was absurd to dream of more than formal resistance. Up in the North in more than one abbey the inmates had armed themselves, and faced the spoilers grimly on the village green; but that was where the whole countryside was with them, and here it was otherwise.

They talked a few minutes longer, and decided that they would neither open nor resist. The monks two were determined to remain there until they were actually cast out; and then the responsibility would rest on other shoulders than theirs.

It was certain of course that by this time tomorrow at the latest they would have been expelled; and it was arranged that the two monks should ride back to Overfield, if they were personally unmolested, and remain there until further plans were decided upon.

The four knew of course that there was a grave risk in provoking the authorities any further, but it was a risk that the two Religious were determined to run.

They broke up presently; Mr. Morris came upstairs to tell them that food was ready in one of the parlors off the cloister; and the two laymen went off with him, while the monks went to sing vespers for the last time.

*A*n hour or two later the two were in the refectory at supper. The evening was drawing in, and the light in the tall windows was fading. Opposite where Chris sat (for Dom Anthony was reading aloud from the pulpit), a row of coats burned in the glass, and he ran his eyes over them. They had been set there, he remembered, soon after his own coming to the place; the records had been searched, and the arms of every prior copied and emblazoned in the panes. There they all were; from Lanzo of five centuries ago, whose arms were conjectural, down to Robert Crowham, who had forsaken his trust; telling the long tale of prelates and monastic life, from the beginning to the close. He looked round beyond the circle of light cast by his own candle, and the place seemed full of ghosts and presences to his fancy. The pale oak paneling glimmered along the walls above the empty seats, from the Prior's to the left, over which the dusky fresco of the Majesty of Christ grew darker still as the light faded, down to the pulpit opposite where Dom Anthony's grave ruddy face with downcast eyes stood out vivid in the candlelight. Ah! surely there was a cloud of witnesses now, a host of faces looking down from the black rafters overhead, and through the glimmering panes, — the faces of those who had eaten here with the same sacramental dignity and graciousness that these two survivors used. It was impossible to feel lonely in this stately house, saturated with holy life; and with a thrill at his heart he remembered how Dom Anthony had once whispered to him at the beginning of the troubles, that if others held their peace the very stones should cry out; and that God was able of those stones to raise up children to His praise. . . .

There was a sound of brisk, hurrying footsteps in the cloister outside, Dom Anthony ceased his reading with his finger on the place, and the eyes of the two monks met.

The door was opened abruptly, and Morris stood there.

"My master has sent me, sir," he said. "They are coming."

Chapter VI
THE LAST STAND

The court outside had deepened into shadows as they came out; but overhead the sky still glowed faintly luminous in a tender translucent green. The evening star shone out clear and tranquil opposite them in the west.

There were three figures standing at the foot of the steps that led down from the cloister; one of the servants with the two gentlemen; and as Chris pushed forward quickly his father turned and lifted his finger for silence.

The town lay away to the right; and over the wall that joined the west end of the church to the gatehouse, there were a few lights visible — windows here and there just illuminated.

For the first moment Chris thought there had been a mistake; he had expected a clamor at the gate, a jangling of the bell. Then as he listened he knew that it was no false alarm.

Across the wall, from the direction of the hills that showed dimly against the evening sky, there came a murmur, growing as he listened. The roads were hard from lack of rain, and he could distinguish the sound of horses, a great company; but rising above this was a dull roar of voices. Every moment it waxed, died once or twice, then sounded out nearer and louder. There was a barking of dogs, the cries of children, and now and again the snatch of a song or a shouted word or two.

Of the group on the steps within not one stirred, except when Sir James slowly lowered his upraised hand; and so they waited.

The company was drawing nearer now; and Chris calculated that they must be coming down the steep road that led from the town; and even as he thought it he heard the sound of hoofs on the bridge that crossed the Winterbourne.

Dom Anthony pushed by him.

"To the gate," he said, and went down the step and across the court followed by the others. As they went the clamor grew loud and near in the road outside; and a ruddy light shone on the projecting turret of the gateway.

Chris was conscious of extraordinary coolness now that the peril was on him; and he stared up at the studded oak doors, at the wicket cut in one of the leaves, and the sliding panel that covered the grill, with little thought but that of conjecture as to how long the destruction of the gate would take. The others, too, though he was scarcely aware of their presence, were silent and rigid at his side, as Dom Anthony stepped up to the closed grill and waited there for the summons.

It came almost immediately.

There was a great crescendo of sound as the party turned the corner, and a flare of light shone under the gate; then the sound of loud talking, a silence of the hoofs; and a sudden jangle on the bell overhead.

The monk turned from the grill and lifted his hand.

Then again the talking grew loud, as the mob swept round the corner after the horses.

Still all was silent within. Chris felt his father's hand seek his own a moment, and grip it; and then above the gabbling clamor a voice spoke distinctly outside.

"Have the rats run, then?"

The bell danced again over their heads; and there was a clatter of raps on the huge door.

Dom Anthony slid back the shutter.

*F*or a moment it was not noticed outside, for the entry was dark. Chris could catch a glimpse on either side of the monk's head of a flare of light, but no more.

Then the same voice spoke again, and with something of a foreign accent.

"You are there, then; make haste and open."

Another voice shouted authoritatively for silence; and the clamor of tongues died.

Dom Anthony waited until all was quiet, and then answered steadily.

"Who are you?"

There was an oath; the tumult began again, but hushed immediately, as the same voice that had called for admittance shouted aloud —

"Open, I tell you, you bloody monk! We come from the King."

"Why do you come?"

A gabble of fierce tongues broke out; Chris pressed up to Dom Anthony's back, and looked out. The space was very narrow, and he could not see much more than a man's leg across a saddle, the brown shoulder of a horse in front, and a smoky haze beyond and over the horse's back. The leg shifted a little as he watched, as if the rider turned; and then again the voice pealed out above the tumult.

"Will you open, sir, for the last time?"

"I will not," shouted the monk through the grill. "You are nothing but —" then he dashed the shutter into its place as a stick struck fiercely at the bars.

"Back to the cloister," he said.

The roar outside was tremendous as the six went back across the empty court; but it fell to a sinister silence as an order or two was shouted outside; and then again swelled with an excited note in it, as the first crash sounded on the panels.

Chris looked at his father as they stood again on the steps fifty yards away. The old man was standing rigid, his hands at his sides, staring out towards the arch of the gateway that now thundered like a drum; and his lips were moving. Once he caught his breath as a voice shouted above the din outside, and half turned to his son, his hand uplifted as if for silence. Then again the voice pealed, and Sir James faced round and stared into Chris's eyes. But neither spoke a word.

Dom Anthony, who was standing a yard or two in front, turned presently as the sound of splintering began to be mingled with the reverberations, and came towards them. His square, full face was steady and alert, and he spoke with a sharp decision.

"You and Sir Nicholas, sir, had best be within. My place will be here; they will be in immediately."

His words were perfectly distinct here in the open air in spite of the uproar from the gate.

There was an indignant burst from the young squire.

"No, no, father; I shall not stir from here."

The monk looked at him; but said no more and turned round.

A sedate voice spoke from the dark doorway behind.

"John and I have fetched out a table or two, father; we can brace this door —"

Dom Anthony turned again.

"We shall not resist further," he said.

Then they were silent, for they were helpless. There was nothing to be done but to stand there and listen to the din, to the crash that splintered more every moment in the cracked woodwork, and to watch the high wall and turret solemn and strong against the stars, and bright here and there at the edges with the light from the torches beneath. The guest-house opposite them was dark, except for one window in the upper floor that glowed and faded with the light of the fire that had been kindled within an hour or two before.

Sir James took his son suddenly by the arm.

"And you, Chris —" he said.

"I shall stay here, father."

There was a rending thunder from the gate; the wicket reeled in and fell, and in a moment through the flimsy opening had sprung the figure of a man. They could see him plainly as he stood there in the light of the torches, a tall upright figure, a feathered hat on his head, and a riding cane in his hand.

The noise was indescribable outside as men fought to get through; there was one scream of pain, the plunging of a horse, and then a loud steady roar drowning all else.

The oblong patch of light was darkened immediately, as another man sprang through, and then another and another; then a pause — then the bright flare of a torch shone in the opening; and a moment later a fellow carrying a flambeau had made his way through.

The whole space under the arch was now illuminated. Overhead the plain moldings shone out and faded as the torch swayed; every brick of the walls was visible, and the studs and bars of the huge doors.

Chris had sprung forward by an uncontrollable impulse as the wicket fell in; and the two monks were now standing motionless on the floor of the court, side by side, in their black habits and scapulars, hooded and girded, with the two gentlemen and the servants on the steps behind.

Chris saw the leaders come together under the arch, as the whole gate began to groan and bulge under the pressure of the crowd; and a moment later he caught the flash of steel as the long rapiers whisked out.

Then above the baying he heard a fierce authoritative voice scream out an order, and saw that one of the gentlemen in front was at the door, his rapier protruded before him; and understood the maneuver. It was necessary that the mad crowd should be kept back.

The tumult died and became a murmur; and then one by one a file of figures came through. In the hand of each was an instrument of some kind, a pick or a bludgeon; and it was evident that it was these who had broken in the gate.

Chris counted them mechanically as they streamed through. There seemed to be a dozen or so.

Then again the man who had guarded the door as they came through slipped back through the opening; and they heard his voice beginning to harangue the mob.

But a moment later they had ceased to regard him; for from the archway, with the torch-bearer beside him, advanced the tall man with the riding-cane who had been the first to enter; and as he emerged into the court Chris recognized his brother.

*H*e was in a plain rich riding-suit with great boots and plumed hat. He walked with an easy air as if certain of himself, and neither quickened nor decreased his pace as he saw the monks and the gentlemen standing there.

He halted a couple of yards from them, and Chris saw that his face was as assured as his gait. His thin lips were tight and firm, and his eyes with a kind of insolent irony looked up and down the figures of the monks. There was not the faintest sign of recognition in them.

"You have given us a great deal of labor," he said, "and to no purpose. We shall have to report it all to my Lord Cromwell. I understand that you were the two who refused to sign the surrender. It was the act of fools, like this last. I have no authority to take you, so you had best be gone."

Dom Anthony answered him in an equally steady voice.

"We are ready to go now," he said. "You understand we have yielded to nothing but force."

Ralph's lips writhed in a smile.

"Oh! if that pleases you," he said. "Well, then —"

He took a little step aside, and made a movement towards the gate where there sounded out still an angry hum beneath the shouting voice that was addressing them.

Chris turned to his father behind, and the voice died in his throat, so dreadful was that face that was looking at Ralph. He was standing as before, rigid it seemed with grief or anger; and his grey eyes were bright with a tense emotion; his lips too were as firm as his son's. But he spoke no word. Sir Nicholas was at his side, with one foot advanced, and in attitude as if to spring; and Morris's face looked like a mask over his shoulder.

"Well, then —" said Ralph once more.

"Ah! you damned hound!" roared the young squire's voice; and his hand went up with the whip in it.

Ralph did not move a muscle. He seemed cut in steel.

"Let us go," said Dom Anthony again, to Chris, almost tenderly; "it is enough that we are turned out by force."

"You can go by the church, if you will," said Ralph composedly. "In fact —" He stopped as the murmur howled up again from the gate — "In fact you had better go that way. They do not seem to be your friends out there."

"We will go whichever way you wish," remarked the elder monk.

"Then the church," said Ralph, "or some other private door. I suppose you have one. Most of your houses have one, I believe."

The sneer snapped the tension.

Dom Anthony turned his back on him instantly.

"Come, brother," he said.

Chris took his father by the arm as he went up the steps.

"Come, sir," he said, "we are to go this way."

There was a moment's pause. The old man still stared down at his elder son, who was standing below in the same position. Chris heard a deep breath, and thought he was on the point of speaking; but there was silence. Then the two turned and followed the others into the cloister.

Chapter VII

AXES AND HAMMERS

*C*hris sat next morning at a high window of a house near Saint Michael's looking down towards the south of the town.

They had escaped without difficulty the night before through the church-entrance, with a man whom Ralph sent after them to see that they carried nothing away, leaving the crowd roaring round the corner of the gate, and though people looked curiously at the monks, the five laymen with them protected them from assault. Mr. Morris had found a lodging a couple of days before, unknown to Chris, in the house of a woman who was favorable to the Religious, and had guided the party straight there on the previous evening.

The two monks had said mass in Saint Michael's that morning before the town was awake; and were now keeping within doors at Sir James's earnest request, while the two gentlemen with one of the servants had gone to see what was being done at the priory.

*F*rom where Chris sat in his black habit at the leaded window he could see straight down the opening of the steep street, across the lower roofs below, to where the great pile of the Priory church less than half-a-mile away soared up in the sunlight against the water-meadows where the Ouse ran to the south of the town.

The street was very empty below him, for every human being that could do so had gone down to the sacking of the priory. There might be pickings, scraps gathered from the hoards that the monks were supposed to have gathered; there would probably be an auction; and there would certainly be plenty of excitement and pleasure.

Chris was himself almost numb to sensation. The coolness that had condensed round his soul last night had hardened into ice; he scarcely realized what was going on, or how great was the catastrophe into which his life was plunged. There lay the roofs before him — he ran his eye from the west tower past the high lantern to the delicate tracery of the eastern apse and chapels — in the hands of the spoilers; and here he sat dry-eyed and steady-mouthed looking down on it, as a man looks at a wound not yet begun to smart.

It was piteously clear and still. Smoke was rising from a fire some-where behind the church, a noise as of metal on stone chinked steadily, and the voices of men calling one to another sounded continually from the enclosure. Now and again the tiny figure of a workman showed clear on the roof, pick in hand; or leaning to call directions down to his fellows beneath.

Dom Anthony looked in presently, breviary in hand, and knelt by Chris on the window-step, watching too; but he spoke no word, glanced at the white face and sunken eyes of the other, sighed once or twice, and went out again.

The morning passed on and still Chris watched. By eleven o'clock the men were gone from the roof; half an hour had passed, and no further figure had appeared.

There were footsteps on the stairs; and Sir James came in.

He came straight across to his son and sat down by him. Chris looked at him. The old man nodded.

"Yes, my son," he said, "they are at it. Nothing is to be left, but the cloister and guest-house. The church is to be down in a week they say."

Chris looked at him dully.

"All?" he said.

"All the church, my son."

Sir James gave an account of what he had seen. He had made his way in with Nicholas and a few other persons, into the court; but had not been allowed to enter the cloister. There was a furnace being made ready in the calefactorium for the melting of the lead, he had been told by one of the men; and the church, as he had seen for himself, was full of workmen.

"And the Blessed Sacrament?" asked Chris.

"A priest was sent for this morning to carry It away to a church; I know not which."

Sir James described the method of destruction.

They were beginning with the apse and the chapels behind the high altar. The ornaments had been removed, the images piled in a great heap in the outer court, and the brasses had been torn up. There were half a dozen masons busy at undercutting the pillars and walls; and as they excavated the carpenters made wooden insertions to prop up the weight. The men had been brought down from London, as the commissioners were not certain of the temper of the Lewes people. Two of the four great pillars behind the high altar were already cut half through.

"And Ralph?"

The old man's face grew tense and bitter.

"I saw him in the roof," he said; "he made as if he did not see me."

They were half-through dinner before Nicholas joined them. He was flushed and dusty and furious.

"Ah! the hounds!" he said, as he stood at the door, trembling. "They say they will have the chapels down before night. They have stripped the lead."

Sir James looked up and motioned him to sit down.

"We will go down again presently," he said.

"But we have saved our luggage," went on Nicholas, taking his seat; "and there was a parcel of yours, Chris, that I put with it. It is all to be sent up with the horses tonight."

"Did you speak with Mr. Ralph?" asked Dom Anthony.

"Ah! I did; the dog! and I told him what I thought. But he dared not refuse me the luggage. John is to go for it all tonight."

He told them during dinner another fact that he had learned.

"You know who is to have it all?" he said fiercely, his fingers twitching with emotion.

"It is Master Gregory Cromwell, and his wife, and his baby. A fine nursery!"

*A*s the evening drew on, Chris was again at the window alone. He had said his office earlier in the afternoon, and sat here again now, with his hands before him, staring down at the church.

One of the servants had come up with a message from Sir James an hour before telling him not to expect them before dusk; and that they would send up news of any further developments. The whole town was there, said the man: it had been found impossible to keep them out. Dom Anthony presently came again and sat with Chris; and Mr. Morris, who had been left as a safeguard to the monks, slipped in soon after and stood behind the two; and so the three waited.

The sky was beginning to glow again as it had done last night with the clear radiance of a cloudless sunset; and the tall west tower stood up bright in the glory. How infinitely far away last night seemed now, little and yet distinct as a landscape seen through a reversed telescope! How far away that silent waiting at the cloister door, the clamor at the gate, the forced entrance, the slipping away through the church!

The smoke was rising faster than ever now from the great chimney, and hung in a cloud above the buildings. Perhaps even now the lead was being cast.

There was a clatter at the corner of the cobbled street below, and Dom Anthony leaned from the window. He drew back.

"It is the horses," he said.

The servant presently came up to announce that the two gentlemen were following immediately, and that he had had orders to procure horses and saddle them at once. He had understood Sir James to say that they must leave that night.

Mr. Morris hurried out to see to the packing.

In five minutes the gentlemen themselves appeared.

Sir James came quickly across to the two monks.

"We must go tonight, Chris," he said. "We had words with Portinari. You must not remain longer in the town."

Chris looked at him.

"Yes?" he said.

"And the chapels will be down immediately. Oh! dear God!"

Dom Anthony made room for the old man to sit down in the window-seat; and himself stood behind the two with Nicholas; and so again they watched.

The light was fading fast now, and in the windows below lights were beginning to shine. The square western tower that dominated the whole priory had lost its splendor, and stood up strong and pale against the meadows. There was a red flare of light somewhere over the wall of the court, and the inner side of the gate-turret was illuminated by it.

A tense excitement lay on the watchers; and no sound came from them but that of quick breathing as they waited for what they knew was imminent.

Outside the evening was wonderfully still; they could hear two men talking somewhere in the street below; but from the priory came no sound. The chink of the picks was still, and the cries of the workmen. Far away beyond the castle on their left came an insistent barking of a dog; and once, when a horseman rode by below Chris bit his lip with vexation, for it seemed to him like the disturbing of a deathbed. A star or two looked out, vanished, and peeped again from the luminous sky, to the south, and the downs beneath were grey and hazy.

All the watchers now had their eyes on the eastern end of the church that lay in dim shadow; they could see the roof of the vault behind where the high altar lay beneath; the flying buttress of a chapel below; and, nearer, the low roof of the Lady-chapel.

Chris kept his eyes strained on the upper vault, for there, he knew the first movement would show itself.

The time seemed interminable. He moistened his dry lips from time to time, shifted his position a little, and moved his elbow from the sharp molding of the window-frame.

Then he caught his breath.

From where he sat, in the direct line of his eyes, the top of a patch of evergreen copse was visible just beyond the roof of the vault; and as he looked he saw that a patch of paler green had appeared below it. All in a moment he saw too the flying buttress crook itself like an elbow and disappear. Then the vault was gone and the roof beyond; the walls sank with incredible slowness and vanished.

A cloud of white dust puffed up like smoke.

Then through the open window came the roar of the tumbling masonry; and shrill above it the clamor of a great crowd.

BOOK III
THE KING'S GRATITUDE

Chapter I
A SCHEME

*T*he period that followed the destruction of Lewes Priory held very strange months for Chris. He had slipped out of the stream into a back-water, from which he could watch the swift movements of the time, while himself undisturbed by them; for no further notice was taken of his refusal to sign the surrender or of his resistance to the Commissioners. The hands of the authorities were so full of business that apparently it was not worth their while to trouble about an inoffensive monk of no particular notoriety, who after all had done little except in a negative way, and who appeared now to acquiesce in silence and seclusion.

The household at Overfield was of a very mixed nature. Dom Anthony after a month or two had left for the Continent to take up his vocation in a Benedictine house; and Sir James and his wife, Chris, Margaret, and Mr. Carleton remained together. For the present Chris and Margaret were determined to wait, for a hundred things might intervene — Henry's death, a changing of his mind, a foreign invasion on the part of the Catholic powers, an internal revolt in England, and such things — and set the clock back again, and, unlike Dom Anthony, they had a home where they could follow their Rules in tolerable comfort.

The country was indeed very deeply stirred by the events that were taking place; but for the present, partly from terror and partly from the great forces that were brought to bear upon English convictions, it gave no expression to its emotion. The methods that Cromwell had employed with such skill in the past were still active. On the worldly side there was held out to the people the hope of relieved taxation, of the distribution of monastic wealth and lands; on the spiritual side the bishops under Cranmer were zealous in controverting the old principles and throwing doubt upon the authority of the Pope. It was impossible for the unlearned to know what to believe; new manifestoes were issued continually by the King and clergy, full of learned arguments and persuasive appeals; and the professors of the old religion were continually discredited by accusations of fraud, avarice, immorality, hypocrisy and the like. They were silenced, too; while active and eloquent preachers like Latimer raged from pulpit to pulpit, denouncing, expounding, convincing.

Meanwhile the work went on rapidly. The summer and autumn of '38 saw again destruction after destruction of Religious Houses and objects of veneration; and the intimidation of the most influential personages on the Catholic side.

In February, for example, the rood of Boxley was brought up to London with every indignity, and after being exhibited with shouts of laughter at Whitehall, and preached against at Paul's Cross, it was tossed down among the zealous citizens and smashed to pieces. In the summer, among others, the shrine of St. Swithun at Winchester was defaced and robbed; and in the autumn that followed the friaries which had stood out so long began to fall right and left. In October the Holy Blood of Hayles, a relic brought from the East in the thirteenth century and preserved with great love and honor ever since, was taken from its resting place and exposed to ridicule in London. Finally in the same month, after St. Thomas of Canterbury had been solemnly declared a traitor to his prince, his name, images and pictures ordered to be erased and destroyed out of every book, window and wall, and he himself summoned with grotesque solemnity to answer the charges brought against him, his relics were seized and burned, and – which was more to the point in the King's view, his shrine was stripped of its gold and jewels and vestments, which were conveyed in a string of twenty-six carts to the King's treasury. The following year events were yet more terrible. The few great houses that survived were one by one brought within reach of the King's hand; and those that did not voluntarily surrender fell under the heavier penalties of attainder. Abbot Whiting of Glastonbury was sent up to London in September, and two months later suffered on Tor hill within sight of the monastery he had ruled so long and so justly; and on the same day the Abbot of Reading suffered too outside his own gateway. Six weeks afterwards Abbot Marshall, of Colchester, was also put to death.

*I*t was a piteous life that devout persons led at this time; and few were more unhappy than the household at Overfield. It was the more miserable because Lady Torridon herself was so entirely out of sympathy with the others. While she was not often the actual bearer of ill news — for she had neither sufficient strenuousness nor opportunity for it — it was impossible to doubt that she enjoyed its arrival.

They were all together at supper one warm summer evening when a servant came in to announce that a monk of St. Swithun's was asking hospitality. Sir James glanced at his wife who sat with passive downcast face; and then ordered the priest to be brought in.

He was a timid, tactless man who failed to grasp the situation, and when the wine and food had warmed his heart he began to talk a great deal too freely, taking it for granted that all there were in sympathy with him. He addressed himself chiefly to Chris, who answered courteously; and described the sacking of the shrine at some length.

"He had already set aside our cross called Hierusalem," cried the monk, his weak face looking infinitely pathetic with its mingled sorrow and anger, "and two of our gold chalices, to take them with him when he went; and then with his knives and hammers, as the psalmist tells us, he hacked off the silver plates from the shrine. There was a fellow I knew very well — he had been to me to confession two days before — who held a candle and laughed. And then when all was done; and that was not till three o'clock in the morning, one of the smiths tested the metal and cried out that there was not one piece of true gold in it all. And Mr. Pollard raged at us for it, and told us that our gold was as counterfeit as the rotten bones that we worshipped. But indeed there was plenty of gold; and the man lied; for it was a very rich shrine. God's vengeance will fall on them for their lies and their robbery. Is it not so, mistress?"

Lady Torridon lifted her eyes and looked at him. Her husband hastened to interpose.

"Have you finished your wine, father?"

The monk seemed not to hear him; and his talk flowed on about the destruction of the high altar and the spoiling of the reredos, which had taken place on the following days; and as he talked he filled his Venetian glass more than once and drank it off; and his lantern face grew flushed and his eyes animated. Chris saw that his mother was watching the monk shrewdly and narrowly, and feared what might come. But it was unavoidable.

"We poor monks," the priest cried presently, "shall soon be cast out to beg our bread. The King's Grace —"

"Is not poverty one of the monastic vows?" put in Lady Torridon suddenly, still looking steadily at his half-drunk glass.

"Why, yes, mistress; and the King's Grace is determined to make us keep it, it seems."

He lifted his glass and finished it; and put out his hand again to the bottle.

"But that is a good work, surely," smiled the other. "It will be surely a safeguard against surfeiting and drunkenness."

Sir James rose instantly.

"Come, father," he said to the staring monk, "you will be tired out, and will want your bed."

A slow smile shone and laded on his wife's face as she rose and rustled down the long hall.

*S*uch incidents as this made life at Overfield very difficult for them all; it was hard for these sore hearts to be continually on the watch for dangerous subjects, and only to be able to comfort one another when the mistress of the house was absent; but above all it was difficult for Margaret. She was nearly as silent as her mother, but infinitely more tender; and since the two were naturally together for the most part, except when the nun was at her long prayers, there were often very difficult and painful incidents.

For the first eighteen months after her return her mother let her alone; but as time went on and the girl's resolution persevered, she began to be subjected to a distressing form of slight persecution.

For example: Chris and his father came in one day in the autumn from a walk through the priory garden that lay beyond the western moat. As they passed in the level sunshine along the prim box-lined paths, and had reached the center where the dial stood, they heard voices in the summer-house that stood on the right behind a yew hedge.

Sir James hesitated a moment; and as he waited heard Margaret's voice with a thrill of passion in it.

"I cannot listen to that, mother. It is wicked to say such things."

The two turned instantly, passed along the path and came round the corner.

Margaret was standing with one hand on the little table, half-turned to go. Her eyes were alight with indignation, and her lips trembled. Her mother sat on the other side, her silver-handled stick beside her, and her hands folded serenely together.

Sir James looked from one to the other; and there fell a silence.

"Are you coming with us, Margaret?" he said.

The girl still hesitated a moment, glancing at her mother, and then stepped out of the summer-house. Chris saw that bitter smile writhe and die on the elder woman's face, but she said nothing.

Margaret burst out presently when they had crossed the moat and were coming up to the long grey-towered house.

"I cannot bear such talk, father," she said, with her eyes bright with angry tears, "she was saying such things about Rusper, and how idle we all were there, and how foolish."

"You must not mind it, my darling. Your mother does not — does not understand."

"There was never anyone like Mother Abbess," went on the girl. "I never saw her idle or out of humor; and — and we were all so busy and happy."

Her eyes overflowed a moment; her father put his arm tenderly round her shoulders, and they went in together.

It was a terrible thing for Margaret to be thrown like this out of the one life that was a reality to her. As she looked back now it seemed as if the convent shone glorified and beautiful in a haze of grace. The discipline of the house had ordered and inspired the associations on which memories afterwards depend, and had excluded the discordant notes that spoil the harmonies of secular life. The chapel, with its delicate windows, its oak rails, its scent of flowers and incense, its tiled floor, its single row of carved woodwork and the crosier by the Abbess's seat, was a place of silence instinct with a Divine Presence that radiated from the hanging pyx; it was these particular things, and not others like them, that had been the scene of her romance with God, her aspirations, tendernesses, tears and joys. She had walked in the tiny cloister with her Lover in her heart, and the glazed laurel-leaves that rattled in the garth had been musical with His voice; it was in her little white cell that she had learned to sleep in His arms and to wake to the brightness of His Face. And now all this was dissipated. There were other associations with her home, of childish sorrows and passions before she had known God, of hunting-parties and genial ruddy men who smelt of fur and blood, of her mother's chilly steady presence — associations that jarred with the inner life; whereas in the convent there had been nothing that was not redolent with efforts and rewards of the soul. Even without her mother life would have been hard enough now at Overfield; with her it was nearly intolerable.

Chris, however, was able to do a good deal for the girl; for he had suffered in the same way; and had the advantage of a man's strength. She could talk to him as to no one else of the knowledge of the interior vocation in both of them that persevered in spite of their ejection from the cloister; and he was able to remind her that the essence of the enclosure, under these circumstances, lay in the spirit and not in material stones.

It was an advantage for Chris too to have her under his protection. The fact that he had to teach her and remind her of facts that they both knew, made them more real to himself; and to him as to her there came gradually a kind of sorrow-shot contentment that deepened month by month in spite of their strange and distracting surroundings.

But he was not wholly happy about her; she was silent and lonely sometimes; he began to see what an immense advantage it would be to her in the peculiarly difficult circumstances of the time, to have some-one of her own sex and sympathies at hand. But he did not see how it could be arranged. For the present it was impossible for her to enter the Religious Life, except by going abroad; and so long as there was the faintest hope of the convents being restored in England, both she and her father and brother shrank from the step. And the hope was increased by the issue of the Six Articles in the following May, by which Transub-stantiation was declared to be a revealed dogma, to be held on penalty of death by burning; and communion in one kind, the celibacy of the clergy, the perpetuity of the vow of chastity, private masses, and auricu-lar confession were alike ratified as parts of the Faith held by the Church of which Henry had made himself head.

Yet as time went on, and there were no signs of the restoration of the Religious Houses, Chris began to wonder again as to what was best for Margaret. Perhaps until matters developed it would be well for her to have some friend in whom she could confide, even if only to relax the strain for a few weeks. He went to his father one day in the autumn and laid his views before him.

Sir James nodded and seemed to understand.

"Do you think Mary would be of any service?"

Chris hesitated.

"Yes, sir, I think so — but —"

His father looked at him.

"It is a stranger I think that would help her more. Perhaps another nun — ?"

"My dear lad, I dare not ask another nun. Your mother —"

"I know," said Chris.

"Well, I will think of it," said the other.

A couple of days later Sir James took him aside after supper into his own private room.

"Chris," he said, "I have been thinking of what you said. And Mary shall certainly come here for Christmas, with Nick; but — but there is someone else too I would like to ask."

He looked at his son with an odd expression.

Chris could not imagine what this meant.

"It is Mistress Atherton," went on the other. "You see you know her a little — at least you have seen her; and there is Ralph. And from all that I have heard of her — her friendship with Master More and the rest, I think she might be the very friend for poor Meg. Do you think she would come, Chris?"

Chris was silent. He could not yet fully dissociate the thought of Beatrice from the memory of the time when she had taken Ralph's part. Besides, was it possible to ask her under the circumstances?

"Then there was one more thing that I never told you;" went on his father, "there was no use in it. But I went to see Mistress Atherton when she was betrothed to Ralph. I saw her in London; and I think I may say we made friends. And she has very few now; she keeps herself aloof. Folks are afraid of her too. I think it would be a kindness to her. I could not understand how she could marry Ralph; and now that is explained."

Chris was startled by this news. His father had not breathed a word of it before.

"She made me promise," went on Sir James, "to tell her if Ralph did anything unworthy. It was after the first news had reached her of what the Visitors were doing. And I told her, of course, about Rusper. I think we owe her something. And I think too from what I saw of her that she might make her way with your mother."

"It might succeed," said Chris doubtfully, "but it is surely difficult for her to come —"

"I know — yes — with Ralph and her betrothal. But if we can ask her, surely she can come. I can tell her how much we need her. I would send Meg to Great Keynes, if I dared, but I dare not. It is not so safe there as here; she had best keep quiet."

They talked about it a few minutes more, and Chris became more inclined to it. From what he remembered of Beatrice and the impression that she had made on him in those few fierce minutes in Ralph's house he began to see that she would probably be able to hold her own; and if only Margaret would take to her, the elder girl might be of great service in establishing the younger. It was an odd and rather piquant idea, and gradually took hold of his imagination. It was a very extreme step to take, considering that she had broken off her betrothal to the eldest son of the house; but against that was set the fact that she would not meet him there; and that her presence would be really valued by at least four-fifths of the household.

It was decided that Lady Torridon should be told immediately; and a day or two later Sir James came to Chris in the garden to tell him that she had consented.

"I do not understand it at all," said the old man, "but your mother seemed very willing. I wonder —"

And then he stopped abruptly.

The letter was sent. Chris saw it and the strong appeal it contained that Beatrice should come to the aid of a nun who was pining for want of companionship. A day or two later brought down the answer that Mistress Atherton would have great pleasure in coming a week before Christmas.

Margaret had a fit of shyness when the day came for her arrival. It was a clear frosty afternoon, with a keen turquoise sky overhead, and she wandered out in her habit down the slope to the moat, crossed the bridge, glancing at the thin ice and the sedge that pierced it, and came up into the private garden. She knew she could hear the sounds of wheels from there, and had an instinctive shrinking from being at the house when the stranger arrived.

The grass walks were crisp to the foot; the plants in the deep beds rested in a rigid stillness with a black blossom or two drooping here and there; and the hollies beyond the yew hedge lifted masses of green lit by scarlet against the pale sky. Her breath went up like smoke as she walked softly up and down.

There was no sound to disturb her. Once she heard the clink of the blacksmith's forge half a mile away in the village; once a blackbird dashed chattering from a hedge, scudded in a long dip, and rose again over it; a robin followed her in brisk hops, with a kind of pathetic impertinence in his round eye, as he wondered whether this human creature's footsteps would not break the iron armor of the ground and give him a chance to live.

She wondered a thousand things as she went; what kind of a woman this was that was coming, how she would look, why she had not married Ralph, and above all, whether she understood — whether she understood!

A kind of frost had fallen on her own soul; she could find no sustenance there; it was all there, she knew, all the mysterious life that had rioted within her like spring, in the convent, breathing its fragrances, bewildering in its wealth of shape and color. But an icy breath had petrified it all; it had sunk down out of sight; it needed a soul like her own, feminine and sympathetic, a soul that had experienced the same things as her own, that knew the tenderness and love of the Savior, to melt that frigid covering and draw out the essences and sweetness again, that lay there paralyzed by this icy environment. . . .

There were wheels at last.

She gathered up her black skirt, and ran to the edge of the low yews that bounded the garden on the north; and as she caught a glimpse of the nodding heads of the postilions, the plumes of their mounts, and the great carriage-roof swaying in the iron ruts, she shrank back again, in an agony of shyness, terrified of being seen.

The sky had deepened to flaming orange in the west, barred by the tall pines, before she unlatched the garden-gate to go back to the house.

The windows shone out bright and inviting from the parlor on the ground-floor and from beneath the high gable of the hall as she came up the slope. Mistress Atherton, she knew, would be in one of these rooms if she had not already gone up stairs; and with an instinct of shyness still strong within her the girl slipped round to the back, and passed in through the chapel.

The court was lighted by a link that flared beside one of the doorways on the left, and a couple of great trunks lay below it. A servant came out as she stood there hesitating, and she called to him softly to know where was Mistress Atherton.

"She is in the parlor, Mistress Margaret," said the man.

The girl went slowly across to the corner doorway, glancing at the parlor windows as she passed; but the curtains were drawn on this side, and she could catch no glimpse of the party within.

The little entrance passage was dark; but she could hear a murmur of voices as she stood there, still hesitating. Then she opened the door suddenly, and went into the room.

Her mother was speaking; and the girl heard those icy detached tones as she looked round the group.

"It must be very difficult for you, Mistress Atherton, in these days."

Margaret saw her father standing at the window-seat, and Chris beside him; and in a moment saw that the faces of both were troubled and uneasy.

A tall girl was in the chair opposite, her hands lying easily on the arms and her head thrown back almost negligently. She was well dressed, with furs about her throat; her buckled feet were crossed before the blaze, and her fingers shone with jewels. Her face was pale; her scarlet lips were smiling, and there was a certain keen and genial amusement in her black eyes.

She looked magnificent, thought Margaret, still standing with her hand on the door — too magnificent.

Her father made a movement, it seemed of relief, as his daughter came in; but Lady Torridon, very upright in her chair on this side, went on immediately.

— "With your opinions, Mistress Atherton, I mean. I suppose all that you consider sacred is being insulted, in your eyes."

The tall girl glanced at Margaret with the amusement still in her face, and then answered with a deliberate incisiveness that equaled Lady Torridon's own.

"Not so difficult," she said, "as for those who have no opinions."

There was a momentary pause; and then she added, as she stood up and Sir James came forward.

"I am very sorry for them, Mistress Torridon."

Before Lady Torridon could answer, Sir James had broken in.

"This is my daughter Margaret, Mistress Atherton."

The two ladies saluted one another.

Chapter II
A DUEL

Margaret watched Beatrice with growing excitement that evening, in which was mingled something of awe and something of attraction. She had never seen anyone so serenely self-possessed.

It became evident during supper, beyond the possibility of mistake, that Lady Torridon had planned war against the guest, who was a representative in her eyes of all that was narrow-minded and contempt-ible. Here was a girl, she seemed to tell herself, who had had every opportunity of emancipation, who had been singularly favored in being noticed by Ralph, and who had audaciously thrown him over for the sake of some ridiculous scruples worthy only of idiots and nuns. Indeed to Chris it was fairly plain that his mother had consented so willingly to Beatrice's visit with the express purpose of punishing her.

But Beatrice held her own triumphantly.

*T*hey had not sat down three minutes before Lady Torridon opened the assault, with grave downcast face and in her silkiest manner. She went abruptly back to the point where the conversation had been interrupted in the parlor by Margaret's entrance.

"Mistress Atherton," she observed, playing delicately with her spoon, "I think you said that to your mind the times were difficult for those who had no opinions."

Beatrice looked at her pleasantly.

"Yes, Mistress Torridon; at least more difficult for those, than for the others who know their own mind."

The other waited a moment, expecting the girl to justify herself, but she was forced to go on.

"Abbot Marshall knew his mind, but it was not easy for him."

(The news had just arrived of the Abbot's execution).

"Do you think not, mistress? I fear I still hold my opinion."

"And what do you mean by that?"

"I mean that unless we have something to hold to, in these troublesome times, we shall drift. That is all."

"Ah! and drift whither?"

Beatrice smiled so genially as she answered, that the other had no excuse for taking offence.

"Well, it might be better not to answer that."

Lady Torridon looked at her with an impassive face.

"To hell, then?" she said.

"Well, yes: to hell," said Beatrice.

There was a profound silence; broken by the stifled merriment of a servant behind the chairs, who transformed it hastily into a cough. Sir James glanced across in great distress at his son; but Chris' eyes twinkled at him.

Lady Torridon was silent a moment, completely taken aback by the suddenness with which the battle had broken, and amazed by the girl's audacity. She herself was accustomed to use brutality, but not to meet it. She laid her spoon carefully down.

"Ah!" she said, "and you believe that? And for those who hold wrong opinions, I suppose you would believe the same?"

"If they were wrong enough," said Beatrice, "and through their fault. Surely we are taught to believe that, Mistress Torridon?"

The elder woman said nothing at all, and went on with her soup. Her silence was almost more formidable than her speech, and she knew that, and contrived to make it offensive. Beatrice paid no sort of attention to it, however; and without looking at her again began to talk cheerfully to Sir James about her journey from town. Margaret watched her, fascinated; her sedate beautiful face, her lace and jewels, her white fingers, long and straight, that seemed to endorse the impression of strength that her carriage and manner of speaking suggested; as one might watch a swordsman between the rounds of a duel and calculate his chances. She knew very well that her mother would not take her first repulse easily; and waited in anxiety for the next clash of swords.

Beatrice seemed perfectly fearless, and was talking about the King with complete freedom, and yet with a certain discretion too.

"He will have his way," she said. "Who can doubt that?"

Lady Torridon saw an opening for a wound, and leapt at it.

"As he had with Master More," she put in.

Beatrice turned her head a little, but made no answer; and there was not the shadow of wincing on her steady face.

"As he had with Master More," said Lady Torridon a little louder.

"We must remember that he has my Lord Cromwell to help him," observed Beatrice tranquilly.

Lady Torridon looked at her again. Even now she could scarcely believe that this stranger could treat her with such a supreme indifference. And there was a further sting, too, in the girl's answer, for all there understood the reference to Ralph; and yet again it was impossible to take offence.

Margaret looked at her father, half-frightened, and saw again a look of anxiety in his eyes; he was crumbling his bread nervously as he answered Beatrice.

"My Lord Cromwell —" he began.

"My Lord Cromwell has my son Ralph under him," interrupted his wife. "Perhaps you did not know that, Mistress Atherton."

Margaret again looked quickly up; but there was still no sign of wincing on those scarlet lips, or beneath the black eyebrows.

"Why, of course, I knew it," said Beatrice, looking straight at her with large, innocent eyes, "that was why —"

She stopped; and Lady Torridon really roused now, made a false step.

"Yes?" she said. "You did not end your sentence?"

Beatrice cast an ironically despairing look behind her at the servants.

"Well," she said, "if you will have it: that was why I would not marry him. Did you not know that, Mistress?"

It was so daring that Margaret caught her breath suddenly; and looked hopelessly round. Her father and brother had their eyes steadily bent on the table; and the priest was looking oddly at the quiet angry woman opposite him.

Then Sir James slid deftly in, after a sufficient pause to let the lesson sink home; and began to talk of indifferent things; and Beatrice answered him with the same ease.

Lady Torridon made one more attempt just before the end of supper, when the servants had left the room.

"You are living on —" she corrected herself ostentatiously — "you are living with any other family now, Mistress Atherton? I remember my son Ralph telling me you were almost one of Master More's household."

Beatrice met her eyes with a delightful smile.

"I am living on — with your family at this time, Mistress Torridon."

There was no more to be said just then. The girl had not only turned her hostess' point, but had pricked her shrewdly in riposte, three times; and the last was the sharpest of all.

Lady Torridon led the way to the oak parlor in silence.

She made no more assaults that night; but sat in dignified aloofness, her hands on her lap, with an air of being unconscious of the presence of the others. Beatrice sat with Margaret on the long oak settle; and talked genially to the company at large.

When compline had been said, Sir James drew Chris aside into the star-lit court as the others went on in front.

"Dear lad," he said, "what are we to do? This cannot go on. Your mother —"

Chris smiled at him, and took his arm a moment.

"Why, father," he said, "what more do we want? Mistress Atherton can hold her own."

"But your mother will insult her."

"She will not be able," said Chris. "Mistress Atherton will not have it. Did you not see how she enjoyed it?"

"Enjoyed it?"

"Why, yes; her eyes shone."

"Well, I must speak to her," said Sir James, still perplexed. "Come with me, Chris."

Mr. Carleton was just leaving the parlor as they came up to its outside door. Sir James drew him into the yard. There were no secrets between these two.

"Father," he said, "did you notice? Do you think Mistress Atherton will be able to stay here?"

He saw to his astonishment that the priest's melancholy face, as the starlight fell on it, was smiling.

"Why, yes, Sir James. She is happy enough."

"But my wife —"

"Sir James, I think Mistress Atherton may do her good. She —" he hesitated.

"Well?" said the old man.

"She — Lady Torridon has met her match," said the chaplain, still smiling.

Sir James made a little gesture of bewilderment.

"Well, come in, Chris. I do not understand; but if you both think so —"

He broke off and opened the door.

Lady Torridon was gone to her room; and the two girls were alone. Beatrice was standing before the hearth with her hands behind her back — a gallant upright figure; as they came in, she turned a cheerful face to them.

"Your daughter has been apologizing, Sir James," she said; and there was a ripple of amusement in her voice. "She thinks I have been hardly treated."

She glanced at the bewildered Margaret, who was staring at her under her delicate eyebrows with wide eyes of amazement and admiration.

Sir James looked confused.

"The truth is, Mistress Atherton, that I too — and my son —"

"Well, not your son," said Chris smiling.

"You too!" cried Beatrice. "And how have I been hardly treated?"

"Well, I thought perhaps, that what was said at supper —" began the old man, beginning to smile too.

"Lady Torridon, and everyone, has been all that is hospitable," said Beatrice. "It is like old days at Chelsea. I love word-fencing; and there are so few who practice it."

Sir James was still a little perplexed.

"You assure me, Mistress, that you are not distressed by — by anything that has passed?"

"Distressed!" she cried. "Why, it is a real happiness!"

But he was not yet satisfied.

"You will engage to tell me then, if you think you are improperly treated by — by anyone — ?"

"Why, yes," said the girl, smiling into his eyes. "But there is no need to promise that. I am really happy; and I am sure your daughter and I will be good friends."

She turned a little towards Margaret; and Chris saw a curious emotion of awe and astonishment and affection in his sister's eyes.

"Come, my dear," said Beatrice. "You said you would take me to my room."

Sir James hastened to push open the further door that led to the stairs; and the two girls passed out together.

Then he shut the door, and turned to his son. Chris had begun to laugh.

Chapter III
A PEACE-MAKER

*I*t was a very strange household that Christmas at Overfield. Mary and her husband came over with their child, and the entire party, with the exception of the duelists themselves, settled down to watch the conflict between Lady Torridon and Beatrice Atherton. Its prolongation was possible because for days together the hostess retired into a fortress of silence, whence she looked out cynically, shrugged her shoulders, smiled almost imperceptibly, and only sallied when she found she could not provoke an attack. Beatrice never made an assault; was always ready for the least hint of peace; but guarded deftly and struck hard when she was directly threatened. Neither would she ever take an insult; the bitterest dart fell innocuous on her bright shield before she struck back smiling; but there were some sharp moments of anxiety now and again as she hesitated how to guard.

A silence would fall suddenly in the midst of the talk and clatter at table; there would be a momentary kindling of glances, as from the tall chair opposite the chaplain a psychological atmosphere of peril made itself felt; then the blow would be delivered; the weapons clashed; and once more the talk rose high and genial over the battlefield.

*T*he moment when Beatrice's position in the house came nearest to being untenable, was one morning in January, when the whole party were assembled on the steps to see the sportsmen off for the day.

Sir James was down with the foresters and hounds at the further end of the terrace, arranging the details of the day; Margaret had not yet come out of chapel, and Lady Torridon, who had had a long fit of silence, was standing with Mary and Nicholas at the head of the central stairs that led down from the terrace to the gravel.

Christopher and Beatrice came out of the house behind, talking cheerfully; for the two had become great friends since they had learnt to understand one another, and Beatrice had confessed to him frankly that she had been wrong and he right in the matter of Ralph. She had told him this a couple of days after her arrival; but there had been a certain constraint in her manner that forbade his saying much in answer. Here they came then, now, in the frosty sunshine; he in his habit and she in her morning house-dress of silk and lace, talking briskly.

"I was sure you would understand, father," she said, as they came up behind the group.

Then Lady Torridon turned and delivered her point, suddenly and brutally.

"Of course he will," she said. "I suppose then you are not going out, Mistress Atherton." And she glanced with an offensive contempt at the girl and the monk. Beatrice's eyes narrowed almost imperceptibly, and opened again.

"Why, no, Lady Torridon."

"I thought not," said the other; and again she glanced at the two — "for I see the priest is not."

There was a moment's silence. Nick was looking at his wife with a face of dismay. Then Beatrice answered smiling.

"Neither are you, dear Lady Torridon. Is not that enough to keep me?"

A short yelp of laughter broke from Nicholas; and he stooped to examine his boot.

Lady Torridon opened her lips, closed them again, and turned her back on the girl.

"But you are cruel," said Beatrice's voice from behind, "and —"

The woman turned once more venomously.

"You do not want me," she said. "You have taken one son of mine, and now you would take the other. Is not my daughter enough?"

Beatrice instantly stepped up, and put her hand on the other's arm.

"Dear Mistress," she said; and her voice broke into tenderness; "she is not enough —"

Lady Torridon jerked her arm away.

"Come, Mary," she said.

*M*atters were a little better after that. Sir James was not told of the incident; because his son knew very well that he would not allow Beatrice to stay another day after the insult; but Chris felt himself bound to consult those who had heard what had passed as to whether indeed it was possible for her to remain. Nicholas grew crimson with indignation and vowed it was impossible. Mary hesitated; and Chris himself was doubtful. He went at last to Beatrice that same evening; and found her alone in the oak parlor, before supper. The sportsmen had not yet come back; and the other ladies were upstairs.

Beatrice affected to treat it as nothing; and it was not till Chris threatened to tell his father, that she told him all she thought.

"I must seem a vain fool to say so;" she said, leaning back in her chair, and looking up at him, "and perhaps insolent too; yet I must say it. It is this: I believe that Lady Torridon — Ah! how can I say it?"

"Tell me," said Chris steadily, looking away from her.

Beatrice shifted a little in her seat; and then stood up.

"Well, it is this. I do not believe your mother is so — so — is what she sometimes seems. I think she is very sore and angry; there are a hundred reasons. I think no one has — has faced her before. She has been obeyed too much. And — and I think that if I stay I may be able — I may be some good," she ended lamely.

Chris nodded.

"I understand," he said softly.

"Give me another week or two," said Beatrice, "I will do my best."

"You have worked a miracle with Meg," said Chris. "I believe you can work another. I will not tell my father; and the others shall not either."

A wonderful change had indeed come to Margaret during the last month. Her whole soul, so cramped now by circumstances, had gone out in adoration towards this stranger. Chris found it almost piteous to watch her — her shy looks, the shiver that went over her, when the brilliant figure rustled into the room, or the brisk sentences were delivered from those smiling lips. He would see too how their hands met as they sat together; how Margaret would sit distracted and hungering for attention, eyeing the ceiling, the carpet, her embroidery; and how her eyes would leap to meet a glance, and her face flush up, as Beatrice throw her a soft word or look.

And it was the right love, too, to the monk's eyes; not a rival flame, but fuel for divine ardor. Margaret spent longer, not shorter, time at her prayers; was more, not less, devout at mass and communion; and her whole sore soul became sensitive and alive again. The winter had passed for her; the time of the singing-birds was come.

*S*he was fascinated by the other's gallant brilliance. Religion for the nun had up to the present appeared a delicate thing that grew in the shadow or in the warm shelter of the cloister; now it blossomed out in Beatrice as a hardy bright plant that tossed its leaves in the wind and exulted in sun and cold. Yet it had its evening tendernesses too, its subtle fragrance when the breeze fell, its sweet colors and outlines — Beatrice too could pray; and Margaret's spiritual instinct, as she knelt by her at the altar-rail or glanced at the other's face as she came down fresh with absolution from the chair in the sanctuary where the chaplain sat, detected a glow of faith at least as warm as her own.

She was astonished too at her friend's gaiety; for she had expected, so far as her knowledge of human souls led to expect anything, a quiet convalescent spirit, recovering but slowly from the tragedy through which Margaret knew she had passed. It seemed to her at first as if Beatrice must be almost heartless, so little did she flinch when Lady Torridon darted Ralph's name at her, or Master More's, or flicked her suddenly where the wound ought to be; and it was not until the guest had been a month in the house that the nun understood.

They were together one evening in Margaret's own white little room above the oak parlor. Beatrice was sitting before the fire with her arms clasped behind her head, waiting till the other had finished her office, and looking round pleased in her heart, at the walls that told their tale so plainly. It was almost exactly like a cell. A low oak bed, red-blanketed, stood under the sloping roof, a prie-dieu beside it, and a cheap little

French image of St. Scholastica over it. There was a table, with a sheet of white paper, a little inkhorn and two quills primly side by side upon it; and at the back stood a couple of small bound volumes in which the nun was accumulating little by little private devotions that appealed to her. A pair of beads hung on a nail by the window over which was drawn an old red curtain; two brass candlesticks with a cross between them stood over the hearth, giving it a faint resemblance to an altar. The boards were bare except for a strip of matting by the bed; and the whole room, walls, floor, ceiling and furniture were speckless and precise.

Margaret made the sign of the cross, closed her book, and smiled at Beatrice.

"You dear child!" she answered.

Margaret's face shone with pleasure; and she put out her hand softly to the other's knee, and laid it there.

"Talk to me," said the nun.

"Well?" said Beatrice.

"Tell me about your life in London. You never have yet, you know."

An odd look passed over the others face, and she dropped her eyes and laid her hands together in her lap.

"Oh, Meg," she said, "I should love to tell you if I could. What would you like to hear?"

The nun looked at her wondering.

"Why — everything," she said.

"Shall I tell you of Chelsea and Master More?"

Margaret nodded, still looking at her; and Beatrice began.

It was an extraordinary experience for the nun to sit there and hear that wonderful tale poured out. Beatrice for the first time threw open her defenses — those protections of the sensitive inner life that she had raised by sheer will — and showed her heart. She told her first of her life in the country before she had known anything of the world; of her father's friendship with More when she was still a child, and of his death when she was about sixteen. She had had money of her own, and had come up to live with Mrs. More's sisters; and so had gradually slipped into intimacy at Chelsea. Then she described the life there — the ordered beauty of it all — and the marvelous soul that was its center and sun. She told her of More's humor, his unfailing gaiety, his sweet cynicism that shot through his talk, his tender affections, and above all — for she knew this would most interest the nun — his deep and resolute devotion to God. She described how he had at one time lived at the Charterhouse, and had seemed to regret, before the end of his life, that he had not become a Carthusian; she told her of the precious parcel that had been sent from the Tower to Chelsea the day before his death, and how she

had helped Margaret Roper to unfasten it and disclose the hair-shirt
that he had worn secretly for years, and which now he had sent back
for fear that it should be seen by unfriendly eyes or praised by flattering
tongues.

Her face grew inexpressibly soft and loving as she talked; more than
once her black eyes filled with tears, and her voice faltered; and the nun
sat almost terrified at the emotion she had called up. It was hardly
possible that this tender feminine creature who talked so softly of divine
and human things and of the strange ardent lawyer in whom both were
so manifest, could be the same stately lady of downstairs who fenced so
gallantly, who never winced at a wound and trod so bravely over sharp
perilous ground.

"They killed him," said Beatrice. "King Henry killed him; for that
he could not bear an honest, kindly, holy soul so near his own. And we
are left to weep for him, of whom — of whom the world was not worthy."

Margaret felt her hand caught and caressed; and the two sat in silence
a moment.

"But — but —" began the nun softly, bewildered by this revelation.

"Yes, my dear; you did not know — how should you? — what a wound
I carry here — what a wound we all carry who knew him."

Again there was a short silence. Margaret was searching for some word
of comfort.

"But you did what you could for him, did you not? And — and even
Ralph, I think I heard —"

Beatrice turned and looked at her steadily. Margaret read in her face
something she could not understand.

"Yes — Ralph?" said Beatrice questioningly.

"You told father so, did you not? He did what he could for Master
More?"

Beatrice laid her other hand too over Margaret's.

"My dear; I do not know. I cannot speak of that."

"But you said —"

"Margaret, my pet; you would not hurt me, would you? I do not think
I can bear to speak of that."

The nun gripped the other's two hands passionately, and laid her
cheek against them.

"Beatrice, I did not know — I forgot."

Beatrice stooped and kissed her gently.

*T*he nun loved her tenfold more after that. It had been before a kind of passionate admiration, such as a subject might feel for a splendid queen; but the queen had taken this timid soul in through the palace-gates now, into a little inner chamber intimate and apart, and had sat with her there and shown her everything, her broken toys, her failures; and more than all her own broken heart. And as, after that evening, Margaret watched Beatrice again in public, heard her retorts and marked her bearing, she knew that she knew something that the others did not; she had the joy of sharing a secret of pain. But there was one wound that Beatrice did not show her; that secret was reserved for one who had more claim to it, and could understand. The nun could not have interpreted it rightly.

*M*ary and Nicholas went back to Great Keynes at the end of January; and Beatrice was out on the terrace with the others to see them go. Jim, the little seven-year-old boy, had fallen in love with her, ever since he had found that she treated him like a man, with deference and courtesy, and did not talk about him in his presence and over his head. He was walking with her now, a little apart, as the horses came round, and explaining to her how it was that he only rode a pony at present, and not a horse.

"My legs would not reach, Mistress Atherton," he said, protruding a small leather boot. "It is not because I am afraid, or father either. I rode Jess, the other day, but not astride."

"I quite understand," said Beatrice respectfully, without the shadow of laughter in her face.

"You see —" began the boy.

Then his mother came up.

"Run, Jim, and hold my horse. Mistress Beatrice, may I have a word with you?"

The two turned and walked down to the end of the terrace again.

"It is this," said Mary, looking at the other from under her plumed hat, with her skirt gathered up with her whip in her gloved hand. "I wished to tell you about my mother. I have not dared till now. I have never seen her so stirred in my life, as she is now. I — I think she will do anything you wish in time. It is useless to feign that we do not understand one another — anything you wish — come back to her Faith perhaps; treat my father better. She — she loves you, I think; and yet dare not —"

"On Ralph's account," put in Beatrice serenely.

"Yes; how did you know? It is on Ralph's account. She cannot forgive that. Can you say anything to her, do you think? Anything to explain? You understand —"

"I understand."

"I do not know how I dare say all this," went on Mary blushing furiously, "but I must thank you too for what you have done for my sister. It is wonderful. I could have done nothing."

"My dear," said Beatrice. "I love your sister. There is no need for thanks."

A loud voice hailed them.

"Sweetheart," shouted Sir Nicholas, standing with his legs apart at the mounting steps. "The horses are fretted to death."

"You will remember," said Mary hurriedly, as they turned. "And — God bless you, Beatrice!"

Lady Torridon was indeed very quiet now. It was strange for the others to see the difference. It seemed as if she had been conquered by the one weapon that she could wield, which was brutality. As Mr. Carleton had said, she had never been faced before; she had been accustomed to regard devoutness as incompatible with strong character; she had never been resisted. Both her husband and children had thought to conquer by yielding; it was easier to do so, and appeared more Christian; and she herself, like Ralph, was only provoked further by passivity. And now she had met one of the old school, who was as ready in the use of worldly weapons as herself; she had been ignored and pricked alternately, and with astonishing grace too, by one who was certainly of that tone of mind that she had gradually learnt to despise and hate.

Chris saw this before his father; but he saw too that the conquest was not yet complete. His mother had been cowed with respect, as a dog that is broken in; she had not yet been melted with love. He had spoken to Mary the day before the Maxwells' departure, and tried to put this into words; and Mary had seen where the opening for love lay, through which the work could be done; and the result had been the interview with Beatrice, and the mention of Ralph's name. But Mary had not a notion how Beatrice could act; she only saw that Ralph was the one chink in her mother's armor, and she left it to this girl who had been so adroit up to the present, to find how to pierce it.

Sir James had given up trying to understand the situation. He had for so long regarded his wife as an irreconcilable that he hoped for nothing better than to be able to keep her pacified; anything in the nature of a conversion seemed an idle dream. But he had noticed the change in her manner, and wondered what it meant; he hoped that the

pendulum had not swung too far, and that it was not she who was being
bullied now by this imperious girl from town.

He said a word to Mr. Carleton one day about it, as they walked in
the garden.

"Father," he said, "I am puzzled. What has come to my wife? Have
you not noticed how she has not spoken for three days. Do you think
she dislikes Mistress Atherton. If I thought that —"

"No, sir," said the priest. "I do not think it is that. I think it is the
other way about. She did dislike her — but not now."

"You do not think, Mistress Atherton is — is a little — discourteous
and sharp sometimes. I have wondered whether that was so. Chris thinks
not, however."

"Neither do I, sir. I think — I think it is all very well as it is. I hope
Mistress Atherton is to stay yet a while."

"She speaks of going in a week or two," said the old man. "She has
been here six weeks now."

"I hope not," said the priest, "since you have asked my opinion, sir."

Sir James sighed, looked at the other, and then left him, to search for
his wife and see if she wanted him. He was feeling a little sorry for her.

A week later the truth began to come out, and Beatrice had the
opportunity for which she was waiting.

They were all gathered before the hall-fire expecting supper; the
painted windows had died with the daylight, and the deep tones of the
woodwork in gallery and floor and walls had crept out from the gloom
into the dancing flare of the fire and the steady glow of the sconces. The
weather had broken a day or two before; all the afternoon sheets of rain
had swept across the fields and gardens, and heavy cheerless clouds
marched over the sky. The wind was shrilling now against the north side
of the hall, and one window dripped a little inside on to the matting
below it. The supper-table shone with silver and crockery, and the
napkins by each place; and the door from the kitchen was set wide for
the passage of the servants, one of whom waited discreetly in the opening
for the coming of the lady of the house. They were all there but she;
and the minutes went by and she did not come.

Sir James turned enquiringly as the door from the court opened, but
it was only a wet shivering dog who had nosed it open, and now crept
deprecatingly towards the blaze.

"You poor beast," said Beatrice, drawing her skirts aside. "Take my place," and she stepped away to allow him to come. He looked gratefully up, wagged his rat-tail, and lay down comfortably at the edge of the tiles.

"My wife is very late," said Sir James. "Chris —"

He stopped as footsteps sounded in the flagged passage leading from the living rooms; and the next moment the door was flung open, and a woman ran forward with outstretched hands.

"O! mon Dieu, mon Dieu!" she cried. "My lady is ill. Come, sir, come!"

Chapter IV

THE ELDER SON

*R*alph had prospered exceedingly since his return from the Sussex Visitation. He had been sent on mission after mission by Cromwell, who had learnt at last how wholly he could be trusted; and with each success his reputation increased. It seemed to Cromwell that his man was more whole-hearted than he had been at first; and when he was told abruptly by Ralph that his relations with Mistress Atherton had come to an end, the politician was not slow to connect cause and effect. He had always regretted the friendship; it seemed to him that his servant's character was sure to be weakened by his alliance with a friend of Master More; and though he had said nothing — for Ralph's manner did not encourage questions — he had secretly congratulated both himself and his agent for so happy a termination to an unfortunate incident.

For the meantime Ralph's fortunes rose with his master's; Lord Cromwell now reigned in England next after the King in both Church and State. He held a number of offices, each of which would have been sufficient for an ordinary man, but all of which did not overtax his amazing energy. He stood absolutely alone, with all the power in his hands; President of the Star Chamber, Foreign Minister, Home-Minister, and the Vicar-General of the Church; feared by Churchmen, distrusted by statesmen and nobles; and hated by all except his own few personal friends — an unique figure that had grown to gigantic stature through sheer effort and adroitness.

And beneath his formidable shadow Ralph was waxing great. He had failed to get Lewes for himself, for Cromwell designed it for Gregory his son; but he was offered his choice among several other great houses. For the present he hesitated to choose; uncertain of his future. If his father died there would be Overfield waiting for him, so he did not wish to tie himself to one of the faraway Yorkshire houses; if his father lived, he did not wish to be too near him. There was no hurry, said Cromwell; there would be houses and to spare for the King's faithful servants; and meantime it would be better for Mr. Torridon to remain in Westminster, and lay his foundations of prosperity deeper and wider yet before building. The title too that Cromwell dangled before him sometimes — that too could wait until he had chosen his place of abode.

Ralph felt that he was being magnificently treated by his master; and his gratitude and admiration grew side by side with his rising fortune. There was no niggardliness, now that Cromwell had learnt to trust in him; he could draw as much money as he wished for the payment of his under-agents, or for any other purpose; and no questions were asked.

The little house at Westminster grew rich in treasures; his bed-coverlet was the very cope he had taken from Rusper; his table was heavy with chalices beaten into secular shape; his fire-screen was a Spanish chasuble taken in the North. His servants were no longer three or four sleeping in the house; there was a brigade of them, some that attended for orders morning by morning, some that skirmished for him in the country and returned rich in documents and hearsay; and a dozen waited on his personal wants.

He dealt too with great folks. Half a dozen abbots had been to see him in the last year or two, stately prelates that treated him as an equal and pleaded for his intercession; the great nobles, enemies of his master and himself, eyed him with respectful suspicion as he walked with Cromwell in Westminster Hall. The King had pulled his ears and praised him; Ralph had stayed at Greenwich a week at a time when the execution of the Benedictine abbots was under discussion; he had ridden down Cheapside with Henry on his right and Cromwell beyond, between the shouting crowds and beneath the wild tossing of gold-cloth and tapestry and the windy pealing of a hundred brazen bells. He had gone up with Norfolk to Doncaster, a mouth through which the King might promise and threaten, and had strode up the steps beside the Duke to make an end of the insurgent-leaders of the northern rebellion.

He did not lack a goad, beside that of his own ambition, to drive him through this desperate stir; he found a sufficient one in his memory. He did not think much of his own family, except with sharp contempt. He did not even trouble to make any special report about Chris or Margaret; but it was impossible to remember Beatrice with contempt. When she had left him kneeling at his table, she had left something besides — the sting of her words, and the bitter coldness of her eyes.

As he looked back he did not know whether he loathed her or loved her; he only knew that she affected him profoundly. Again and again as he dealt brutally with some timid culprit, or stood with his hand on his hip to direct the destruction of a shrine, the memory whipped him on his raw soul. He would show her whether he were a man or no; whether he depended on her or no; whether her woman's tongue could turn him or no.

*H*e was exercised now with very different matters. Religious affairs for the present had fallen into a secondary place, and home and foreign politics absorbed most of Cromwell's energies and time. Forces were gathering once more against England, and the Catholic powers were coming to an understanding with one another against the country that had thrown off allegiance to the Pope and the Empire. There was an opportunity, however, for Henry's propensity to marriage once more to play a part in politics; he had been three years without a wife; and Cromwell had hastened for the third time to avail himself of the King's passions as an instrument in politics. He had understood that a union between England and the Lutheran princes would cause a formidable obstacle to Catholic machinations; and with this in view had excited Henry by a description and a picture of the Lady Anne, daughter of the Duke of Cleves and sister-in-law of the Elector of Saxony. He had been perfectly successful in the first stages; the stout duchess had landed at Deal at the end of December; and the marriage had been solemnized a few days later. But unpleasant rumor had been busy ever since; it was whispered far and wide that the King loathed his wife, and complained that he had been deceived as to her charms; and Ralph, who was more behind the scenes than most men, knew that the rumor was only too true. He had been present at an abominable incident the day after the marriage had taken place, when the King had stormed and raved about the council-room, crying out that he had been deceived, and adding many gross details for the benefit of his friends.

Cromwell had been strangely moody ever since. Ralph had watched his heavy face day after day staring vacantly across the room, and his hand that held the pen dig and prick at the paper beneath it.

Even that was not all. The Anglo-German alliance had provoked opposition on the continent instead of quelling it; and Ralph saw more than one threatening piece of news from abroad that hinted at a probable invasion of England should Cromwell's schemes take effect. These too, however, had proved deceptive, and the Lutheran princes whom he had desired to conciliate were even already beginning to draw back from the consequences of their action.

Ralph was in Cromwell's room one day towards the end of January, when a courier arrived with dispatches from an agent who had been following the Spanish Emperor's pacific progress through France, undertaken as a kind of demonstration against England.

Cromwell tore open the papers, and glanced at them, running his quick attentive eye over this page and that; and Ralph saw his face grow stern and white. He tossed the papers on to the table, and nodded to the courier to leave the room.

Then he took up a pen, examined it; dashed it point down against the table; gnawed his nails a moment, and then caught Ralph's eye.

"We are failing," he said abruptly. "Mr. Torridon, if you are a rat you had better run."

"I shall not run, sir," said Ralph.

"God's Body!" said his master, "we shall all run together, I think; — but not yet."

Then he took up the papers again, and began to read.

It was a few days later that Ralph received the news of his mother's illness.

She had written to him occasionally, telling him of his father's tiresome ways, his brother's arrogance, his sister's feeble piety, and finally she had told him of Beatrice's arrival.

"I consented very gladly," she had written, "for I thought to teach my lady a lesson or two; but I find her very pert and obstinate. I do not understand, my dear son, how you could have wished to make her your wife; and yet I will grant that she has a taking way with her; she seems to fear nothing but her own superstitions and folly, but I am very happy to think that all is over between you. She never loved you, my Ralph; for she cares nothing when I speak your name, as I have done two or three times; nor yet Master More either. I think she has no heart."

Ralph had wondered a little as he read this, at his mother's curious interest in the girl; and he wondered too at the report of Beatrice's callousness. It was her damned pride, he assured himself.

Then, one evening as he arrived home from Hackney where he had slept the previous night; he found a messenger waiting for him. The letter had not been sent on to him, as he had not left word where he was going.

It contained a single line from his father.

"Your mother is ill. Come at once. She wishes for you."

*I*t was in the stormy blackness of a February midnight that he rode up through the lighted gatehouse to his home. Above the terrace as he came up the road the tall hall-window glimmered faintly like a gigantic luminous door hung in space; and the lower window of his father's room shone and faded as the fire leapt within.

A figure rose up suddenly from before the hall-fire as he came in, bringing with him a fierce gust of wet wind through the opened door; and when he had slipped off his dripping cloak into his servant's hands, he saw that his father was there two yards away, very stern and white, with outstretched hands.

"My son," said the old man, "you are too late. She died two hours ago."

It was a fierce shock, and for a moment he stood dazed, blinking at the light, holding his father's warm slender hands in his own, and trying to assimilate the news. He had been driven inwards, and his obstinacy weakened, during that long ride from town through the stormy sunset into the black, howling night; memories had reasserted themselves on the strength of his anxiety; and the past year or two slipped from him, and left him again the eldest son of the house and of his two parents.

Then as he looked into the pale bearded face before him, and the eyes which had looked into his own a few months ago with such passionate anger, he remembered all that was between them, dropped the hands and went forward to the fire.

His father followed him and stood by him there as he spread his fingers to the blaze, and told him the details, in short detached sentences.

She had been seized with pain and vomiting on the previous night at supper time; the doctor had been sent for, and had declared the illness to be an internal inflammation. She had grown steadily worse on the following day, with periods of unconsciousness; she had asked for Ralph an hour after she had been taken ill; the pain had seemed to become fiercer as the hours went on; she had died at ten o'clock that night.

Ralph stood there and listened, his head pressed against the high mantelpiece, and his fingers stretching and closing mechanically to supple the stiffened joints.

"Mistress Atherton was with her all the while," said his father; "she asked for her."

Ralph shot a glance sideways, and down again.

"And —" he began.

"Yes; she was shriven and anointed, thank God; she could not receive Viaticum."

Ralph did not know whether he was glad or sorry at that news. It was a proper proceeding at any rate; as proper as the candles and the shroud and the funeral rites. As regards grief, he did not feel it yet; but he was aware of a profound sensation in his soul, as of a bruise.

There was silence for a moment or two; then the wind bellowed suddenly in the chimney, the tall window gave a crack of sound, and the smoke eddied out into the room. Ralph turned round.

"They are with her still," said Sir James; "we can go up presently."

The other shook his head abruptly.

"No," he said, "I will wait until tomorrow. Which is my room?"

"Your old room," said his father. "I have had a truckle-bed set there for your man. Will you find your way? I must stay here for Mistress Atherton."

Ralph nodded sharply, and went out, down the hill.

*I*t was half an hour more before Beatrice appeared; and then Sir James looked up from his chair at the sound of a footstep and saw her coming up the matted floor. Her face was steady and resolute, but there were dark patches under her eyes, for she had not slept for two nights.

Sir James stood up, and held out his hands.

"Ralph has come," he said. "He is gone to his room. Where are the others?"

"The priests are at prayers and Meg too," she said, "It is all ready, sir. You may go up when you please."

"I must say a word first," said Sir James. "Sit down, Mistress Atherton."

He drew forward his chair for her; and himself stood up on the hearth, leaning his head on his hand and looking down into the fire.

"It is this," he said: "May our Lord reward you for what you have done for us."

Beatrice was silent.

"You know she asked my pardon," he said, "when we were left alone together. You do not know what that means. And she gave me her forgiveness for all my folly —"

Beatrice drew a sharp breath in spite of herself.

"We have both sinned," he went on; "we did not understand one another; and I feared we should part so. That we have not, we have to thank you —"

His old voice broke suddenly; and Beatrice heard him draw a long sobbing breath. She knew she ought to speak, but her brain was bewildered with the want of sleep and the long struggle; she could not think of a word to say; she felt herself on the verge of hysteria.

"You have done it all," he said again presently. "She took all that Mr. Carleton said patiently enough, he told me. It is all your work. Mistress Atherton —"

She looked up questioningly with her bright tired eyes.

"Mistress Atherton; may I know what you said to her?"

Beatrice made a great effort and recovered her self-control.

"I answered her questions," she said.

"Questions? Did she ask you of the Faith? Did she speak of me? Am I asking too much?"

Beatrice shook her head. For a moment again she could not speak.

"I am asking what I should not," said the old man.

"No, no," cried the girl, "you have a right to know. Wait, I will tell you —"

Again she broke off, and felt her own breath begin to sob in her throat. She buried her face in her hands a moment.

"God forgive me," said the other. "I —"

"It was about your son Ralph," said Beatrice bravely, though her lips shook.

"She — she asked whether I had ever loved him at all — and —"

"Mistress Beatrice, Mistress Beatrice, I entreat you not to say more."

"And I told her — yes; and, yes — still."

Chapter V
THE MUMMERS

*I*t was a strange meeting for Beatrice and Ralph the next morning. She saw him first from the gallery in chapel at mass, kneeling by his father, motionless and upright, and watched him go down the aisle when it was over. She waited a few minutes longer, quieting herself, marshaling her forces, running her attention over each movement or word that might prove unruly in his presence; and then she got up from her knees and went down.

It had been an intolerable pain to tell the dying woman that she loved her son; it tore open the wound again, for she had never yet spoken that secret aloud to any living soul, not even to her own. When the question came, as she knew it would, she had not hesitated an instant as to the answer, and yet the answer had materialized what had been impalpable before.

As she had looked down from the gallery this morning she knew that she hated, in theory, every detail of his outlook on life; he was brutal, insincere; he had lied to her; he was living on the fruits of sacrilege; he had outraged every human tie he possessed; and yet she loved every hair of his dark head, every movement of his strong hands. It was that that had broken down the mother's reserve; she had been beaten by the girl's insolence, as a dog is beaten into respect; she had only one thing that she had not been able to forgive, and that was that this girl had tossed aside her son's love; then the question had been asked and answered; and the work had been done. The dying woman had surrendered wholly to the superior personality; and had obeyed like a child.

*S*he had a sense of terrible guilt as she went downstairs into the passage that opened on the court; the fact that she had put into words what had lain in her heart, made her fancy that the secret was written on her face.

Then again she drove the imagination down by sheer will; she knew that she had won back her self-control, and could trust her own discretion.

Their greeting was that of two acquaintances. There was not the tremor of an eyelid of either, or a note in either voice, that betrayed that their relations had once been different. Ralph thanked her courteously for her attention to his mother; and she made a proper reply. Then they all sat down to breakfast.

Then Margaret had to be attended to, for she was half-wild with remorse; she declared to Beatrice when they went upstairs together that she had been a wicked daughter, that she had resented her mother's words again and again, had behaved insolently, and so forth. Beatrice took her in her arms.

"My dear," she said, "indeed you must leave all that now. Come and see her; she is at peace, and you must be."

The bedroom where Lady Torridon had died was arranged as a *chapelle ardente;* the great bed had been moved out into the center of the room. Six tall candlesticks with escutcheons and yellow tapers formed a slender mystical wall of fire and light about it; the windows were draped a couple of kneeling desks were set at the foot of the bed. Chris was kneeling at one beside his father as they went in, and Mary Maxwell, who had arrived a few hours before death had taken place, was by herself in a corner.

Beatrice drew Margaret to the second desk, pushed the book to her, and knelt by her. There lay the body of the strange, fierce, lonely woman, with her beautiful hands crossed, pale as wax, with a crucifix between them; and those great black eyebrows beyond, below which lay the double reverse curve of the lashes. It seemed as if she was watching them both, as her manner had been in life, with a tranquil cynicism.

And was she at peace, thought Beatrice, as she had told her daughter just now? Was it possible to believe that that stormy, vicious spirit had been quieted so suddenly? And yet that would be no greater miracle than that which death had wrought to the body. If the one was so still, why not the other? At least she had asked pardon of her husband for those years of alienation; she had demanded the sacraments of the Church!

Beatrice bowed her head, and prayed for the departed soul.

She was disturbed by the soft opening of a door, and lifted her eyes to see Ralph stand a moment by the head of the bed, before he sank on his knees. She could watch every detail of his face in the candlelight;

his thin tight lips, his heavy eyebrows so like his mother's, his curved nostrils, the clean sharp line of his jaw.

She found herself analyzing his processes of thought. His mother had been the one member of his family with whom he had had sympathy; they understood one another, these two bitter souls, as no one else did, except perhaps Beatrice herself. How aloof they had stood from all ordinary affections; how keen must have been their dual loneliness! And what did this snapped thread mean to him now? To what, in his opinion, did the broken end lead that had passed out from the visible world to the invisible? Did he think that all was over, and that the one soul that had understood his own had passed like a candle flame into the dark? And she too — was she crying for her son, a thin soundless sobbing in the world beyond sight? Above all, did he understand how alone he was now — how utterly, eternally alone, unless he turned his course?

A great well of pity broke up and surged in her heart, flooding her eyes with tears, as she looked at the living son and the dead mother; and she dropped her head on her hands again, and prayed for his soul as well as for hers.

*I*t was a very strange atmosphere in the house during the day or two that passed before the funeral. The household met at meals and in the parlor and chapel, but seldom at other times. Ralph was almost invisible; and silent when he appeared. There were no explanations on either side; he behaved with a kind of distant courtesy to the others, answered their questions, volunteered a word or two sometimes; made himself useful in small ways as regarded giving orders to the servants, inspecting the funeral standard and escutcheons, and making one or two arrangements which fell to him naturally; and went out by himself on horseback or on foot during the afternoon. His contempt seemed to have fallen from him; he was as courteous to Chris as to the others; but no word was spoken on either side as regarded either the past and the great gulf that separated him from the others, or the future relations between him and his home.

The funeral took place three days after death, on the Saturday morning; a requiem was sung in the presence of the body in the parish church; and Beatrice sat with the mourners in the Torridon chapel behind the black hearse set with lights, before the open vault in the center of the pavement. Ralph sat two places beyond her, with Sir James between; and she was again vividly conscious of his presence, of his movements as he knelt and sat; and again she wondered what all the solemn ceremonies meant to him, the yellow candles, the black vestments, the mysterious hallowing of the body with incense and water — counteracting, as it were, with fragrance and brightness, the corruption and darkness of the grave.

She walked back with Margaret, who clung to her now, almost desperately, finding in her sane serenity an antidote to her own remorse; and as she walked through the garden and across the moat, with Nicholas and Mary coming behind, she watched the three men going in front, Sir James in the middle, the monk on his left, and the slow-stepping Ralph on his right, and marveled at the grim acting.

There they went, the father and his two sons, side by side in courteous silence — she noticed Ralph step forward to lift the latch of the garden-gate for the others to pass through — and between them lay an impassable gulf; she found herself wondering whether the other gulf that they had looked into half an hour before were so deep or wide.

She was out again with Sir James alone in the evening before supper, and learnt from him then that Ralph was to stay till Monday.

"He has not spoken to me of returning again," said the old man, "Of course it is impossible. Do you not think so, Mistress Atherton."

"It is impossible," she said. "What good would be served?"

"What good?" repeated the other.

The evening was falling swiftly, layer on layer of twilight, as they turned to come back to the house. The steeple of the church rose up on their left, slender and ghostly against the yellow sky, out of the black yews and cypresses that lay banked below it. They stopped and looked at it a moment, as it aspired to heaven from the bones that lay about its base, like an eternal resurrection wrought in stone. There all about it were the mortal and the dead; the stones and iron slabs leaned, as they knew, in hundreds about the grass; and round them again stood the roofs, beginning now to kindle under the eaves, where the living slept and ate. There was a rumbling of heavy carts somewhere beyond the village, a crack or two of a whip, the barking of a dog.

Then they turned again and went up to the house.

*I*t was the chaplain who was late this evening for supper. The others waited a few minutes by the fire, but there was no sign of him. A servant was sent up to his room and came back to report that he had changed his cassock and gone out; a boy had come from the parish-priest, said the man, ten minutes before, and Mr. Carleton had probably been sent for.

They waited yet five minutes, but the priest did not appear, and they sat down. Supper was nearly over before he came. He came in by the side-door from the court, splashed with mud, and looking pale and concerned. He went straight up to Sir James.

"May I speak with you, sir?" he said.

The old man got up at once, and went down the hall with him.

The rest waited, expecting them to return, but there was no sign of them; and Ralph at last rose and led the way to the oak-parlor. As they passed the door of Sir James's room they heard the sound of voices within.

Conversation was a very difficult matter that evening. Ralph had behaved with considerable grace and tact, but Nicholas had not responded. Ever since his arrival on the day before the funeral he had eyed Ralph like a strange dog intruded into a house; Mary had hovered round her husband, watchful and anxious, stepping hastily into gaps in the conversation, sliding in a sentence or two as Nicholas licked his lips in preparation for a snarl; once even putting her hand swiftly on his and drowning a growl with a word of her own. Ralph had been wonderfully self-controlled; only once had Beatrice seen him show his teeth for a moment as his brother-in-law had scowled more plainly than usual.

The atmosphere was charged tonight, now that the master of the house was away; and as Ralph took his seat in his father's chair, Beatrice had caught her breath for a moment as she saw the look on Nicholas's face. It seemed as if the funeral had lifted a stone that had hitherto held the two angry spirits down; Nicholas, after all, was but a son-in-law, and Ralph, to his view at least, a bad son. She feared that both might think that a quarrel did not outrage decency; but she feared for Nicholas more than for Ralph.

Ralph appeared not to notice the other's scowl, and leaned easily back, his head against the carved heraldry, and rapped his fingers softly and rhythmically on the bosses of the arms.

Then she heard Nicholas draw a slow venomous breath; and the talk died on Mary's lips. Beatrice stood up abruptly, in desperation; she did not know what to say; but the movement checked Nicholas, and he glanced at her a moment. Then Mary recovered herself, put her hand sharply on her husband's, and slid out an indifferent sentence. Beatrice saw Ralph's eyes move swiftly and sideways and down again, and a tiny wrinkle of a smile show itself at the corners of his mouth. But that danger was passed; and a minute later they heard the door of Sir James's room opposite open, and the footsteps of the two men come out.

Ralph stood up at once as his father came in, followed by the priest, and stepped back to the window-seat; there was the faintest hint in the slight motion of his hands to the effect that he had held his post as the eldest son until the rightful owner came. But the consciousness of it in Beatrice's mind was swept away as she looked at the old man, standing with a white stern face and his hands clenched at his sides. She could see that something impended, and stood up quickly.

"Mr. Carleton has brought shocking news," he said abruptly; and his eyes wandered to his eldest son standing in the shadow of the curtain. "A company of mummers has arrived in the village — they — they are to give their piece tomorrow."

There was a dead silence for a moment, for all knew what this meant.

Nicholas sprang to his feet.

"By God, they shall not!" he said.

Sir James lifted his hand sharply.

"We cannot hinder it," he said. "The priests have done what they can. The fellow tells them —" he paused, and again his eyes wandered to Ralph — "the fellow tells them he is under the protection of my Lord Cromwell."

There was a swift rustle in the room. Nicholas faced sharply round to the window-seat, his hands clenched and his face quivering. Ralph did not move.

"Tell them, father," said Sir James.

The chaplain gave his account. He had been sent for by the parish priest just before supper, and had gone with him to the barn that had been hired for the performance. The carts had arrived that evening from Maidstone; and were being unpacked. He had seen the properties; they were of the usual kind — all the paraphernalia for the parody of the Mass that was usually given by such actors. He had seen the vestments, the friar's habit, the red-nosed mask, the woman's costume and wig — all the regular articles. The manager had tried to protest against the priests' entrance; had denied at first that any insult was intended to the Catholic Religion; and had finally taken refuge in defiance; he had flung out the properties before their eyes; had declared that no one could hinder him from doing as he pleased, since the Archbishop had not protested; and Lord Cromwell had given him his express sanction.

"We did all we were able," said the priest. "Master Rector said he would put all the parishioners who came, under the ban of the Church; the fellow snapped his fingers in his face. I told them of Sir James's wishes; the death of my Lady — it was of no avail. We can do nothing."

The priest's sallow face was flushed with fury as he spoke; and his lips trembled piteously with horror and pain. It was the first time that the mummers had been near Overfield; they had heard tales of them from other parts of the country, but had hoped that their own village would escape the corruption. And now it had come.

He stood shaking, as he ended his account.

"Mr. Carleton says it would be of no avail for me to go down myself. I wished to. We can do nothing."

Again he glanced at Ralph, who had sat down silently in the shadow while the priest talked.

Nicholas could be restrained no longer. He shook off his wife's hand and took a step across the room.

"And you — you sit there, you devil!" he shouted.

Sir James was with him in a moment, so swiftly that Beatrice did not see him move. Margaret was clinging to her now, whispering and sobbing.

"Nick," snapped out the old man, "hold your tongue, sir. Sit down."

"God's Blood!" bellowed the squire. "You bid me sit down."

Sir James gripped him so fiercely that he stepped back.

"I bid you sit down," he said. "Ralph, will you help us?"

Ralph stood up instantly. He had not stirred a muscle as Nick shouted at him.

"I waited for that, sir," he said. "What is it you would have me do?"

Beatrice saw that his face was quite quiet as he spoke; his eyelids drooped a little; and his mouth was tight and firm. He seemed not to be aware of Nicholas's presence.

"To hinder the play-acting," said his father.

There fell a dead silence again.

"I will do it, sir," said his son. "It — it is but decent."

And in the moment of profound astonishment that fell, he came straight across the room, passed by them all without turning his head, and went out.

Beatrice felt a fierce emotion grip her throat as she looked after him, and saw the door close. Then Margaret seized her again, and she turned to quiet her.

She was aware that Sir James had gone out after his son, after a moment of silence, and she heard his footsteps pass along the flags outside.

"Oh! God bless him!" sobbed Margaret.

Sir James came back immediately, shook his head, went across the room, and sat down in the seat that Ralph had left. A dreadful stillness fell. Margaret was quiet now. Mary was sitting with her husband on the other side of the hearth. Chris rose presently and sat down by his father, but no one spoke a word.

Then Nicholas got up uneasily, came across the room, and stood with his back to the hearth warming himself. Beatrice saw him glance now and again to the shadowed window-seat where the two men sat; he hummed a note or two to himself softly; then turned round and stared at the fire with outstretched hands.

The bell rang for prayers, and still without a word being spoken they all got up and went out.

In the same silence they came back. Ralph's servant was standing by the door as they entered.

"If you please, sir, Mr. Ralph is come in. He bade me tell you that all is arranged."

The old man looked at him, swallowed once in his throat; and at last spoke.

"It is arranged, you say? It will not take place?"

"It will not take place, sir."

"Where is Mr. Ralph?"

"He is gone to his room, sir. He bade me tell you he would be leaving early for London."

Chapter VI

A CATASTROPHE

*R*alph rode away early next morning, yet not so early as to escape an interview with his father. They met in the hall, Sir James in his loose morning gown and Ralph booted and spurred with his short cloak and tight cap. The old man took him by the sleeve, drawing him to the fire that burned day and night in winter.

"Ralph — Ralph, my son," he said, "I must thank you for last night."

"You have to thank yourself only, sir, and my mother. I could do no otherwise."

"It is you —" began his father.

"It is certainly not Nick, sir. The hot fool nearly provoked me."

"But you hate such mummery yourself, my son?"

Ralph hesitated.

"It is not seemly —" began his father again.

"It is certainly not seemly; but neither are the common folk seemly."

"Did you have much business with them, my son?" Ralph smiled in the firelight.

"Why, no, sir. I told them who I was. I charged myself with the burden."

"And you will not be in trouble with my Lord?"

"My Lord has other matters to think of than a parcel of mummers."

Then they separated; and Ralph rode down the drive with his servants behind him. Neither father nor son had said a word of any return. Neither had Ralph had one private word with Beatrice during his three days' stay. Once he had come into the parlor to find her going out at the other door; and he had wondered whether she had heard his step and gone out on purpose. But he knew very well that under the superficial courtesy between him and her there lay something deeper — some passionate emotion vibrated like a beam between them; but he did not know, even on his side and still less on hers, whether that emotion were one of love or loathing. It was partly from the discomfort of the charged atmosphere, partly from a shrinking from thanks and explanations that he had determined to go up to London a day earlier than he had intended; he had a hatred of personal elaborateness.

*H*e found Cromwell, on his arrival in London, a little less moody than he had been in the previous week; for he was busy with preparations for the Parliament that was to meet in April; and to the occupation that this gave him there was added a good deal of business connected with Henry's negotiations with the Emperor. The dispute, that at present centered round the treatment of Englishmen in Spain, and other similar matters, in reality ran its roots far deeper; and there were a hundred details which occupied the minister. But there was still a hint of storm in the air; Cromwell spoke brusquely once or twice without cause, and Ralph refrained from saying anything about the affair at Overfield, but took up his own work again quietly.

A fortnight later, however, he heard of it once more.

He was sitting at a second table in Cromwell's own room in the Rolls House, when one of the secretaries came up with a bundle of reports, and laid them as usual before Ralph.

Ralph finished the letter he was engaged on — one to Dr. Barnes who had preached a Protestant sermon at Paul's Cross, and who now challenged Bishop Gardiner to a public disputation. Ralph was telling him to keep his pugnacity to himself; and when he had done took up the reports and ran his eyes over them.

They were of the usual nature — complaints, informations, protests, appeals from men of every rank of life; agents, farm-laborers, priests, ex-Religious, fanatics — and he read them quickly through, docketing their contents at the head of each that his master might be saved trouble.

At one, however, he stopped, glanced momentarily at Cromwell, and then read on.

It was an illiterate letter, ill-spelt and smudged, and consisted of a complaint from a man who signed himself Robert Benham, against "Mr. Ralph Torridon, as he named himself," for hindering the performance of a piece entitled "The Jolly Friar" in the parish of Overfield, on Sunday, February the first. Mr. Torridon, the writer stated, had used my Lord Cromwell's name and authority in stopping the play; expenses had been incurred in connection with it, for a barn had been hired, and the transport of the properties had cost money; and Mr. Benham desired to know whether these expenses would be made good to him, and if Mr. Torridon had acted in accordance with my Lord's wishes.

Ralph bit his pen in some perplexity, when he had finished making out the document. He wondered whether he had better show it to Cromwell; it might irritate him or not, according to his mood. If it was destroyed surely no harm would be done; and yet Ralph had a disinclination to destroy it. He sat a moment or two longer considering; once he took the paper by the corners to tear it; then laid it down again; glanced once more at the heavy intent face a couple of yards away, and then by a sudden impulse took up his pen and wrote a line on the corner explaining the purport of the paper, initialed it, and laid it with the rest.

Cromwell was so busy during the rest of the day that there was no opportunity to explain the circumstances to him; indeed he was hardly in the room again, so great was the crowd that waited on him continually for interviews, and Ralph went away, leaving the reports for his chief to examine at his leisure.

*T*he next morning there was a storm.

Cromwell burst out on him as soon as he came in.

"Shut the door, Mr. Torridon," he snapped. "I must have a word with you."

Ralph closed the door and came across to Cromwell's table and stood there, apparently imperturbable, but with a certain quickening of his pulse.

"What is this, sir?" snarled the other, taking up the letter that was laid at his hand. "Is it true?"

Ralph looked at him coolly.

"What is it, my Lord? Mr. Robert Benham?"

"Yes, Mr. Robert Benham. Is it true? I wish an answer."

"Certainly, my Lord. It is true."

"You hindered this piece being played? And you used my name?"

"I told them who I was — yes."

Cromwell slapped the paper down.

"Well, that is to use my name, is it not, Mr. Torridon?"

"I suppose it is."

"You suppose it is! And tell me, if you please, why you hindered it."

"I hindered it because it was not decent. My mother had been buried that day. My father asked me to do so."

"Not decent! When the mummers have my authority!"

"If your Lordship does not understand the indecency, I cannot explain it."

Ralph was growing angry now. It was not often that Cromwell treated him like a naughty boy; and he was beginning to resent it.

The other stared at him under black brows.

"You are insolent, sir."

Ralph bowed.

"See here," said Cromwell, "my men must have no master but me. They must leave houses and brethren and sisters for my sake. You should understand that by now; and that I repay them a hundredfold. You have been long enough in my service to know it. I have said enough. You can sit down, Mr. Torridon."

Ralph went to his seat in a storm of fury. He felt he was supremely in the right — in the right in stopping the play, and still more so for not destroying the complaint when it was in his hands. He had been scolded like a school-child, insulted and shouted down. His hand shook as he took up his pen, and he kept his back resolutely turned to his master. Once he was obliged to ask him a question, and he did so with an icy aloofness. Cromwell answered him curtly, but not unkindly, and he went to his seat again still angry.

When dinner-time came near, he rose, bowed slightly to Cromwell and went towards the door. As his fingers touched the handle he heard his name called; and turned round to see the other looking at him oddly.

"Mr. Torridon — you will dine with me?"

"I regret I cannot, my Lord," said Ralph; and went out of the room.

*T*here were no explanations or apologies on either side when they met again; but in a few days their behavior to one another was as usual. Yet underneath the smooth surface Ralph's heart rankled and pricked with resentment.

*A*t the meeting of Parliament in April, the business in Cromwell's hands grow more and more heavy and distracting.

Ralph went with him to Westminster, and heard him deliver his eloquent little speech on the discord that prevailed in England, and the King's determination to restore peace and concord.

"On the Word of God," cried the statesman, speaking with extraordinary fervor, his eyes kindling as he looked round the silent crowded benches, and his left hand playing with his chain, "On the Word of God His Highness' princely mind is fixed; on this Word he depends for his sole support; and with all his might his Majesty will labor that error shall be taken away, and true doctrines be taught to his people, modeled by the rule of the Gospel."

Three days later when Ralph came into his master's room, Cromwell looked up at him with a strange animation in his dark eyes.

"Good-day, sir," he said; "I have news that I hope will please you. His Grace intends to confer on me one more mark of his favor. I am to be Earl of Essex."

It was startling news. Ralph had supposed that the minister was not standing so high with the King as formerly, since the unfortunate incident of the Cleves marriage. He congratulated him warmly.

"It is a happy omen," said the other. "Let us pray that it be a constellation and not a single star. There are others of my friends, Mr. Torridon, who have claim to His Highness' gratitude."

He looked at him smiling; and Ralph felt his heart quicken once more, as it always did, at the hint of an honor for himself.

The business of Parliament went on; and several important bills became law. A land-act was followed by one that withdrew from most of the towns of England the protection of a sanctuary in the case of certain specified crimes; the navy was dealt with; and then in spite of the promises of the previous years a heavy money-bill was passed. Finally five more Catholics, four priests and a woman, were attainted for high treason on various charges.

*R*alph was not altogether happy as May drew on. There began to be signs that his master's policy with regard to the Cleves alliance was losing ground in the councils of the State; but Cromwell himself seemed to acquiesce, so it appeared as if his own mind was beginning to change. There was a letter to Pate, the ambassador to the Emperor, that Ralph had to copy one day, and he gathered from it that conciliation was to be used towards Charles in place of the old defiance.

But he did not see much of Parliament affairs this month.

Cromwell had told him to sort a large quantity of private papers that had gradually accumulated in Ralph's own house at Westminster; for that he desired the removal of most of them to his own keeping.

They were an enormous mass of documents, dealing with every sort and kind of the huge affairs that had passed through Cromwell's hands for the last five years. They concerned hundreds of persons, living and dead — statesmen, nobles, the foreign Courts, priests, Religious, farmers, tradesmen — there was scarcely a class that was not represented there.

Ralph sat hour after hour in his chair with locked doors, sorting, docketing, and destroying; and amazed by this startling object-lesson of the vast work in which he had had a hand. There were secrets there that would burst like a bomb if they were made public — intrigues, bribes, threats, revelations; and little by little a bundle of the most important documents accumulated on the table before him. The rest lay in heaps on the floor.

Those that he had set aside beneath his own eye were a miscellaneous set as regarded their contents; the only unity between them lay in the fact that they were especially perilous to Cromwell. Ralph felt as if he were handling gunpowder as he took them up one by one or added to the heap.

The new coronet that my Lord of Essex had lately put upon his head would not be there another day, if these were made public. There would not be left even a head to put it upon. Ralph knew that a great minister like his master was bound to have a finger in very curious affairs; but he had not recognized how exceptional these were, nor how many, until he had the bundle of papers before him. There were cases in which persons accused and even convicted of high treason had been set at liberty on Cromwell's sole authority without reference to the King; there were commissions issued in his name under similar conditions; there were papers containing drafts, in Cromwell's own hand of statements of doctrine declared heretical by the Six Articles, and of which copies had been distributed through the country at his express order; there were copies of letters to country-sheriffs ordering the release of convicted heretics and the imprisonment of their accusers; there were evidences of enormous bribes received by him for the perversion of justice.

Ralph finished his task one June evening, and sat dazed with work and excitement, his fingers soiled with ink, his tired eyes staring at the neat bundle before him.

The Privy Council, he knew, was sitting that afternoon. Even at this moment, probably, my Lord of Essex was laying down the law, speaking in the King's name, silencing his opponents by sheer force of will, but with the Royal power behind him. And here lay the papers.

He imagined to himself with a fanciful recklessness what would happen if he made his way into the Council-room, and laid them on the table. It would be just the end of all things for his master. There would be no more bullying and denouncing then on that side; it would be a matter of a fight for life.

The memory of his own grudge, only five months old, rose before his mind; and his tired brain grew hot and cloudy with resentment. He took up the bundle in his hand and wielded it a moment, as a man might test a sword. Here was a headsman's axe, ground and sharp.

Then he was ashamed; set the bundle down again, leaned back in his chair and stretched his arms, yawning.

What a glorious evening it was! He must go out and take the air for a little by the river; he would walk down towards Chelsea.

He rose up from his chair and went to the window, threw it open and leaned out. His house stood back a little from the street; and there was a space of cobbled ground between his front-door and the uneven stones of the thoroughfare. Opposite rose up one of the tall Westminster houses, pushing forward in its upper stories, with a hundred diamond panes bright in the slanting sunshine that poured down the street from the west. Overhead rose up the fantastic stately chimneys, against the brilliant evening sky, and to right and left the street passed out of sight in a haze of sunlight.

It was a very quiet evening; the men had not yet begun to stream homewards from their occupations; and the women were busy within. A chorus of birds sounded somewhere overhead; but there was not a living creature to be seen except a dog asleep in the sunshine at the corner of the gravel.

It was delicious to lean out here, away from the fire that burned hot and red in the grate under its black mass of papers that had been destroyed, — out in the light and air. Ralph determined that he would let the fire die now; it would not be needed again.

He must go out, he told himself, and not linger here. He could lock up the papers for the present in readiness for their transport next day;

and he wondered vaguely whether his hat and cane were in the entrance-hall below.

He straightened himself, and turned away from the window, noticing as he did so the dog at the corner of the street sit up with cocked ears. He hesitated and turned back.

There was a sound of furious running coming up the street. He would just see who the madman was who ran like this on a hot evening, and then go out himself.

As he leaned again the pulsating steps came nearer; they were coming from the left, the direction of the Palace.

A moment later a figure burst into sight, crimson-faced and hatless, with arms gathered to the sides and head thrown back; it appeared to be a gentleman by the dress — but why should he run like that? He dashed across the opening and disappeared.

Ralph was interested. He waited a minute longer; but the footsteps had ceased; and he was just turning once more from the window, when another sound made him stand and listen again.

It came from the same direction as before; and at first he could not make out what it was. There was a murmur and a pattering.

It came nearer and louder; and he could distinguish once more running footsteps. Were they after a thief? he wondered. The murmur and clatter grew louder yet; and a second or two later two men burst into sight; one, an apprentice with his leather apron flapping as he ran, the other a stoutish man like a merchant. They talked and gesticulated as they went.

The murmur behind swelled up. There were the voices of many people, men and women, talking, screaming, questioning. The dog was on his feet by now, looking intently down the street.

Then the first group appeared; half a dozen men walking fast or trotting, talking eagerly. Ralph could not hear what they said.

Then a number surged into sight all at once, jostling round a center, and a clamor went up to heaven. The dog trotted up suspiciously as if to enquire.

Ralph grew excited; he scarcely knew why. He had seen hundreds of such crowds; it might mean anything, from a rise in butter to a declaration of war. But there was something fiercely earnest about this mob. Was the King ill?

He leaned further from the window and shouted; but no one paid him the slightest attention. The crowd shifted up the street, the din growing as they went; there was a sound of slammed doors; windows opened opposite and heads craned out. Something was shouted up and the heads disappeared.

Ralph sprang back from the window, as more and more surged into sight; he went to his door, glancing at his papers as he ran across; unlocked the door; listened a moment; went on to the landing and shouted for a servant.

There was a sound of footsteps and voices below; the men were already alert, but no answer came to his call. He shouted again.

"Who is there? Find out what the disturbance means."

There was an answer from one of his men; and the street door opened and closed. Again he ran to the window, and saw his man run out without his doublet across the court, and seize a woman by the arm.

He waited in passionate expectancy; saw him drop the woman's arm and turn to another; and then run swiftly back to the house.

There was something sinister in the man's very movements across that little space; he ran desperately, with his head craning forward; once he stumbled; once he glanced up at his master; and Ralph caught a sight of his face.

Ralph was on the landing as the steps thundered upstairs, and met him at the head of the flight.

"Speak man; what is it?"

The servant lifted a face stamped with terror, a couple of feet below Ralph's.

"They — they say —"

"What is it?"

"They say that the King's archers are about my Lord Essex's house."

Ralph drew a swift breath.

"Well?"

"And that my Lord was arrested at the Council today."

Ralph turned, and in three steps was in his room again. The key clacked in the lock.

Chapter VII
A QUESTION OF LOYALTY

*H*e did not know how long he stood there, with the bundle of papers gripped in his two hands; and the thoughts racing through his brain.

The noises in the street outside waned and waxed again, as the news swept down the lanes, and recoiled with a wave of excited crowds following it. Then again they died to a steady far-off murmur as the mob surged and clamored round the Palace and Abbey a couple of hundred yards away.

At last Ralph sat down; still holding the papers. He must clear his brain; and how was that possible with the images flashing through it in endless and vivid succession? For a while he could not steady himself; the shock was bewildering; he could think of nothing but the appalling drama. Essex was fallen!

Then little by little the muddy current of thought began to run clear. He began to understand what lay before him; and the question that still awaited decision.

His first instinct had been to dash the papers on to the fire and grind them into the red heart of the wood; but something had checked him. Very slowly he began to analyze that instinct.

First, was it not useless? He knew he did not possess one hundredth part of the incriminating evidence that was in existence. Of what service would it be to his master to destroy that one small bundle?

Next, what would be the result to himself if he did? It was known that he was a trusted agent of the minister's; his house would be searched; papers would be found; it would be certainly known that he had made away with evidence. There would be records of what he had, in the other houses. And what then?

On the other hand if he willingly gave up all that was in his possession, it would go far to free him from complicity.

Lastly, like a venomous snake lifting its head, his own private resentment looked him in the eyes, and there was a new sting added to it now. He had lost all, he knew well enough; wealth, honor and position had in a moment shrunk to cinders with Cromwell's fall, and for these cinders he had lost Beatrice too. He had sacrificed her to his master; and his master had failed him. A kind of fury succeeded to his dismay.

Oh, would it not be sweet to add even one more stone to the mass that was tottering over the head of that mighty bully, that had promised and not performed?

He blinked his eyes, shocked by the horror of the thought, and gripped the bundle yet more firmly. The memories of a thousand kindnesses received from his master cried at the door of his heart. The sweat dropped from his forehead; he lifted a stiff hand to wipe it away, and dropped it again into its grip on the papers.

Then he slowly recapitulated to himself the reasons for not destroying them. They were overwhelming, convincing! What was there to set against them? One slender instinct only, that cried shrill and thin that in honor he must burn that damning evidence — burn it — burn it — whether or no it would help or hinder, it must be burned!

Then again he recurred to the other side; told himself that his instinct was no more than a ludicrous sentimentality; he must be guided by reason, not impulse. Then he glanced at the impulse again. Then the two sides rushed together, locked in conflict. He moaned a little, and lay back in his chair.

*T*he bright sunlight outside had faded to a mellow evening atmosphere before he moved again; and the fire had died to one dull core of incandescence.

As he stirred, he became aware that bells were pealing outside; a melodious roar filled the air. Somewhere behind the house five brazen voices, shouting all together, bellowed the exultation of the city over the great minister's fall.

He was weary and stiff as he stood up; but the fever had left his brain; and the decision had been made. He relaxed his fingers and laid the bundle softly down on the table from which he had snatched it a couple of hours before.

They would be here soon, he knew; he wondered they had not come already.

Leaving his papers there, he went out, taking the key with him, and locking the door after him. He called up one of his men, telling him he would be ready for supper immediately in the parlor downstairs, and that any visitors who came for him were to be admitted at once.

Then he passed into his bedroom to wash and change his clothes.

*H*alf an hour later he came upstairs again.

He had supped alone, listening and watching the window as he ate; but no sign had come of any arrival. He had dressed with particular care, intending to be found at his ease when the searchers did arrive; there must be no sign of panic or anxiety. He had told his man as he rose from table, to say to any that came for him that they were expected, and to bring them immediately upstairs.

He unlocked the door of his private room, and went in. All was as he had left it; the floor between the window and table was white with ordered heaps of papers; the bundle on the table itself glimmered where he had laid it.

The fire had sunk to a spark. He tenderly lifted off the masses of black sheets that crackled as he touched them; it had not occurred to him before that these evidences of even a harmless destruction had better be removed; and he slid them carefully on to a broad sheet of paper, folded it, shaking the ashes together as he did so, and stood a moment, wondering where he should hide it.

The room was growing dark now; he put the package down; went to the fire and blew it up a little, added some wood, and presently the flames were dancing on the broad hearth.

As he stood up again he heard the knocker rap on his street-door. For a moment he had an instinct to run to the window and see who was there; but he put it aside; there was scarcely time to hide the ashes; and it was best too to give no hint of anxiety. He lifted the package of burned papers once more, and stood hesitating; a press would be worse than useless as a hiding place; all such would of course be searched. Then a thought struck him; he stood up noiselessly on his chair. The Holbein portrait of Cromwell in his furred gown and chain leaned forward from the tapestry over the mantelpiece. Ralph set one hand against the wall at the side; and then tenderly let the package fall behind the portrait. As he did so the painted and living eyes were on a level; it seemed strange to him that the faces were so near together at that moment; and it struck him with a grim irony that the master should be so protecting the servant under these circumstances.

Then he dropped lightly to the ground, and sat quickly in the chair, snatching up the bundle of papers from the table as he did so.

The steps were on the landing now; he heard the crack of the balustrade; but it seemed they were coming very quietly.

There was a moment's silence; the muscles of his throat contracted sharply, then there came the servant's tap; the handle was turned.

Ralph stood up quickly, still holding the papers, as the door opened, and Beatrice stepped forward into the room. The door shut noiselessly behind her.

*S*he stood there, with the firelight playing on her dark loose-sleeved mantle, the hood that surrounded her head, her pale face a little flushed, and her black steady eyes. Her breath came quickly between her parted lips.

Ralph stared at her, dazed by the shock, still gripping the bundle of papers. She moved forward a step; and the spell snapped.

"Mistress Beatrice," he said.

"I have come," she said; "what is it? You want me?"

She came round the table, with an air of eager expectancy.

"I — I did not know," said Ralph.

"But you wanted me. What is the matter? I heard you call."

Ralph stared again, bewildered.

"Call?" he said.

"Yes, I heard you. I was in my room at my aunt's house — ah! a couple of hours ago. You called me twice. 'Beatrice! Beatrice!' Then — then they told me what had happened about my Lord Essex."

"I called you?" repeated Ralph.

"Yes — you called me. Your voice was quite close to me, at my ear; I thought you were in the room. Tell me what it is."

She loosened her hold of her mantle as she stood there by the table; and it dropped open, showing a sparkle of jewels at her throat. She threw back her hood, and it dropped on to her shoulders, leaving visible the coiled masses of her black hair set with knots of ribbon.

"I did not call," said Ralph dully. "I do not know what you mean, Mistress Atherton."

She made a little impatient gesture.

"Ah! yes," she said, "it is something. Tell me quickly. I suppose it has to do with my Lord. What is it?"

"It is nothing," said Ralph again.

They stood looking at one another in silence. Beatrice's eyes ran a moment up and down his rich dress, the papers in his hands, then wandered to the heaped floor, the table, and returned to the papers in his hands.

"You must tell me," she said. "What is that you are holding?"

An angry terror seized Ralph.

"That is my affair, Mistress Atherton. What is your business with me?"

She came a step nearer, and leant her left hand on his table. He could see those steady eyes on his face; she looked terribly strong and controlled.

"Indeed you must tell me, Mr. Torridon. I am come here to do something. I do not know what. What are those papers?"

He turned and dropped them on to the chair behind him.

"I tell you again, I do not know what you mean."

"It is useless," she said. "Have they been to you yet? What do you mean to do about my Lord? You know he is in the Tower?"

"I suppose so," said Ralph, "but my counsel is my own."

"Mr. Torridon, let us have an end of this. I know well that you must have many secrets against my lord —"

"I tell you that what I know is nothing. I have not a hundredth part of his papers."

He felt himself desperate and bewildered, like a man being pushed to the edge of a precipice, step by step. But those black eyes held and compelled him on. He scarcely knew what he was saying.

"And are these papers all his? What have you been doing with them?"

"My Lord told me to sort them."

The words were drawn out against his own will.

"And those in your hand — on the chair. What are they?"

Ralph made one more violent effort to regain the mastery.

"If you were not a woman, Mistress Atherton, I should tell you you were insolent."

Not a ripple troubled those strong eyes.

"Tell me, Mr. Torridon, what are they?"

He stood silent and furious.

"I will tell you what they are," she said; "they are my Lord's secrets. Is it not so? And you were about to burn them. Oh! Ralph, is it not so?"

Her voice had a tone of entreaty in it. He dropped his eyes, overcome by the passion that streamed from her.

"Is it not so?" she cried again.

"Do you wish me to do so?" he said amazed. His voice seemed not his own; it was as if another spoke for him. He had the same sensation of powerlessness as once before when she had lashed him with her tongue in the room downstairs.

"Wish you?" she cried. "Why, yes; what else?"

He lifted his eyes to hers; the room seemed to have grown darker yet in those few minutes. He could only see now a shadowed face looking at him; but her bright passionate eyes shone out from it and dominated him.

Again he spoke, in spite of himself.

"I shall not burn them," he said.

"Shall not? shall not?"

"I shall not," he said again.

There was silence. Ralph's soul was struggling desperately within him. He put out his hand mechanically and took up the papers once more, as if to guard them from this fierce, imperious woman. Beatrice's eyes followed the movement; and then rested once more on his face. Then she spoke again, with a tense deliberateness that drove every word home, piercing and sharp to the very center of his spirit.

"Listen," she said, "for this is what I came to say. I know what you are thinking — I know every thought as if it were my own. You tell yourself that it is useless to burn those secrets; that there are ten thousand more — enough to cast my lord. I make no answer to that."

"You tell yourself that you can only save yourself by giving them up to his enemies. I make no answer to that."

"You tell yourself that it will be known if you destroy them — that you will be counted as one of His Highness's enemies. I make no answer to that. And I tell you to burn them."

She came a step nearer. There was not a yard between them now; and the fire of her words caught and scorched him with their bitterness.

"You have been false to every high and noble thing. You have been false to your own conscience — to your father — your brother — your sister — your Church — your King and your God. You have been false to love and honor. You have been false to yourself. And now Almighty God of His courtesy gives you one more opportunity — an opportunity to be true to your master. I say nothing of him. God is his judge. You know what that verdict will be. And yet I bid you be true to him. He has a thousand claims on you. You have served him, though it be but Satan's service; yet it is the highest that you know — God help you! He is called friendless now. Shall that be wholly true of him? You will be called a traitor presently — shall that be wholly true of you? Or shall there be one tiny point in which you are not false and treacherous as you have been in all other points?"

She stopped again, looking him fiercely in the eyes.

*F*rom the street outside there came the sound of footsteps; the ring of steel on stone. Ralph heard it, and his eyes rolled round to the window; but he did not move.

Beatrice was almost touching him now. He felt the fragrance that hung about her envelop him for a moment. Then he felt a touch on the papers; and his fingers closed more tightly.

The steps outside grew louder and ceased; and the house suddenly reverberated with a thunder of knocking.

Beatrice sprang back.

"Nay, you shall give me them," she said; and stood waiting with outstretched hand.

Ralph lifted the papers slowly, stared at them, and at her.

Then he held them out.

*I*n a moment she had snatched them; and was on her knees by the hearth. Ralph watched her, and listened to the steps coming up the stairs. The papers were alight now. The girl dashed her fingers among them, grinding, tearing, separating the heavy pages.

They were almost gone by now; the thick smoke poured up the chimney; and still Beatrice tore and dashed the ashes about.

There was a knocking at the door; and the handle turned. The girl rose from her knees and smiled at Ralph as the door opened, and the pursuivants stood there in the opening.

Chapter VIII

TO CHARING

Chris had something very like remorse after Ralph had left Overfield, and no words of explanation or regret had been spoken on either side. He recognized that he had not been blameless at the beginning of their estrangement — if, indeed, there ever had been a beginning — for their inflamed relations had existed to some extent back into boyhood as far as he could remember; but he had been responsible for at least a share in the fierce words in Ralph's house after the death of the Carthusians. He had been hotheaded, insolent, theatrical; and he had not written to acknowledge it. He had missed another opportunity at Lewes — at least one — when pride had held him back from speaking, for fear that he should be thought to be currying favor. And now this last opportunity, the best of all — when Ralph had been accessible and courteous, affected, Chris imagined, by the death of his mother — this too had been missed; and he had allowed his brother to ride away without a word of regret or more than formal affection.

He was troubled at mass, an hour after Ralph had gone; the distraction came between him and the sweet solemnity upon which he was engaged. His soul was dry and moody. He showed it in his voice. As a younger brother in past years; as a monk and a priest now, he knew that the duty of the first step to a reconciliation had lain with him; and that he had not taken it.

It had been a troubled household altogether when Ralph had gone. There was first the shock of Lady Torridon's death, and the hundred regrets that it had left behind. Then Beatrice too, who had helped them all so much, had told them that she must go back to town — her aunt was alone in the little house at Charing, for the friend who had spent Christmas there was gone back to the country; and Margaret, consequently, had been almost in despair. Lastly Sir James himself had been troubled; wondering whether he might not have been warmer with Ralph, more outspoken in his gratitude for the affair of the mummers, more ready to welcome an explanation from his son. The shadow of Ralph then rested on the household, and there was something of pathos in it. He was so much detached now, so lonely, and it seemed that he was content it should be so.

*T*here were pressing matters too to be arranged; and, weightiest of all, those relating to Margaret's future. She would now be the only woman besides the servants, in the house; and it was growing less and less likely that she would be ever able to take up the Religious Life again in England. There seemed little reason for her remaining in the country, unless indeed she threw aside the Religious habit altogether, and went to live at Great Keynes as Mary preferred. Beatrice made an offer to receive her in London for a while, but in this case again she would have to wear secular dress.

The evening before Beatrice left, the two sat and talked for a couple of hours. Margaret was miserable; she cried a little, clung to Beatrice, and then was ashamed of herself.

"My dear child," said the other. "It is in your hands. You can do as you please."

"But I cannot," sobbed the nun. "I cannot; I do not know. Let me come with you, Beatrice."

Beatrice then settled down and talked to her. She told her of her duty to her father for the present; she must remember that he was lonely now. In any case she must not think of leaving home for another six months. In the meantime she had to consider two points. First, did she consider herself in conscience bound to Religion? What did the priest tell her? If she did so consider herself, then there was no question; she must go to Bruges and join the others. Secondly, if not, did she think herself justified in leaving her father in the summer? If so, she might either go to Great Keynes, or come up for at least a long visit to Charing.

"And what do you think?" asked the girl piteously.

"Do you wish me to tell you!" said Beatrice.

Margaret nodded.

"Then I think you should go to Bruges in July or August."

Margaret stared at her; the tears were very near her eyes again.

"My darling; I should love to have you in London," went on the other caressing her. "Of course I should. But I cannot see that King Henry his notions make any difference to your vows. They surely stand. Is it not so, my dear?"

And so after a little more talk Margaret consented. Her mind had told her that all along; it was her heart only that protested against this final separation from her friend.

Chris too agreed when she spoke to him a day or two later when Beatrice had gone back. He said he had been considering his own case too; and that unless something very marked intervened he proposed to follow Dom Anthony abroad. They could travel together, he said. Finally, when the matter was laid before their father he also consented.

"I shall do very well," he said. "Mary spoke to me of it; and Nicholas has asked me to make my home at Great Keynes; so if you go, my son, with Meg in the summer, I shall finish matters here, lease out the estate, and Mr. Carleton and I shall betake ourselves there. Unless" — he said — "unless Ralph should come to another mind."

*A*s the spring and early summer drew on, the news, as has been seen, was not reassuring.

In spite of the Six Articles of the previous year by which all vows of chastity were declared binding before God, there was no hint of making it possible for the thousands of Religious in England still compelled by them to return to the Life in which such vows were tolerable. The Religious were indeed dispensed from obedience and poverty by the civil authority; it was possible for them to buy, inherit, and occupy property; but a recognition of their corporate life was as far as ever away. It was becoming plainer every day that those who wished to pursue their vocation must do so in voluntary exile; and letters were already being exchanged between the brother and sister at home and the representatives of their respective communities on the Continent.

Then suddenly on the eleventh of June there arrived the news of Cromwell's fall and of all that it involved to Ralph.

They were at dinner when it came.

There was a door suddenly thrust open at the lower end of the hall; and a courier, white with dust and stiff with riding, limped up the matting and delivered Beatrice's letter. It was very short.

"Come," she had written. "My Lord of Essex is arrested. He is in the Tower. Mr. Ralph, too, is there for refusing to inform against him. He has behaved gallantly."

There followed a line from Mistress Jane Atherton, her aunt, offering rooms in her own house.

A wild confusion fell upon the household. Men ran to and fro, women whispered and sobbed in corners under shadow of the King's displeasure that lay on the house, the road between the terrace and the stable buzzed with messengers, ordering and counter-ordering, for it was not certain at first that Margaret would not go. A mounted groom dashed up for instructions and was met by Sir James in his riding-cloak on the terrace who bade him ride to Great Keynes with the news, and entreat Sir Nicholas Maxwell to come up to London and his wife to Overfield; there was not time to write. Sir James's own room was in confusion; his clothes lay tumbled on the ground and a distraught servant tossed them this way and that; Chris was changing his habit upstairs, for it would mean disaster to go to town as a monk. Margaret was on her knees in chapel, silent and self-controlled, but staring piteously at the compassionate figure of the great Mother who looked down on her with Her Son in Her arms. The huge dog under the chapel-cloister lifted his head and bayed in answer, as frantic figures fled across the court before him. And over all lay the hot June sky, and round about the deep peaceful woods.

A start was made at three o'clock.

Sir James was already in his saddle, as Chris ran out; an unfamiliar figure in his plain priest's cloak and cap and great riding boots beneath. A couple of grooms waited behind, and another held the monk's horse. Margaret was on the steps, white and steadied by prayer; and the chaplain stood behind with a strong look in his eyes as they met those of his patron.

"Take care of her, father; take care of her. Her sister will be here tonight, please God. Oh! God bless you, my dear! Pray for us all. Jesu keep us all! Chris, are you mounted?"

Then they were off; and the white dust rose in clouds about them.

*I*t was between eight and nine as they rode up the north bank of the river from London Bridge to Charing.

It had been a terrible ride, with but few words between the two, and long silences that were the worst of all; as, blotting out the rich country and the deep woods and the meadows and heathery hills on either side of the road through Surrey, visions moved and burned before them, such as the King's vengeance had made possible to the imagination. From far away across the Southwark fields Chris had seen the huddled buildings of the City, the princely spire that marked them, and had heard the sweet jangling of the thousand bells that told the Angelus;

but he had thought of little but of that high gateway under which they must soon pass, where the pikes against the sky made palpable the horrors of his thought. He had given one swift glance up as he went beneath; and then his heart sickened as they went on, past the houses and St. Thomas's chapel with gleams of the river seen beneath. Then as he looked his breath came sharp; far down there eastwards, seen for a moment, rose up the somber towers where Ralph lay, and the saints had suffered.

The old Religious Houses, stretching in a splendid line upwards, from the Augustinian priory near the river-bank, along the stream that flowed down from Ludgate, caught the last rays of sunlight high against the rich sky as the riders went along towards Charing between the sedge-brinked tide and the slope of grass on their right; and the monk's sorrowful heart was overlaid again with sorrow as he looked at them, empty now and desolate where once the praises of God had sounded day and night.

They stopped beneath the swinging sign of an inn, with Westminister towers blue and magical before them, to ask for Mistress Atherton's house, and were directed a little further along and nearer to the water's edge.

It was a little old house when they came to it, built on a tiny private embankment that jutted out over the flats of the river-bank; of plaster and timber with overhanging storeys and windows beneath the roof. It stood by itself, east of the village, and almost before the jangle of the bell had died away, Beatrice herself was at the door, in her house-dress, bare-headed; with a face at once radiant and constrained.

She took them upstairs immediately, after directing the men to take the horses, when they had unloaded the luggage, back to the inn where they had enquired the way: for there was no stable, she said, attached to the house.

Chris came behind his father as if in a dream through the dark little hall and up the two flights on to the first landing. Beatrice stopped at a door.

"You can say what you will," she said, "before my aunt. She is of our mind in these matters."

Then they were in the room; a couple of candles burned on a table before the curtained window; and an old lady with a wrinkled kindly face hobbled over from her chair and greeted the two travelers.

"I welcome you, gentlemen," she said, "if a sore heart may say so to sore hearts."

There was no news of Nicholas, they were told; he had not been heard of.

*T*hey heard the story so far as Beatrice knew it; but it was softened for their ears. She had found Ralph, she said, hesitating what to do. He had been plainly bewildered by the sudden news; they had talked a while; and then he had handed her the papers to burn. The magistrate sent by the Council had arrived to find the ashes still smoking. He had questioned Ralph sharply, for he had come with authority behind him; and Ralph had refused to speak beyond telling him that the bundles lying on the floor were all the papers of my Lord Essex that were in his possession. They had laid hands on these, and then searched the room. A quantity of ashes, Beatrice said, had fallen from behind a portrait over the hearth when they had shifted it. Then the magistrate had questioned her too, enquired where she lived, and let her go. She had waited at the corner of the street, and watched the men come out. Ralph walked in the center as a prisoner. She had followed them to the river; had mixed with the crowd that gathered there; and had heard the order given to the wherryman to pull to the Tower. That was all that she knew.

"Thank God for your son, sir. He bore himself gallantly."

There was a silence as she ended. The old man looked at her wondering and dazed. It was so sad, that the news scarcely yet conveyed its message.

"And my Lord Essex?" he said.

"My Lord is in the Tower too. He was arrested at the Council by the Duke of Norfolk."

The old lady intervened then, and insisted on their going down to supper. It would be ready by now, she said, in the parlor downstairs.

They supped, themselves silent, with Beatrice leaning her arms on the table, and talking to them in a low voice, telling them all that was said. She did not attempt to prophesy smoothly. The feeling against Cromwell, she said, passed all belief. The streets had been filled with a roaring crowd last night. She had heard them bellowing till long after dark. The bells were pealed in the City churches hour after hour, in triumph over the minister's fall.

"The dogs!" she said fiercely. "I never thought to say it, but my heart goes out to him."

Her spirit was infections. Chris felt a kind of half-joyful recklessness tingle in his veins, as he listened to her talk, and watched her black eyes hot with indignation and firm with purpose. What if Ralph were cast? At least it was for faithfulness — of a kind. Even the father's face grew steadier; that piteous trembling of the lower lip ceased, and the horror left his eyes. It was hard to remain in panic with that girl beside them.

They had scarcely done supper when the bell of the outer door rang again, and a moment later Nicholas was with them, flushed with hard riding. He strode into the room, blinking at the lights, and tossed his riding whip on to the table.

"I have been to the Lieutenant of the Tower," he said; "I know him of old. He promises nothing. He tells me that Ralph is well-lodged. Mary is gone to Overfield. God damn the King!"

He had no more news to give. He had sent off his wife at once on receiving the tidings, and had started half an hour later for London. He had been ahead of them all the way, it seemed; but had spent a couple of hours first in trying to get admittance to the Tower, and then in interviewing the Lieutenant; but there was no satisfaction to be gained there. The utmost he had wrung from him was a promise that he would see him again, and hear what he had to say.

Then Nicholas had to sup and hear the whole story from the beginning; and Chris left his father to tell it, and went up with Beatrice to arrange about rooms.

Matters were soon settled with the old lady; Nicholas and Chris were to sleep in one room, and Sir James in an another. Two servants only could be accommodated in the house; the rest were to put up at the inn. Beatrice went off to give the necessary orders.

Mistress Jane Atherton and Chris had a few moments together before the others came up.

"A sore heart," said the old lady again, "but a glad one too. Beatrice has told me everything."

"I am thankful too," said Chris softly. "I wonder if my father understands."

"He will, father, he will. But even if he does not — well, God knows all."

It was evident when Sir James came upstairs presently that he did not understand anything yet, except that Beatrice thought that Ralph had behaved well.

"But it is to my Lord Essex — who has been the worker of all the mischief — that my son is faithful. Is that a good thing then?"

"Why, yes," said Chris. "You would not have him faithless there too?"

"But would he not be on God's side at last, if he were against Cromwell?"

The old man was still too much bewildered to understand explanations, and his son was silent.

*C*hris could not sleep that night, and long after Nicholas lay deep in his pillow, with open mouth and tight eyes, the priest was at the window looking out over the river where the moon hung like a silver shield above Southwark. The meadows beyond the stream were dim and colorless; here and there a roof rose among trees; and straight across the broad water to his feet ran a path of heaving glory, where the strong ripple tossed the silver surface that streamed down upon it from the moon.

London lay round him as quiet as Overfield, and Chris remembered with a stir at his heart his moonlight bathe all those years ago in the lake at home, when he had come back hot from hunting and had slipped down with the chaplain after supper. Then the water had seemed like a cool restful gulf in the world of sensation; the moon had not been risen at first; only the stars pricked above and below in air and water. Then the moon had come up, and a path of splendor had smitten the surface into sight. He had swum up it, he remembered, the silver ripple washing over his shoulders as he went.

And now those years of monastic peace and storm had come and gone, sifting and penetrating his soul, washing out from it little by little the heats and passions with which he had plunged. As he looked back on himself he was astonished at his old complacent smallness. His figure appeared down that avenue of years, a tiny passionate thing, gesticulating, feverish, self-conscious. He remembered his serene certainty that he was right and Ralph wrong in every touch of friction between them, his own furious and theatrical outburst at the death of the Carthusians, his absurd dignity on later occasions. Even in those first beginnings of peace when the inner life had begun to well up and envelop him he had been narrow and self-centered; he had despised the common human life, not understanding that God's Will was as energetic in the bewildering rush of the current as in the quiet sheltered back-waters to which he himself had been called. He had been awakened from that dream by the fall of the Priory, and that to which he opened his eyes had been forced into his consciousness by the months at home, when he had had that astringent mingling of the world and the spirit, of the interpenetration of the inner by the outer. And now for the first time he stood as a balanced soul between the two, alight with a tranquil grace within, and not afraid to look at the darkness without. He was ready now for either life, to go back to the cloister and labor there for the world at the springs of energy, or to take his place in the new England and struggle at the tossing surface.

He stood here now by the hurrying turbulent stream, a wider and more perilous gulf than that that had lain before him as he looked at the moonlit lake at Overfield and yet over it brooded the same quiet shield of heaven, gilding the black swift flowing forces with the promise of a Presence greater than them all.

He stood there long, staring and thinking.

Chapter IX

A RELIEF-PARTY

*T*he days that followed were very anxious and troubled ones for Ralph's friends at Charing. They were dreadful too from their very uneventfulness.

On the morning following their arrival Chris went off to the Temple to consult a lawyer that the Lieutenant had recommended to Nicholas, and brought him back with him an hour later. The first need to be supplied was their lack of knowledge as to procedure; and the four men sat together until dinner, in the parlor on the first floor looking over the sunlit river; and discussed the entire situation.

The lawyer, Mr. Herries, a shrewd-faced Northerner, sat with his back to the window, fingering a quill horizontally in his lean brown fingers and talking in short sentences, glancing up between them, with patient silences as the others talked. He seemed the very incarnation of the slow inaction that was so infinitely trying to these anxious souls.

The three laymen did not even know the crime with which Ralph was charged, but they soon learnt that the technical phrase for it was misprision of treason.

"Mr. Torridon was arrested, I understand," said the lawyer, "by order of Council. He would have been arrested in any case. He was known to be privy to my Lord Essex's schemes. You inform me that he destroyed evidence. That will go against him if they can prove it."

He drew the quill softly through his lips, and then fell to fingering it again, as the others stared at him.

"However," went on Mr. Herries, "that is not our affair now. There will be time for that. Our question is, when will he be charged, and how? My Lord Essex may be tried by a court, or attainted in Parliament. I should suppose the latter. Mr. Torridon will be treated in the same way. If it be the former, we can do nothing but wait and prepare our case. If it be the latter, we must do our utmost to keep his name out of the bill."

He went on to explain his reasons for thinking that a bill of attainder would be brought against Cromwell. It was the customary method, he said, for dealing with eminent culprits, and its range had been greatly extended by Cromwell himself. At this moment three Catholics lay in the Tower, attainted through the statesman's own efforts, for their supposed share in a conspiracy to deliver up Calais to the invaders who had threatened England in the previous year. Feeling, too, ran very high against Cromwell; the public would be impatient of a long trial; and a bill of attainder would give a readier outlet to the fury against him.

This then was the danger; but they could do nothing, said the lawyer, to avert it, until they could get information. He would charge himself with that business, and communicate with them as soon as he knew.

"And then?" asked Chris, looking at him desperately, for the cold deliberate air of Mr. Herries gave him a terrible sense of the passionless process of the law.

"I was about to speak of that," said the lawyer. "If it goes as I think it will, and Mr. Torridon's name is suggested for the bill, we must approach the most powerful friends we can lay hold on, to use their influence against his inclusion. Have you any such, sir?" he added, looking at Sir James sharply over the quill.

The old man shook his head.

"I know no one," he said.

The lawyer pursed his lips.

"Then we must do the best we can. We can set aside at once all of my Lord Essex's enemies — and — and he has many now. Two names come to my mind. Master Ralph Sadler — the comptroller; and my Lord of Canterbury."

"Ah!" cried Chris, dropping his hand, "my Lord of Canterbury! My brother has had dealings with him."

Sir James straightened himself in his chair.

"I will ask no favor of that fellow," he said sternly.

The lawyer looked at him with a cocked eyebrow.

"Well, sir," he said, "if you will not you will not. But I cannot suggest a better. He is in high favor with his Grace; they say he has already said a word for my Lord Essex — not much — much would be too much, I think; but still 'twas something. And what of Master Sadler?"

"I know nothing of him," faltered the old man.

There was silence a moment.

"Well, sir," said Mr. Herries, "you can think the matter over. I am for my Lord of Canterbury; for the reasons I have named to you. But we can wait a few days. We can do nothing until the method of procedure is known."

Then he went; promising to let them know as soon as he had information.

*R*umors began to run swiftly through the City. It was said, though untruly at that time, that Cromwell had addressed a letter to the King at Henry's own request, explaining his conduct, utterly denying that he had said certain rash words attributed to him, and that His Majesty was greatly affected by it. There was immense excitement everywhere; a crowd assembled daily outside Westminster Hall; groups at every corner of the streets discussed the fallen minister's chances; and shouts were raised for those who were known to be his enemies, the Duke of Norfolk, Rich, and others — as they rode through to the Palace.

Meanwhile Ralph's friends could do little. Nicholas rode down once or twice to see the Lieutenant of The Tower, and managed to extract a promise that Ralph should hear of their presence in London; but he could not get to see him, or hear any news except that he was in good health and spirits, and was lodged in a private cell.

Then suddenly one afternoon a small piece of news arrived from Mr. Herries to the effect that Cromwell was to be attainted; and anxiety became intense as to whether Ralph would be included. Sir James could eat nothing at supper, but sat crumbling his bread, while Beatrice talked almost feverishly in an attempt to distract him. Finally he rose and went out, and the others sat on, eyeing one another, anxious and miserable.

In desperation Nicholas began to talk of his visit to the Tower, of the Lieutenant's timidity, and his own insistence; and they noticed nothing, till the door was flung open, and the old man stood there, his eyes bright and his lips trembling with hope. He held a scrap of paper in his hand.

"Listen," he cried as the others sprang to their feet.

"A fellow has just come from Mr. Herries with this" — he lifted the paper and read, — "Mr. Torridon's name is not in the bill. I will be with you tomorrow."

"Thank God!" said Chris.

*T*here was another long discussion the following morning. Mr. Herries arrived about ten o'clock to certify his news; and the four sat till dinner once again, talking and planning. There was not the same desperate hurry now; the first danger was passed.

There was only one thing that the lawyer could do, and that was to repeat his advice to seek the intercession of the Archbishop. He observed again that while Cranmer had the friendship of the fallen minister, he had not in any sense been involved in his fall; he was still powerful with the King, and of considerable weight with the Council in consequence. He was likely therefore to be both able and willing to speak on behalf of Cromwell's agent.

"But I would advise nothing to be done until the bill of attainder has come before Parliament. We do not know yet how far Mr. Torridon's action has affected the evidence. From what you say, gentlemen, and from what I have heard elsewhere, I should think that the papers Mr. Torridon destroyed are not essential to a conviction. My Lord's papers at his own house are sufficient."

But they had some difficulty in persuading Sir James to consent to ask a favor of the Archbishop. In his eyes, Cranmer was beyond the pale of decency; he had lived with two women, said the old man, whom he called his wives, although as a priest he was incapable of marriage; he had violated his consecration oath; he had blessed and annulled the frequent marriages of the King with equal readiness; he was a heretic confessed and open on numberless points of the Catholic Faith.

Mr. Herries pointed out with laborious minuteness that this was beside the question altogether. He did not propose that Sir James Torridon should go to the Archbishop as to a spiritual superior, but as to one who chanced to have great influence; — if he were a murderer it would make no difference to his advice.

Chris broke in with troubled eyes.

"Indeed, sir," he said to his father, "you know how I am with you in all that you say; and yet I am with Mr. Herries too. I do not understand —"

"God help us," cried the old man. "I do not know what to do."

"Will you talk with Mistress Beatrice?" asked Chris.

Sir James nodded.

"I will do that," he said.

*T*he next day the bill was passed; and the party in the house at
Charing sat sick at heart within doors, hearing the crowds roaring down
the street, singing and shouting in triumph. Every cry tore their hearts;
for was it not against Ralph's master and friend that they rejoiced? As
they sat at supper a great battering broke out at the door that looked
on to the lane; and they sprang up to hear a drunken voice bellowing
at them to come out and shout for liberty. Nicholas went crimson with
anger; and he made a movement towards the hall, his hand on his hilt.

"Ah! sit down, Nick," said the monk. "The drunken fool is away
again."

And they heard the steps reel on towards Westminster.

*I*t was not until a fortnight later that they went at last to Lambeth.

Sir James had been hard to persuade; but Beatrice had succeeded at
last. Nicholas had professed himself ready to ask a favor of the devil
himself under the circumstances; and Chris himself continued to support the lawyer's opinion. He repeated his arguments again and again.

Then it was necessary to make an appointment with the Archbishop;
and a day was fixed at last. My Lord would see them, wrote a secretary,
at two o'clock on the afternoon of July the third.

Beatrice sat through that long hot afternoon in the window-seat of
the upstairs parlor, looking out over the wide river below, conscious
perhaps for the first time of the vast weight of responsibility that rested
on her.

She had seen them go off in a wherry, the father and son with
Nicholas in the stern, and the lawyer facing them on the cross-bench;
they had been terribly silent as they walked down to the stairs; had stood
waiting there without a word being spoken but by herself, as the wherry
made ready; and she had talked hopelessly, desperately, to relieve the
tension. Then they had gone off. Sir James had looked back at her over
his shoulder as the boat put out; and she had seen his lips move. She
had watched them grow smaller and smaller as they went, and then when
a barge had come between her and them, she had gone home alone to
wait for their return, and the tidings that they would bring.

And she, in a sense was responsible for it all. If it had not been for
her visit to Ralph, he would have handed the papers over to the
authorities; he would be at liberty now, no doubt, as were Cromwell's
other agents; and, as she thought of it, her tortured heart asked again
and again whether after all she had done right.

She went over the whole question, as she sat there, looking out over the river towards Lambeth, fingering the shutter, glancing now and again at the bent old figure of her aunt in her tall chair, and listening to the rip of the needle through the silk. Could she have done otherwise? Was her interference and advice after all but a piece of mad chivalry, unnecessary and unpractical?

And yet she knew that she would do it again, if the same circumstances arose. It would be impossible to do otherwise. Reason was against it; Mr. Herries had hinted as much with a quick lifting of his bushy eyebrows as she had told him the story. It would have made no difference to Cromwell — ah! but she had not done it for that; it was for the sake of Ralph himself; that he might not lose the one opportunity that came to him of making a movement back towards the honor he had forfeited.

But it was no less torture to think of it all, as she sat here. She had faced the question before; but now the misery she had watched during these last three weeks had driven it home. Day by day she had seen the old father's face grow lined and haggard as the suspense gnawed at his heart; she had watched him at meals — had seen him sit in bewildered grief, striving for self-control and hope — had seen him, as the light faded in the parlor upstairs, sink deeper into himself; his eyes hidden by his hand, and his grey pointed beard twitching at the trembling of his mouth. Once or twice she had met his eyes fixed on hers, in a questioning stare, and had known what was in his heart — a simple, unreproachful wonder at the strange events that had made her so intimately responsible for his son's happiness.

She thought of Margaret too, as she sat there; of the poor girl who had so rested on her, believed in her, loved her. There she was now at Overfield, living in a nightmare of suspense, watching so eagerly for the scanty letters, disappointed every time of the good news for which she hoped. . . .

*T*he burden was an intolerable one. Beatrice was scarcely conscious of where she sat or for what she waited. She was living over again every detail of her relations with Ralph. She remembered how she had seen him at first at Chelsea; how he had come out with Master More from the door of the New Building and across the grass. She had been twisting a grass-ring then as she listened to the talk, and had tossed it on to the dog's back. Then, day by day she had met him; he had come at all hours; and she had watched him, for she thought she had found a man. She remembered how her interest had deepened; how suddenly her heart had leapt that evening when she came into the hall and found him sitting in the dark. Then, step by step, the friendship had grown till it had revealed its radiant face at the bitterness of Chris's words in the house at Westminster. Then her life had become magical; all the world cried "Ralph" to her; the trumpets she heard sounded to his praise; the sunsets had shone for him and her. Then came the news of the Visitors' work; and her heart had begun to question her insistently; the questions had become affirmation; and in one passionate hour she had gone to him, scourged him with her tongue, and left him. She had seen him again once or twice in the years that followed; had watched him from a window hung with tapestries in Cheapside, as he rode down beside the King; and had not dared to ask herself what her heart so longed to tell her. Then had come the mother's question; and the falling of the veils.

Then he had called her; she never doubted that; as she sat alone in her room one evening. It had come, thin and piteous; — "Beatrice, Beatrice." He needed her, and she had gone, and meddled with his life once more.

And he lay in the Tower. . . .

*B*eatrice, my child."

She turned from the window, her eyes blind with tears; and in a moment was kneeling at her aunt's side, her face buried in her lap, and felt those kindly old hands passing over her hair. She heard a murmur over her head, but scarcely caught a word. There was but one thing she needed, and that —

Then she knelt suddenly upright listening, and the caressing hand was still.

"Beatrice, my dear, Beatrice."

*T*here were footsteps on the stairs outside, eager and urgent. The girl rose to her feet, and stood there, swaying a little with a restrained expectation.

Then the door was open, and Chris was there, flushed and radiant, with the level evening light full on his face.

"It is all well," he cried, "my Lord will take us to the King."

Chapter X

PLACENTIA

*T*he river-front of Greenwich House was a magnificent sight as the four men came up to it one morning nearly three weeks later. The long two-storied row of brick buildings which Henry had named Placentia, with their lines of windows broken by the two clusters of slender towers, and porticos beneath, were fronted by broad platforms and a strip of turf with steps leading down to the water, and at each of these entrances there continually moved brilliant figures, sentries with the sunlight flashing on their steel caps and pike-points, servants in the royal livery, watermen in their blue and badges.

Here and there at the foot of the steps rocked gaudy barges, a mass of gilding and color, with broad low canopies at the stern, and flags drooping at the prow; wherries moved to and fro, like water-beetles, shooting across from bank to bank with passengers, above and below the palace, or pausing with uplifted oars as the stream swept them down, for the visitors to stare and marvel at the great buildings. Behind rose up the green masses of trees against the sloping park. And over all lay the July sky, solemn flakes of cloud drifting across a field of intense blue.

There had been a delay in the fulfillment of the Archbishop's promise; at one time he himself was away in the country on affairs, at another time the King was too much pressed, Cranmer reported, to have such a matter brought before him; and then suddenly a messenger had come across from Lambeth with a letter, bidding them present themselves at Greenwich on the following morning; for the day following that had been fixed for Cromwell's execution, and the Archbishop hoped that the King would be ready to hear a word on behalf of the agent whose loyalty had failed to save his master.

*T*he boatman suddenly backed water with his left-hand oar, took a stroke or two with his right, glancing over his shoulder; and the boat slid up to the foot of the steps.

A couple of watermen were already waiting there, in the Archbishop's livery, and steadied the boat for the four gentlemen to step out; and a moment later the four were standing on the platform, looking about them.

They were at one of the smaller entrances to the palace, up-stream. A hundred yards further down was the royal entrance, canopied and carpeted, with the King's barge rocking at the foot, a number of servants coming and going on the platform, and the great state windows overlooking all; but here they were in comparative quiet. A small doorway with its buff and steel-clad sentry before it opened on their right into the interior of the palace.

One of the watermen saluted the party.

"Master Torridon?" he said.

Chris assented.

"My Lord bade me take you through to him, sir, as soon as you arrived."

He went before them to the door, said a word to the guard, and then the party passed on through the little entrance-hall into the interior. The corridor was plainly and severely furnished with matting underfoot, chairs here and there set along the wainscot, pieces of stuff with crossed pikes between hanging on the walls; through the bow windows they caught a glimpse now and again of a little court or two, a shrubbery and a piece of lawn, and once a vista of the park where Henry in his younger days used to hold his May-revels, a gallant and princely figure all in green from cap to shoes, breakfasting beneath the trees.

Continually, as they went, first in the corridor and then through the waiting rooms at the end, they passed others going to and fro, servants hurrying on messages, leisurely and magnificent persons with their hats on, pages standing outside closed doors; and twice they were asked their business.

"For my Lord of Canterbury," answered the waterman each time.

It seemed to Chris that they must have gone an immense distance before the waterman at last stopped, motioning them to go on, and a page in purple livery stepped forward from a door.

"For my Lord of Canterbury," said the waterman for the last time.

The page bowed, turned, and threw open the door.

They found themselves in a square parlor, carpeted and hung with tapestries from floor to ceiling. A second door opened beyond, in the window side, into another room. A round table stood in the center, with brocaded chairs about it, and a long couch by the fireplace. Opposite rose up the tall windows through which shone the bright river with the trees and buildings on the north bank beyond.

They had hardly spoken a word to one another since they had left Charing, for all that was possible had been said during the weeks of waiting for the Archbishop's summons.

Cranmer had received them kindly, though he had not committed himself beyond promising to introduce them to the King, and had expressed no opinion on the case.

He had listened to them courteously, had nodded quietly as Chris explained what it was that Ralph had done, and then almost without comment had given his promise. It seemed as if the Archbishop could not even form an opinion, and still less express one, until he had heard what his Highness had to say.

Chris walked to the window and the lawyer followed him.

"Placentia!" said Mr. Herries, "I do not wonder at it. It is even more pleasing from within."

He stood, a prim, black figure, looking out at the glorious view, the shining waterway studded with spots of color, the long bank of the river opposite, and the spires of London city lying in a blue heat-haze far away to the left.

Chris stared at it too, but with unseeing eyes. It seemed as if all power of sensation had left him. The suspense of the last weeks had corroded the surfaces of his soul, and the intensity to which it was now rising seemed to have paralyzed what was left. He found himself picturing the little house at Charing where Beatrice was waiting, and, he knew, praying; and he reminded himself that the next time he saw her he would know all, whether death or life was to be Ralph's sentence. The solemn quiet and the air of rich and comfortable tranquility which the palace wore, and which had impressed itself on his mind even in the hundred yards he had walked in it, gave him an added sense of what it was that lay over his brother, the huge passionless forces with which he had become entangled.

Then he turned round. His father was sitting at the table, his head on his hand; and Nicholas was staring round the grave room with the solemnity of a child, looking strangely rustic and out of place in these surroundings.

It was very quiet as Chris leaned against the window-shutter, in his secular habit, with his hands clasped behind his back, and looked. Once a footstep passed in the corridor outside, and the floor vibrated slightly to the tread; once a horn blew somewhere far away; and from the river now and again came the cry of a waterman, or the throb of oars in rowlocks.

Sir James looked up once, opened his lips as if to speak; and then dropped his head on to his hand again.

The waiting seemed interminable.

Chris turned round to the window once more, slipped his breviary out of his pocket, and opened it. He made the sign of the cross and began —

"In nomine Patris et Filii. . . ."

Then the second door opened; he turned back abruptly; there was a rustle of silk, and the Archbishop came through in his habit and gown.

Chris bowed slightly as the prelate went past him briskly towards the table where Sir James was now standing up, and searched his features eagerly for an omen. There was nothing to be read there; his smooth large-eyed face was smiling quietly as its manner was, and his wide lips were slightly parted.

"Good-day, Master Torridon; you are in good time. I am just come from His Highness, and will take you to him directly."

Chris saw his father's face blanch a little as he bowed in return. Nicholas merely stared.

"But we have a few minutes," went on the Archbishop. "Sir Thomas Wriothesly is with him. Tell me again sir, what you wish me to say."

Sir James looked hesitatingly to the lawyer.

"Mr. Herries," he said.

Cranmer turned round, and again made that little half-deprecating bow to the priest and the lawyer. Mr. Herries stepped forward as Cranmer sat down, clasping his hands so that the great amethyst showed on his slender finger.

"It is this, my Lord," he said, "it is as we told your Lordship at Lambeth. This gentleman desires the King's clemency towards Mr. Ralph Torridon, now in the Tower. Mr. Torridon has served — er — Mr. Cromwell very faithfully. We wish to make no secret of that. He destroyed certain private papers — though that cannot be proved against him, and you will remember that we were doubtful whether his Highness should be informed of that —"

Sir James broke in suddenly.

"I have been thinking of that, my Lord. I would sooner that the King's Grace knew everything. I have no wish that that should be kept from him."

The Archbishop who had been looking with smiling attention from one to the other, now himself broke in.

"I am glad you think that, sir. I think so myself. Though it cannot be proved as you say, it is far best that His Grace should know all. Indeed I think I should have told him in any case."

"Then, my Lord, if you think well," went on Mr. Herries, "you might lay before his Grace that this is a free and open confession. Mr. Torridon did burn papers, and important ones; but they would not have served anything. Master Cromwell was cast without them."

"But Mr. Torridon did not know that?" questioned the Archbishop blandly.

"Yes, my Lord," cried Sir James, "he must have known — that my Lord Cromwell —"

The Archbishop lifted his hand delicately.

"Master Cromwell," he corrected.

"Master Cromwell," went on the old man, "he must have known that Mr. Cromwell had others, more important, that would be certainly found and used against him."

"Then why did he burn them? You understand, sir, that I only wish to know what I have to say to his Grace."

"He burned them, my Lord, because he could not bear that his hand should be lifted against his master. Surely that is but loyal and good!"

The Archbishop nodded quietly three or four times.

"And you desire that his Grace will take order to have Mr. Torridon released?"

"That is it, my Lord," said the lawyer.

"Yes, I understand. And can you give any pledge for Mr. Torridon's good behavior?"

"He has served Mr. Cromwell," answered the lawyer, "very well for many years. He has been with him in the matter of the Religious Houses; he was one of the King's Visitors, and assisted in the — the destruction of Lewes priory; and that, my Lord, is a sufficient —"

Sir James gave a sudden sob.

"Mr. Herries, Mr. Herries —"

Cranmer turned to him smiling.

"I know what you feel, sir," he said. "But if this is true —"

"Why, it is true! God help him," cried the old man.

"Then that is what we need, sir; as you said just now. Yes, Mr. Herries?"

The lawyer glanced at the old man again.

"That is sufficient guarantee, my Lord, that Mr. Ralph Torridon is no enemy of his Grace's projects."

"I cannot bear that!" cried Sir James.

Nicholas, who had been looking awed and open-mouthed from one to the other, took him by the arm.

"You must, father," he said. "It — it is devilish; but it is true. Chris, have you nothing?"

The monk came forward a step.

"It is true, my Lord," he said. "I was a monk of Lewes myself."

"And you have conformed," put in the Archbishop swiftly.

"I am living at home peaceably," said Chris; "it is true that my brother did all this, but — but my father wishes that it should not be used in his cause."

"If it is true," said the Archbishop, "it is best to say it. We want nothing but the bare truth."

"But I cannot bear it," cried the old man again.

Chris came round behind the Archbishop to his father.

"Will you leave it, father, to my Lord Archbishop? My Lord understands what we think."

Sir James looked at him, dazed and bewildered.

"God help us! Do you think so, Chris."

"I think so, father. My Lord, you understand all?"

The Archbishop's bowed again slightly.

"Then, my Lord, we will leave it all in your hands."

There was a tap at the door.

The Archbishop rose.

"That is our signal," he said. "Come, gentlemen, his Grace will be ready immediately."

Mr. Herries sprang to the door and opened it, bowing as the Archbishop went through, followed by Sir James and Nicholas. He and Chris followed after.

*T*here was a kind of dull recklessness in the monk's heart as he went through. He knew that he was in more peril than any of the others, and yet he did not fear it. The faculty of fear had been blunted, not sharpened, by his experiences; and he passed on towards the King's presence, almost without a tremor.

The room was empty, except for a page by the further door, who opened it as the party advanced; and beyond was a wide lobby, with doors all round, and a staircase on the right as they came out. The

Archbishop made a little motion to the others as he went up, gathering his skirts about him, and acknowledging with his disengaged hand the salute of the sentry that stood in the lobby.

At the top of the stairs was a broad landing; then a corridor through which they passed, and on. They turned to the left, and as they went it was apparent that they were near the royal apartments. There were thick leather rugs lying here and there; along the walls stood magnificent pieces of furniture, inlaid tables with tall dragon-jars upon them, suits of Venetian armor elaborately worked in silver, and at the door of every room that opened on the corridor there was standing a sentry or a servant, who straightened themselves at the sight of the Archbishop. He carefully acknowledged each salutation, and nodded kindly once or twice.

There was a heavy odor in the air, warm and fragrant, as of mingled stuffs and musk, which even the wide windows set open towards the garden on the right hand did not wholly obliterate.

For the first time since leaving Charing, Chris's heart quickened. The slow stages of approach to the formidable presence had begun to do their work; if he had seen the King at once he would not have been moved; if he had had an hour longer, he would have recovered from his emotion; but this swift ordered approach, the suggestiveness of the thick carpets and furniture, the sight of the silent figures waiting, the musky smell in the air, all combined now to work upon him; he began to fancy that he was drawing nearer the presence of some great carrion-beast that had made its den here, that was guarded by these discreet servitors, and to which this smooth prelate, in the rôle of the principal keeper, was guiding him. Any of these before him might mark the sanctuary of the labyrinth, where the creature lurked; one might open, and a savage face look out, dripping blood and slaver.

A page threw back a door at last, and they passed through; but again there was a check. It was but one more waiting room. The dozen persons, folks of all sorts, a lawyer, a soldier, and others stood up and bowed to the prelate.

Then the party sat down near the further door in dead silence, and the minutes began to pass.

There were cries from the river once or twice as they waited; once a footstep vibrated through the door, and twice a murmur of voices sounded and died again.

Then suddenly a hand was laid on the handle from the other side, and the Archbishop rose, with Sir James beside him.

There was still a pause. Then a voice sounded loud and near, and there was a general movement in the room as all rose to their feet. The door swung open and the Garter King-at-Arms came through, bland and smiling, his puffed silk sleeves brushing against the doorpost as he passed. A face like a mask, smooth and expressionless, followed him, and nodded to the Archbishop.

Cranmer turned slightly to his party, again made that little movement, and went straight through.

Chris followed with Mr. Herries.

Chapter XI

THE KING'S HIGHNESS

*A*s Chris knelt with the others, and the door closed behind him, he was aware of a great room with a tall window looking on to the river on his left, tapestry-hung walls, a broad table heaped with papers in the center, a high beamed ceiling, and the thick carpet under his knees.

For a moment he did not see the King. The page who had beckoned them in had passed across the room, and Chris's eyes followed him out through an inner door in the corner.

Then, still on his knees, he turned his eyes to see the Archbishop going towards the window, and up the step that led on to the dais that occupied the floor of the oriel.

Then he saw the King.

A great figure was seated opposite the side door at which they had entered on the broad seat that ran round the three sides of the window. The puffed sleeves made the shoulders look enormous; a gold chain lay across them, with which the gross fingers were playing. Beneath, the vast stomach swelled out into the slashed trunks, and the scarlet legs were crossed one over the other. On the head lay a broad plumed velvet cap, and beneath it was the wide square face, at once jovial and solemn, with the narrow slits of eyes above, and the little pursed mouth fringed by reddish hair below, that Chris remembered in the barge years before. The smell of musk lay heavy in the air.

Here was the monstrous carrion-beast then at last, sunning himself and waiting.

So the party rested a moment or two, while the Archbishop went across to the dais; he knelt again and then stood up and said a word or two rapidly that Chris could not hear.

Henry nodded, and turned his bright narrow eyes on to them; and then made a motion with his hand. The Archbishop turned round and repeated the gesture; and Chris rose in his place as did the others.

"Master Torridon, your Grace," explained the Archbishop, with a deferential stoop of his shoulders. "Your Grace will remember —"

The King nodded abruptly, and thrust his hand out.

Chris touched his father behind.

"Go forward," he whispered; "kiss hands."

The old man went forward a hesitating step or two. The Archbishop motioned sharply, and Sir James advanced again up to the dais, sank down, and lifted the hand to his lips, and fell back for the others.

When Chris's turn came, and he lifted the heavy fingers, he noticed for a moment a wonderful red stone on the thumb, and recognized it. It was the Regal of France that he had seen years before at his visit to St. Thomas's shrine at Canterbury. In a flash, too, he remembered Cromwell's crest as he had seen it on the papers at Lewes — the demi-lion holding up the red-gemmed ring.

Then he too had fallen back, and the Archbishop was speaking.

"Your Grace will remember that there is a Mr. Ralph Torridon in the Tower — an agent of Mr. Cromwell's —"

The King's face moved slightly, but he said nothing.

— "Who is awaiting trial for destroying evidence. It is that, at least, your Grace, that is asserted against him. But it has not been proved. Master Torridon here tells me, your Highness, that it cannot be proved, but that he wishes to acknowledge it freely on his son's behalf."

Henry's eyes shot back again at the old man, ran over the others, and settled again on Cranmer's face, who was standing beside him with his back to the window.

"He is here to plead for your Grace's clemency. He wishes to lay before your Grace that his son erred through overfaithfulness to Mr.

Cromwell's cause; and above all that the evidence so destroyed has not affected the course of justice —"

"God's Body!" jarred in the harsh voice suddenly, "it has not. Nor shall it."

Cranmer waited a moment with downcast eyes; but the King was silent again.

"Master Torridon has persuaded me to come with him to your Grace to speak for him. He is not accustomed —"

"And who are these fellows?"

Chris felt those keen eyes running over him.

"This is Master Nicholas Maxwell," explained the Archbishop, indicating him. "Master Torridon's son-in-law; and this, Mr. Herries —"

"And the priest?" asked the King.

"The priest is Sir Christopher Torridon, living with his father at Overfield."

"Ha! has he always lived there then?"

"No, your Grace," said Cranmer smoothly, "he was a monk at Lewes until the dissolution of the house."

"I have heard somewhat of his name," mused Henry. "What is it, sir, that I have beard of you?"

"It was perhaps Mr. Ralph Torridon's name that your Grace —" began Cranmer.

"Nay, nay, it was not. What was it, sir?"

Chris's heart was beating in his ears like a drum now. It had come, then, that peril that had always been brooding on the horizon, and which he had begun to despise. He had thought that there could be no danger in his going to the King; it was so long since Lewes had fallen, and his own part had been so small. But his Grace's memory was good, it seemed! Danger was close to him, incarnate in that overwhelming presence. He said nothing, but stood awaiting detection.

"It is strange," said Henry. "I have forgot. Well, my Lord?"

"I have told your Grace all," explained the Archbishop. "Mr. Ralph Torridon has not yet been brought to trial, and his father hopes that your Grace will take into consideration these two things: that it was a mistake of overfaithfulness that his son committed; and that it has not hindered the course of justice."

"Well, well," said Henry, "and that sounds to be in reason. We have none too much of either faithfulness or justice in these days. And there is no other charge against the fellow?"

"There is no other charge, your Grace."

There fell a complete silence for a moment or two.

Chris glanced up at his father, his own heart uplifted by hope, and saw the old man's face trembling with it too. The wrinkled eyes were full of tears, and his lips quivered; and Chris could feel the short cloak that hung against him shaking at his hand. Nicholas's crimson face showed a mingling of such emotion and solemnity that Chris was seized with an internal hysterical spasm; but it suddenly died within him as he brought his eyes round, and saw that the King was staring at him moodily. . . .

The Archbishop's voice broke in again.

"Are we to understand, your Grace, that your Grace's clemency is extended to Mr. Ralph Torridon?"

"Eh! then," said the King peevishly, "hold your tongue, my Lord. I am trying to remember. Where is Michael?"

"Shall I call him, your Grace?"

"Nay, then; let the lawyer ring the bell!"

Mr. Herries sprang to the table at the King's gesture, and struck the little hand-bell that stood there. The door where the page had disappeared five minutes before opened silently, and the servant stood there.

"Michael," said the King, and the page vanished.

There was an uncomfortable silence. Cranmer stood back a little with an air of patient deference, and his quick eyes glanced up now and again at the party before him. There was a certain uneasiness in his manner, as Chris could see; but the monk presently dropped his eyes again, as he saw that the King was once more looking at him keenly, with tight pursed lips, and a puzzled look on his forehead.

The thoughts began to race through Chris's brain. He found himself praying with desperate speed that Michael, whoever he was, might not know; and that the King might not remember; and meanwhile through another part of his being ran the thought of the irony of his situation. Here he was, come to plead for his brother's life, and on the brink of having to plead for his own. The quiet room increased his sense of the irony. It seemed so safe and strong and comfortable, up here in the rich room, with the tall window looking on to the sunlit river, in a palace girt about with guards; and yet the very security of it was his danger. He had penetrated into the stronghold of the great beast that ruled England: he was within striking distance of those red-stained claws and teeth.

Then suddenly the creature stirred and snarled.

"I know it now, sir. You were one of the knaves that would not sign the surrender of Lewes."

Chris lifted his eyes and dropped them again.

"God's Body," said the King, "and you come here!"

Again there was silence.

Chris saw his father half turn towards him with a piteous face, and perceived that the lawyer had drawn a little away.

The King turned abruptly to Cranmer.

"Did you know this, my Lord?"

"Before God, I did not!" — but his voice shook as he answered.

Chris was gripping his courage, and at last spoke.

"We were told it was a free-will act, your Grace."

Henry said nothing to this. His eyes were rolling up and down the monk's figure, with tight, thoughtful lips. Cranmer looked desperately at Sir James.

"I did not know that, your Grace," he said again. "I only knew that this priest's brother had been very active in your Grace's business."

Henry turned sharply.

"Eh?" he said.

Sir James's hands rose and clasped themselves instinctively. Cranmer again looked at him almost fiercely.

"Mr. Ralph Torridon was one of the Visitors," explained the Archbishop nervously.

"And this fellow a monk!" cried the King.

"They must have met at Lewes, your Grace."

"Ah! my Lord," cried Sir James suddenly. "I entreated you —"

Henry turned on him suddenly.

"Tell us the tale, sir. What is all this?"

Sir James took a faltering step forward, and then suddenly threw out his hands.

"Ah! your Grace, it is a bitter tale for a father to tell. It is true, all of it. My son here was a monk at Lewes. He would not sign the surrender. I — I approved him for it. I — I was there when my son Ralph cast him out —"

"God's blood!" cried the King with a beaming face. "The one brother cast the other out!"

Chris saw the Archbishop's face suddenly lighten as he watched the King sideways.

"But I cannot bear that he should be saved for that!" went on the old man piteously. "He was a good servant to your Grace, but a bad one to our Lord —"

The Archbishop drew a swift breath of horror, and his hands jerked. But Henry seemed not to hear; his little mouth had opened in a round hole of amazed laughter, and he was staring at the old man without hearing him.

"And you were there?" he said. "And your wife? And your aunts and sisters?"

"My wife is dead," cried the old man. "Your Grace —"

"And on **which** side was she?"

"She was — was on your Grace's side."

Henry threw himself back in his chair.

*F*or one moment Chris did not know whether it was wrath or laughter that shook him. His face grew crimson, and his narrow eyes disappeared into shining slits; his fat hands were on his knees, and his great body shook. From his round open mouth came silent gusts of quick breath, and he began to sway a little from side to side.

Across the Archbishop's face came a deferential and sympathetic smile, and he looked quickly and nervously from the King to the group and back again. Sir James had fallen back a pace at the King's laughter, and stood rigid and staring. Chris took a step close to him and gripped his hand firmly.

There was a footstep behind, and the King leaned forward again, wiping the tears away with his sleeve.

"Oh, Michael, Michael!" he sobbed, "here is a fine tale."

A dark-dressed man stepped forward from behind, and stood expectant.

"God! What a happy family!" said the King. "And this fellow here?"

He motioned towards Nicholas, with a feeble gesture. He was still weak with laughter.

The young squire moved forward a step, rigid and indignant.

"I am against your Grace," he said sharply.

Henry grew suddenly grave.

"Eh! that is no way to speak," he said.

"It is the only way I can speak," said Nicholas, "if your Grace desires the truth."

The King looked at him a moment; but the humor still shone in his eyes.

"Well, well. It is the truth I want. Michael, I sent for you to know about the priest here; but I know now. And is it true that his brother in the Tower — Ralph Torridon — was one of the Visitors?"

The man pursed his lips a moment. He was standing close to Chris, a little in front of him.

"Yes, your Majesty."

"Oh! well. We must let him out, I suppose — if there is nothing more against him. You shall tell me presently, Michael."

The Archbishop looked swiftly across at the party.

"Then your Grace extends —"

"Well, Michael, what is it?" interrupted the King.

"It is a matter your Majesty might wish to hear in private," said the stranger.

"Oh, step aside, my Lord. And you, gentlemen."

The King motioned down to the further end of the room, as Michael came forward.

The Archbishop stepped off the low platform, and led the way down the floor; and the others followed.

*C*hris was in a whirl of bewilderment. He could see the King's great face interested and attentive as the secretary said something in his ear, and then suddenly light up with amusement again.

"Not a word, not a word," whispered Henry harshly. "Very good, Michael."

The secretary then whispered once more. Chris could hear the sharp sibilants, but no word. The King nodded once more, and the man stepped down off the dais.

"Prepare the admission, then," said the King after him.

The secretary bowed as he turned and went out of the room once more.

Henry beckoned.

"Come, gentlemen."

He watched them with a solemn joviality as they came up, the Archbishop in front, the father and son together, and the two others behind.

"You are a sad crew," began the King, eyeing them pleasantly, and sitting forward with a hand on either knee, "and I am astonished, my Lord of Canterbury, at your companying with them. But we will have mercy, and remember your son's services, Master Torridon, in the past. That alone will excuse him. Remember that. That alone. He is the stronger man, if he turned out the priest there. And I remember your son very well, too; and will forgive him. But I shall not employ him again. And his forgiveness shall cover yours, Master Priest; but you must be off — you must be off, sir," he barked suddenly, "out of these realms in a week. We will have no more treason from you."

The fierce overpowering personality flared out as he spoke, and Chris felt his heart beat sick at the force of it.

"And you two gentlemen," went on the King, still smoldering, "you two had best hold your tongues. We will not hear such talk in our presence or out of it. But we will excuse it now. There, sir, have I said enough?"

Sir James dropped abruptly on his knees.

"Oh! God bless your Grace!" he began, with the tears running down.

Henry made an abrupt gesture.

"You shall go to your son," he said, "and see how he fares, and tell him this. And she shall have the order of release presently, from me or another."

Again the little mouth creased and twitched with amusement.

"And I hope he will be happy with his mother. You may tell him that from me."

The Archbishop looked up.

"Mistress Torridon is dead, your Grace," he said softly and questioningly.

"Oh, well," said the King; and thrust out his hand to be kissed.

Chris did not know how they got out of the room. They kissed hands again; the old man muttered out his thanks; but he seemed bewildered by the rush of events, and the supreme surprise. Chris, as he backed away from the presence, saw for the last time those narrow royal eyes fixed on him, still bright with amusement and expectancy, and the great red-fringed cheeks creased about the tiny mouth with an effort to keep back laughter. Why was the King laughing, he wondered?

They waited a few minutes in the anteroom for the order that the Archbishop had whispered to them should be sent out immediately. They said nothing to one another — but the three sat close, looking into one another's eyes now and again in astonishment and joy, while Mr. Herries stood a little apart solemn and happy at the importance of the rôle he had played in the whole affair, and disdaining even to look at the rest of the company who sat on chairs and watched the party.

The secretary came to them in a few minutes, and handed them the order.

"My Lord of Canterbury is detained," he said; "he bade me tell you gentlemen that he could not see you again."

Sir James was standing up and examining the order.

"For four?" he said.

"Why, yes," said the secretary, and glanced at the four men.

Chris put his hand on his father's arm.

"It is all well," he whispered, "say nothing more. It will do for Beatrice."

Chapter XII

THE TIDINGS AT THE TOWER

*T*hey debated as they stood on the steps in the sunlight five minutes later, as to whether they should go straight to the Tower, or back to Charing and take Beatrice with them. They spoke softly to one another, as men that have come out from darkness to light, bewildered by the sense of freedom and freshness that lay round them. Instead of the musk-scented rooms, the formidable dominating presence, the suspense and the terror, the river laughed before them, the fresh summer breeze blew up it, and above all Ralph was free, and that, not only of his prison, but of his hateful work. It had all been done in those few sentences; but as yet they could not realize it; and they regarded it, as they regarded the ripples at their feet, the lapping wherry, and far-off London city, as a kind of dazzling picture which would by and bye be found to move and live.

The lawyer congratulated them, and they smiled back and thanked him.

"If you will put me to shore at London Bridge," said Mr. Herries — "I have a little business I might do there — that is, if you will be going so far."

Chris looked at his father, whose arm he was holding.

"We must take her with us," he said. "She has earned it."

Sir James nodded, dreamily, and turned to the boat.

"To the London Bridge Stairs first," he said.

*T*here was a kind of piquant joy in their hearts as they crept up past the Tower, and saw its mighty walls and guns across the water. He was there, but it was not for long. They would see him that day, and tomorrow — tomorrow at the latest, they would all leave it together.

There were a hundred plans in the old man's mind, as he leaned gently forward and back to the motion of the boat and stared at the bright water. Ralph and he should live at Overfield again; his son would surely be changed by all that had come to him, and above all by his own response to the demands of loyalty. They should learn to understand one another better now — better than ever before. The hateful life lay behind them of distrust and contempt; Ralph would come back to his old self, and be again as he had been ten years back before he had been dazzled and drugged by the man who was to die next day. Then he thought of that man, and half-pitied him even then; those strong walls held nothing but terror for him — terror and despair; the scaffold was already going up on Tower Hill — and as the old man thought of it he leaned forward and tried to see over the wharf and under the trees where the rising ground lay; but there was nothing to be seen — the foliage hid it.

Chris, also silent beside him, was full of thoughts. He would go abroad now, he knew, with Margaret, as they had intended. The King's order was the last sign of God's intention for him. He would place Margaret with her own sisters at Bruges, and then himself go on to Dom Anthony and take up the life again. He knew he would meet some of his old brethren in Religion — Dom Anthony had written to say that three or four had already joined him at Cluny; the Prior — he knew — had turned his back forever on the monastic life, and had been put into a prebendal stall at Lincoln.

And meanwhile he would have the joy of knowing that Ralph was free of his hateful business; the King would not employ him again; he would live at home now, and rule Overfield well: he and his father together. Ah! and what if Beatrice consented to rule it with him! Surely now — He turned and looked at his father as he thought of it, and their eyes met.

Chris leaned a little closer.

"Beatrice!" he said. "What if she — ?"

The old man nodded tenderly, and his drawn eyes shone in his face.

"Oh! Chris — I was thinking that —"

Then Nicholas came out of his maze.

Ever since his entrance into the palace, except when he had flared out at the King, he had moved and stood and sat in a solemn bewilderment. The effect of the changed atmosphere had been to paralyze his simple and sturdy faculties; and his face had grown unintelligent during the process. More than once Chris had been seized with internal laughter, in spite of the tragedy; the rustic squire was so strangely incongruous with the situation. But he awoke now.

"God bless me!" he said wonderingly. "It is all over and done. God —"
Chris gave a short yelp of laughter.

"Dear Nick," he said, "yes. God bless you indeed! You spoke up well!"

"Did I do right, sir," said the other to Sir James, "I could not help it. I —"

"Oh! Nick," said the old man, and leaned forward and put his hand on his knee.

Nicholas preened himself as he sat there; he would tell Mary how he had bearded his Majesty, and what a diplomatist was her husband.

"You did very well, sir," put in Mr. Herries ironically. "You terrified his Grace, I think."

Chris glanced at the lawyer; but Nicholas took it all with the greatest complacency; tilted his hilt a little forward, smoothed his doublet, and sat smiling and well-pleased.

They reached the Stairs presently and put Mr. Herries ashore.

"I will be at your house tomorrow, sir," he said, "when you go to take Mr. Ralph out of prison. The order will be there by the morning, I make no doubt."

He bowed and smiled and moved off, a stiff figure deliberately picking its way up the oozy steps to the crowded street overhead.

*B*eatrice's face was at the window as they came up the tide half-an-hour later. Chris stood up in the wherry, when he saw it, and waved his cap furiously, and the face disappeared.

She was at the landing stage before they reached it, a slender brilliant figure in her hood and mantle, with her aunt beside her. Chris stood up again and cried between his hands across the narrowing space that all was well; and her face was radiant as the boat slipped up to the side, and balanced there with the boatman's hand on the stone edging.

"It is all well," said Chris again as he stood by her a moment later. "He is to go free, and we are to tell him."

He dared not look at her; but he was aware that she stood very still and rigid, and that her eyes were on his father's.

"Oh! Mistress Beatrice —"

Chris began to understand it all a little better, a few minutes later, as the boat was once again on its way downstream. He and Nicholas had moved to the bows of the wherry, and the girl and the old man sat alone in the stern.

They were all very silent at first; Chris leaned on his elbow and stared out at the sliding banks, the trees on this side and that, the great houses with their high roofs and towers behind, and their stone steps in front, the brilliant glare on the water, the hundreds of boats — great barges flashing jewels from their dozen blades, spidery wherries making this way and that; and his mind was busy weaving pictures. He saw it all now; there had been that in Beatrice's face during the moment he had looked at her, that was more than sympathy. In the shock of that great joy the veils had fallen, and her soul had looked out through her black tearful eyes.

There was little doubt now as to what would happen. It was not for their sake alone, or for Ralph's, that she had looked like that; she had not said one word, but he knew what was unspoken.

As they passed under London Bridge he turned a little and looked across the boatmen's shoulder at the two as they sat there in the stern, and what he saw confirmed him. The old man had flung an arm along the back of the seat, and was leaning a little forward, talking in a low voice, his face showing indeed the lines and wrinkles that had deepened more than ever during these last weeks, but irradiated with an extraordinary joy. And the girl was beside him, smiling with downcast eyes, turning a quick look now and again as she sat there. Chris could see her scarlet lips trembling, and her hands clasped on her knee, shifting a little now and again as she listened. It was a strange wooing; the father courting for the son, and the woman answering the son through the father; and Chris understood what was the answer that she was giving.

Nicholas was watching it too; and presently the two in the stern looked up suddenly; first Beatrice and then Sir James, and their eyes flashed joy across and across as the four souls met.

*F*ive minutes later again they were at the Tower Stairs.

Mr. Morris, who had been sent on by Mistress Jane Atherton when she had heard the news, was there holding his horse by the bridle; and behind him had collected a little crowd of idlers. He gave the bridle to one of them, and came down the steps to help them out of the boat.

"You have heard?" said Chris as he stepped out last.

"Yes, father," said the servant.

Chris looked at him; and his masklike face too seemed strangely lighted up. There was still across his cheek the shadow of a mark as of an old whip-cut.

As they passed up the steps they became aware that the little crowd that had waited at the top was only the detached fringe of a multitude that had assembled further up the slope. It stretched under the trees as far as they could see to right and left, from the outer wall of the Tower on the one side, to where the rising ground on the left was hidden under the thick foliage in the foreground. There was a murmur of talking and laughter, the ringing of hand-bells, the cracking of whips and the cries of children. The backs of the crowd were turned to the steps: there was plainly something going on higher up the slope, and it seemed somewhat away to the left.

For a moment Chris did not understand, and he turned to Morris. "What is it?" he asked.

"The scaffold," said the servant tersely.

At the same moment high above the murmur of the crowd came the sound of heavy resounding blows, as of wood on wood.

Then Chris remembered; and for one moment he sickened as he walked. His father turned and looked over his shoulder as he went with Beatrice in front, and his eyes were eloquent.

"I had forgotten," said Chris softly. "God help him!"

*T*hey turned in towards the right almost immediately to the low outer gate of the fortress; and those for the first time remembered that the order they carried was for four only.

Nicholas instantly offered to wait outside and let Morris go in. Morris flatly refused. There was a short consultation, and then Nicholas went up to the sentry on guard with the order in his hand.

The man looked at it, glanced at the party, and then turned and knocked with his halberd on the great door behind, and in a minute or two an officer came out in his buff and feathers. He took the order and ran his eyes over it.

Nicholas explained.

The officer looked at him a moment without answering.

"And the lady too?" he said.

"Why, yes," said Nicholas.

"The lady wishes —" then he broke off. "You will have to see the Lieutenant," he went on. "I can let you all through to his lodgings."

They passed in with a yeoman to conduct them under the low heavy vaulting and through to the open way beyond. On their right was the wall between them and the river, and on their left the enormous towers and battlements of the inner court.

Chris walked with Morris behind, remembering the last time he was here with the Prior all those years before. They had walked silently then, too, but for another reason.

They passed the low Traitor's Gate on their right; Chris glanced at the green lapping water beneath it as he went — Ralph had landed there — and turned up the steep slope to the left under the gateway of the inner court; and in a minute or two more were at the door of the Lieutenant's lodgings.

There seemed a strange suggestiveness in the silence and order of the wide ward that lay before them. The great White Tower dominated the whole place on the further side, huge and menacing, pierced by its narrow windows set at wide intervals; on the left, the row of towers used as prisons diminished in perspective down to where the wall turned at right angles and ran in behind the keep; and the great space enclosed by the whole was almost empty. There were soldiers on guard here and there at the doorways; a servant hurried across the wide sunlit ground, and once, as they waited, a doctor in his short gown came out of one door and disappeared into another.

And here they waited for an answer to their summons, silent and happy in their knowledge. The place held no terrors for them.

The soldier knocked again impatiently, and again stood aside.

Chris saw Nicholas sidle up to the man with something of the same awe on his face that had been there an hour ago.

"My Lord — Master Cromwell?" he heard him whisper, correcting himself.

The man jerked a thumb over his shoulder.

"There," he said.

There were three soldiers, Chris noticed, standing at the foot of one of the Towers a little distance off. It was there, then, that Thomas Cromwell, wool-carder, waited for death, hearing, perhaps, from his window the murmur of the crowd beyond the moat, and the blows of mallet on wood as his scaffold went up.

Then the door opened, and after a word or two the soldier motioned them in.

*A*gain they had to wait.

The Lieutenant, they were told, had been called away. He was expected back presently.

They sat down, still in silence, in the little ground-floor parlor. It was a pleasant little room, with a wide hearth, and two windows looking on to the court.

But the suspense was not like that of the morning. Now they knew how it must end. There would be a few minutes more, long perhaps to

Ralph, as he sat in his cell somewhere not far from them, knowing nothing of the pardon that was on its way; and then the door would open, where day by day for the last six weeks the jailer had come and gone; and the faces he knew would be there, and it would be from their lips that he would hear the message.

The old man and the girl still sat together in the window-seat, silent now like the others. They had had their explanations in the boat, and each knew what was in the other's heart. Chris and Nicholas stood by the hearth, Mr. Morris by the door; and there was not the tremor of a doubt in any of them as to what the future held.

Chris looked tranquilly round the room, at the little square table in the center, the four chairs drawn close to it, with their brocade panels stained and well-worn showing at the back, the dark ceiling, the piece of tapestry that hung over the side-table between the doors — it was a martial scene, faded and discolored, with ghostly bare-legged knights on fat prancing horses all in inextricable conflict, a great battleaxe stood out against the dusky foliage of an autumn tree; and a stag with his fore feet in the air, ramped in the foreground, looking over his shoulder. It was a ludicrously bad piece of work, picked up no doubt by some former Lieutenant who knew more of military than artistic matters, and had hung there — how long? Chris wondered.

He found himself criticizing it detail by detail, comparing it with his own designs in the antiphonary; he had that antiphonary still at home; he had carried it off from Lewes, when Ralph — Ralph! — had turned him out. He had put it up into a parcel on the afternoon of the spoilers' arrival. He would show it to Ralph again now — in a day or two at Overfield; they would laugh over it together; and he would take it with him abroad, and perhaps finish it there. God's work is not so easily hindered after all.

But all the while, the wandering stream of his thought was lighted and penetrated by the radiant joy of his heart. It was all true, not a dream!

He glanced again at the two in the window-seat.

His father was looking out of the lattice; but Beatrice raised her eyes to his, and smiled at him.

Sir James stood up.

"The Lieutenant is coming," he said.

A moment later there were steps in the flagged passage; and a murmur of voices. The soldier who had brought them to the lodgings was waiting there with the order of admission, and was no doubt explaining the circumstances.

Then the door opened suddenly; and a tall soldierly-looking man, grey-haired and clean-shaven, in an officer's dress, stood there, with the order in his hand, as the two in the window-seat rose to meet him.

"Master Torridon," he said abruptly.

Sir James stepped forward.

"Yes, sir."

"You have come to see Mr. Ralph Torridon whom we have here?"

"Yes, sir — my son."

Nicholas stepped forward, and the Lieutenant nodded at him.

"Yes, sir," said the officer to him, "I could not admit you before —" he stopped, as if embarrassed, and turned to Beatrice.

"And this lady too?"

"Yes, Master Lieutenant," said the old man.

"But — but — I do not understand —"

He looked at the radiant faces before him, and then dropped his eyes.

"I suppose — you have not heard then?"

Chris felt his heart leap, and then begin to throb furiously and insistently. What had happened? Why did the man look like that? Why did he not speak?

The Lieutenant came a step forward and put his hand on the table. He was looking strangely from face to face.

Outside the court was very still. The footstep that had passed on the flagstones a minute before had ceased; and there was no sound but the chirp of a bird under the eaves.

"You have not heard then?" said the Lieutenant again.

"Oh! for God's sake —" cried the old man suddenly.

"I have just come from your son," said the other steadily. "You are only just in time. He is at the point of death."

Chapter XIII
THE RELEASE

*I*t was morning, and they still sat in Ralph's cell.

*T*he attendant had brought in stools and a tall chair with a broken back, and these were grouped round the low wooden bed; the old man in the chair on one side, from where he could look down on his son's face, with Beatrice beside him, Chris and Nicholas on the other side. Mr. Morris was everywhere, sitting on a form by the door, in and out with food and medicine, at his old master's bedside, lifting his pillow, turning him in bed, holding his convulsive hands.

He had been ill six days, the Lieutenant told them. The doctor who had been called in from outside named the disease *phrenitis*. It was certain that he would not recover; and a message to that effect had been sent across on the morning before, with the usual reports to Greenwich.

They had supped as they sat — silently — on what the jailer brought; and had slept by turns in the tall chair, wakening at a sound from the bed; at the movement of the light across the floor as Morris slipped to and fro noiselessly; at the chirp of the birds and the noises of the stirring City as the daylight broadened on the wall, and the narrow window grew bright and luminous.

And now the morning was high, and they were waiting for the end.

A little table stood by the door, white-covered, with two candles, guttering now in their sockets, and a tall crucifix, ivory and black, lifting its arms in the midst. Before it stood two veiled vessels.

"He will speak before he passes," the doctor had told them the evening before; "I do not know whether he will be able to receive Viaticum."

Chris raised himself a little in his chair — he was stiff with leaning elbows on knees; and he stretched out his feet softly; looking down still at the bed.

His brother lay with his back to him; the priest could see the black hair, longer than Court fashion allowed now, the brown sinewy neck beneath; and one arm outlined over his hip beneath the piled clothes. The fingers were moving a little, contracting and loosening, contracting and loosening; and he could hear the long slow breaths.

Beyond sat Beatrice, upright and quiet, one hand in her lap, and the other holding the father's. The old man was bowed with his head on his other hand, as he had been for the last hour, his back bent forward with the burden, and his feet crossed before him.

From outside the noises grew louder as the morning advanced. There had been the sound of continual coming and going since it was light. Wheels had groaned and rattled up out of the distance and ceased abruptly; and the noise of hoofs had been like an endless patter over the stone-paving. And now, as the hours passed a murmur had been increasing, a strange sound like the wind in dry trees, as the huge crowd gathered.

Beatrice raised her eyes suddenly.

The fortress itself which had been quiet till now seemed to awaken abruptly.

The sound seemed to come to them up the stairs, but they had learnt during those hours that all sounds from within came that way. There was a trumpet-note or two, short and brazen; a tramp of feet for a moment, the throb of drums; then silence again; then the noise of moving footsteps that came and went in an instant. And as the sound came, Ralph stirred.

He swayed slowly over on to his back; his breath came in little groans that died to silence again as he subsided, and his arm drew out and lay on the bedclothes. Chris could see his face now in sharp profile against Beatrice's dark skirt, white and sharp; the skin was tightly stretched over the nose and cheekbones, his long thin lips were slightly open, there was a painful frown on his forehead, and his eyes squinted terribly at the ceiling.

A contraction seized the priest's throat as he watched; the face was at once so august and so pitiable.

The lips began to move again, as they had moved during the night; it seemed as if the dying man were talking and listening. The eyelids twitched a little; and once he made a movement as if to rise up. Chris was down on his knees in a moment, holding him tenderly down; he felt the thin hands come up and fumble with his own, and noticed lines deepen between the flickering eyelids. Then the hands lay quiet.

Chris lifted his eyes and saw his father's face and Beatrice's watching. Something of the augustness of the dying man seemed to rest on the grey bearded lips and solemn eyes that looked down. Beatrice's face was steady and tender, and as the priest's eyes met hers, she nodded.

"Yes, speak to him," she said.

Chris threw a hand across the bed and rested it on the wooden frame, and then lowered himself softly till his mouth was at the other's ear.

"Ralph," he said, "Ralph, do you hear me?"

Then he raised his face a little and watched.

The eyelids were rising slowly; but they dropped again; and there came a little faint babbling from the writhing lips; but no words were intelligible. Then they were silent.

"He hears," said Beatrice softly.

The priest bent low again; and as he did so, from outside came a strange sound, as of a long monstrous groan from a thousand throats. Again the dying man stirred; his hand sought his brother's arm and gripped it with a kind of feeble strength; then dropped again on to the coverlet.

Chris hesitated a moment, and again glanced up; and as he did so, there was a sound on the stairs. He threw himself back on his heels and looked round, as the doctor came in with Morris behind him.

He was a stout ruddy man, and moved heavily across the floor; but Ralph seemed not to hear it.

The doctor came to the end of the bed, and stood staring down at the dying man's face, frowning and pursing his lips; Chris watched him intently for some sign. Then he came round by Beatrice, leaned over the bed, and took Ralph's wrist softly into his fingers. He suddenly seemed to remember himself, and turned his face abruptly over his shoulder to Sir James.

"There is a man come from the palace," he whispered harshly. "I suppose it is the pardon." And Chris saw him arch his eyebrows and purse his lips again. Then he bent over Ralph once more.

Then again the doctor jerked his head towards the window behind and spoke across to Chris.

"They have him out there," he said; "Master Cromwell, I mean."

Then he rose abruptly.

"He cannot receive Viaticum; and he will not be able to make his confession. I should shrive him at once, sir, and anoint him."

"At once?" whispered Chris.

"The sooner the better," said the doctor; "there is no telling."

Chris rose swiftly from his knees, and made a sharp sign to Morris. Then he sank down once more, looking round, and lifted the purple stole from the floor where he had laid it the evening before; and even as he did so his soul revolted.

He looked up at Beatrice. Would not she understand the unchivalry of the act? But the will in her eyes compelled him. — Yes, yes! Who could set a limit to mercy?

He slipped the strip over his shoulders, and again bent down over his brother, with one arm across the motionless body. Beatrice and Sir James were on their knees by now. Nicholas was busy with Morris at the further end of the room. The doctor was gone.

There was a profound silence now outside as the priest bent lower and lower till his lips almost touched the ear of the dying man; and every word of the broken abrupt sentences was audible to all in the room.

"Ralph — Ralph — dear brother. You are at the point of death. I must shrive you. You have sinned very deeply against God and man. I shall anoint you afterwards. Make an act of sorrow in your heart for all your sins; it will stand for confession. Think of Jesu's love, and of His death on the bitter cross — the wounds that He bore for us in love. Give me a sign if you can that you repent."

Chris spoke rapidly, and leaned back a moment. Now he was terrified of waiting — he did not know how long it would be; but for an intent instant he stared down on the shadowed face.

Again the eyelids flickered; the lips formed words, and ceased again.

The priest glanced up, scarcely knowing why; and then again lowered himself that if it were possible Ralph might hear.

Then he spoke, with a tense internal effort as if to drive the grace home. . . .

"*Ego te absolvo ab omnibus censuris et peccatis, in nomine Patris —*" He raised himself a little and lifted his hand, moving it sideways across and down as he ended — "*et Filii et Spiritus Sancti.*"

*T*he priest rose up once more, his duty driving his emotion down; he did not dare to look across at the two figures beyond the bed, or even to question himself again as to what he was doing.

The two men at the further end of the room were waiting now; they had lifted the candles and crucifix off the table, and set them on the bench by the side.

Chris went swiftly across the room, dropped on one knee, rose again, lifted the veiled vessel that stood in the center, with the little linen cloth beneath, and set it all down on the bench. He knelt again, went a step aside back to the table, lifted the other vessel, and signed with his head.

The two men grasped the ends of the table, and carried it across the floor to the end of the bed. Chris followed and set down the sacred oils upon it.

"The cross and one candle," he whispered sharply.

A minute later he was standing by the bed once more.

"*Oremus* —" he began, reading rapidly off the book that Beatrice held steadily beneath his eyes.

"*Almighty Everlasting God, who through blessed James Thy Apostle, hast spoken, saying, Is any sick among you, let him call the priests of the Church* —" (The lips of the dying man were moving again at the sound of the words; was it in protest or in faith?) — " *. . . that is what is done without through our ministry, may be wrought within spiritually by Thy divine power, and invisibly by Thy healing; through our Lord Jesus Christ. Amen.*"

The lips were moving faster than ever on the pillow; the head was beginning to turn from side to side, and the mouth lay open.

"*Usquequo, Domine*" . . . began Beatrice.

Chris dipped his thumb in the vessel, and sank swiftly on to his knees.

"*Per istam sanctam Unctionem*" — "*through this holy unction. . . .*"

(The old man leaned suddenly forward on to his knees, and steadied that rolling head in his two hands; and Chris signed firmly on the eyelids, pressing them down and feeling the fluttering beneath his thumb as he did so.)

" *. . . And His most loving mercy, may the Lord forgive thee whatsoever thou hast sinned through sight.*"

Ah! that was done — dear God! those eyes that had drooped and sneered, that had looked so greedily on treasure — their lids shone now with the loving-kindness of God.

Chris snatched a morsel of wool that Morris put forward from behind, wiped the eyelids, and dropped the fragment into the earthen basin at his side.

"Per istam sanctam Unctionem. . . ."

And the ears were anointed — the ears that had listened to Layton's filth, to Cromwell's plotting; and to the cries of the oppressed.

The nostrils; the lips that had lied and stormed and accused against God's people, compressed now in his father's fingers — they seemed to sneer even now, and to writhe under the soft oil; the hands that had been laid on God's portion, that had torn the vessels from the altar and the cloth of gold from the treasury — those too were signed now, and lay twitching on the coverlet.

The bed clothes at the foot of the wooden framework were lifted and laid back as Chris passed round to the end, and the long feet, icy cold, were lying exposed side by side.

Per Istam sanctam Unctionem, et suam piissimam misericordiam, indulgeat tibi Domimus quidquid peccasti per incessum pedum. Amen.

Then they too were sealed with pardon, the feet that had been so swift and unwearied in the war with God, that had trodden the sanctuary in His despite, and trampled down the hearts of His saints — they too were signed now with the mark of Redemption and lay again under the folded coverlet at the end of their last journey.

A convulsion tore at the priest's heart.

*T*hen suddenly in the profound silence outside there broke out an indescribable clamor, drowning in an instant the murmur of prayers within. It seemed as if the whole world of men were there, and roaring. The sound poured up through the window, across the moat; the boards of the flooring vibrated with the sound. There was the throb of drums pulsating through the long-drawn yell, the screams of women, the barking of dogs; and a moment later, like some devilish benediction, the bells of Barking Church pealed out, mellow and jangling, in an exultation of blood.

Ralph struggled in his bed; his hands rose clutching at his throat, tearing open his shirt before Beatrice's fingers could reach them. The breath came swift and hoarse through his open teeth, and his eyelids flickered furiously. Then they opened, and his face grew quiet, as he looked out across the room.

"My — my Lord!" he said.

THE END

Printed in the United States
100168LV00003B/126/A

9 781598 189964